ADVENTURES
IN TIME
AND SPACE
WITH
MAX MERRIWELL

ALSO BY PAT MURPHY

The Shadow Hunter
The Falling Woman
The City, Not Long After
Nadya: The Wolf Chronicles
There and Back Again
Wild Angel

ADVENTURES
IN TIME
AND SPACE
WITH
MAX MERRIWELL

PAT MURPHY

TOR®

A TOM DOHERTY ASSOCIATES BOOK
NEW YORK

This is a work of fiction. All the characters and events portrayed in this book are either products of the author's imagination or are used fictitiously.

ADVENTURES IN TIME AND SPACE WITH MAX MERRIWELL

Copyright © 2001 by Pat Murphy

Edited by Beth Meacham

A Tor Book
Published by Tom Doherty Associates, LLC
175 Fifth Avenue
New York, NY 10010

www.tor.com

Tor® is a registered trademark of Tom Doherty Associates, LLC.

ISBN 0-812-54173-1
Library of Congress Catalog Card Number: 2001042325

First edition: November 2001
First mass market edition: December 2002

Printed in the United States of America

0 9 8 7 6 5 4 3 2 1

ONE

"Are we lost?" the young woman asked.
The Captain looked up from the chart he had been examin-
ing. "How can you be lost when you don't know where
you're going?" he asked, with an air of imperturbable calm.
    —from *Here Be Dragons*
       by Mary Maxwell

Susan was lost. She stood in the corridor, peering first in
one direction and then in the other, hoping to see something
that would give her a clue about what deck she was on this
time.

The ship's engines hummed softly underfoot. The faint
vibration served as a constant reminder that she was aboard
the *Odyssey*, a cruise ship that was about to set sail. She
had hoped to find her stateroom and rendezvous with her
friend Pat before that happened, but at this point, the odds
didn't look good.

Susan took another look at the map in her hand. Just half
an hour before, when she had blithely accepted it from the
man at the top of the gangway, this map had seemed so
promising and trustworthy. Such a festive map, showing all
ten of the ship's decks in bright tropical colors. Half an
hour in her hands, and the map was already dog-eared and
wrinkled and she was lost.

A few doors down the way, sunlight shone through an
open door onto the turquoise blue carpet. Voices—men's
voices—drifted down the corridor. She could smell fresh-
brewed coffee. Tucking her purse firmly under her arm, she
headed for the open door, determined to ask directions.

"But Mr. Merrimax," a man's voice was saying. "I just
don't see—"

"The name is Merriwell," said a patient voice. "Max Merriwell. Weldon Merrimax is one of my pen names."

Susan stopped in the doorway, looking into the room. It was an office. A balding man in a Hawaiian shirt sat behind the desk. He looked flustered. The etched glass nameplate on the desk identified him as "Gene Culver, Cruise Director." A bearded man sat in the upholstered chair across from him. Neither of the men looked in her direction; they were absorbed in their own conversation.

Susan recognized the bearded man as Max Merriwell from the author photos on his books. He looked like an author, with his wire-rimmed glasses, bushy eyebrows, gray hair, and gray beard. In the photos, he always wore a tweed sports coat with suede patches on the elbows.

Max Merriwell looked a bit less imposing in person than he did in his photos. He was a short man. His hair needed combing. He was wearing a tweed sports coat, but the patches on the elbows were shiny with wear.

"A pen name. Of course." Gene rubbed his balding head. "But the company contracted with Weldon Merrimax to teach a writing workshop aboard the *Odyssey*."

Max Merriwell nodded in agreement. "I understand that. My agent made the arrangements. But I'm sure he explained that my name is Max Merriwell. I write books as Max Merriwell, as Mary Maxwell, and as Weldon Merrimax."

Gene shook his head, frowning. "I don't know. All that paperwork went through company headquarters in Los Angeles. But I need to use Weldon Merrimax's name in the ship's newsletter. We have a lot of mystery fans aboard who will recognize that name. We have to let them know that Weldon Merrimax will be teaching a workshop."

Max looked, Susan thought, rather uncomfortable. "I'm afraid that's not possible."

"But you are Weldon Merrimax."

Max shook his head. "No, I'm not." An edge had crept into his voice. "I write as Weldon Merrimax, but I'm not Weldon Merrimax. That's not the same thing at all."

Gene was fidgeting with a pen on his otherwise empty desk. "I just don't see . . . it seems to me that you're splitting hairs, Mr. Merriwell. What difference does it make whether we call you Max Merriwell or Weldon Merrimax?"

"It makes a great deal of difference to me," Max said.

"You're putting me in a very difficult position. I have a contract that says Weldon Merrimax will teach a workshop."

Max frowned at Gene. Susan sympathized. She didn't like the way that Gene was trying to bully the writer. She was pleased that Max rose to the challenge.

He stood up. "Well, you'll have to take that up with Weldon Merrimax if you can find him," he said. "I guess I'd better get back on shore while I still can."

"Hold on," Gene said unhappily. "Can't you just teach as Weldon Merrimax?"

Max picked up his battered leather suitcase. "That wouldn't be right."

"But I have passengers who are looking forward to this writing workshop." Gene was clearly unhappy that Max had called his bluff. "I suppose you could teach under your own name."

Max put his suitcase down and pushed up his glasses, which had slid down his nose. "That's what I was planning to do," Max said. "That is, if you think anyone would want to take a workshop from me."

"Well, I certainly would," Susan said.

Both men turned to stare at her. She felt her cheeks grow hot. Interested in the discussion, she had forgotten that she was eavesdropping. "Oh, I'm so sorry. I was just walking by—I'm lost, you see." She held up the map that she still clutched in her hand, feeling like a complete idiot. "I was going to ask directions and I heard you talking. I didn't mean to interrupt. I'm so sorry, but I love Mr. Merriwell's work. I've read all your books." She knew she was babbling. Feeling the heat rise from her cheeks to her ears, she took a step backward into the corridor and bumped into someone, dropping her map. "Excuse me!" She turned to face a man in a crisp white uniform with black-and-gold striped epaulets. "I'm so sorry."

Tom Clayton, the *Odyssey*'s chief security officer, had been on his way to the bridge when the woman bumped into him. He smiled politely and stooped to pick up her map.

"No problem," he said, handing her the map. "I should have remembered to be on my guard when passing Gene's office. Pretty women are always rushing out. He's a very busy man." Tom peered in the open door. "Isn't that so, Gene?"

Gene looked pained. Tom had overheard a bit of the conversation as he came down the hall. Something about Max Merriwell. He had noticed that name on the list of additional staff for this cruise. He wondered if the tweedy gentleman in Gene's office was Max Merriwell, and if Mr. Merriwell were giving Gene a hard time. That seemed strange. The tweedy gentleman didn't look like the sort to give anyone a hard time.

"Tom, perhaps you could assist this lady," Gene said. "She seems to be lost."

"Of course. I'd be happy to." Tom closed the office door and turned back to the woman who waited in the corridor. She had curly, red-gold hair fastened at the nape of her neck with a large silver hair clip. Wisps of hair had escaped this restraint and curled around her face. She wore dark gray slacks, a forest-green V-necked sweater that looked very soft and very expensive, and a light gray blazer. She clutched an oversized black leather purse under one arm.

She looked good. If she had relaxed and smiled, she would have looked great. But her forehead wrinkled in the hint of a frown; her mouth was tight with worry.

She wasn't wearing any makeup. She had the kind of fair skin that freckles and burns, the kind that shows a blush. She was blushing like mad.

"Now where are you trying to go?" Tom asked.

"I was trying to find my stateroom." The woman's

cheeks were still flaming red. She shook her head. "I'm always getting lost. My husband says . . . my husband used to say that my sense of direction was installed backward. If I said turn left, we should turn right. I guess he had a point."

He nodded politely. She was fidgeting nervously with the wedding ring on her left hand.

"That map is enough to get anyone lost," he told her. "None of the companionways are marked, so it's a wonder that anyone can find their way from one deck to the next. Now what deck is your stateroom on?" He started down the hallway and she trailed him, for all the world like a wayward child who had been caught out of school.

"Calypso Deck. Stateroom number 144. Where am I now?"

"In the officers' quarters, right by the bridge."

He glanced back in time to catch another wave of color flooding her cheeks. "Completely off limits to passengers, I'm sure."

"No harm done." He held the door open for her. "And you really weren't too far off. Calypso Deck is just two decks below the bridge."

"Well, I took a stairway that wasn't on the map—I thought it might be a short cut. I should have known better."

"Right down here," he said. "By the way, aboard a ship, stairways are called companionways."

"I like that." Her voice echoed from the bare metal and concrete. A service companionway, this route had none of the carpeting and wood paneling of the passengers' areas. "It sounds so friendly. I guess I took the wrong companionway." She sounded a little less breathless; she was starting to relax a bit.

He opened a door into a corridor on the Calypso Deck. "This is your deck," he said. "Now your stateroom is right down—"

"Don't tell me," she said. "I can find the way from here." She was peering at the map, turning it around in her hands.

"In fact, I'll bet it's right down here." She turned to the left.

He reached around and took her arm, gently steering her in the opposite direction. "Actually, it's this way." He walked her down to where the corridor turned. "Straight down that way, on the right," he said. "You can't miss it."

"Really?" She frowned at the map again.

Looking over her shoulder, he took the map from her hand and turned it around, so its orientation matched that of the ship. "The bow is that way. The stern is that way. We're right here."

She contemplated the map for a moment, then nodded tentatively. "All right," she said, as if agreeing to a sort of compromise.

"It'll all make sense to you in no time," he said.

"I'm sure it will." She seemed to have about as much confidence in that as she did in his orientation of the map. "Thank you so much for your help. Sorry to be such a bother."

"No bother at all."

"I've got it straight now." She folded the map neatly and tucked it into her purse. She pushed her hair back out of her eyes, straightened her shoulders, and smiled at him bravely. "I'm sure I'll get it all sorted out." She held out her hand and gave him a firm handshake. "Thank you again."

He watched her walk down the corridor to her room. She smiled, waved, and disappeared from view. With almost two thousand passengers aboard, he probably wouldn't see her again.

Susan found Pat already in the stateroom, already unpacked. They both lived in San Francisco, but Susan had flown into New York City just that morning. Pat had spent the last week in the city, visiting friends.

Now Pat sat cross-legged on one of the twin beds. Pat's hair was cropped short in a spiky crew cut. While she was in New York, she had had it bleached white, then dyed a blue-violet shade that she called "electric blue." In the sunlight that shone through the sliding glass door that led to their balcony, Pat's hair seemed to glow, like a psychedelic poster under black light.

Having boarded at the earliest opportunity, Pat had already explored the *Odyssey* thoroughly. Pat had already unpacked—their suitcases, she informed Susan, had been delivered to the stateroom by a cheerful steward named Mario.

Working together at one of San Francisco's branch libraries, Pat and Susan had become close friends. In the two years that Susan had known Pat, her hair had rarely remained the same color for more than a few months at a stretch.

Susan recognized that the other folks who worked at the library thought she and Pat were an unlikely pair of friends. In matters of the heart, Susan was cautious and Pat was impulsive, given to sudden passions. In matters of fashion, Pat was trendy where Susan was conservative. But Susan admired Pat's self-assurance and her bold enthusiasm.

At twenty-six, Pat was a few years younger than Susan. She was a graduate student in theoretical physics at University of California, Berkeley. Currently, she was writing her dissertation. Until recently, she had been working part time at the library—maintaining the library's computers and Internet connection. Actually, as far as Susan could tell, Pat wasn't working on her dissertation much. She had had a falling out with her advisor. Pat said he was an idiot with no imagination.

Two months back, Pat and Susan had both been laid off because of budget cutbacks. Since the layoff, Pat had been doing temp work and writing copy for a Web site called The Bad Grrlz' Guide to Physics (www.badgrrlzguide. com). The Web site, Pat had told Susan, would provide bad girls (or bad grrlz) with a justification to do what they wanted to do anyway. Susan had her doubts about the project, but working on it seemed to make Pat happy, so Susan kept her reservations to herself.

In a raffle sponsored by a writers' magazine Susan had won a cruise on the *Odyssey*—from New York to England, with stops in Bermuda and the Azores. She had invited Pat to come along, and Pat had accepted with enthusiasm.

While Susan unpacked, Pat read aloud from a brochure that she had found in the "Welcome Aboard" fruit basket. "The *Odyssey* offers its fun-loving, adventurous passengers a fully equipped gymnasium, an aerobics studio with classes running from early morning to late evening, two dining rooms, three swimming pools, five restaurants (including a pizzeria), and eight bars. The *Odyssey* crew wants to make your stay with us a memorable experience, an adventure in luxury."

Susan hung the last of her sundresses in the tiny closet. She felt neither fun-loving nor adventurous. Instead, she felt more than a bit timid and uncertain.

"Why are you still wearing that?" Pat asked her.

Susan glanced down at her hands and realized that she was twisting her wedding ring on her finger, a nervous habit that she had developed in the past few months. Her divorce had been finalized just before she left for the cruise.

"I thought you signed the divorce papers," Pat said.

Susan nodded. "Just before I left."

Pat frowned. "So you're not married anymore."

Susan stared down at the ring on her hand. "I guess I haven't figured out what to do with it."

"Stick it in a drawer until you figure it out," Pat advised. "Who knows—you might meet some cute guy."

Susan gave her friend a warning glance. She had made Pat promise not to play matchmaker on the cruise. Susan wasn't in the mood—and she certainly didn't trust Pat's opinions about men.

But Pat was probably right about wearing the ring. Susan tugged it off her finger and shoved it into her pocket.

———

At 6:15, the pilot who had guided the *Odyssey* from the harbor to the open ocean disembarked, boarding the pilot boat and heading back home. Tom Clayton watched the pilot boat head for New York and relaxed a little. Escorting the pilot off the ship was his last duty related to the ship's departure from New York City.

Tom always liked putting out to sea. The ship was at its most vulnerable when it was in port. Port was where the trouble was. People could bring contraband aboard; stowaways could sneak aboard. Once they were at sea, the ship was isolated from the rest of the world. Tom enjoyed that sense of autonomy.

The *Odyssey* was a grand old lady with a checkered past. She had been built in 1961, at a time when the shipyards of France were turning out grand ocean liners. But the *Odyssey* had been built in a Yugoslavian shipyard, ordered by a Brazilian coffee company that wanted to get into the cruise business. Christened *Thetis,* after the sea nymph of Greek mythology, the ship had been sold just a year after delivery, a victim of a bad year for the Brazilian coffee crop.

The British company that purchased her renamed her *Wendolyn,* an Anglo-Saxon name meaning "wanderer." The *Wendolyn* made a number of transatlantic voyages, a solid, reliable passenger liner. The company that owned her was perpetually undercapitalized, a bad position for any player in the cruise industry. As a result, the standards aboard the *Wendolyn* never quite measured up to those set by the *Queen Elizabeth,* the *Norway,* and the other great ocean liners.

After a number of years of faithful service, the *Wendolyn* was sold again, this time to a British-based, Ukranian-owned cruise operator. Renamed the *Happy Traveler* (a sad fate for a former sea goddess), the ship was retrofitted to accommodate more passengers. For a number of years, she cruised the Mediterranean, a budget cruise ship for the family market, a grand ship that had fallen on hard times.

Finally, with the collapse of the Soviet Union, a

California-based, Italian-owned shipping company purchased the ship at a bargain price. She had been retrofitted, upgraded, renamed the *Odyssey,* and relaunched as a luxury cruise ship.

Having spent five years as second in command of security aboard one of Princess Cruises' megaships, Tom had signed on to be the *Odyssey*'s chief security officer. He had, over the past three years aboard, grown fond of the *Odyssey.* According to the engineering staff, the ship still suffered from her years of neglect. In the latest retrofit, they said, money that should have been spent on upgrading engineering and infrastructure had gone to cosmetic improvements of the passenger areas. The *Odyssey* had her problems, but she was still a solid and dependable vessel.

Tom figured this cruise for an easy run. It was a repositioning cruise; the company was moving the ship from the Caribbean to the Mediterranean for the winter. They would reach England on November first. He had scanned the passenger list and had noticed no obvious troublemakers. A large convention of historians from California had booked their cabins together at a discounted group rate, but he didn't figure them for trouble. Probably a group of stuffy academics on their way to tour Europe. There was the usual assortment of savvy cruisers who had sought out the repositioning cruise for its bargain price.

Tom glanced at his watch. He had just enough time to stop by the security office for a final check before he got dressed for dinner.

The security office was near the bridge—a small room furnished with two desks and a filing cabinet full of forms, procedure sheets, and company memos. Tom kept his desk clear, dealing with each day's paperwork as it came in. He didn't much like spending time in the office; he felt he could do a better job on his feet—talking to people, keeping an eye on things.

The other desk in the office was currently occupied by Ian G. Macabbee, a blonde Californian computer expert in his mid-twenties. Officially, Ian's title was "Information

Management System Analyst/Integrator." The company had supplied him with an official etched glass name plate with that title. But Ian had covered the official title with a different title, neatly printed in large, block letters. It said "Consulting Propellerhead."

Ian had been aboard the *Odyssey* for just over two months, installing and debugging the "A Pass" system, a computerized security system that tracked passengers, crew, and all visitors as they boarded and exited the ship. Each passenger and crew member had a key card that served as a pass to the ship and a key to their stateroom. Each gangway was equipped with a card reader. The system read the cards as people boarded the ship or disembarked and noted who was aboard and who was missing. Passengers also used their cards, known aboard ship as "cruise cards," to charge drinks and services that were not included in the cruise package. Ian had set the system up and had been monitoring its performance.

Though he'd been cruising in the Caribbean for weeks, Ian retained the pallor of a man who spent his life in front of a computer screen, living on coffee and junk food. During his first week aboard, Ian had ordered only coffee, turkey sandwiches, and fries from the galley. After a week of this, Osvaldo, the steward who took care of the bridge staff, had taken on the task of improving Ian's diet. Ian still drank too much coffee, but he ate what Osvaldo brought him— and his diet now included fresh fruit and an occasional salad. Ian was still thin, but he no longer looked quite as malnourished.

When Tom stepped through the security office door, Ian looked up from his computer screen and grinned. "So who is she?" He spoke quickly, as always, riding as he did on a constant caffeine buzz.

Tom frowned. "Who is who?"

"The beautiful redhead you were escorting to her stateroom," Ian asked.

Tom sat down at his desk, shaking his head. "How do

you know about that?" Then he held up a hand. "No, wait—let me guess."

Ian grinned and poured himself another cup of coffee from the pot on his desk. The coffeepot was on a tray from the galley. By the aroma, it was quite fresh.

"The coffee was delivered by someone who talked to someone who saw me."

Ian nodded. "Osvaldo delivered the coffee. He had talked to Mario who was making up a stateroom on the Calypso deck when you passed by. According to Osvaldo, Mario said she's quite attractive."

In his first week aboard the *Odyssey,* Ian had taken it upon himself to know everything that happened aboard the ship. He wanted to know who was sleeping with whom, who was angry about what and why. He had an astounding predilection for gossip and intrigue. He was, he explained to Tom, very fond of information.

"Just a lost passenger who found her way onto the bridge somehow. She was asking Gene Culver for directions when I passed by."

"Why didn't Gene escort her himself?" The cruise director, the man in charge of the ship's entertainment and passenger activities, had a reputation as a ladies' man. Ian knew that, of course.

Tom smiled. Ian was grilling him, but Tom was willing to indulge the younger man. "Gene was not having a good day. He was talking to a tweedy looking chap about a writing workshop."

"Max Merriwell," Ian said. "Excellent science fiction writer. He also writes fantasy as Mary Maxwell and mystery as Weldon Merrimax." Ian opened one of his desk drawers, pulled out a hardcover book, and tossed it to Tom. "That's his latest. I just finished reading it last night. Wonderful book."

"Seems like he has too many names," Tom said.

Ian shrugged. "He writes in different genres under different names. He doesn't want to confuse his readers."

Tom laughed. "Then I'd say he's going about it the wrong way."

"Well, his pseudonyms are not common knowledge." Ian sipped his coffee, smiling a self-satisfied smile. He was, Tom had noticed, fond of knowing things that were not common knowledge.

"How did you find out?" Tom asked.

"I'm on an Internet mailing list with people who make it their business to know this sort of thing. When I found out Max Merriwell was coming aboard, I asked about him."

Tom nodded and glanced at the book in his hand. *There and Back Again,* by Max Merriwell. On the cover, a woman with a tattooed face gazed into a cube in which stars swirled.

"You can borrow it," Ian said.

"I don't read much fiction." Tom handed the book back to Ian and sat down at his desk. He glanced at the stack of papers in the center of the desk—Ian's print-out from the A Pass system. Over the past month, Tom's security staff had been trained in the new system and had simultaneously maintained the old system, relying on roster sheets and paper records. On this cruise, the switch to the new system would be complete and security would rely on the A Pass system.

Tom glanced at the print-out, knowing that Ian would tell him what he needed to know before he could ask.

"Everything went smoothly," Ian said, not waiting for Tom to review the print-out. "All crew accounted for. Last visitor disembarked at 4:15 with minutes to spare."

"Great. I checked at the gates, and there didn't seem to be any problems there."

Ian nodded, sipping his coffee.

Tom glanced at his watch, then stood up. "I've got to get ready for dinner." On the *Odyssey,* company policy required officers to dine with the passengers, making small talk and serving, according to company memos, as "ambassadors for Odyssey Lines."

Ian nodded. "I'll see you there."

"Really?" Tom was surprised. As a consultant, Ian was exempt from this requirement. He had, on all the earlier cruises, opted to eat with the rest of the crew, rather than dining with the passengers.

"I decided it might be interesting. So I checked with the purser and he signed me up."

"Interesting?" Tom shook his head. "You have an optimistic streak I'd never noticed before. You'll probably be seated with six little old ladies." Some officers enjoyed presiding over a table at dinner; Tom regarded it as a necessary part of his job.

"Watch your tongue," Ian said. "If they're passengers, those little old ladies are vertically challenged senior citizens." The company had recently sent out a memo on the politically correct terms to be used for passengers.

"Have it your way." Tom left the office, closing the door firmly behind him.

Ian returned to his computer screen. With a few key strokes, he called up the list of passengers dining in the Ithaca Dining Room at the eight-fifteen seating. They were listed by table; he searched for Tom's table. Eight passengers and Tom.

He tapped a few keys to call up the passenger list. According to Mario, the beautiful redhead was in stateroom 144. Two women occupied that stateroom: Susan Galina and Pat Murphy. For good measure, he located Max Merriwell, too. He returned to the seating chart, bumped four passengers to other tables, and inserted himself, the women from stateroom 144, and Max Merriwell.

He smiled. Much better, he thought. He liked Tom, but he thought the security officer could use a bit of loosening up. It had been more than a year since Tom had had a girlfriend; that's what Mario had told Ian. Tom had dated a singer for a while, but she'd transferred to another ship, and he'd been on his own ever since. Ian thought Tom deserved good company at dinner, and Ian was happy to

arrange it. And even happier to set wheels in motion and
see what happened.

It was shaping up to be an interesting cruise, he thought
happily. He was looking forward to meeting Max Merriwell; he was looking forward to seeing what, if anything,
developed between Tom and the redhead. And the ship was
heading into the Bermuda Triangle.

For the past few weeks, Ian had been reading up on the
Bermuda Triangle. He didn't believe all the stories about
ships and planes that had disappeared there, but he was
interested in them, just as he was interested in anything that
smacked of conspiracy and cover-up. He didn't believe in
the mystical power of the Bermuda Triangle, but he enjoyed the fervor of those who did. He tried to keep an open
mind.

Yes, he thought, it was bound to be an interesting cruise.

TWO

She slit open the belly of a fish while cleaning it for dinner, and found a gold ring. The ring was inscribed "With all my love." She considered the ring, muttered her thanks to whatever god sent it her way, and sold it in the market. It was a lovely ring and a lovely sentiment, but when it got right down to it, she felt she'd be better off with the cash.

—from *Here Be Dragons*
by Mary Maxwell

The Ithaca Dining Room on the Lotus Deck had the look and feel of an expensive steak house: dark wooden paneling on the walls, heavy wooden chairs upholstered in leather, white linen tablecloths. Candles burned on every table; in the ceiling, tiny lights twinkled like stars. It all looked so solid, so stable. But Susan could feel the ship rocking beneath her, a subtle shifting that made her feel unsteady, as if she had already had too much to drink. A little dizzy, a little disoriented.

"Welcome to the *Odyssey*," the head waiter said, smiling at the two of them. Susan noticed that he blinked once at Pat's hair—blinked as if checking his vision. But then he simply smiled—a precise smile of professional greeting. He did not mention Pat's hair; he did not mention her jeans. He simply checked their cruise cards and consulted a computer print out. "Ah, yes—you're at one of the officer's tables. Nicholas will show you the way."

Susan and Pat followed Nicholas to their assigned table. A placard in the center of the table said "233." Six people smiled at Susan expectantly; three seats were still empty. Susan forced herself to smile back at the people, but her smile faltered when she noticed that Max Merriwell was seated at one end of the table and the officer who had shown her to her stateroom was at the other.

"I see you found your way to the dining hall," the officer was saying, and she could feel her cheeks reddening. She hoped that the light was dim enough that no one would notice. She felt like fleeing, but Pat was already taking the seat next to Max Merriwell. Susan reached for the back of one of the remaining seats, leaving an empty chair between herself and the officer. But before she could pull out the chair and seat herself, a man came hurrying up. He was just a few years older than Pat. Like Pat, he was dressed in jeans and a T-shirt.

"Allow me," he said, smiling at her, and pulled out the chair next to the officer.

Susan hesitated, then took the seat, not wanting to make a scene.

"We weren't properly introduced before," the officer said, still smiling. "I'm Tom Clayton, ship's security officer."

"Susan Galina," she murmured. She felt tongue-tied and self-conscious. She had made a fool of herself earlier; she just hoped she could make it through dinner without embarrassing herself further.

"So sorry I'm late," said the man who had pulled out her chair. "I'm Ian Macabbee. Consulting Propellerhead."

Susan blinked, wondering if she had heard him right. But she didn't have a chance to ask. Ian was already turning to Pat, murmuring something about her fabulous hair.

"I've decided that the Captain has us all pegged as troublemakers," said the balding man on the other side of the table. He was grinning. "That's why we're all at Tom's table. This way, he can keep an eye on us."

"You're the troublemaker, Bill," said the woman beside him, shaking her head fondly. "Don't go dragging the rest of us into it."

"Well, clearly Tom has already met this young lady," said a red-headed man at the far end of the table. "If that isn't suspicious I don't know what is." He was a large, prosperous-looking fellow who appeared to be used to living the good life. "I'm Charles Rafferty," he told Susan.

Then everyone introduced themselves, a great confusion of names and identities. Bill Carver, the balding joker at the end of the table, and his wife Alberta were from Cleveland, Ohio. Charles Rafferty was a banker from Boston. His wife, a slim Asian woman named Lily, was an antique dealer.

Ian Macabbee smiled at Susan sympathetically and she wondered if she looked a bit panicked. "It's always hard to keep track of all the names at the first dinner," he murmured. "It'll get easier."

"Max here seems determined to make it harder than usual." Bill Carver said jovially. "He has more than his share of names."

Susan glanced shyly at Max. Beside Bill Carver, he looked even shorter and shabbier. She imagined how difficult it could be to explain all his pen names to people like Bill and Charles.

Susan had been reading Max's science fiction novels since she was ten years old. They were wonderful tales that had let her escape from the demands of her family into a world of adventure where anything was possible.

At about the same age, she had discovered Mary Maxwell's novels, stories in which girls and women led heroic lives. It wasn't until she became a librarian that she discovered that Mary Maxwell was a pseudonym for Max Merriwell. She knew some women who had been disappointed to learn that a man had written Mary Maxwell's books, but she still thought that the books were marvelous and that the man who wrote them must be equally extraordinary. On the cruise, she had brought Max's latest novel, a rollicking space adventure titled *There and Back Again,* and *Wild Angel,* a new book by Mary Maxwell.

She knew Max had also written books as Weldon Merrimax, but she hadn't read them. She'd started one once, but it was so bleak she had set it aside.

"Really, Max," Charles chimed in. "It does seem like you

are going out of your way to be confusing. I really don't see the point."

"Now let's see if I've got it straight," Bill said. "You're Max Merriwell when you write that wild sci-fi stuff. You're Mary Maxwell when you write fantasy. And you're Weldon Merrimax when you write best-sellers." Bill rubbed his head, pretending he was baffled. "Of course, I don't read all that far-out stuff. I've heard of Weldon, at least. But keeping track of all those names is too much for me."

Susan thought she saw a flicker of irritation cross Max's face at the mention of Weldon Merrimax. Clearly, Bill was the sort of person who didn't read science fiction, but felt he knew all about it. He knew it was trashy and a waste of time. Kid stuff. Susan felt she had to speak up.

"I don't have any problem with all the names," she said abruptly. "I already know his names because I know his books. I'm looking forward to your workshop, Mr. Merriwell."

"Call me Max," he said, rewarding her with a small smile.

She managed to smile back, startled by her own audacity.

"A workshop," Alberta said, leaning forward a little. She was a stout woman with obviously bleached hair and an earnest and determined manner. "What sort of workshop?"

"I'll be teaching a writing workshop on board," Max said.

"Really," Alberta said. She clasped her hands in front of her like a child anticipating a treat. "I'd love to come to that. I've always wanted to write a novel. I have so many stories to tell." She glanced at Susan and Pat. "Are you both writers?"

"Only if you count writing a dissertation on quantum mechanics," Pat said. "My advisor tells me I might as well be writing a science fiction novel, so maybe that counts."

Susan shook her head. "I'm a librarian, and I love books. I really don't think I can write one, but I thought I'd go to Max's workshop anyway."

"A cruise is a lovely place to try new things," Alberta

said briskly. "Last year, Bill and I tried swing dancing and I took a boxing class in the aerobics studio. There's so much to do on board."

Susan nodded, imagining Alberta throwing a punch. It wasn't difficult. She would, Susan thought, approach boxing with the same earnest doggedness that she approached conversation.

Their waiter arrived with menus, and the conversation turned to food.

"The smoked salmon with caviar cream sounds lovely to start with," Alberta was saying. "Then perhaps the grilled eggplant salad."

"The rack of lamb could be good," Charles said. "Tom, what can you tell me about the prime rib."

Susan realized, listening to the conversation, that Bill, Alberta, Charles, and Lily had all been on many cruises before. Charles was praising the wine selection on Celebrity Cruises and Bill was maintaining that Norwegian Cruise Lines had the best chefs. Susan kept her eyes on her menu, having nothing to add to the conversation and feeling a little out of her depth.

"It'll all calm down after a bit," Ian said to her softly. She glanced up to find him studying her. "They're just jockeying for position. Like a pack of wolves. They're establishing the pack hierarchy. Who's the alpha male, who's beta, and so on."

She glanced at Charles and Bill, who had engaged Tom in a conversation about wine, while their wives discussed their salad selection. Pat and Max were studying their menus.

"Everyone will sort it out to their satisfaction soon enough," Ian said. "Then they'll all calm down. We'll just have to lay low until that happens."

Susan watched as Charles asked the waiter a complex question about the sauce on the veal. He wanted to know where the juniper berries used in the sauce had come from, something that apparently affected the flavor. Then he had a few questions about the wine. He did seem to be establishing his credentials as a gourmet.

"Who do you suppose will win?" she asked Ian softly.

"I'd put my money on Tom. He wins by not playing."

"You're not playing either," she said.

"I play a different game," Ian said. "I watch."

Charles and Lily and Bill and Alberta continued discussing the menu, with comments designed to demonstrate their knowledge of food and wine and cruises. Following Ian's lead, Susan watched and listened. Bill and Charles dominated the conversation, talking about activities on board and comparing them with other cruises. Among the women, Alberta seemed to be the one who kept the conversation going, asking questions and waiting for the answers with her head cocked attentively.

Tom participated in the conversation mostly by joking. Susan agreed with Ian's assessment—he wasn't playing, but he would win. The others were jockeying for second position in the pecking order, since Tom seemed so clearly in charge.

Tom glanced in Susan's direction when she was studying him, and she dropped her eyes to her water glass, then busied herself with her salad.

She managed to stay out of the conversation, eating her dinner quietly, until they were just finishing the main course. Then Alberta turned her attention to Susan. "So, Susan, what do you do and where are you from?"

"I'm a librarian," Susan said. "I live in San Francisco."

"Oh, that's a lovely city," Alberta said. "How nice that you two girls could come on the cruise together. No men to tie you down."

"You are leaping to conclusions, dear," Bill said. "How do you know that Susan doesn't have someone special back home?"

Alberta laughed. "Women's intuition," she said. She looked at Susan. "You aren't married, are you?"

Susan hesitated. That question, once so normal, now confused her. It was an innocent question, she knew that. But it felt like a demand for a long explanation. I was married for many years, but then my husband ran off with his personal trainer, a buffed blonde with a perfect smile. I don't really understand why—my friends all say it was some kind of mid-life crisis, but he was only thirty. I thought that was supposed to happen at forty. I keep wondering if it was my fault, if maybe we should have had kids, if maybe I should have done something different. I just don't know. I kept thinking we'd get back together but then we got divorced. But you know, I still don't feel divorced. I don't feel married either. I feel like I don't belong anywhere. I feel like a part of me is missing. Not my husband. I think I've gotten over missing him. But a part of myself that I used to have. That's gone somewhere, and I don't know how to get it back.

"No," Susan said. "I'm not married."

She avoided looking at Tom, remembering suddenly that she had mentioned her husband in their earlier conversation.

"So you can just do whatever you want." Alberta smiled, relentlessly cheerful. "What fun!"

Susan managed to nod. Everyone was looking at her. She didn't know what to say.

"Have you decided what you're having for dessert?" Tom asked Alberta. Susan glanced at Tom, grateful for the interruption. She wondered if he had asked solely to divert Alberta's attention. While the others debated the relative merits of Grand Marnier soufflé, chocolate raspberry roulade, and apple fritters with vanilla-cinnamon sauce, Susan pushed back her chair.

"I'm sure you'll all excuse me." Susan smiled brightly at the others. "I need to get some air."

"Do you want me to come with you?" Pat asked.

"Oh, no—I'll be fine. You stay and enjoy dessert." She turned away quickly, before Pat could insist, and hurried out of the restaurant.

"I think she may be feeling a little seasick," she heard

Tom saying. She didn't know why he was covering for her, but she was grateful that he was.

As she stepped out of the dining room into the atrium, she felt the ship move beneath her. In the atrium, three decks were connected by a spiral staircase. The decor was hard-edged and slick—all marble and glass and chrome. Stained glass fixtures in the ceiling appeared to be sky-lights, but she knew there was another deck up there. Mock skylights, just another illusion. One level up, there were boutiques selling souvenirs and "cruise wear," extremely expensive casual clothing.

She climbed the spiral staircase up one level, to the promenade deck. Opposite her, a glass elevator filled with passengers dressed in cruise wear rose toward the next deck.

The ship moved again. Looking up at the elevator, she felt a wave of vertigo. In her nervousness, she had had two glasses of wine with dinner, and she felt the effects now. She turned away from the atrium blindly, pushing through a door.

A gust of cool air slapped her in the face as she stepped onto the promenade, a wooden deck that ran around the ship. She took a deep breath, glad to be out of the over-heated dining room. She stepped to the railing and looked out over the dark waters. The moon was not yet up, and the stars glittered in the black sky.

Sailors, she knew, had once navigated by the stars. She looked up at the sky and wondered where she was going.

Tom made his way along the walkway around the ship's uppermost deck. He was heading toward the bow of the ship, where there was an observation platform called Cy-clops' Lookout.

The ship's movement created a steady wind that cut through his windbreaker. He walked close to the side wall—the outer wall of Penelope's, one of the *Odyssey*'s five restaurants.

The walkway was deserted. It was almost midnight—
past time for bed after a long day—but one of the security
guards had notified him of a potential problem, and he had
to check it out. A woman was standing on the observation
platform at the bow of the ship. She was alone, the guard
had said, and she didn't seem to be doing anything—just
standing there and staring out to sea.

Tom had been on the security staff of cruise ships for
the past eight years. Three times, he had been aboard a ship
where someone decided to jump. Once, when he was a
security guard, he had been the one to find a pile of folded
clothes, set neatly beside the railing, with a note tucked
into one of the shoes.

Tom remembered holding that shoe, a burgundy leather
wingtip, and thinking that its owner had never intended to
travel in the tropics. This man had come on the cruise,
planning to leave it permanently in the middle of the ocean,
planning to dive overboard a few hundred miles from New
York harbor, out where his body would never be found.

Tom was an easy-going guy, but that had pissed him off.
Why had that man chosen to kill himself aboard Tom's
ship? And if he insisted on killing himself, why had he left
his clothes behind for Tom to find?

Tom did not like loose ends, and those clothes were a
loose end, a disruption in the smooth workings of the ship.
Tom's job was to keep order aboard, and those clothes,
however neatly folded, were a symbol of disorder. Those
clothes had generated no end of trouble for the security
office. It had taken two days to figure out who was missing.
Then there had been stacks of paperwork—people to be
notified, explanations to be made, letters to be written.

For weeks afterward, Tom had found himself noting the
shoes of the passengers, unconsciously on the lookout for
shoes inappropriate to cruising. If he had spotted someone
in leather wingtips, he didn't know what he would have
done. Fortunately, the other passengers wore sandals and
running shoes and other appropriate footwear.

The *Odyssey* was patrolled regularly by security watchmen. Every area of the ship was visited by a guard at least once an hour. When Tom had become head of ship's security, he had increased patrols in the areas where people might be likely to jump. If a security guard spotted a potential jumper, he alerted Tom. It didn't happen often.

Tom stepped onto the observation platform and a blast of cold wind stung his face. The woman was standing at the railing to one side of the deck, staring out over the water. The wind was whipping her curly hair into tangles. She was, he noted with an odd sense of relief, wearing casual, rubber-soled shoes that were perfectly appropriate to a cruise. She had her arms wrapped around herself, hugging herself for warmth.

"Excuse me, ma'am," he said. "Are you all right?"

She turned to look at him, and the wind whipped her hair into her face. She pushed it back and he realized that it was Susan. "I'm fine," she said.

He leaned against the railing beside her. From where he stood, he could look straight down into the dark waves. The half-moon was rising. In its silver light, the ocean water moved like a living thing, restless and uneasy. If he looked toward the bow of the ship, he could see the sundeck, where a maze of glass wind screens created many small wind shelters. On a sunny day, each one would be occupied by sunbathing passengers. They were deserted now.

"I really wasn't seasick," Susan said. "I just didn't want to answer any more questions about who I am and what I do and where I live. I don't want to answer those right now."

Tom could sympathize with that. He could guess at some of the reasons she didn't want to answer questions. On the bridge, she had mentioned her husband, and he had noticed that she was wearing a wedding band. But at dinner, she wasn't wearing the ring, and she was clearly uncomfortable talking about her life. Trouble in her marriage, he figured.

"I guessed as much," he said.

"You did?" She looked worried. "I hope Alberta didn't realize it."

He shook his head. "Alberta didn't notice a thing." Alberta, he thought, probably wouldn't have noticed anything was amiss unless Susan had burst into tears at the table.

"Thanks for covering for me," she said. She wasn't smiling, but she seemed more relaxed than she had been at dinner. She had lost her beleaguered look, and the tension around her eyes had eased.

Tom nodded sympathetically. "No reason you have to answer anyone's questions," he said. "Your life is nobody's business but your own."

She looked out to sea. Then she said, "I threw my wedding ring overboard."

Tom blinked, startled by the sudden admission. She continued watching the water for a moment, then turned to look at him. "Aren't you going to ask why?"

"I guess you didn't want it anymore," he said carefully.

She considered that. "You're right. I just got divorced. I figured it didn't belong to me anymore. And I didn't want to sell it or anything. It was jinxed."

"I can see how you might feel that way," he said.

"It's so strange not to be wearing it," she said. "Harry and I weren't always happy—in fact, I guess we were unhappy a lot of the time. But he was my anchor. Being married kept me grounded."

"Sometimes an anchor is a good thing," Tom said. "And sometimes it just drags you down." He shrugged. "But what do I know about it. I'm just a sea-going cop in a fancy uniform."

She studied him thoughtfully. "Are you married?"

He shook his head. "Not now. I was married once, a long time ago. Just for a few years."

"What happened?"

A simple question. The answer hadn't seemed simple at the time of his divorce, but now it seemed simple enough. "I was a cop in Boston at the time, and I worked nights. She decided she didn't want to be married to someone who wasn't around to party with. I decided I didn't want to be married to someone who couldn't deal with my job. So we got divorced. Then I quit being a cop and I joined the merchant marine."

"Why did you do that?" she asked.

"I needed to do something different," he said.

She nodded, staring at the waves. "I know what you mean. I'm glad I threw it overboard." She touched her left hand with her right, as if feeling for the ring. "I like it out here. We're moving; we're off on an adventure. It feels like anything could happen."

Tom smiled. He had felt that way when he shipped out with the merchant marine at age twenty-five. Back then, standing in the icy wind on a midnight shift had been part of the adventure. He had loved every minute of it.

"I know what you mean," he said.

She glanced at him, frowning just a little, as if she were trying to figure him out. She didn't quite believe him, he thought.

"I felt like that on my first trip out," he said. "But to-night's too cold a night for me to be looking for adventure. I'm heading back inside. Do you need help finding your stateroom?"

"I know exactly where it is. But I suppose I should go in. Pat will be worried." She bit her lip, still staring out to sea. "I hope I can get to sleep," she said, half to herself. "I haven't been sleeping well, lately."

"I've always found that I sleep very well aboard," Tom said. "The waves rock me to sleep."

She followed him as he headed back past Penelope's. It turned out that she didn't really know where her stateroom was. He stopped her from making two wrong turns and took her to the right corridor. At her stateroom, she let herself in and he said good night.

It was just past midnight. Tom knew that the casino would be hopping. The bars, he was certain, would be full of passengers drinking bon voyage drinks. In the all-night restaurant, passengers would be ordering midnight snacks.

But here, where there were only staterooms, it was quiet. Just one man at the end of the corridor, hurrying away. Tom caught a flash of pale skin as the man glanced back over his shoulder, then he disappeared around the corner.

Strange that the man was in such a hurry, that he had glanced over his shoulder like someone who didn't want to be caught. Tom walked quickly to the corner and glanced down the adjoining corridor. No one was there. The recessed lamps in the ceiling filled the corridor with a soft, even light, leaving no shadows, no dark corners.

Pat was already asleep when Susan slipped into the stateroom. The curtains were open and moonlight shone through the sliding glass door. Susan undressed quietly and pulled on her cotton nightshirt.

Lying in bed, she touched her left hand. She could still feel the impression that the ring had left on her finger—a valley where the ring had been, a slightly callused ridge of flesh beside that valley.

She wondered what would happen to the ring. She imagined the circle of gold sinking in the dark water, buffeted by waves. Maybe a fish would eat it. Maybe someone would catch the fish and find the gold ring inside. She imagined that and smiled. The ring, which had brought her bad luck, might be someone else's good luck.

She closed her eyes and felt the ship rocking beneath her. Rocking her to sleep, she thought. Lulled by the steady motion, soothed by the rumbling of the ship's engines far below, she drifted into sleep and dreamed of a gold ring, sinking in the deep ocean waters, a golden circle drifting in the darkness. In her dreams, it changed from a golden ring in the dark ocean waters to a golden space ship, a flying saucer against the night sky, humming with a rhythm that matched the *Odyssey*'s engines.

BAD GRRLZ' GUIDE TO PHYSICS

OBSERVATIONS REGARDING THE HEAT DEATH OF THE UNIVERSE

It's my first morning on the *Odyssey*, and I'm up at dawn, observing a skirmish in the ongoing struggle for the destiny of the universe.

I'm on the sundeck, which is on the same level as our stateroom. I'm leaning against the railing and sipping a cup of cappuccino from the Olympus Eatery, the ship's twenty-four-hour cafeteria.

Here at the bow of the ship, the decks are staggered like the layers on a wedding cake. One level up is the observation deck, labeled on the map as Cyclops' Lookout. Above that is the bridge. The windows of the bridge reflect the rising sun. Around me, the maze of glass wind screens on the sundeck cast interesting shadows in the dawn light.

From my vantage point, I can observe the battle that is being waged here on the *Odyssey,* an ancient war between two opposing forces. No, not good and evil. That's the old Judeo-Christian view of the world and really kind of a waste of time. Take philosophy if you want to worry about that stuff. I'm a physicist and as a physicist I'm concerned with a more significant struggle—the struggle between order and chaos.

The cruise ship staff is on the side of order. From where I stand, I can see them bustling about and cleaning things up. There's a guy hosing down the deck, washing off the salt spray. There's another guy painting one of the white railings. The railing is already white, but he's making it even whiter, so white that it will be blinding in the noonday sun. There is another guy polishing the wooden railings and still another guy washing the glass sunscreens.

Everywhere I go on this ship, it's startlingly clean. For someone who lives in a seedy section of San Francisco's Mission District, this is both refreshing and unnerving. I am accustomed to deterioration and dirt. Where I live, there is dog shit on the sidewalks, graffiti on the buildings, and a thin coating of urban grime on everything.

As any physicist can tell you, grime is a natural occurrence. Disorder and decay are the way of the universe. The second Law of Thermodynamics says so. Entropy—the tendency for things to become disordered—always increases. Basically, everything goes to shit.

Eventually, the second Law will lead to the Heat Death of the Universe. Death, decay, and disorder are inevitable. There's no changing that. You can put all the energy you want into a system—cleaning up your desk, washing the dishes, doing the laundry, finding a place for everything and putting everything in its goddamn place. But in the end, entropy will win.

Suppose you decide to clean house—a futile endeavor if you ask me. As you work to battle disorder in your house, your efforts are fueled by the food you've eaten. Your body breaks down orderly sugars into simpler, more chaotic forms, adding to the disorder in the universe. Your body produces heat, a disordered form of energy. Ultimately, all your efforts create a small pocket of order—a house that is temporarily clean. But you have, with all your work, increased the disorder in the universe as a whole. As you fight the good fight, you are aiding the enemy.

The ocean is a corrosive force: salt water rusts metal, peels paint, grimes glass. Yet here on the *Odyssey,* the brave crew is at war with the ocean's entropic effect.

Last night, after dinner, I asked Tom, the friendly officer who dined with us, about this obsession with cleanliness, having noted it on my first day aboard. Tom says that this obsession is Company Policy. (I swear he said it in capital letters, just like that.) The Company will not tolerate rust or dirt or decay. Their goal is a perfect ship, so sparkling clean you'd think it had just been dipped in bleach.

When I pointed out the futility of this endeavor, Tom nodded. He seemed to realize that they are battling in vain. The Heat Death of the Universe will win.

There are some on the ship who have not aligned themselves with the forces promoting order and tidiness. Ian, the ship's self-styled "Consulting Propellerhead" appears to be a force for chaos. Max Merriwell, the author who is teaching the writing workshop, may be another troublemaker. At first glance, he appears to be a friendly, dumpy, good-natured, old fellow. But he has more than his share of names, and I think he bears further observation.

I'm not sure about Officer Tom. His job is that of security officer, a position dedicated to keeping order. But I sense in him an easy-going nature and a fondness for joking that seems at odds with a sincere dedication to order.

As I stand and watch, another member of deck staff scurries about, setting up deck chairs behind each wind screen. On each chair, he places a fluffy, clean, freshly laundered towel.

I know that passengers will disrupt this order, shaking the towels free of their tidy folds, using the fluffy terry cloth to dry themselves, then leaving the towels in rumpled heaps on the deck. The deck staff will bustle about, picking up the wet towels and replacing them with neatly folded ones. They will not permit the untidiness of wet towels to mar the perfection of the ship.

I watch the deck guy with his towels and I think about which side I am on. On my desk at home, where the completion of my dissertation seems an ever more distant goal, disorder is winning.

The choice is clear to me. I believe it is clear to any Bad Grrl. I sympathize with the staff of the *Odyssey*, but I will never join their futile cause. I will not become a slave to cleanliness and tidiness and order. I choose to align myself with a winner. I'm for Heat, Entropy, Chaos, and Disorder.

THREE

"I love to watch a good liar at work," she said. *"Not your average, workaday liar, but an extravagant, industrious, experienced liar railing against imagined wrongs, weeping for illusory sorrows. A good lie, well-told, is a truly admirable thing."*

—from *Here Be Dragons*
by Mary Maxwell

When Susan woke, Pat's bed was empty, a jumble of tangled blankets and sheets. Susan sat up and stretched, glancing out the sliding glass door that led to the balcony. A sunny day, with no land in sight; dark blue ocean swells, stretching to the horizon.

She had slept soundly for the first time in weeks. The gentle rocking of the ship had lulled her to sleep. She could feel the engines humming far below her, a vibration that had penetrated her dreams.

On the desk beside the sliding glass doors, she found a scrawled note from Pat. "Gone to explore. Back at 10."

Her stomach growled, reminding her that she hadn't eaten much dinner. She hadn't been eating well lately. She'd lost weight since Harry had left her. Her friends said she was on the Misery Diet: no sleep and no food. The clock on the bedside table said it was 9:15.

Her stomach growled again, and she decided she couldn't wait for Pat. She'd go to one of the ship's eight restaurants and break the Misery Diet once and for all.

She took a shower and quickly dressed in black slacks and a tailored shirt. Uncertain as to what clothes would be appropriate, she followed advice her mother had given her long ago: "It's always better to be overdressed than under-dressed."

On the dressing table, she found the brochure that Pat had been reading aloud. She checked the list of the the ship's restaurants and decided to head for Circe's Kitchen, where the brochure claimed she would find "casual dining with a magnificent view." She picked up her copy of *Wild Angel* by Mary Maxwell, and took it with her so that she'd have something to read as she ate. Then she headed out the door.

As she stepped into the corridor, the door to the state-room next to hers opened and Max Merriwell stepped out. He glanced at her, then looked both ways down the corridor. He held a piece of paper in his hand, and he looked puzzled.

"Good morning," she said. "Is something wrong?" Since she was frequently lost herself, she had a great deal of sympathy for anyone who was confused.

"Not really." He looked at the paper in his hand and shook his head. "I found this note under my door. I wonder . . . you didn't see who left it."

"No, I just got here. I didn't see anyone. What does it say?" She asked without thinking, then immediately added, "Oh, it's none of my business, of course." She could feel her cheeks reddening as Max put the note in her hands.

At the top of the note was a set of lines, arranged like this:

Beneath the lines, someone had printed: "A one-eyed man treads on the tail of the tiger. The tiger bites the man. Misfortune." The paper was from one of the ship's notepads. The words were printed in a large, angular hand, like that of a child who has only recently learned to print.

"The hexagram is from the *I Ching*," Max said. He tapped a finger on the lines. "You know, the *Book of Changes*. Ordinarily, I throw the yarrow sticks each morning. I find it clears my mind. The oracle is so wonderfully ambiguous. It offers so many possibilities if you are open to them."

When Susan was in college, her roommate had experimented with the ancient Chinese oracle known as the *I Ching*. Rather than throwing yarrow sticks, her roommate had flipped pennies to select the six lines of the hexagram. The advice the *Book of Changes* gave always seemed rather vague to Susan. You could interpret it in so many ways.

"Don't you find its advice confusing?" Susan asked.

"Not at all. I find it liberating. A high tolerance for ambiguity is a very useful trait. Unfortunately, in my haste to pack I didn't bring my copy of the book." He took the note back from her, pushed his glasses up on his nose, and studied it again. "I recognize the hexagram, of course. It warns of a difficult situation ahead. One is handling wild and intractable people."

"Why would someone leave you a fortune from the *I Ching*?" she wondered aloud.

"A sort of fan mail, I imagine." Max smiled vaguely and stuffed the note into his pocket. "Or a warning—perhaps the workshop will be filled with intractable people."

"Well, I'll be there and I promise to be cooperative," she said, smiling.

"Then I won't worry about it."

She hesitated, then said, "I was just going to breakfast. Would you like to join me?"

"Well, I was heading to breakfast myself." He glanced at the book in her hand. "But you look like you were planning to read."

She held up the book so that he could see the cover. "Given the choice of reading the book or having breakfast with the author, I'll choose the author," she said.

In Circe's Kitchen, a casual restaurant with red-checkered tablecloths and a long breakfast menu, they sat at a table by a window that looked out on the Promenade. Joggers passed the window at regular intervals.

"You know," Max said, studying the menu, "they really should be more careful about how they name restaurants. Circe was the one who turned men into swine. Hardly a recommendation for an eatery."

Susan laughed. She felt lucky to be having breakfast with Max. When the waiter came, she ordered a Belgian waffle and he ordered pigs in a blanket. She suppressed a giggle and got a funny look from the waiter. Max smiled, obviously glad to be entertaining her.

Max picked up the book she had set on the table. "You mentioned at dinner you had read all my books."

"All the books you've written as Max Merriwell or as Mary Maxwell except for the latest two, *Wild Angel* and *There and Back Again.* I haven't read any of the books you've written as Weldon Merrimax."

Max waved a hand, as if dismissing Weldon's work as unimportant. "That's fine. Frankly, Weldon's work can be rather depressing. Not everyone's cup of tea."

"I love Mary Maxwell's books." She hesitated. "I guess I should say I love all the books you've written as her."

He shook his head. "You were right the first time. Those are Mary's books."

She frowned, remembering the conversation she had overheard on the bridge. Max made a distinction between himself and his pen names. "So you don't think of yourself as Mary?"

"Not really. Mary writes books with a woman's perspective. My books are very different from hers. I really prefer writing science fiction, but fantasy is so popular. So I put some time into thinking about Mary Maxwell, a sort of alter ego of mine. Then one night, I met her in a dream and she started telling me a story."

Susan nodded, frowning. He talked about Mary as if she were real. Susan decided to play along. "So what's Mary like?" she asked. "I've always wondered."

"She's a very self-confident woman," he said. "A bit younger than I am. Totally fearless. She likes to travel— she's always taking off for exotic places, always getting into trouble. But she's quite capable of getting out of any trouble she gets into. In fact, I rather think she likes trouble. If there isn't any trouble around, chances are she'll stir some up. So she always has fascinating stories to tell."

Susan smiled. He seemed very fond of Mary. "And what about Weldon?" she asked.

Max shook his head, looking like a disappointed father. He wasn't as happy with Weldon, she thought. "Weldon's another story," he said. "A very rough character. His parents were carnival grifters. His mother told fortunes. His dad played three-card monte, standing at a folding table on the edge of the midway. 'Find the queen,' his dad would say, 'Find the lucky lady and double your money.' As a kid, Weldon shilled for his dad, making bets and winning repeatedly, convincing the marks that they could win. If that kid could win, they figured anyone could.

"But they couldn't and they didn't because somehow the queen was never where they thought she'd be—maybe because they didn't think she'd be up Weldon's father's sleeve or in his pocket."

"That sounds like a hard life," Susan said.

Max nodded. "Weldon began contributing to the family income when he was sixteen. His dad was in prison for a few years—a con had gone wrong. So Weldon was playing three-card monte at the edge of the midway, just as his dad had. 'Find the lucky lady,' Weldon crooned. 'Maybe it's your lucky day.' Another carnival brat was serving as his shill, and the kid had won a few bucks."

"It was a slow night and Weldon was just about to give up. The midway was starting to close down when half a dozen workers from one of the steel plants came by and started gambling with their pay—betting big and losing big.

Weldon was doing great—until the steel workers decided he was cheating. His shill ran for help, but the kid didn't run fast enough. The steel workers broke both Weldon's hands, stomping them beneath heavy boots and fracturing the fingers that had manipulated the cards so nimbly. By the time Weldon's friends found him, the steel workers were gone. Weldon's mother nursed him back to health, but his hands have never been the same."

"How terrible," Susan said, forgetting for a moment that he was talking about an imaginary character.

Max shrugged. "When Weldon recovered, he stole a car, went back to the town, waited at the back gate to the steel mill, and shot the three men as they came out. Killed two, left the third paralyzed from the waist down, and took off before anyone knew what was happening. Then disappeared into the carny world and got away with it. Don't waste your sympathy on him. He's a ruthless man."

Susan stared at Max, horrified at the story. Then Max laughed. "You said you didn't read Weldon's books and here I am, telling you Weldon Merrimax stories."

Susan managed a smile, remembering that Weldon was an imaginary character. There was no Weldon Merrimax, no steel workers. The waiter brought their breakfast just then. Susan dug into the Belgian waffle with enthusiasm.

"You've got a better appetite than you did last night," Max said. "You're feeling better?"

"Well, I wasn't really seasick," she began, feeling a little foolish. She looked up from the waffle. "I just . . ." She hesitated, then continued, "I just didn't want to answer a lot of personal questions."

Max nodded as if he had known it all along. "Of course," he said.

"Tom figured it out and covered for me," Susan said. She looked down at her plate. If her discomfort had been so obvious that both Tom and Max had realized what was going on, surely others had noticed. "I hope the others didn't think . . ." she began.

Max waved his hand, interrupting her. "The others didn't

notice a thing. Oh, perhaps that young fellow, Ian, and your friend, Pat, figured it out. But the rest . . ." He shook his head. "Most people walk around as if they were half asleep. They don't notice half of what's going on around them. Cops and writers pay attention to things that other people don't. I watch people and make up lies. Cops watch people and figure out when they're lying. I have the easier job, I think."

She sipped her coffee and thought perhaps she had underestimated Max. He was rather sharp about noticing what was going on around him.

When she looked up from her coffee, she caught him studying her face. "You know, I have a suggestion for you," he said.

"A suggestion?"

He was watching her carefully. "I think you need to learn to lie."

"I beg your pardon?" She stared at him, taken aback.

"I think you need to learn to lie. You're really much too honest."

"I didn't think a person could be too honest," she said.

"Oh, I disagree. Take that conversation with Alberta at dinner. She was asking personal questions to find out who you were so that she could figure out how to treat you. That was what dinner was all about, you know. Sizing people up and jockeying for position."

"Well . . ." Susan was reluctant to accept this assessment. She would like to have a better opinion of her fellow passengers than that. "That seems rather harsh. I'm sure she was trying to get to know me . . ."

Max interrupted. "Of course. She wanted to get to know you so she'd know where you fit into the scheme of things. You'd been very quiet and she wanted to know how to treat you. Should she patronize you, bully you, or treat you with respect? She knows you're a librarian and you're not currently married, so I think she's inclined to patronize you at this point, but you could change that."

Susan frowned, startled again. "You said I'm not currently married. What makes you think I was ever married?"

He smiled again, looking rather pleased with himself. "I told you, Susan. I watch people. When you told Alberta that you weren't married, you touched your left hand, as if feeling for a wedding ring that wasn't there. When I mentioned your marital status just now, you did it again. I would guess that you used to wear a ring, but gave it up quite recently."

Susan looked down at her hands and caught herself in the act of feeling for her ring—her right hand was on top on her left, touching the ring finger. She carefully set her hands on the table on either side of her water glass.

"Don't worry about it," Max said. "Most people wouldn't notice. It's a matter of careful observation."

She nodded, looking up from her hands. "So you figure Alberta is going to patronize me because I'm a divorced librarian. Well, if she thinks being a librarian is unimportant, I don't see how . . ."

"Where are you a librarian? Wait—don't tell me!" He held up his hand. "This is an opportunity to reinvent yourself. You can be any number of different people, depending on how you answer." He leaned closer. "Your answer determines your status. If you are a librarian at Stanford University, that's one thing. Or if you manage the private law library for a wealthy attorney. Or perhaps . . ." He let his voice drop. "Perhaps you run the library for a government security agency—not the CIA, something much more secret. You can't really talk about your work—that's always useful."

She realized the advantages of his line of thinking. "If I can't talk about it, then I don't have to lie," she said.

"That's true. But it's important to realize that the way that you refuse to talk about it will be very different than if you were—oh, say—out of work. Keep in mind—it's not that you won't talk about it. You can't talk about it. So you quickly redirect the conversation, and people will know you are not saying all you can. That creates a hint of mystery, a bit of intrigue.

She was smiling now. "You talk as if my life were a story."

"It is, isn't it?" he said. "It's your story. You're making it up as you go along. So tell me: where do you work?"

She pursed her lips, suppressing a grin, and tried to look serious. "I'm afraid I'm not at liberty to say." She laughed. "Besides, why would anyone want to talk about work on such a beautiful day?"

BAD GRRLZ' GUIDE TO PHYSICS

ABOUT PHYSICS AND BAD GRRLZ

Some people are surprised when I tell them I'm a physicist. They seem to think that being a physicist and being a Bad Grrl are somehow incompatible.

They couldn't be more wrong.

Physicists and Bad Grrlz have a great deal in common. They both ask many questions. Why not dye my hair blue? What's wrong with eating chocolate cake for dinner? What is the basic nature of matter?

Oh, the questions may be different, but the impulse underlying them is the same. Bad Grrlz and physicists question things that other people take for granted.

For example, you're probably sitting in a chair as you are reading this. You're sitting in a chair and thinking nothing of it. Your butt presses against the chair and the chair supports your butt. So simple. So straightforward.

But it's really not simple at all. That chair you're sitting on is 99.9% empty space. For that matter, so is your butt. Your butt and that chair are both made of molecules which are made of protons and neutrons and electrons—with a whole lot of space between them. Why then doesn't your butt slide right through that chair, with molecules of the chair sliding through the empty space in your butt and vice versa?

As a physicist, I can tell you the answer. You owe your comfortable seat to electromagnetic forces. All that empty space between the electrons and protons and neutrons of the chair is electrically charged. So is the empty space between the electrons and protons and neutrons of your butt. Electrical charge pushes on electrical charge and your butt rests on the chair, rather than falling through.

To be a physicist, you need to believe in forces that you can't see and you don't really understand—forces like electricity and magnetism. As a Bad Grrl, you often have to

deal with people who would rather not see you and who
certainly don't understand you—like the maître d' at the
Ithaca Dining Room, who was so very determined not to
stare at my hair. Not the same thing, but strangely related.
As a Bad Grrl, I figure I am like electricity and magnetism,
an invisible force acting on society in mysterious ways.

And being a physicist has proven very useful to this Bad
Grrl. After all, the game of pool is nothing more than ap-
plied physics and geometry. It's all about angles and spin
and momentum. Thanks to physics (and a bunch of ill-
informed men who were willing to bet that a cute little lady
could never beat them at pool) I made it through my un-
dergraduate years without taking out a single student loan.

FOUR

"In a just universe, I would never win at cards," the man said. "Fortunately this is not a just universe." He laid his cards on the table and smiled.

—from *Here Be Dragons*
by Mary Maxwell

The *Odyssey*, the sole cruise ship of Odyssey Lines, was a temporary resting place for cruise industry workers who were on their way up—or on their way down. Take Gene Culver, the cruise director. This man was pictured in every *Odyssey* brochure, wearing a smile that displayed far too many teeth. Gene Culver believed he was on his way up. Gene believed in himself with the confidence of a graduate from a Dale Carnegie course.

In the first issue of the *Ship's Log*, the *Odyssey's* daily newsletter, Gene's "Welcome Aboard" letter explained that the *Odyssey* was on the cutting edge of cruise ship entertainment. On this cruise—on this very cruise!—passengers would be treated to two "innovative concepts in cruise entertainment." One was a Gold Rush–style melodrama, staged in honor of the convention of California historians that was on board. The other was the *Star Ship Odyssey*, an original work created just for the *Odyssey*. Gene's letter promised that passengers would be amazed, would be astounded, would be delighted by the show.

Gene was frantic in his desire to be noticed by the Powers That Be at Celebrity, at Princess, oh, even at Carnival Cruises (known in the industry as Cannibal Cruises). To that end, Gene had brought aboard entertainers ("talent" as they say in show biz) that offered something other than run-of-the-mill cruise entertainment. That was why Max was on board—Gene thought that offering a writing workshop by a popular novelist would attract the attention of those who mattered.

But passengers wouldn't miss out on more typical cruise fare: a magician who did card tricks, a hypnotist who told bad jokes; lounge singers and their backup bands, Vegas-style stage shows with more than their share of sequins and feathers. Gene was trying to strike a delicate balance, getting the attention of the Big Boys with his innovations while hiding any disasters that resulted from his experiments. Maintaining this balance made Gene very nervous.

At the other end of the spectrum was Antonio, the man in charge of fruit sculptures, ice sculptures, and the champagne fountain that was required on every luxury cruise. Antonio was on his way down. He had worked for Celebrity Cruises for many years, but he had quit after an altercation with a French chef.

For the final dinner on a two-week Celebrity Cruise, Antonio had planned an elaborate fruit sculpture of a dragon, complete with flaming breath. Antonio had planned to carve the flames from mango, a fruit with precisely the right color and consistency. He had personally selected a case of mangos, choosing fruit that would be ripe, but not overripe when the time came to carve them. He had checked to make sure that the case of mangos was on board and properly stored in the galley's supply room.

But when Antonio went to get the fruit and begin work on the carving, the case of mangos was nowhere to be found. It seemed that the French chef had appropriated them for a special dessert sauce. When Antonio confronted the chef, the man dismissed Antonio's concerns.

"But what about the flames," Antonio protested.

"Carve them from cantaloupe," the chef said with a Gallic shrug. His tone dripped with contempt. "What difference does it make?"

Antonio was an artist. Antonio would not substitute cantaloupe for mangos—carefully chosen mangos, his very own mangos. Antonio would not tolerate disrespect from a

French pig of a chef who thought of food only as something to be eaten, not the substance of art.

They argued. Somehow, the argument, which began with mangos, delved into the role of Italy in the Second World War, into the cowardice of the French, into the personal habits of the Italians, into the sexual impotence of the French, into any number of subjects that might seem, on first examination, to have little to do with mangos or dessert sauce or fruit sculpture.

The galley of a cruise ship was no place for a such a heated argument. At some point, Antonio grabbed his carving knife. The chef snatched up a cleaver. There was much shouting and waving of blades and ship's security intervened.

Though Antonio explained that the Frenchman was at fault, Antonio was blamed for the fight. A fruit sculptor, however talented, was more expendable than a French chef. Bitter and angry, Antonio left Celebrity Cruises and signed on with the *Odyssey*.

People on their way up and people on their way down. And a few, just a few, people who liked it right where they were. Tom was one of the latter.

Being the security chief on a cruise ship was a bit like being the sheriff of a town with a population of just over two thousand people. Three quarters of the population were passengers; the other six hundred and some were crew members who were working hard to keep those passengers happy.

The *Odyssey* was an incredibly diverse small town. Tom had counted fifteen different nationalities among the crew, last time he had bothered to check. Most of the officers were British or Italian. Most of the passengers were American, as was the purser's staff. Galley staff tended to be French and Italian. The dining room staff came from all over—Italians, Greeks, Arabs, a few Irish, a few Scots. The staff in the ship's many bars were Irish and Scottish and English and Australian with one Norwegian and one Dane. The accommodation staff—the stewards and butlers who tended to the staterooms and room service—were Filipino, for the most part, with a few Mexicans. The casino manager was American, the head of the beauty salon was Dutch, the manager of the boutiques was Swiss, and the ship's doctor was German.

Occasionally, the diversity lead to trouble—an American woman became upset at the way an Italian man hit on her; a Greek and a Turk were unable to work in the same department; a French woman flirted a little much with an Australian man and had her intentions misunderstood. Many members of the crew were young, out to see the world and have a good time. There were cabin parties and drinking that sometimes got out of control.

But generally, Tom had little trouble dealing with the crew. Members of the crew respected him; when he shut down a cabin party, he rarely had to return and do it again.

The passengers were another story. They expected luxury. They expected the crew to cater to their every whim. To "pamper" them, to be exact—the advertising brochures promised that all the *Odyssey*'s passengers would be "pampered." The passengers read these brochures and believed them. The crew did their best to meet passengers' expectations of pampering.

Except for Tom. Tom was the one who had to intervene when the shouts of a squabbling couple disturbed passengers in the adjoining staterooms; when a drunken passenger insisted on picking a fight; when a party in a passenger's stateroom got out of hand. Unlike the crew, the *Odyssey*'s passengers did not always accept Tom's authority gracefully. They felt entitled to whatever they wanted—and Tom occasionally had to be the one to tell them that they couldn't have it.

Fortunately, Tom was an even-tempered, easygoing sort of guy. He did his best to smooth over any minor difficulties, and there was rarely any real trouble.

When Tom woke on the second morning of the cruise, he was hoping for a quiet day at sea. Since they wouldn't be landing in Bermuda until the next day, he had no port officials to deal with, no visitors and passengers coming and going, no new paperwork cluttering his desk.

He got to the security office before Ian arrived. He filed all the paperwork related to their departure from New York Harbor. He was checking to make sure that their forms were in order for entry to Bermuda when his phone rang.

It was the purser's office, letting him know that a passenger complaint required security attention. The games room, a lovely, little, wood-paneled room that was occupied each afternoon by blue-haired ladies playing bridge, had apparently been the site of a poker game on the previous evening. A passenger was complaining that he had lost a lot of money and was demanding that the purser do something about it.

Tom went to the purser's office and talked with the passenger, a square-jawed, white-haired man who seemed accustomed to getting his own way. "My wife was in the theater watching the show," the man told Tom. "I was heading for the casino when I ran into this fellow. We had a drink at the Alehouse, then decided to play a friendly game or two." The man frowned. "He took me for five hundred dollars."

Tom nodded gravely, doing his best to convey that he was taking this matter very seriously. He knew that it would do no good to ask the man why on earth he had felt the need to carry five hundred dollars in cash during a cruise where he could pay for everything with his cruise card. Tom also knew that what he was going to say was not going to make the man happy.

"I can certainly understand your unhappiness, sir," he said.

"I want you to find him and arrest him," the man said.

"I understand that," Tom said patiently. "But I'm afraid that's not possible. You see, nothing illegal has happened here. If two passengers wish to gamble privately, that's not my business. Of course, we'd prefer you gamble in the casino, where the games are regulated. But if you choose to set up your own game . . ."

"He was cheating," the passenger interrupted. "Some kind of a card shark, I'm sure of that."

Tom nodded again. The man had lost and he was unhappy. Therefore, it must be someone else's fault. That was human nature.

"I'm afraid that there's nothing we can do to get your money back. But I would be happy to contact the other party and suggest that he confine his gambling to the casino." Tom took out a notepad. He had started doing that after watching a number of Columbo reruns from the ship's video library. He'd found that people seemed to find it reassuring when he wrote information down. "Did you get the other man's name?"

Of course he hadn't. The other fellow had said, "Call me Max," and that was good enough for this fellow.

Tom got a description, which he patiently wrote down: the other player had been a man in his forties with brown hair and blue eyes. Medium height, a mustache but no beard, casually dressed. Then Tom listened to a great deal of bluster about how this sort of thing shouldn't happen. Tom politely agreed that such things shouldn't happen. The passenger, according to Company Policy, was always right.

Eventually, Tom assured the passenger that he would look into the matter and gently repeated his suggestion that the man restrict his gambling to the casino, where the *Odyssey* staff could ensure a fair game.

Ian was tapping furiously on his keyboard when Tom returned to the security office. Tom asked him to search the passenger list for anyone named Max, but the only Max on the list was Max Merriwell. The writer didn't match the passenger's description of the hustler. While Tom considered other possibilities, Ian continued to tap on his keyboard.

Tom reviewed the previous night's security log to determine who had been patrolling the area where the incident had occurred. He called the guard who had been on duty. The man had noticed the card game, but it had appeared at that time to be a friendly game, involving no money. He had advised the players that gambling was restricted to the ship's casino. The players had assured him that they were just playing for fun.

The guard was new. Tom advised him that there was no such thing as a friendly poker game. Of course they had been playing for fun. But invariably some people had more fun than others. The guy who lost didn't have any fun at all. The guy who won had quite a lot of fun.

Tom hung up, shaking his head. He'd tell his staff to keep a better eye on the games room for other friendly games of poker. He'd check the casino for the alleged card shark and have a quiet word with the man if he found him. If a professional gambler was aboard, Tom wanted to advise the man that he was being watched before any more problems developed. Just a friendly tip—Tom figured that's all it would take. Tom pushed his chair back, planning to take a stroll through the casino.

"Uh, Tom . . ." Ian held his cup of coffee in both hands, his eyes narrowed in concentration as he stared at the computer screen. "I didn't find another Max, but I did find something else very interesting. I was checking the records for last night and I found an anomaly. Last night, at Aphrodite's Alehouse, someone paid for a drink with a cruise card that isn't in the system." Aphrodite's Alehouse was one of the ship's eight bars.

Tom frowned at Ian. "A cruise card that isn't in the system? What do you mean?"

Ian was smiling ever so slightly. He sipped his coffee. "A name that's not on the passenger list. A cruise card that doesn't exist in the system. There's no record of the person with this cruise card getting on the ship. No photo on file."

"How can that be? Someone has a counterfeit cruise card?" Tom shook his head. Ian's computerized cruise card system was supposed to track who was on board and who wasn't. Tom didn't see the need for the new technology. The old method of controlling who was on board—a checklist at each gangway—had worked just fine from Tom's point of view. But all the competitors' ships had cruise cards, so the Company had decided that the *Odyssey* should have them, too. Now, after two shakedown cruises, Ian had found a problem.

Tom wasn't worried: he had not yet discontinued the old checklist system. Don, his second in command, had insisted that they keep the old system going until they were certain the new system worked flawlessly. Don was an old Navy master-at-arms, and he tended to be conservative. So thanks to the checklist system, Tom know who was on the ship. There were no extra passengers aboard.

"I don't think it's a counterfeit card," Ian said, still smiling. "More likely it's some kind of mistake. You see, the name on the cruise card is Weldon Merrimax."

"That's one of Max Merriwell's names," Tom said.

"That's right."

"So where else has Weldon Merrimax been?"

"I can't tell you. A card only shows up on the system when the person charges something. Since most of the ship's services are included in the cruise, there's no charge. I could have set up the system to track whenever a card was used to enter a stateroom, but some people were concerned about passengers' privacy." Ian shrugged. "You'll have to wait until he buys something else."

Tom frowned. "Gene Culver wanted Max Merriwell to teach that writing workshop as Weldon Merrimax," he said. "Maybe Gene issued Max a cruise card in that name."

"Maybe," Ian said. "I can check into that."

"You do that," Tom said. "In the meantime, maybe I'll ask Max if he charged a drink in Aphrodite's last night."

Ian consulted his computer screen. "His workshop is in the library," Ian said. "He'll be teaching for another half hour. You could catch him there."

Tom nodded. "I guess I'll do that."

On his way to the library, Tom visited the accounting office where a clerk made him a copy of the charge slip that Weldon Merrimax had signed. The signature was printed more than written. "Weldon Merrimax," it said, in square, angular letters. Tom noted the name of the bartender who had signed off on the tab, then pocketed the copy and headed for the library.

Susan sat in a comfortable chair in the ship's library, listening to Max talk about writing.

The library was furnished like a gentleman's club with upholstered easy chairs and oak tables. The windows along one wall looked onto the Promenade, where passengers strolled and jogged. The other wall was lined with bookshelves on which Max's work was prominently displayed—books by Max Merriwell, Mary Maxwell, and Weldon Merrimax.

Max sat in an upholstered leather chair at one end of a heavy oak table. A dozen or so passengers sat around the table. Alberta was there. So were two little old ladies, one with her knitting and one with her embroidery. A brooding teenage boy with a ragged haircut and rumpled clothes slumped in his chair and glowered out the window at the joggers who passed on the promenade. Susan guessed he was a Weldon Merrimax fan even before she noticed the paperback copy of *Tell Me No Lies* on the table in front of him.

Cindy, a young woman wearing a Hawaiian shirt, turquoise blue trousers, and the blue blazer that served as the uniform of the cruise staff, had introduced Max with an air of breathless enthusiasm. "I'm so glad you all came to the first ever *Odyssey* writers' workshop," she said to the group. "I think it's so exciting that we have an internationally known author here to teach us."

"I want to introduce Max Merriwell, the author of many, many books." It was clear to Susan that Cindy had not read any of Max's books. The young woman seemed more impressed by the number of books than their content. "We are pleased and honored that he'll be teaching this workshop," she concluded.

Max regarded the group benignly. "It's very nice to see you all here today," he said. "You may think that I'm going to teach you to write, but what I'm really going to do is help you exercise your imaginations. I've found that relatively few adults ever exercise their imaginations at all, let alone give them the kind of strenuous workout that writing a story demands."

He talked for a while about paying attention to the world around you, about learning to listen to your inner voice, about the power of your imagination.

"I assume that each of you is here because you have a story to tell. You may not know what that story is, but if you try, you'll figure it out. Every one of us has many stories that make up our lives. I'm going to help you learn to tell those stories. So let's get started. Everyone needs a pencil and paper."

Some people had brought notebooks; others had not. Cindy bustled around, getting everyone what they needed. She was relieved, Susan thought, to have something to do.

"First off, I don't want you to confuse me with your high school English teacher. I didn't much like my high school English teachers and I certainly never wanted to be one. I'm not here to correct your grammar and put periods in the right places. I have a healthy respect for a well-placed period, but I don't think the world will end if a period is out of place. I don't even care much about the words. What I care about is the imagination. That's what matters."

"Now I want you to think about something that matters to you. An object of some sort that you have strong feelings about. Something you love or something you hate—I don't care which—but something that matters to you. Write down what you are thinking about."

In her notebook, Susan scrawled, "My wedding ring."

"Write down a couple of lines about that object. Describe it. You don't have to write in sentences. I don't care about that. Just write something."

Susan wrote: "Solid gold. Heavy. Valuable." She hesitated for a moment, tapping her pen on the page nervously, then crossed out the word valuable and wrote "Expensive." Not quite the same thing, she thought. It was worth money, but it wasn't valuable to her, or she wouldn't have thrown it away. She caught herself in the act of feeling for the ring with the thumb of her left hand, touching the callus where the ring had once rested. "Familiar," she wrote. "Gone."

"Now write a few words about how that object makes you feel," Max said.

She stared at the page, her eyes focusing on the last word she had written. "Gone." How did she feel? She remembered staring at the horizon as the ship headed across the ocean, far from land. "Adventurous," she wrote. "Bold."

"Don't worry if some of the feelings are contradictory," Max said. "That's just the way it is, sometimes."

"Afraid," Susan wrote. "Lost. Confused."

"All right," Max said. "Now I want you to put all that together into a scene. A very short scene involving the object you have described. A scene that comes out of your feelings about the object."

Susan wrote: "A woman stood on the deck of a ship, staring out at the ocean waves. In her hand, she held a golden ring, her wedding ring. Staring out at the waves, she threw the ring overboard, threw it as hard as she could. At the moment it left her hand, she wished that she could snatch it back. Too late. Her hand was empty; the ring was gone. She felt lost. She felt lonely. She felt like anything could happen."

Tom stepped into the ship's library and stood just inside the doorway. The class was ending. Max was saying, "Now, if nobody has any more questions, we'll wrap it up for today."

People stood, stretched, and began talking. As Tom made his way to the front of the room, he overheard a few comments about writing, but most of the people were talking about where they should go for lunch. That didn't surprise him; in his experience, passengers talked more about food than about anything else.

Tom saw Susan and Pat standing by the table, gathering

their things. Susan looked up, saw Tom, and quickly
stepped toward him. "I'm glad you're here," she said. "I
thought about trying to talk Max into going to see you, but
I don't know if he would have. He got a strange note this
morning."

"A note? What sort of note?"

"A note with a hexagram from the *I Ching*," she said.
Tom frowned, and she explained a little more. "The *Book
of Changes*. It's a system of Chinese fortune-telling. Max
said the note was nothing to worry about, but it seemed
kind of threatening to me. Someone slipped it under his
door last night."

Seems like last night was a busy night, Tom thought.
Max was talking to a frowning teenager, who seemed to be
complaining about something.

"Maybe you could rescue poor Max," Pat said. "He's
talking to a Weldon Merrimax fan."

"That's bad?" Tom asked.

"That would be my guess."

From Max's pained expression, Tom had to agree.

"Better go save him," Susan said.

Tom stepped toward the writer. "Max, I need to have a
word with you." He glanced at the teenager. "I hope you'll
excuse us."

"Sure," the kid mumbled. "I was looking for Weldon
Merrimax, anyway." He turned and walked away.

Max shook his head, looking unhappy.

Tom frowned. "I thought you were Weldon," he said.

"I write as Weldon," Max said. He was fumbling in his
pocket. After a moment, he pulled out a pipe and a lighter.

"Remember, Mr. Merriwell." Cindy's clear voice came
from the back of the room. "No smoking in the library!"

"Perhaps we could step outside," Max said, glancing at
Cindy with the weary expression of a smoker who had been
denied too long. Tom followed Max onto the promenade
deck.

Outside, Tom leaned against the rail, waiting for Max to
fill his pipe. The sun was warm on his face. Joggers in

brightly colored sweat suits pounded past him. Passengers aboard the *Odyssey* were always jogging. A nearby sign read: "Three times around the promenade deck is one mile."

Max tamped down the tobacco in his pipe and took his time lighting it, cupping his hand around the bowl, holding the lighter just so, and puffing diligently until the tobacco caught. It took quite a while. Once it was lit, Max looked up from his pipe and smiled.

"Just as well the young man didn't find Weldon," Max said. "I'm much nicer to my fans than Weldon would be." Max puffed on his pipe. "Now what was it that you wanted to talk with me about?"

"I was hoping you could help me out with a bit of a mystery," Tom said. "Could I take a look at your cruise card?"

"My cruise card? Why's that?"

"Well, it seems that Weldon Merrimax charged a drink on a cruise card last night."

Max stopped puffing on his pipe and narrowed his eyes. "Really? Weldon Merrimax?"

"The charge showed up on a tab at Aphrodite's. I thought perhaps Gene issued you a cruise card with the wrong name."

Max pulled out his cruise card and handed it to Tom. Tom glanced at the cruise card—issued to Max Merriwell. The photo showed Max, staring into the camera, and the embossed name identified it as belonging to Max Merriwell.

"I assume it's all in order," Max said. "In any case, I didn't go out for a drink last night. I stayed in my cabin. I'm just starting to work on my next book."

Tom nodded and returned Max's card. "It looks just fine. Now tell me about this mysterious note you received."

"Did Susan mention that to you? It's nothing to trouble you about," Max said. "Just a joke, I'm sure."

"Susan seemed to think it was threatening."

"Such a sweet girl," Max said. He fumbled in his pocket

again. This time, he pulled out a sheet of ship's stationery and handed it to Tom.

"It is a hexagram from the *I Ching*," Max said. "You're familiar with that, of course?"

"Chinese fortune-telling," Tom said.

Max squinted from beneath bushy eyebrows, looking rather like a professor whose student has delivered an incomplete answer. "Not just fortune-telling," Max said. "The *I Ching* is an oracle, true, but it is also a book of wisdom. You throw the yarrow sticks to generate a hexagram. That hexagram provides the reader with a set of possibilities—and recommends a course of action."

"What course of action does this one recommend?" Tom asked.

Max peered at the hexagram. "The lower trigram—that's the bottom three lines—is Tui, the joyous—cheerful but weak. The upper trigram is Ch'ien, the creative, large and strong. This deals with power relationships. The weak treads upon the strong."

"And so what does that tell you to do?"

"It describes a dangerous enterprise. The superior man has the power to carry it through, but this power must be combined with caution. One must be resolute but conscious of danger."

Tom shook his head. It sounded like a fortune cookie to him, but he thought it best not to share that opinion with Max. "Are you about to begin a dangerous enterprise?" Tom asked.

Max nodded thoughtfully. "As I said, I am beginning work on a book."

Tom smiled. "That hardly seems hazardous."

"There's always an element of danger there," Max said, quite seriously. "It's an unpredictable process. Anything could happen."

Tom nodded. "Well, that's not the sort of danger that usually involves ship's security." Tom continued examining the note. The printing was quite distinctive. Tom reached into his pocket and pulled out the copy of the charge slip that Weldon Merrimax had signed. "You know, the printing on your note is very similar to Weldon Merrimax's signature on the charge slip." He glanced up at Max as he said that.

Max bit down on his pipe, looking thoughtful. "How interesting. Perhaps the same person wrote both."

"Do you have any idea who might want to leave a note for you?" Tom asked.

Max shrugged and puffed on his pipe. "As a writer, one gets used to this sort of thing."

Tom nodded, studying Max's face. He had dealt with many liars in his time as a cop and his time as a security officer. He prided himself on his ability to spot a liar. Tom didn't think Max was lying. No, he seemed like a nice, old guy.

Tom held up the note. "Do you mind if I hang onto this?"

"Be my guest," Max said.

Tom left Max tranquilly puffing on his pipe as the joggers ran past.

Pat and Susan had lunch at the poolside bar on the recreation deck. The sun was out and the afternoon promised to be warm.

Over a burger and fries, Susan told Pat about her breakfast with Max. "He said I was too honest," Susan told Pat. "He told me I needed to learn how to lie."

Pat laughed. "Sounds like great advice. I've been telling you for the past year that you're way too nice."

Susan shook her head. Pat thought most people were way too nice. "It's strange. I just met him, but it feels like I've known him for years. I feel like he's an uncle I never met."

"The black sheep of the family," Pat suggested.

"Yeah—not because he was bad, but because the rest of the family couldn't figure him out. He's a little odd, but in an interesting sort of way. Anyway, he feels like an old friend. Maybe it's because I've read so many of his books.

He's sharper than you might expect, too. He figured out that I had been divorced recently."

Pat leaned back in her chair, studying Susan. "I hate to tell you this, Susan, but it's not all that hard to figure out."

Susan shrugged, feeling uncomfortable. "Well, I'm done with that now. I threw the ring overboard, and now it's fish food."

Pat lifted her beer in a toast. "Best thing you ever did," she said.

INTRODUCING QUANTUM MECHANICS

My Ph.D. dissertation deals with a mathematical synthesis of the Everett-DeWitt Many Worlds theory and the Wigner Interpretation. My work could revolutionize quantum physics and change our view of the universe. Or it could be dismissed as a totally crackpot scheme. (My advisor, unfortunately, seems inclined toward the second view.)

Both outcomes are possible—and that's only appropriate since possibilities are what quantum mechanics is all about.

Classical Newtonian physics is all about nuts and bolts. It focuses on actualities—something is or it isn't. In classical Newtonian physics, you look at facts that you can measure and quantify and pin down like butterflies in a collector's box. Newtonian physics is about actualities—what *is*.

Quantum physics, on the other hand, is also about what *might be*—the potentiality of any situation. In any system—whether it's an atom about to absorb some light or a bingo game about to begin—there's the actuality and there's the potentiality—that is, the reality waiting to be born as the system evolves, the range of realities that are lurking in the system. Actuality and potentiality are equally real.

Consider, for example, an electron that's orbiting an atom. I'm sure you've seen those lovely retro diagrams of electrons whizzing around a lumpy nucleus.

Now an electron orbiting an atom has a bunch of different orbits to choose from. When a passing light beam of just the right frequency hits an atom, the electron absorbs some energy and moves into a new orbit. But before the electron makes its move, while it's still deciding which orbit to take, it temporarily moves into all possible orbits at the same time.

Yes, it really does. That electron really is in several places at once. In fact, it's smeared all over time and space as it makes trial runs into the future, testing out potentialities.

You don't want to think about electrons? OK, try it this way. Suppose you're a Bad Grrl at a party and you meet three interesting guys—call them Moe, Larry, and Curly. All three guys are hot to date you and they all ask you out for the following Friday night.

If you were like that electron, you could date them all simultaneously. Hey, you could even set up housekeeping with all three, living in three different houses at the same time, a Bad Grrl's dream come true.

You see, quantum entities can experience more than one reality at the same time. In fact, quantum systems are just throwing out possibilities right and left, always making trial runs into the future. Quantum physicists call this 'superposition,' where one reality is superposed on another.

So you've got a reality that consists of a bunch of superposed possibilities, smeared all over time and space. Now suppose that an electron decides on a particular orbit—or you decide that Moe is the guy for you. You don't want to continue your simultaneous existence with Larry and Curly. So you dump those boys and all of a sudden these many possibilities disappear and become one single actuality: the electron is in one orbit and you are with Moe, living happily ever after.

It's a bit tough to wrap your head around, but in the quantum world, those potential realities aren't just possibilities. They interact with one another, evolving and interfering with each other and changing over time. Those potential realities can be described by the Schrödinger Equation, which explores the range of things that might happen, calculating the probability of each.

Those potentialities are real—and that's what makes them interesting.

FIVE

"You can call me Max," he said.
"Is that your name?" she asked. She had learned a thing or two along the way.
He smiled and shook his head. "No. But it will do for now."
          —from *Here Be Dragons*
          by Mary Maxwell

When Tom left the library, it was still too early to find the bartender who had served Weldon Merrimax the night before. So he stopped by the casino.

On the Promenade Deck, it was early afternoon, but in the *Odyssey*'s small casino, it was night. It was always night in the casino.

The casino had no windows. The room's mirrored walls made it appear larger than it actually was. If it weren't for the hum of the engines underfoot and the slow rocking of the ship on the swells, he could have been in Las Vegas.

The bright screens of the video poker machines shone steadily in the dim light. An elderly woman fed a quarter into a slot machine and pulled the lever. The reels spun and the machine jangled, a chaotic collection of musical notes that Tom suspected was designed to keep the players on edge and a little confused. The woman watched the reels, as if mesmerized. "Come on, cherries," she said to the slot machine, half joking, half serious. "Make me a winner." Her husband stood at her elbow, watching her with a tolerant smile.

Casual gamblers who didn't expect to win, Tom thought. That was true of most passengers. They'd drop a few dollars in a slot machine, lose a few at poker or craps. Nothing serious. All in good fun.

He paused near the blackjack table to consider the men playing. There were two young guys, egging each other on, and two men of the right age for the card shark. One was blond; the other, too tall to match the description.

Tom stopped by the casino manager's office. Lisa Hackett, the casino manager, was a blonde in her early forties who had worked her way up from cocktail waitress to blackjack dealer to manager. Tom told her about the illicit poker game and the angry passenger.

"Nothing illegal," Tom said. "But the sort of behavior we'd like to discourage." He advised her to keep her eyes open for the man. "In the bar, he claimed his name was Weldon Merrimax."

"Weldon Merrimax? I've read his books," Lisa said. "Great stuff. It figures he'd be a card shark. His books are all about crooks—swindlers, con artists, thieves, and murderers. He seems to know an awful lot about swindles and cons."

"Well, actually, Max Merriwell writes those books," Tom said. "Weldon Merrimax is a pen name."

Lisa frowned. "I thought you were looking for Weldon Merrimax," she said.

"Yes, I am. But Max Merriwell is the writer who is on board, teaching a workshop. He writes as Weldon Merrimax. Weldon Merrimax doesn't really exist."

"Hang on—you said that's who you were looking for."

"I'm looking for someone who is pretending to be Weldon Merrimax," Tom said.

"But that's what you said Max Merriwell did—pretend to be Weldon Merrimax."

"Max Merriwell writes books as Weldon Merrimax, but he doesn't pretend to be Weldon Merrimax."

Lisa shook her head. "That's a pretty fine line if you ask me," she said. "All right, then. I'll ask my staff to keep an eye out for the man who doesn't exist but somehow manages to win at cards."

———

Shortly after two, Tom reached Aphrodite's Alehouse, where Frank Robinson, the bartender who had waited on Weldon Merrimax, had just come on shift. The bar had the ambiance of an upscale English pub—dark walls, wooden tables, a fire in the fireplace. If it was always night in the casino, it was always late afternoon in the Alehouse. A long lazy afternoon, perfect for a game of darts or hoisting a few pints with a friend.

Frank Robinson, a black man who had been tending bar at the Alehouse for as long as Tom had been chief security officer, was drawing a pint for a passenger at the far end of the bar. Tom sat down and waited until Frank headed in his direction, stopping en route to pour a club soda and add a twist of lemon. Frank set the drink in front of Tom.

"Afternoon, Tom." Frank was from Trinidad. He'd been working on the ship long enough that "dat" and "de" had become "that" and "the," but the lilting accent of the island was still with him. "I thought you'd be coming my way."

"How's that?"

"The manager said that charge slip was no good." Frank shrugged. "The man told me he had forgotten his cruise card. But I knew his name. Heard about this writer teaching on board. So I just did it the way I used to—filled out the slip and all. No problem."

Tom frowned wearily, not wanting to get into another discussion of Max's pseudonyms. "You're not supposed to do that anymore. You have to use the passenger's cruise card. That's the new policy."

"I should tell the man he can't have a drink?" Frank shook his head. "Better give him a drink than have a passenger unhappy." Frank knew the Company Policy—the customer was always right.

"So what did this man look like?"

Frank gave a description that sounded familiar: a white man in his forties, brown hair and blue eyes, mustache, medium height, casually dressed.

"He was here with another fellow," Frank said.

"What did the other fellow look like?"

"White hair. Square chin. Talked too loud," Frank said. "Not like Mr. Merrimax."

Tom frowned. The description matched the passenger who had complained about the card shark. "What was Mr. Merrimax like?"

"Mutton dressed up like lamb," Frank said softly.

Tom nodded. He knew the Caribbean expression: Frank thought Weldon was pretending to be better than he was.

Frank was shaking his head. "Eyes like a snake. Not a man I'd play cards with."

"Were he and the other fellow planning to play cards?"

"I heard Mr. Merrimax say something about it."

Tom nodded. Weldon Merrimax, the mysterious passenger, was also the card shark. How odd that his two problems should overlap. Far from making matters tidier, it seemed to him to make more of a mess.

Susan chose a lounge chair on the side of the pool farthest from the bar. The balmy air was scented with suntan lotion and ocean spray.

Susan sat in the shade provided by a large umbrella. The sun was bright in a cloudless sky. Susan had put on number 25 sunscreen, but she was taking no chances. Many of the chairs in the sun were already occupied by folks who had obviously never heard of a connection between tanning and skin cancer.

Susan draped a towel over her legs, feeling a little self-conscious about her body. She was pale—San Francisco's foggy climate wasn't conducive to tanning—and she had never much liked how she looked in a swimsuit. She had lost weight during the divorce negotiations, but in her estimation she had managed to make the transition from too chubby to too thin without passing through acceptable. It didn't seem fair, but there it was.

Pat was at a line-dancing class. She had told Susan that she wanted to try it out and see if there was something she could write up for the Bad Grrlz' Guide. She had asked

Susan to join her, but Susan had declined. She didn't like dancing. In any group dancing endeavor, she would step to the left when everyone else was stepping right or go forward when everyone else was going back.

She hadn't told Pat any of that, of course. She had just said that she was looking forward to reading *Wild Angel*, by Mary Maxwell. And that was true.

Mary Maxwell's books were always page-turners. The first page of *Wild Angel* introduced young Sarah McKensie, a toddler whose parents have come to California in 1850, searching for gold. By page five, there had been a stagecoach robbery, three murders, and the savage killing of a litter of defenseless wolf pups. Sarah's parents were dead and the little girl had been adopted by the mother wolf whose pups had been killed.

Susan read for more than an hour. Sarah McKensie lived among the wolves, growing up to become an amazing young savage. She was at home in the wilderness—she could bring down a deer with her lasso, kill a grizzly with a bow and arrow, hunt with the wolf pack and howl at the moon.

It was a wonderful and totally unlikely story. Susan particularly enjoyed the descriptions of the Ancient Order of E Clampus Vitus, a wildly improbable secret society:

> *The Ancient Order of E Clampus Vitus claimed origins in 4004 B.C. Some spoilsports said that the Order had been created in the late 1850s as a drunken response to the Masons, the Odd Fellows, and other fraternal orders. Not so, said the Clampers. Adam, the Clampers said, was the Order's first Noble Grand Humbug, the title given to the leader of a chapter. The society counted among its past members such luminaries as Solomon, George Washington, and Henry Ward Beecher. Since these individuals were conveniently dead, they could neither confirm nor deny their membership in the order.*
>
> *The Clampers' motto was Credo Quia Absurdum,*

"I believe because it is absurd." Their meeting hall
was designated the Hall of Comparative Ovations.
Their symbol was the Staff of Relief. Upon initiation,
all members were given *"titles of equal importance."*
Their avowed goal was to assist widows and orphans,
particularly the widows. Their primary activity was
initiating new candidates in extravagant and drunken
rituals. They were reputed to also do good works, but
the truth of that was difficult to ascertain. Since no
Clamper could ever recall the events of a meeting on
the following day, the activities of the society were
assured of remaining secret.

At the sound of shouting from the poolside bar, Susan
looked up from the book. A group of men were drinking
and shouting about something. She frowned, wondering
who they were.

SIX

> *"We're in the Bermuda Triangle," the Captain said. "Better watch what you drink. I've heard that the affects of alcohol are intensified here."*
>
> *"I hear a lot of things," said the woman, mixing herself another Rum Monkey. "Some are true; some aren't. I make a point of choosing which ones to believe." She smiled. "I choose not to believe that one."*
>
> —from *Here Be Dragons*
> by Mary Maxwell

Back in the security office, Ian grinned when Tom told him what Frank Bender had done. There wasn't really anyone on board with a Weldon Merrimax cruise card, Tom told Ian. Someone had used Weldon Merrimax's name and managed to score a free drink.

"So it isn't a computer problem at all," Ian said happily. "It's human error. That's just great!"

Tom went on to say that the person masquerading as Weldon appeared to be the man who had played poker with the angry passenger. "So our card shark is Weldon Merrimax, a man who doesn't exist."

"Wonderful!" Ian said. *"Non sunt multiplicanda entia praeter necissitatem."*

"What on earth are you talking about?" Tom asked in a mild tone.

"Ockham's razor, the principle stated in the thirteenth century by the noted philosopher William of Ockham. The Latin translates as: 'Entities are not to be multiplied beyond necessity.' That is, you should always seek the simplest solution to any problem. And there's your answer. Weldon Merrimax is the card shark!"

"Where do you come up with these things?" Tom asked.

"I was a philosophy major before I got into computer programming," Ian said. "Philosophy is a great excuse to stay up all night talking about ridiculous things."

Tom nodded. He could see how Ian would enjoy something like that. From his pocket, he pulled the note that Max had received and tossed it down on Ian's desk. "All right, here's something else to try to tie into the mess."

Ian unfolded the note and smiled. "An *I Ching* hexagram," he said.

Tom nodded. "A bunch of gibberish."

"Oh, no," Ian said. "The *Book of Changes* isn't gibberish at all. It's really quite wonderful. It's a book of potentialities and possibilities."

Tom squinted at Ian. "You sure know a lot about some wacky stuff."

"I keep an open mind," Ian said. "That's all. Besides, how do you know the *I Ching* is wacky. You haven't tried it."

"Yeah," Tom said. "Max told me you generate a hexagram by throwing yarrow sticks—and I don't seem to have brought along any yarrow sticks."

"Oh, it doesn't have to be yarrow sticks," Ian said quickly. "I've got a random number generator that works just as well. Why don't you give it a try?"

"Give it a try? What do you mean?"

"You come up with a question and I'll generate a hexagram for you."

"And then this ancient Chinese book will tell me what's going to happen?"

"I prefer to think of the *I Ching* as a method for exploring your unconscious thoughts. It's a book of interesting advice. It encourages careful scrutiny of a situation in light of one's own character, attitude, and motives. Come on— what could it hurt? It often provides some interesting insights."

Tom glanced at his watch. "I'd love to, but I have to meet with the purser and let him know that I'm on top of this gambling problem. I'll just have to struggle on in ignorance."

Ian was persistent. "Well, if you were going to ask a question, what would you ask?"

"My question? What's the deal with Max Merriwell and Weldon Merrimax?"

Ian frowned. "Don't you want to be more specific?"

"I think that's specific enough," Tom said. "It's what I'd like to know. Hey—I've got to run."

After Tom left, Ian consulted the *I Ching*.

He had a program that generated a hexagram and provided interpretation and commentary from several translations of the original Chinese texts. Ian's favorite translation was the Wilhelm/Baynes edition, which had been translated from Chinese to German by Richard Wilhelm and from German to English by Cary F. Baynes.

Before generating the hexagram, Ian considered the question he wished to ask the oracle. What's the deal with Max Merriwell and Weldon Merrimax? One always formulated a question before casting the yarrow sticks (or running the random number generator). One then analyzed the resulting hexagram in relation to that question.

Ian turned to his computer and typed in a few characters. A set of six lines appeared on the screen. Beneath it were a few paragraphs of text with the heading: "The Wanderer."

The hexagram was made up of two trigrams, each a set of three lines. The lower trigram was Ken, the mountain. The upper trigram was Li, the fire. As the commentary explained, the two could be together only briefly. The flame goes upward, the mountain presses downward. The flame represents the wanderer, who does not linger in one place. He is in a foreign land and can't find his place. He has few friends. He must be cautious and reserved to protect himself from evil.

Ian was willing to accept that description of Max.

The third line of the hexagram was a changing line,

which meant that it became its opposite—changing from a
solid line to a broken line, from yin to yang, from light to
dark. That change affected the interpretation of the hexagram.

According to the commentary, a changing line in the
third place meant danger. The inn where the wanderer had
lodged burns down. Through his arrogance, the wanderer
loses the loyalty of his servant. He draws misfortune upon
himself.

Ian nodded. His servant could be Weldon Merrimax.

Ian hit another key on the keyboard to change the third
line and generate a new hexagram. The new hexagram appeared on his screen, with its commentary.

The upper trigram was still Li, fire. The lower trigram
was now K'un, the earth. The commentary explained that
fire over the earth represented sunrise. As the sun rises, the
light grows brighter and all becomes clear. For Tom's sake,
Ian hoped that would be the case.

Tom met with the purser, dressed for dinner, and got to the
Ithaca dining room a few minutes early, before the doors
opened to the passengers. Just inside the entrance, Antonio
was putting the final touches on the evening's fruit sculpture.

Tom liked Antonio, a wizened old Italian who took his
work very seriously. Antonio regarded fruit sculpture as a
form of artistic expression overlooked by the unimagina-
tive fools of the art world. "People have no imagination,"
Antonio had told Tom. "If it is not paint, not marble, they
think it is nothing. They do not understand. I carve and I
make the fruit beautiful. It does not last—but beauty can-
not last. The most beautiful woman someday grows old."

From pieces of fresh coconut, painstakingly carved and
neatly stacked, Antonio had created a replica of the *Odyssey*
that was about a foot long. The miniature ship sailed on a
bed of crushed ice. It was sailing toward the Bermuda Islands, constructed from mounds of grapes and identified by

a small sign at the apex of the mound. Red ribbon, tied to the necks of three bottles of white wine set in the ice, marked a large triangle. The ship was sailing under the ribbon.

"The Bermuda Triangle," Antonio told Tom when he paused to admire the Italian's creation. "Ian told me that we entered it last night."

Tom was the last to arrive at the table. The others were already seated. It was one of the ship's formal dinners. People had, for the most part, dressed for the cocktail party that would be held in the Atrium that evening. Max was in his usual tweedy sport coat; Charles and Bill were in suits. Lily was elegant in flame red silk; Alberta wore something with far too many sequins. Susan wore a forest green velvet dress, the same color as the sweater she'd been wearing when he met her. It was a good color for her. Pat wore black jeans and a silk shirt that matched her hair. Ian was in jeans and a T-shirt, as usual.

"Hello, Tom," Bill Carver called. "Just what we need— an expert opinion. We were talking about the Bermuda Triangle."

"I'm hardly an expert on that." Tom took his seat.

"But you've been through it before," Bill persisted.

"More than once," Tom said. He glanced at Ian, who was grinning. Tom was certain Ian had started the conversation. He had seen Ian do it before, tossing an odd topic into a group like a fisherman chumming for sharks. Invariably, people rose to the bait.

"Ian tells us that hundreds of ships and planes have disappeared here," Alberta said. "Vanished without a trace."

Tom shrugged. "No real mystery there. Weather is unpredictable in this part of the world. Storms can come up fast and ships and planes can go down." He smiled reassuringly. "Of course, we won't have any problem with the weather. Satellites warn us about any storm systems. And even if they didn't, no storm is going to swamp the *Odyssey*."

Bill chimed in then, supporting his wife. "Sounds pretty

mysterious though. Ian was telling us that one plane went missing on a perfectly clear day, right after the pilot radioed to say he'd be arriving in Bermuda on schedule. Back in 1941, a navy ship vanished on its way from the Virgin Islands to Florida—and a month later, the same thing happened to another ship."

"And then you've got the *Mary Celeste*," Ian said cheerfully. "It passed near the Bermuda Triangle and everyone aboard vanished."

Tom glanced around the table. Pat seemed amused; Susan, politely interested. Lily wore an expression of mocking tolerance; she clearly thought the conversation was silly. Charles and Bill were listening to Ian. Max had taken refuge behind his menu.

Leaning back in his chair, obviously enjoying himself, Ian told the group about the *Mary Celeste*. On December 14, 1872, the 103-foot brigantine en route from New York to Genoa had been found abandoned and drifting, some 590 miles west of Gibraltar. The ship's captain, his wife, and the seven-member crew were missing. The last position recorded in the log placed her a hundred miles west of the Azores, a path that took her close to the Bermuda Triangle.

Tom had heard all this from Ian, over the past few weeks. Ian delighted in sharing the stranger bits that he found on the Internet. He was particularly fond of the story of *Mary Celeste*.

"The ship was in perfect shape," Ian said, his voice pitched as low as a man telling a ghost story. "The table was set for breakfast. No sign of any foul weather. Something strange had happened—and no one knows what it was."

Tom watched as Charles looked up from the wine list. Tom could see that Charles was thinking about how to turn this conversation to his advantage. "So what's your explanation, Bill?" he asked, a touch of challenge in his voice.

More posturing, Tom thought. He had watched on the

previous night when Bill and Charles had played one-upmanship, and he could see the same thing happening again. Charles had noticed Bill's support of this mystery, and now he was trying to nudge Bill into a position where he'd propose a theory that Charles could ridicule.

Bill shook his head, unwilling to be nudged. "I'm no expert," he said. "But we do have an expert at the table. You write about this weird stuff all the time, don't you, Max? I bet you have an explanation."

Tom frowned as Bill and Charles leaned back in their chairs, grinning. Bill had sidestepped Charles neatly. Now they were both eager, Tom thought, to watch Max make a fool of himself describing some crackpot theory. That would make them feel superior and they'd enjoy that.

Max looked up from his menu and took off his reading glasses. "An explanation for the Bermuda Triangle?" Max set his glasses on the table beside his menu. "Well, I am, actually, a bit of an expert on this topic."

Tom noticed that Susan was biting her lip, looking concerned. She was worried for Max. Bill and Charles were waiting, smiling like wolves waiting for a comrade to fall.

"So what's the explanation?" Bill asked.

"People have proposed any number of explanations," Max said in a serious tone. He had the manner of a professor lecturing his students. "Some say that the islands in this area are the mountain tops of the sunken continent of Atlantis, and that the seismic disturbances that sank Atlantis millions of years ago will occasionally capture a ship. There are others who blame sea monsters—giant squid or other monstrous animals dragging ships down. Others prefer an extraterrestrial explanation: UFOs and alien abductions. There's one fellow who has written to me a few times: he thinks that there are tiny wormholes under the water—those are black holes that lead to white holes, you know. Anyway, these micro-wormholes open up and suck people into other dimensions. He claims he has found evidence of this in the form of magnetic anomalies." Max paused to take a sip of water.

"Very interesting," Charles said. "Do you think that's the case?" He was hoping, Tom knew, that Max would say yes.

Max set down his glass. "No, I have my own theory," he said. "It's really quite simple. I'm surprised more people haven't figured it out. But I suppose the truth is always difficult to see."

Tom saw Charles and Bill exchange glances. They were in league now, ready to be amused.

Max smiled at them, then said simply, "People lie."

"What?" Charles exclaimed, as if stung. "What do you mean?"

"People make up stories. They lie." Max studied Charles with an air of benign puzzlement. "Surely it can't come as a shock to you. As a banker, you must come across this all the time."

"Well, yes, of course." Charles was sputtering now. "People lie when it's to their advantage. But there's no advantage to lying about things like this. Why would they?"

Tom grinned as he watched Max tilt his head and study Charles. It was clear who had the upper hand. The banker was uncomfortable now; Max took his time.

"People are always lying," Max said. "They lie for fun. They lie to make a better story. The crew of the *Mary Celeste* probably abandoned ship in the lifeboat and then were lost in a storm. There's a lot of evidence to support that. All that business about the table being set for breakfast, the ship being in perfect shape—all that was added later on. The historical record shows that the ship's lifeboat was missing, and that the ship had endured some heavy weather. The cargo was a couple of thousand barrels of unrefined alcohol—and there's some evidence that a few barrels exploded. So you can understand why the crew might have abandoned ship.

"But Conan Doyle got a hold of the story of the *Mary Celeste,* wove it into one of his books, and made it much more interesting. Doyle was an excellent liar, you know.

People liked the story he told better than the truth, so that's what they remembered."

Max picked up his menu and smiled innocently. "Fiction writers are all liars," he said. "People tend to forget that."

SEVEN

You say I'm a liar? I say you're a liar. And who's to say we aren't both right."

—from *Here Be Dragons*
by Mary Maxwell

"So what are we supposed to do here?" Susan said. She and Pat stood by the spiral staircase on the uppermost deck of the Atrium, leaning against the railing and looking down. Their position gave them a good view of the deck below.

"This is the 'Welcome Aboard' party," Pat said. "We're supposed to mingle and have a good time. We can meet the captain if you like. There he is, right over there."

Susan glanced in the direction that Pat had nodded. The captain was surrounded by well-dressed women and their husbands. He was smiling and nodding, but Susan thought he looked bored. She didn't see any reason to meet him. "What else can we do?"

"We can get our picture taken by the ship's photographer." Pat gestured to the photographer at the bottom of the stairs. A matronly woman in a gold lamé dress posed on the stairs, showing a fearsome array of teeth. The photographer snapped her photograph, then she continued down the stairs and a matronly woman wrapped in flowered silk took her place. "Apparently they always take people's pictures at these things. Later, they sell the print to you for five bucks. You can look at the prints in the photo gallery, down near the theater. Have you seen that yet? They've got a photo of you, that one they snapped when you were getting aboard."

Susan shook her head. She remembered being asked to pose beside a big cardboard cutout of a palm tree while someone official had snapped her picture, but she'd been in a rush and hadn't asked why. She hadn't seen the photo gallery and hadn't found the theater yet. She was still having some trouble finding her way around the ship. Restaurants and shops and pools and corridors—it was all very confusing. She found it difficult to remember sometimes that she was on board a ship. It felt more like an enormous hotel.

On the far side of the lower deck, she saw a flurry of activity surrounding a man in a cowboy hat. Light glittered on the silver star he wore on his chest. As the crowd shifted, she saw a woman dressed in an historic gown and a man in a top hat. She saw a flash of light as another photographer snapped a picture.

"What's going on over there?" she said, staring at the group below.

"Some folks from the show that's playing tomorrow night in the Singing Sirens Theater," Pat said. "Some kind of musical melodrama set in Gold Rush California."

Susan stared at her.

"Hey, don't look at me. I don't make this up. Apparently there are a bunch of California historians on board—some kind of convention."

"How do you know this stuff?"

"It's all in the *Ship's Log*," Pat said. "Hey, there's Tom." Susan saw Tom moving through the crowd below. "Want to go down and say hi?"

Susan shook her head. "He looks busy."

Pat gave her an appraising look. Pat had commented on Tom more than once, and Susan knew that her friend thought Susan and Tom would make a good couple.

"There's Ian," Susan said, waving at the computer programmer. He was watching the couples on the dance floor.

"You want to go see what he's up to?" Pat asked.

"You go. I'll meet you later." Susan could tell that Pat really wanted to get to know Ian a little better.

"What are you going to do?"

Susan shrugged. "Explore the ship a little. Maybe I'll go

check out the photo gallery. If I don't run into you later, I'll meet you in the stateroom."

"Are you sure?" Pat asked.

"Absolutely."

Pat shrugged. "If you say so." Pat headed downstairs, pausing at the photographer to have her picture taken. Susan stayed where she was, watching the crowd below.

She saw Charles and Lily Rafferty making their way toward the captain. Of course, Charles would want to introduce himself. She hadn't seen Bill and Alberta yet; she was hoping to avoid them if she did. At dinner, conversation had focused on the Bermuda Triangle and she hadn't had to answer any questions about herself. She was still thinking about Max's suggestion that she lie. He made it sound like such harmless fun. Reinvent yourself.

She thought about heading down the spiral staircase, but then she saw Alberta and Bill coming up. She turned away before they could see her and headed toward the bow of the ship to look for the photo gallery that Pat had mentioned.

It took a while, but she found her way to the photo gallery, one deck down and toward the bow of the ship. The gallery was in a corridor near Aphrodite's Alehouse. The walls of the corridor were covered with photos under glass—hundreds of photos of passengers standing beside that silly cardboard palm tree, teeth bared in insincere smiles. The counter where you ordered copies of your photo was closed, and no one else was in the gallery. A placard at the end of the corridor pointed the way to the Singing Sirens Theater, where a magician and a comic were currently performing.

Susan could hear music from the Alehouse—a woman singing a Barbara Streisand song about people who need people. Susan thought about going to the bar for a drink. She had long since finished her rum swizzle from the cocktail party. But she didn't want to sit in a bar alone.

Susan studied the walls of photos, idly looking for herself. In most of the photos, a couple or a group of people stood by the silly palm, grinning at the camera or at each other. There were, she thought, so few photos of solitary travelers. So many couples and family groups and groups of friends. She stared at one photo—a balding man in his fifties and his chubby wife. They looked genuinely happy, she thought. The woman was leaning on the man's shoulder and they were both smiling. A little tired from waiting to board, but she was sure that they hadn't been snapping at each other while they waited. No, they had been doing their best to be cheerful. They had probably been chatting amiably with the other folks who were waiting.

She and Harry had not been a happy couple. She did not know why they hadn't been happy. She thought they should have been. When they were in college, Harry had said he loved her. He had asked her to marry him, and she had said yes. She couldn't remember exactly how she felt when she said yes, but she thought that she must have been happy.

Her memories of her wedding day were hazy. She remembered her mother fussing with her hair; she remembered her father walking her down the aisle; she remembered a reception filled with people, all admiring her dress, all wishing her the best of luck. She remembered feeling dazed. She remembered feeling that she was there, but not quite there—as if this were happening to someone else.

They must have been happy then. But if they had been, it hadn't lasted. Somewhere along the way, Harry had grown impatient with her. She didn't understand why. He became an ambitious lawyer. Maybe a bookish librarian was not the ideal wife for him.

It seemed to her that Harry was always angry. He was angry with the other lawyers in his practice, angry at other drivers, angry when they had to wait in line—always angry. Sometimes, he was angry with her, but she tried not to give him any reason for that.

It hadn't been a terrible marriage. Harry was a civilized man—he rarely raised his voice, never raised his hand in anger. But even when he wasn't angry over anything in particular, she had been aware of anger simmering just below the surface, waiting to boil over. It wasn't easy and comfortable being with Harry.

She studied the picture of the balding man and his chubby wife. They looked happy. She couldn't imagine Harry smiling, however wearily, after waiting to board the *Odyssey*.

She touched her left hand, aware once again of the absence of a wedding ring. It had been silly to throw it overboard, she thought. The ring had been expensive—she remembered Harry telling her so. Throwing it overboard was a foolish and extravagant gesture, but thinking about it, she smiled.

"Over here," a man's voice said. She glanced toward the sound. She hadn't noticed the man entering the gallery. "You were looking for your picture, weren't you?"

She nodded, a little startled.

"Right here," he said.

He was in his late forties—a man with a thin face, a neatly trimmed mustache, and curly brown hair. Not handsome, exactly, but attractive in a roguish sort of way. Blue eyes that studied her with just a little too much interest. She thought he looked a bit like the sort of fellow Pat tended to date.

He was wearing khaki pants and a polo shirt—not exactly cruise wear. She imagined that he had skipped the Captain's Welcome Party; he was a bit too casually dressed for that. He looked a little out of place, as if he didn't really belong on a cruise. She could sympathize with that.

She hesitated, feeling uncomfortable, but not willing to be rude. Reluctantly, she stepped over to him and glanced at the photo he indicated. It was her all right. She remembered that moment now—her cab from the airport had been caught traffic and she had been late, rushed, a bit panicked. In the photo, her hair was a mess. She had smiled when the photographer said, "Say cheese," but just barely. She was looking past the camera at the gangway, her eyes wide and distracted.

"Oh, dear," she said.

"It's not that bad," the man said pleasantly. "It looks like you were in a bit of a rush, that's all."

"I was late," she said. "I was meeting my fiancé on board. I knew he'd be worried."

It was an experiment. When she started the sentence, she had intended to say "my friend," rather than "my fiancé." But she wanted to discourage this man if he was thinking what she was afraid he might be thinking. And she didn't want to insult him if he was just a helpful fellow with no ulterior motives. Max had said she needed to learn to lie, so she was giving it a try.

The man laughed sympathetically. "Your fiancé will get used to it. My wife is late all the time." His tone, when he mentioned his wife, was affectionate.

Susan returned the man's smile. He was married; she could relax. "Maybe yours turned out better," she said, glancing at the photo wall.

He shook his head. "I doubt that. Haven't had any luck finding it anyway."

She turned to the photo wall to see if she could spot his picture. Instead, she saw a photo of Max. He was standing by the cardboard palm tree, looking extremely uncomfortable. He hadn't even bothered to smile. "There's Max," she said without thinking.

"Your fiancé?" The man peered at the photo and frowned.

"Oh, no. That's Max Merriwell. He's teaching a writing workshop on board. He writes books as Max Merriwell, Mary Maxwell, and Weldon Merrimax."

"How interesting," the man said. "Are you attending this workshop he's teaching?"

"Oh, yes."

"You're a writer, then?"

She shook her head. "No, I just thought it would be interesting. I love Max's books."

The man glanced toward the Alehouse and Susan realized that the singing had stopped. "Sounds like the musicians are taking a break," he said. "It's safe to get a beer."

She laughed. "Low tolerance for lounge music?"

"Low tolerance for cruise ship entertainment in general," he said. "My wife is watching the magician. Card tricks and bad jokes." He made a face. "I told her I'd meet her in the bar when he was done. So where's your fiancé? What's he thinking, letting you wander around by yourself?"

"He's a little under the weather." She didn't hesitate to lie a second time. Maybe Max was right. There were times when lying was a fine idea. It was fun—and she was starting to feel a bit like a woman with a fiancé. She remembered how wonderful it had been to be engaged. Everyone had been so happy for her.

"He's seasick?"

"Just a little queasy. I stayed with him for a while, but I got restless."

The man nodded, studying her face. "Let me hazard a guess about something and make a suggestion. Maybe you'd like a drink, but you know that if you go into the bar unattended you'll get some guy hitting on you and you don't want that. If you let me buy you a drink, I'll protect you from the other guys and you can keep me company until that magician pulls the last rabbit from his hat and my wife comes to claim me."

Susan blinked, startled at how well he had guessed her thoughts. "That's a very good guess," she said slowly.

"So will you join me for a drink? You can tell me about this writing workshop."

She smiled with the confidence of a happily engaged woman, almost believing for a moment that that's who she was. "All right. But only if you let me buy the drinks. After all, you're serving as my bodyguard."

The Alehouse wasn't crowded. They found a table that was near the fireplace and as far as they could get from the stage and the dance floor.

"So tell me about Max Merriwell's work. You seem to like his books."

"Oh, yes. I've read all Max's science fiction novels. Rollicking adventures about people blasting off across the galaxy. And I've read all the books he's written as Mary Maxwell. Great action adventure stories about young women."

He nodded. "And the books by Weldon Merrimax?"

She shook her head. "I haven't read any of those. They're gritty, urban thrillers. Not my sort of thing."

"Not your sort of thing," the man repeated. The firelight flickered over his face. He frowned. "But you like the rest of his work so much. I would think you'd at least give Weldon's work a try."

She shrugged. "I've taken a look at some of the books. But they're all dark and depressing. All about sleazy criminals cheating people and committing crimes. I don't want to read about that."

"You'd rather read about people blasting off across the galaxy." Susan thought he sounded angry. But that didn't make sense. Why would he care that Susan hadn't read Weldon Merrimax's work. "So tell me about this writing workshop," he said. "What have you learned?"

"Well," she said hesitantly. "There's only been one meeting so far. Max talked about the creative process. He talked about how the writer creates his own world. He's a god in his own universe. He said that the advantage of writing science fiction is that you have to make everything up. And the disadvantage is that you have to make everything up."

"Interesting," the man said.

"And he told us that a writer has to be a good observer. He told us that we needed to watch the people around us, to consider their gestures, their body language. We need to learn to read them so that we can describe them in our work. He gave us that as a homework assignment."

"Have you done your homework yet?" the man asked.

Susan laughed. "Not yet."

"Well, I've always thought bars were great places to

watch people." He looked around the room, then jerked his head toward a couple sitting two tables away. "So what do you make of them?"

Susan glanced in the direction he had gestured and saw a heavyset man with dark hair sitting with a thin blonde woman. They were both in their mid-twenties. She was wearing a silk shirt and a skirt that matched and he was in a Hawaiian shirt and Dockers. The waitress had just brought their drinks: a beer for him and a frothy pink drink with an umbrella and a shish kabob of fruit for her. The man smiled at the waitress as she walked away; the woman sipped her drink.

"I don't know," she said. "A young couple on their first cruise, I guess."

The man smiled. "Oh, I think we can figure out more than that. Take a look at their hands."

Susan glanced at the couple again. The woman was laughing at something the man had said. She was playing with her wedding ring, twisting it on her finger. "She's playing with her ring," Susan said. "And she has a nice manicure," she said.

"His nails look nice, too," the man said. "I'd guess they're just married. A wedding is about the only time most men will let themselves be talked into a manicure. She suggested it so his hands would look nice for the wedding pictures."

Susan glanced at the couple again: his nails did look nice.

"You can tell that she comes from money," he went on.

"She is dressed nicely," Susan said. That silk shirt wasn't cheap.

"Here's a tip: Don't just look at her clothes," he said. "It's the shoes that tell you the most. Hers are top quality. That woman is used to nice things. Now look at his shoes."

He was wearing athletic shoes of a brand she didn't recognize.

"He shops the sales and doesn't care about appearances, as long as the shoes are comfortable." The man shook his head sadly. "I'll give the marriage two years, tops."

Susan was suddenly painfully aware that her own shoes could use polishing. She was starting to feel a little guilty at the way the man was passing judgments on the other couple. "You think their marriage is going to fail because he doesn't buy the right shoes?" she asked in dismay.

"The shoes are just a part of it," he said. "Look at how the two of them are sitting. No body contact; no connection between them."

The woman had her legs crossed; she sat at an angle on the chair, gazing at the fire. The man was leaning back in his chair, staring toward the stage.

"Now consider the way she's eating that cherry."

The woman had taken a small bite from the cherry on the fruit shish kabob.

"That's no way to eat a cherry," the man said. "A woman who would eat a cherry like that has no enthusiasm for sex. I'd guess that within a year she'll be spending more money than he makes and he'll be flirting with a waitress who can tie a cherry stem in a knot with her tongue."

Susan blushed, glad that she had ordered a beer so that her cherry-eating would not be analyzed. The frightening thing was, she suspected the man was right about that couple. The woman was laughing again, tossing her blond hair back. Susan suspected it was a gesture the woman had practiced in front of the mirror. "You're good at this," she said. "Max told me this morning that cops and writers pay attention to things that other people don't. So if you're not a cop, you must be a writer."

The man laughed. "I'm certainly not a cop. I've written a few books."

"Really. What's your name? Maybe I've seen your work."

The man shook his head. "I don't think it would be to your taste." He smiled, but it wasn't a friendly smile. It was a superior smirk, as if he knew something she didn't. "In fact, I'm sure of it."

Susan frowned. He seemed to be enjoying himself. He

knew that he was making her uncomfortable, and he liked that.

The man was still talking. "But that's not the real reason I'm good at reading people. You see, I used to tell fortunes for a living. Reading people was an occupational requirement." Suddenly, he leaned across the table, taking her left hand in both of his. "I'll tell your fortune now," he said.

His hands were large and strong and crisscrossed with old scars. She laughed awkwardly and tried to tug her hand free. He gripped her hand harder, so hard it brought tears to her eyes.

He wasn't looking at her hand; he was staring at her face, studying her with unblinking intensity. "I can tell a lot about you," he said. "I can tell that you're a liar. That's easy to see."

She tried again to pull her hand away. This time, he let her go.

"You're the sort of person who would lie to a perfect stranger for no reason at all."

She stared at him, unable to speak.

"You don't have a sick fiancé. You've been lying to me since we met. My guess is that you've been married, but you recently got dumped and you're still dealing with that."

"But . . ." Susan started to protest.

"Don't dig yourself deeper," he said, waving a hand. "You'd better practice more if you're going to make a habit of lying. First, never hesitate before you lie. You gave yourself away right there."

She clutched her drink, feeling like a fool. "I just . . ."

He ignored her attempt to interrupt. "No ring," he said, tapping the ring finger of her left hand. She flinched at his touch. "That was another sign. And you didn't bother to look for your fiancé's photo."

"I . . . I didn't think you'd be interested," she said weakly.

He shook his head. "No happily engaged woman would miss a chance to point out her fiancé's photo." He studied her for a moment. "Besides, if you had been telling the truth, you wouldn't be blushing and stammering right now. You'd be indignant."

She sat up straight in her chair, trying to muster a little dignity. "I don't see . . ."

"I know that. But I see." He stared at her. "I see right through you." He pushed back his chair. "But you probably don't even realize that I started lying to you as soon as you started lying to me. I don't have a wife." He stood up. "But unlike you, I know how to lie." He walked away, leaving her sitting alone at the table by the fire, stunned and confused.

The piano player returned to the stage. The woman singer took the microphone from the stand and began a line of easy patter—about what a wonderful night it was, what a wonderful audience they were. The singer was halfway through her first number when Tom Clayton tapped Susan on the shoulder.

Tom had been shutting down a noisy party in the crew quarters when he got the call from Frank Bender at the Alehouse saying that the fellow who called himself Weldon Merrimax was in the bar. It had taken Tom a few minutes to make his way up to the Promenade Deck and forward to the Alehouse. By the time he arrived, Weldon was gone.

"He left about ten minutes ago. He was sitting with that lady there," Frank said. "She bought the drinks, so I didn't see him at first."

Tom recognized Susan, sitting at a table alone. There was a glass of beer in front of her, and an empty glass in front of the chair across the table. She looked upset and confused; she looked as if she might be ready to burst into tears. "Thanks, Frank."

Tom got on the radio and advised Don, the security guard who was patrolling the sector that included the Games Room, to check that room for poker players. "If Weldon Merrimax shows up, I'd like to have a word with him," Tom told Don.

Susan was staring into space and she didn't notice Tom until he touched her shoulder. Then she jumped, startled.

"Hello, Susan." He slid into the seat across from her.

She blinked at him. "What are you doing here?"

He shrugged. "Looking for trouble. It's my job."

She managed a tremulous smile. "Is there trouble here?"

"That's what I was going to ask you," he said. "I had a few questions about the gentleman you were drinking with."

She frowned at him. He had her attention now, he thought. "He was no gentleman," she said.

"Really? What happened?"

She told him a rather confusing story about meeting the man in the photo gallery and lying about her fiancé. Max had told her she should practice lying and she had decided to give it a try. Watching her, Tom knew she was a rotten liar.

"I didn't want him to get the wrong idea," she said. "But he said he was waiting for his wife—and he invited me for a drink." She flushed then, looking down at her hands. "I figured it would be okay, since he was married and I was engaged—or he thought I was engaged. But then he got really angry."

Tom nodded. All this was beside the point. He really just needed to find the man and ask him about a few things. But Susan seemed to need to talk. "What was he angry about?" Tom asked.

She shook her head, still frowning. "I don't know. We were talking about Max's books. I said something about Weldon Merrimax. And then he told me I was a liar and he left."

"Did he say where he was going?"

She shook her head again. "Even if he had, I wouldn't put much stock in it. He admitted he was a liar—he didn't really have a wife or a daughter. He seemed okay until we started talking about Max's work. I said I hadn't read the books Max had written as Weldon Merrimax because I'd heard they were too depressing. And then he got downright mean. It was weird. Why are you looking for him?"

"A little confusion over his cruise card," Tom said easily. "An identification problem, that's all."

She was still frowning.

"But I think you're right—he's certainly not a gentleman. Unfortunately, that's not considered a crime on the *Odyssey*."

EIGHT

There was a dragon in the cave, she was sure of that. But she knew the monster's name. And that gave her a certain advantage.

—from *Here Be Dragons*
by Mary Maxwell

Susan had the Promenade to herself. Tom had sat and talked with her while she finished her beer, then offered to walk her to her stateroom. She had declined his offer. Too restless to sleep, she thought she'd walk around the Promenade once before heading up to her stateroom.

The ocean was dark. Beside the doors that led from the ship's interior to the Promenade, electric lightbulbs set in fixtures designed to look like antique lanterns glowed brightly. Near the doors, light shone on the fat white bellies of the lifeboats that hung overhead, glistened on the damp, wooden boards of the deck. Away from the doors, the deck was thick with shadows. Here and there, a window cast a bright rectangle of light, but the stretches of deck between the windows were dark.

Susan walked briskly, moving from light to shadow and back to light again. As she walked, she thought about how Tom had a knack for appearing at just the wrong time. "What happened?" he had asked her, and she had told him everything.

He must think she was a complete idiot—lying about being engaged, having a drink with a man who was some sort of criminal. But Tom had simply listened to her. And he had done his best to reassure her that she had done nothing wrong. "Just relax," he had told her. "Have a good time. Why let one encounter with a jerk spoil your vacation? It seems like you need a vacation."

She did need a vacation, and she was perfectly willing to have a good time. But it seemed that in five years of marriage, she'd forgotten how. Maybe she could remember.

At the stern of the ship, she forced herself to stop walking. The air felt warm and tropical. In the morning, they would make port in Hamilton, Bermuda, one of the ship's two ports of call on the way to London. She leaned against the railing, looking out at the ship's wake. Illuminated by lights at the stern of the ship, the wake made a white path in the dark water.

Relax, she told herself. Why let one jerk spoil your vacation? She imagined telling Pat about her encounter with the man in the bar. Pat would laugh, Susan thought. Pat would approve of Susan's lie—Pat felt that Susan needed to cut loose and make trouble. Pat would be amused that Susan had lied to a liar. Pat wouldn't waste any time stewing about her lies—or about the arrogance of the man she had met.

Behind her, Susan heard a burst of music from one of the ship's bars. Someone had opened a door that led onto the Promenade. The music was muffled again as the door swung shut, drowned out by the hum of the engines.

Susan did not look around. She did not want to talk with anyone. She watched the churning bubbles of the wake. From behind her, she heard a thump—as if something had struck the side of the ship. Then she saw a dark object bobbing and swirling in the ship's wake. Startled, she glanced behind her. No one was there. She looked at the wake again, but the object, whatever it was, was out of sight.

Hesitant, but curious, she walked along the railing in the direction from which the sound had come. On the side of the ship, just around the corner from where she had stood, she noticed a bright smear of red. It looked like blood, she thought.

Then the lights went out.

Tom was heading for his cabin when he got a radio call from Don, requesting assistance. "Possible 245 in the Games Room." That was the code for aggravated assault.

When Tom reached the Games Room, he found Don sitting with a male passenger on a bench in the corridor outside the room. The passenger, a large man in his fifties, was pale. His face was wet with sweat and his hands were shaking. "It was a friendly game," he was telling Don. The man was drunk, and Tom could tell from Don's expression that this was not the first time the man had told him about how friendly the game had been.

"This is Mr. Perkins," Don told Tom. "He's reported the incident. I've called for backup and I've secured the room, but I thought I'd better stay with Mr. Perkins until you got here."

Tom nodded. Mr. Perkins started talking again.

"Patrick said Weldon was cheating, and then Weldon stabbed him. Just like that. Not a bit of warning. Just stabbed him. He killed him; I'm sure he killed him. Then he looked at me like I might be next." Mr. Perkins looked like he might be about to cry. "I ran out the door before he could go after me."

"I was coming by to check on the Games Room," Don said. "I found Mr. Perkins running down the corridor. By the time we got back here, the other poker players were gone. I secured the room and called you."

Tom flicked on his radio to call the ship's doctor to see if the victim had come in for medical treatment. And then the lights went out.

Susan froze in the sudden darkness. She couldn't see a thing. The ship's engines still rumbled underfoot; she could hear the rush of water past the ship's hull, far below. She could hear her own heart pounding. She was alone in the darkness. She felt cold, despite the warmth of the air around her.

She turned away from the sound of rushing water. Arms outstretched, she took a few tentative steps in what she thought was the direction of the doors. Her hand brushed against the wall, and she groped her way along the wall to find a door.

She pulled the door open a crack and heard voices, people shouting and laughing. "Hey, who turned out the lights?"

"Anyone have a flashlight?"

"What's going on?"

"I don't know, but I can't find my drink."

Susan opened the door and stepped into the corridor. In the distance, she could see a light. Someone was holding up a cigarette lighter, which cast a pool of flickering light, and people were gathering around, talking and laughing. No one seemed particularly alarmed.

She headed toward the man with the cigarette lighter. "We should go to our muster stations," he was saying to the people who had gathered around him. "That's what we're supposed to do in an emergency."

Susan's eyes were beginning to adjust to the dark. She could make out the people surrounding the man with the cigarette lighter.

"Is this an emergency?" a woman asked.

"Where are our muster stations?" asked someone else.

"Hello," Susan said to the group gathered around the cigarette lighter. "Does anyone know what's going on?"

"Hello! Hello!" A bright flashlight beam shone from the far end of the corridor. The young man holding the flashlight wore the red jacket that designated him as a member of the purser's staff. People peppered the young man with questions.

"Is something wrong with the ship?"

"Should we have our life jackets?"

"What should we do?"

"Just a little problem with the electrical system," the

young man said. "No big deal. The engineering staff is busy fixing it right now. You could go to bed. Or you could come to Apollo's Court, if you like."

"That's our muster station," said the man with the cigarette lighter in a satisfied tone. He seemed to be the sort of fellow who liked knowing what was going on.

There was much discussion then—with some people going to bed and some deciding to accompany the crew member to Apollo's Court, the large buffet-style restaurant not far from where they were.

Susan hesitated, her arms wrapped around herself. She didn't know what to do.

"Are you all right, ma'am?" the crew member asked her.

She bit her lip, thinking about what she'd seen. A splash of red on the railing. Blood? More likely a strawberry daquiri, spilled by a drunk. She weighed the odds and decided on the innocent explanation. It couldn't have been blood.

"I'm fine," she said and followed the man with the flashlight to Apollo's Court.

Sitting in the darkness, Mr. Perkins told Tom that a man named Patrick Murphy had been stabbed by a man named Weldon Merrimax during the course of a poker game in the Games Room. Patrick Murphy, according to Mr. Perkins, was a tall fellow with a mustache. Patrick had been dressed in what Mr. Perkins called "old timey" clothes. "Maybe he's one of those historians," Mr. Perkins suggested. Mr. Perkins' description of Weldon matched Frank Bender's description of Weldon Merrimax.

Mr. Perkins had met Weldon in the Lotus Eaters' Lounge, the bar closest to the Games Room. Weldon had seemed like such a friendly sort, Mr. Perkins said. The conversation turned to cards, and Patrick Murphy, who was also sitting at the bar, had joined in. Patrick was the one who had suggested a hand of poker, Mr. Perkins said. Weldon was the one who suggested that they go to the Games Room.

The ship's procedures offered little guidance in this matter. Most fights aboard the ship were simple matters. Someone smacked someone else around; Tom separated the protagonists and usually that ended the matter. There had been knife fights between members of the crew, but the combatants in those had been easily identified, fired, and removed from the ship at the first opportunity. This was another matter.

During the confusion of the blackout, Tom did what he could. He ascertained that no stabbing victim had visited the ship's doctor. Security staff conducted a flashlight search of all the open decks, service areas, and public areas. They found no victim, but one guard found the cause of the blackout in the course of the search. An electrical panel in a staff area had been torn open and shorted out. "Smells like Scotch," said the guard who found it. According to Mr. Perkins, the poker players had all been drinking rather heavily. Weldon had supplied them with Scotch.

Tom nodded. So the man calling himself Weldon had torn open the panel to turn off the lights, giving himself plenty of time to get away.

Tom secured the Games Room. There was some evidence of a fight in the room: a chair had been knocked over; drinks had been spilled, cards scattered on the floor. But no blood stains on the carpet; no bloody knife left conveniently behind. In Tom's experience, the little old ladies had left worse messes after a rubber of bridge.

Apollo's Court was illuminated by candles. As Susan walked across the restaurant, she heard Max calling to her.

"Hey, Susan." The writer was sitting at a booth with a young woman and a little girl. "Come join us," Max said. "This is Jody." He gestured to the little girl, who sat on one of the benches, a blanket draped around her shoulders like a cape. "And this is Nancy, Jody's nanny."

"Pleased to meet you," Nancy said. Her voice had an

Irish lilt. In the candlelight, both Jody and Nancy looked young and frightened.

"Do you know when they are going to turn the lights back on?" Jody asked Susan. "I don't like this. I'm scared of the dark."

"Now, Jody," Nancy said. "There's nothing to be scared of."

The little girl looked up at Nancy, her eyes round. "I'm scared," she said again.

Susan sat on the bench beside Max. She agreed with Nancy—there was nothing to be scared of. But she sympathized with Jody. Susan didn't much like the darkness either.

"What are you scared of?" Max asked Jody.

"Monsters," the little girl said.

Max nodded. "Yeah, I'm scared of monsters, too."

Susan watched the little girl's face in the candlelight. She seemed puzzled by this grownup who believed in monsters.

"Where do your monsters live?" Max asked.

The little girl frowned, thinking about her answer. "Under the bed," she said. "In the closet."

Max nodded. "Places where it's dark. Monsters like to hide in the dark."

The restaurant was filled with shadows. The candles on the tables created pools of light, but the room was dark between the tables. As the candle flames flickered and danced, the shadows wavered and moved. So many places for monsters to hide, Susan thought.

"You know where the monsters come from?" Max asked.

The little girl shook her head.

"Out of your head. You make them up."

"No!" Jody protested. She had obviously been through this before. She could see what was coming: your monsters are imaginary so they're nothing to be afraid of. "They're real!"

"Of course they're real," Max said. "Just because you make them up doesn't mean they aren't real."

Susan glanced at Nancy. The young woman was leaning

back, half asleep, paying no attention to Max and Jody.

"I make things up all the time," Max said. "And some of the things I've made up are very real. You know why?"

"Why?" Jody asked.

"Because I believe in them. That's what makes them strong. Your monsters are strong because you believe in them and you think they're strong."

"Really strong," agreed the little girl.

"That's the power of the imagination," Max said. "If you believe in something, you can make it real."

"The monster under the bed is real," Jody said.

Max nodded. "What does that monster look like?"

"All covered with scales," Jody said without hesitation. "Lots of teeth and big claws. It wants to grab me."

"What's its name?"

Jody hesitated. Susan guessed that the little girl had never considered being on a first name basis with her monsters. "I don't know."

"It's good to name your monsters," Max said. "Maybe we should call him Henry."

Susan watched as Jody thought about this for a moment. She guessed that the little girl was considering the possibility, perhaps thinking that this man seemed to know a lot about monsters. "Okay," Jody agreed after a moment.

"So Henry lives under the bed," Max said. "That's not a very big space. Especially not on this ship. That's where I put my suitcases."

Jody nodded. "That's where Nancy put my suitcases."

"How many suitcases do you have?"

"Two."

"Hmm. That doesn't leave much room under there. Could you get under the bed when your suitcases are there?"

Susan remembered that there was just a foot or so to spare after she shoved her own suitcases under the bed.

Jody shook her head. "There's not enough room."

Max nodded thoughtfully. "So Henry is smaller than you are."

Jody nodded. "Yeah, I guess so."

"I wonder if the other monsters pick on Henry because he's so small."

Jody stared at Max. Obviously, she had never thought about Henry's problems.

"I think the other monsters would pick on a little monster like Henry," Max continued.

Jody frowned. She was working through this new view of Henry, a small, scaly monster who had problems with his peers. It was a struggle, but her sympathy lay with the underdog.

"That's not nice," Jody said. "It's not nice to pick on someone smaller than you are."

Max shrugged. "Well, some monsters can be kind of mean. I don't know whether Henry is or not, but those other monsters might be."

Jody was still frowning.

"I wonder why Henry hides under your bed," Max mused. "It can't be very comfortable down there."

Jody thought about this. "I think he's hiding from the other monsters," she said at last.

"And he figures he's safe under the bed because it's dark and the other monsters can't find him there." Max nodded. "I think you're right."

Jody bit her lip, considering that possibility. She was, Susan thought, growing fond of Henry—and angry at those other monsters, the mean ones.

Max leaned back, looking out the window at the dark ocean waters. "Sometimes, darkness can be useful," he said. "It hides many things."

At that moment, the lights came on.

Nancy smiled. "Oh, good." She spoke to Jody. "Now I can take you back to bed."

The little girl went without a protest. She was, Susan thought, still deep in thought about Henry and the other monsters.

"You did a good job with Jody," Susan told Max as they

walked to their staterooms. "Seems like you really know your monsters."

Max shrugged. "It's part of the business," he said. "As a writer, you have to know the bad guys as well as the good guys."

"I think you had Jody feeling sorry for Henry by the end," Susan said.

Max nodded. "Oh, Henry isn't such a bad fellow," he said. "A sweetheart, as monsters go."

After the lights came back on, Tom checked the passenger list. No one named Patrick Murphy was on the list. As Tom already knew, Weldon Merrimax was not on the list either. A check of the crew roster revealed no Patrick Murphy. He had been dressed in old-fashioned clothes, which suggested that he might be part of the melodrama performance, but no member of the entertainment staff matched Mr. Perkins' description of Patrick.

It was past midnight by the time Tom completed his interview with Mr. Perkins and arranged for the man to come to his office in the morning. As each passenger boarded the ship, an ID photo was taken. Tom figured Ian could sort out the photos of men of the appropriate age— which would probably be a few hundred individuals. Tom would have Mr. Perkins review the photos in the unlikely chance that he might spot Weldon or Patrick.

Tom had more faith in the memory of Nic, the bartender at the Lotus Eaters' Lounge. A bright-eyed young Irishman, Nic remembered both men—Weldon had paid cash for his drink, an unusual occurrence on the cruise ship. And the other fellow had offered to pay for his drink with gold dust.

"I figured him for one of those historians or a player in the show," Nic said. "It was either that or he was off in the head."

The man had been wearing a cowboy hat and a sheriff's star. "He came up to the bar, looking wild," Nic said. "He told me 'I reckon this is the strangest dream I've ever had.'

So I laughed and asked him what he wanted to drink." The man had ordered a whiskey. When Nic asked for his cruise card, the man asked him what the hell he was talking about.

Nic shrugged. "I told him it was a card with his name on it—but if he gave me his name, I'd see what I could do. He told me his name was Pat Murphy, so I punched him into the computer, found his name on the list, and charged his account."

"Pat Murphy?" Tom said.

"That's right. Stateroom 144."

Tom nodded wearily. The drink had been charged to Susan's friend, Pat.

"So d'you really think he killed that fella?" the bartender asked.

Tom shrugged. "Hard to say: no blood, no sign of the body."

"Well, that's easy enough to explain," Nic said. "Over the side, splash, and the body's long gone."

Tom nodded. Hoist the body over the railing and drop it in the ocean. Few people were out on deck after dark. Even if the crime were discovered and the engines were cut immediately, momentum would carry the ship half a mile or more before it stopped. No one would ever find the body. "Easy to dispose of the body, but not so easy to get away with it," Tom said. "If there's a murderer aboard, he's not going anywhere."

Nic nodded.

"Keep your eyes open," Tom advised the bartender. "Let me know if you spot anything unusual. I'll be talking to the captain about a bonus for anyone who supplies information that helps me with this."

Nic nodded solemnly. Tom left him, knowing that word about the incident would spread fast. The *Odyssey* was a small town, and gossip was a way of life. By morning, everyone in the crew would be on the lookout for Weldon.

Tom left a message for the purser—asking him to tell the cabin stewards of the situation and to alert Tom if anyone noticed evidence of a wounded passenger: bloody towels, a cabin that the steward was not allowed to clean. Then, just a few hours before the time Tom usually got up, he went to bed.

Until Tom located Weldon and Patrick, it would be difficult for him to proceed. Until he found or identified the victim, Tom couldn't question the victim's friends and acquaintances. Without the body, he had little physical evidence. He bagged the playing cards and the drinking glasses. If it ever became clear that a crime had actually taken place, Tom might use fingerprints on those items to link the criminal to the crime.

But so far, all he had was the mumbled testimony of a drunken man. Nothing more.

That night, as Susan fell asleep, she thought about Jody's monster. All covered with scales, the little girl had said. Lots of teeth and big claws.

Susan remembered a monster like that from Maurice Sendak's children's book, *Where the Wild Things Are*. A fierce but cuddly sort of monster, she thought.

When Susan was growing up, she had had a monster under her bed, too. Her monster had been one of the ones that carried away bad little girls. Her mother had told her about those monsters. They snatched little girls who were untidy or noisy or bossy, little girls who stayed up too late or asked too many questions. Susan's mother hadn't said exactly what the monsters did to the bad little girls. She didn't have to. Susan had had an excellent imagination, something that her mother had deplored. Susan had known the monsters did something dreadful to the little girls they captured.

Susan's mother had not really liked children much. Susan realized that now. Her mother had wanted a little girl who was tidy, quiet, and compliant, who went to bed without complaint and accepted her mother's pronouncements without question. Susan had done her best to be that child, but it had always been an imperfect imitation.

Susan fell asleep imagining Jody's monster crouching under her bed, hiding from the larger, meaner monsters. She preferred Jody's monster to her own.

BAD GRRLZ' GUIDE TO PHYSICS

CONSIDERING THE POSSIBILITIES

It's shaping up to be a very promising cruise. At the dance last night, I ran into Ian, the cute programmer who is seated at our table at dinner. Just my type—a little nerdy, a little too smart for his own good, obviously aware of both my intelligence and my feminine charms and therefore sweetly attentive.

We had a few glasses of champagne and we ended up sitting out by the pool, beneath a canopy of brilliant stars, talking about quantum mechanics, the nature of reality, the Bermuda Triangle, and Weldon Merrimax.

He asked me what my dissertation was about, and I told him in detail, not sparing him the mathematical analysis. He listened intently with an earnest expression of geeky concentration. Ah, the way to this Bad Grrl's heart is through her dissertation. He seemed quite intrigued by the notion of superposed realities.

I asked him what he was doing on the *Odyssey,* and he told me about the cruise card system and how it tracked passengers. And he told me about an intriguing glitch in the system. It seems that Max Merriwell's pseudonym, Weldon Merrimax, had bought a drink and bilked a fellow passenger at poker.

"I thought it might be a problem in the system," Ian said. "But it turned out that the bartender let someone sign as Weldon without checking the computer. Just human error." He shrugged. "But it still could get interesting. You know about that note that Max received this morning?"

Susan had told me about it, of course. Apparently Tom had shown the note to Ian.

"The handwriting on the note matches the signature on the charge slip," Ian said, smiling that charming, geek-boy smile. "And it all happened just as the ship moved into the Bermuda Triangle."

Ian is quite enthusiastic about the Bermuda Triangle. He told me more than I cared to know about the hundreds of ships that sailed into the Triangle, never to emerge. He looked quite mischievous as he described planes that had vanished without a trace. I asked him point blank if he believed the stories about paranormal phenomena in the Bermuda Triangle and he grinned. "I enjoy them," he said, and he wouldn't say a word one way or the other about belief.

In that same spirit, I told him that he didn't need to look to the Bermuda Triangle for an explanation of Weldon Merrimax's sudden appearance. "I don't think you need to look any farther than Max Merriwell," I said. "The man is a vortex of possibilities. He spins around and flings out possible realities, inhabited by Mary Maxwell, Weldon Merrimax, and god knows what other versions of himself." I explained to him that under certain circumstances, quantum phenomena could intrude into our experience. (The Bose-Einstein Condensation is one example of such a phenomena.)

Around about then, the lights went out. We stayed where we were and continued to talk about possibilities. I rather hoped he might take advantage of the darkness to make a pass, but he seemed a little too intrigued by the possibilities of quantum mechanics and the *I Ching* and the Bermuda Triangle. We kept talking until the lights came back on.

NINE

"Now you tell me a story," the dragon said. "Make it an interesting one. Make sure there's a dragon in it."
The woman hesitated for a moment, considering all the stories involving dragons that she had heard over the years. In most of them, the dragon met an untimely end. She thought it prudent to avoid telling any of those.
"There was once a young woman who left her home and family and went to seek her fortune," she began.

—from *Here Be Dragons*
by Mary Maxwell

Susan woke just as the *Odyssey* was entering the harbor of Hamilton, the capital city of Bermuda. She sat up in bed, rubbing her eyes. Through the sliding glass doors, she could see Pat on the balcony, sitting in one of the two lounge chairs. A coffee pot and a plate of pastries were on the small round table beside her.

Susan pulled on a plush white terry cloth robe with the *Odyssey* logo on the pocket and joined her. The air was warm. In the distance, she could see the roofs of houses in Hamilton.

"I was beginning to wonder if you'd ever get up," Pat said. "Want some coffee?"

Pat poured Susan a cup of coffee and told her to help herself to one of the pastries. "I ordered them from room service. And it's all free. Isn't that great?" Pat had a starving graduate student's appreciation of free food.

Susan sipped her coffee. "So where were you when the lights went out?" she asked Pat.

"Out by the pool, talking with Ian."

Susan raised her eyebrows, inviting her friend to say more.

"We just hung out and talked about physics, the Bermuda Triangle, and that note Max got from Weldon Merrimax."

Susan stared at Pat. "What?"

Pat grinned, enjoying Susan's surprise. "Well, Ian said it was from Weldon. The handwriting matches the charge slip that Weldon Merrimax signed."

"Wait a second. Weldon Merrimax signed a charge slip?"

"Yeah, someone posing as Weldon bought a drink in Aphrodite's Alehouse the other night, then cheated some other passenger at poker." Pat shrugged. "Weird, huh? Anyway, the lights went out, Ian and I talked for a while, then the lights came on, and I came to bed."

"I wonder if that's the guy Tom was looking for," Susan murmured.

"What guy?" Pat asked.

Susan described her encounter with the guy in the bar.

"So then you were sitting alone in the bar and Tom showed up?"

Susan took another bite of her cheese Danish and licked sugar from her fingers. "I got the impression that the bartender called him. He wanted to talk to that guy I'd been talking to. He said something about some confusion over a cruise card." Susan poured a second cup of coffee.

"So you had a drink with Weldon Merrimax, and then Tom showed up." Pat was delighted.

Susan shook her head. "Tom was just doing his job. Remember, I didn't bring you along to play matchmaker."

"I'm just making an observation, that's all. Max told us to make careful observations of the world around us. That's all I'm doing."

Susan shook her head again, smiling. Pat was irrepressible. Looking out over the sparkling water, Susan admired the houses, painted in beautiful pastel shades of blue and pink and yellow.

"Hey, I found out that we can take a one-day scuba-diving class while we're here," Pat said. "I figured I'd go to Max's workshop and then go diving. Do you want to come?"

Susan shook her head. She wasn't a strong swimmer and the idea of going underwater with a tank strapped to her back didn't appeal to her. "I don't think so. But you go ahead."

"What are you going to do?"

Susan frowned. She wanted to explore the town, but she was hesitant to do it alone. "I had thought about doing some shopping in Hamilton." She hesitated. "I guess I could buy a map in the gift shop. But I'll probably get lost."

Pat studied her face. "So what if you do get lost," she said. "You can ask somebody the way. Bermuda used to be a British colony, so everybody speaks English." Pat shrugged. "If you're really worried about it, I could skip the dive class."

"Oh, no, don't be silly. I'll be fine on my own." Susan smiled, determined to give it a try. "Hey, we'd better get to workshop if we're going," she said.

"I had a long conversation about monsters last night," Max was saying. They sat around the library table and the tropical sunshine streamed in the windows. "Everyone has monsters. Some people have monsters that live under the bed; some people have monsters that live in the closet. Most people do their best to keep their monsters in the dark. Most people don't want to look at their monsters."

"As a writer, you need your monsters. You need to examine them carefully and use them in your writing," Max continued. "You can't go hiding your monsters in the dark. You need to believe in your monsters and bring them to life. You need to make them real."

Max talked about the unconscious, about finding and using your monsters. Then he gave them a writing exercise.

"Most people have monsters that are vague, incompletely imagined. As a writer, you need to look at things very carefully, describe the impossible in detail to convince your readers that it's real."

"Get out your notebooks," Max said. "I want you to write about a monster."

"What do you mean, a monster?" Alberta asked.

"Something that scares you—really terrifies you. We all have dark places where frightening things live. I want you to go to one of those places and find something you don't like to think about. Something that gets under your skin and sends a chill up your spine. I can't tell you what it would be. That's something only you know."

"What if we can't think of anything?" Alberta asked.

Of course, Susan thought. Alberta would ask that.

"Then start with a childhood monster," Max said. "Something that scared you when you were little. Chances are that your childhood monsters have grown up along with you. They've changed shape, but they're with you still. Follow your childhood fears and see what you find.

"It's hard to face your monsters directly, so here's what I suggest. Write a scene in which the monster is just out of sight. But you know it's there. Write about how the monster makes you feel."

"Can it be something real?" Pat asked.

Max nodded. "Of course. All monsters are real."

He opened his own notebook and began writing. Susan stared at the blank page in front of her.

Childhood monsters, Susan thought, remembering the monsters that snatched bad girls. How had those monsters grown up? What happened to bad girls now?

The answer came suddenly and she shivered, though the room was warm. She thought of Alice, a woman she had known in college.

Susan had attended the University of California at Santa Cruz, a rural campus in the hills above the beachside community. It was a beautiful campus, tucked among redwood groves, isolated from town by miles of rolling hills.

Susan had met Alice in an American Literature seminar. At the second meeting of the class, Alice told the instructor that she thought the reading list didn't have enough women authors and suggested a few that he could add. It was something that the women in the class had talked about amongst themselves, but no one else had summoned the nerve to mention it to the professor.

Susan lingered after class to thank Alice for speaking up. They had gone out for coffee—just that one time. Susan remembered sitting in the coffee shop and thinking about how much she admired Alice.

Alice didn't seem to be afraid of anything. She had traveled in Europe the previous summer, working as a camp counselor for two months and then traveling alone through France and England and Ireland. She was thinking of traveling in Nepal next summer; she was trying to line up a job with a travel company to fund the trip.

A year older than Susan, Alice lived in town, rather than in a dormitory on campus. When they left the coffee shop, Susan realized that it would be half an hour until the next bus to town. It was a rainy February night. Susan asked Alice if she wanted company waiting at the bus stop.

Alice shook her head. "I'll stick out my thumb and catch a ride," she said. "Lots of people are heading to town this time of night."

Susan frowned.

Alice laughed at Susan's expression. "Oh, don't worry," she said. "I'm careful. I only ride with folks with University parking stickers."

Susan left Alice at the bus stop, her thumb out to catch a ride.

Susan never saw Alice again. Alice disappeared. A month later, a serial killer confessed to her murder and led police to her headless, dismembered body. Alice was one of the killer's eight victims. Six of them were young women, about Alice's age, picked up hitchhiking. The seventh and eighth victim were the murderer's mother and her friend.

The newspapers had carried graphic stories of the killer's atrocities. The man had killed the young women in many different ways. He had shot them, strangled them, suffocated them. Some had died quickly; others had fought and suffered. He had raped their dead bodies. He had cut them to pieces. He had kept their heads and hands and disposed of them separately, to thwart any efforts to identify the bodies.

Susan had read the newspaper accounts. She could not help herself. She could not help imagining Alice's death.

Alice hadn't died immediately. The killer had shot her several times to kill her. He had taken her lifeless body into his apartment and had sex with her corpse. He had cut off her head. He had cut off her hands.

For months after reading the newspaper account, Susan kept imagining Alice's hands, separated from her body, lying on the shelf of the refrigerator in the killer's apartment. She didn't know that he kept Alice's head and hands in the refrigerator—the newspapers had only said that he kept them for a few days before disposing of them. But Susan always imagined them in the refrigerator, their bloody stumps wrapped in plastic. Alice's hands, one curled into a fist, one limp, with fingers outstretched.

A monster, she thought. She studied her hands—left hand holding the notebook, right hand holding the pen. She remembered the weeks after the murderer had confessed to the killings.

"I am afraid," she wrote. "I am afraid to go out in a world where there are monsters.

"The newspapers say that this man killed Alice and the other women. But I don't think he's a man. Surely a person with a mother and a father, a person with blood pumping through his veins, a person who can feel pain could not have done such terrible things to Alice. No, I think Alice was killed by a monster, some kind of machine maybe, an alien construction that feels no pain and therefore can't comprehend the pain of others."

Susan looked at what she had written so far. The monster should be just out of sight, Max had said.

"During the day," she wrote, "I can go out to the cafeteria for meals; I can go to class. But at night, when darkness comes, I stay in my dorm room with the door closed and locked.

"Sometimes, late at night, I hear things. I hear metal scraping on metal, like the sound of a knife being sharpened. The knife that cut off Alice's hands must have been very, very sharp. I think of the knife, glinting in the moonlight as the monster sharpens it. I think of the monster, lovingly stroking it on the steel sharpener, admiring the glittering blade. Sometimes, late at night, I catch the scent of rotting meat, and I think of Alice's hands. Maybe the monster didn't keep them in the refrigerator. Maybe he left them out in his living room, someplace warm. Maybe they started to decay, breaking down slowly, going bad.

"My mother warned that bad things happened to girls who behaved badly. She didn't tell me what the bad things were, but now I know what they are. Killers stalk women; monsters threaten them. Madmen cut them apart with chain saws, with hatchets, with knives. Women are raped, tortured, killed. Good girls stay home where they can be safe.

"The monster waits outside the door. I can hear its raspy breathing, smell a whiff of putrefying flesh."

"It's always useful to think about what your characters want," Max said. "Think about what your monster wants."

"The monster wants my hands," Susan wrote. "He wants to take my hands and my heart."

"And think about what the monster fears," Max said. "What could keep the monster away?"

Susan stared at the words she had written. She had not thought about Alice for years. Now she remembered the first time after Alice's death that she had gone out at night.

It had been with Harry. He had been in one of her classes. He had asked her if she'd come help him study for the midterm. He knew she took good notes and he would really appreciate her help. She had hesitated, then shaken her head. "I'm not going out at night," she had told him. She had explained, as calmly as she could, that Alice's death had left her shaken, that she didn't feel safe at night.

A puzzled expression had crossed Harry's broad, all-American face. He had heard of the murders, of course, but it hadn't occurred to him that there was anything to be afraid of.

"That's no good," he said. "You can't just stay in at night."

She shrugged. She had stayed in at night since Alice's death and it seemed to her that she could go on doing so.

"I'll come get you," he said. "And I'll bring you back to your room. You'll be safe with me."

He had kept his word. She had been safe with him—that night and on subsequent nights when they went out on dates. For all his faults, Harry had kept her safe, had helped her forget about the monster lurking in the dark. She had worn Harry's wedding ring and she had been safe.

TEN

"And so she found her heart's desire," the woman said. "But she didn't know it at first."

—from *Here Be Dragons*
by Mary Maxwell

After workshop, Pat went to her scuba-diving class and Susan set off with a guidebook from the ship's boutique, determined to explore Hamilton. It was a beautiful, sunny day, and she knew there was nothing to be afraid of.

According to the guidebook, Court Street offered "a fascinating potpourri of smaller stores and services." The book went on to say that the section north of Church Street was good for "a cultural experience and a 'different' shopping excursion." It sounded intriguing.

On the map, the way to Court Street was quite clear—Susan could follow Front Street, which ran right along the waterfront, to Court Street. Even she couldn't get lost.

Susan left the ship late in the morning, dressed in a sundress and sandals, with the guidebook and her camera tucked into her purse. Most passengers going on shore excursions had already left. At the top of the gangplank, a security guard ran her cruise card through a card reader. "Have a nice time ashore," he said.

She strolled down the gangplank. "Taxi," called a man in baggy Bermuda shorts and a T-shirt. She shook her head and continued down the waterfront past booths offering snorkeling trips and other excursions, past vendors selling cheap jewelry and tourist trinkets, past a stand where a gray horse stood by a carriage for hire. "No, thank you," Susan said to the vendors who hailed her. "Maybe later."

The waterfront had a holiday atmosphere. Flowers

bloomed in planter boxes along the waterfront. A dark-skinned woman with a basket of coconuts smiled at Susan. A man in Bermuda shorts was selling ice cream bars to a group of children.

Susan noticed a number of tourists from the cruise ship: half a dozen older women were inspecting the jewelry; a young couple was discussing the merits of a carriage ride; two other couples were talking to a man in a booth about a snorkeling trip.

She walked along the waterfront, leaving the tourists behind, and found her way to Court Street without incident. On Court Street, she headed north, past government buildings. She passed a group of men dressed in the business attire she had read was standard here during the warm months—button-down shirts, jackets, ties, and baggy Bermuda shorts that ended just above the knee.

Seeing the men gave her a dreamy sense of dislocation. The setting looked so normal—stone government buildings, wide green lawns. From the waist up, the men would have looked fine on the streets of downtown San Francisco. And from the waist down, they just looked silly, giving the scene a strangely surreal quality.

When she crossed Church Street, the official buildings gave way to shops selling fabric, ready-made clothing, umbrellas, toys. The shops had a crowded, jumbled feel to them. The sidewalks were filled with shoppers—men in shorts, housewives in colorful dresses—all local people, she was sure.

She wandered down the street, strolling through the shops. There didn't seem to be anyone else from the cruise ship shopping here. She made her way through the crowd, happy to have left the other tourists behind. She bought a keychain flashlight in one store—the kind that lit up when squeezed. It said "Souvenir of Bermuda" on the side, but she bought it just in case there was another blackout.

She took a few pictures: a shop with brightly colored clothing hanging in the window, the crowded street. She could imagine sharing this with her friends back home.

"This street was a little off the beaten track," she would say. "Just locals, no tourists."

She was getting tired and starting to think about lunch. The sun was overhead and the day was getting a little too hot, when she saw a side street that looked intriguing. She'd go just a little farther, she decided as she turned onto it.

Trucks filled with produce were parked along both sides of the narrow street, leaving just enough space for a vehicle to pass between them. In the trucks and on the crowded sidewalks beside the stores, mangos, bananas, coconuts, papayas, and tropical fruits she could not name spilled from boxes and bins. The smell of ripe fruit was almost over-powering.

Men pushed carts filled with produce through the crowd; women carrying shopping baskets negotiated with shop-keepers. The men selling the produce watched her as she passed; the shopping housewives glanced at her. She was out of place here. She knew that. The people around her spoke English, but she couldn't understand half of it, so thick were the accents; so abundant, the slang terms.

As she passed a shop doorway, she noticed a group of teenaged boys watching her a little too closely. One of them said something she didn't understand, and the others laughed. She hurried past them, glad of the crowd of house-wives around her.

She felt dizzy with the heat. She needed something cool to drink, a place to sit down. Maybe she should turn back. She glanced back in the direction from which she had come, but two of the teenagers were walking after her. Looking forward, she could see bright sunlight where the street ended at another street or a square. She continued down the narrow street.

"Excuse me," she said. "Pardon me." She was squeezing through a crowd of chattering housewives—big black women in colorful clothing who had gathered around a pro-duce stall. Susan had to make her way past them to reach the light. She clutched her purse under her arm, remem-bering now that the guidebook had warned against pickpockets and purse snatchers. It was too hot, too crowded, too loud with unintelligible chatter. "Excuse me. Pardon me."

She had almost reached the end of the alley when she heard a rumble of drums and a shrieking of whistles. "It's the gombey," she heard a woman say—or at least that's what it sounded like.

People jostled against her. The crowd moved and she was carried along with them, like a swimmer caught in a current. She tried to resist, struggling toward the light at the end of the alley. "Please," she said. "Excuse me. I need to go this way."

"Gombey," someone else was saying. "It's the gombey."

"Please let me through," Susan said. She just wanted to get to an open space where she could get a breath of air. "Please."

Some of the people around her tried to help. "Look sharp there—let the tourist lady through," said a woman.

More chatter around her—she didn't catch much of it, something about the tourist lady, something about a good view—and she found herself pushed to the front of the crowd, facing the bright mouth of the alley. The drums were thundering around her, echoing from the walls; the whistles were shrieking like lost souls. She could see strange figures coming toward her, silhouetted against the light. They were impossibly tall, and the light reflected from them, sparkling on their faces and bodies. She squinted, trying to make out details, and she saw leering faces with bright, staring eyes. One figure brandished a hatchet in her direction. The monstrous creatures around him wielded whips, raising them high. They stalked toward her, waving their weapons.

She clutched her purse and her camera, confused by the pounding of the drums, frightened and dizzy. She couldn't run—the alley behind her was packed with people; in front of her, the creatures blocked the way. She didn't know what to do.

She felt a hand on her shoulder. "Your camera," said a

woman's voice. "Take his picture." Susan glanced at the woman beside her—a smiling American woman in a brilliantly flowered dress.

Susan raised her camera and snapped a picture.

"It's the local gombey troop," the woman was saying. "They're dancers, practicing for a festival next week. Take another picture."

Susan lifted her camera and snapped a picture of a gyrating creature in a feathered headdress. She could see now that it was a man in a costume decorated with beads and sequins and fringe and tassels. They were costumed dancers, nothing to be afraid of. She took another photo.

"That's it," said the woman beside her. "People let you to the front so you could get a good view."

Susan nodded and managed a smile. "Yes," she said. She glanced around her at the smiling faces. "Very nice of them."

Susan was almost finished with the roll of film, when the gombey dancers moved on. Some of the crowd surged around her, moving to follow the dancers. Others returned to their shopping.

Susan turned to the woman beside her. "I'm sure glad you came along," Susan said. "I didn't know what was going on."

The woman laughed. "The gombey can be startling," she said.

Susan nodded. "That's for sure. By the way, I'm Susan Galina."

"Pleased to meet you," the woman said. "I'm Mary. I was just thinking of getting some lunch. Do you want to join me?"

Mary led the way through a series of narrow streets and somehow, miraculously it seemed to Susan, they emerged on Front Street. She could see the *Odyssey* in the distance, looming over the buildings along the waterfront, shining white and clean in the sunshine. "There's the ship!" she said. It was strangely comforting to see the *Odyssey,* so substantial and familiar.

"There's an Irish pub up this way," Mary said. "Good beer and good food. Does that sound all right to you?"

"Sounds wonderful."

Susan followed the woman into a building and up a flight of stairs to Flanagan's. The room was cool and dimly lit, a relief after the heat of the day. The air was perfumed with the rich scent of Guinness and grilling steak. Susan realized how hungry she was. The cheese Danish she'd had for breakfast had been a long time ago.

They took a table by the window, where Susan could look out at the tourists and vendors on the waterfront below. A few other tables were occupied by tourists and locals. The honeymooning couple from the *Odyssey* was two tables down.

"I recommend the fish chowder," Mary said. "I've been told it's the best on the island."

While they ordered—fish chowder and Guinness for Mary and a steak and Guinness for Susan—Susan studied the woman. Her shoulder-length black hair was almost as unruly as Susan's. She was a few years older than Susan.

No wedding ring—Susan looked for that. Mary wore dangling earrings and a charm bracelet that jingled when she gestured, which she did frequently. Her jewelry, her clothing, her gestures, her expressions all indicated that this woman was confident and comfortable with her body and her self.

"You certainly seem to know your way around," Susan said. "Have you been here before?"

"Oh, yes," Mary said. "I've visited Hamilton before, spent some time here. I like Bermuda. I often dream of the island."

Susan nodded. She could imagine that—dreaming of tropical beaches when she was back at home. "Well, I'm glad you came along when you did," Susan said.

Mary nodded. "You looked a little overwhelmed."

"Well, I had just realized that I was completely lost. And

I didn't know what to make of those dancers."

"The gombey dancers can be startling. Back in the early 1900s, there was a move to outlaw them, because so many of the white settlers found them intimidating."

Susan nodded. She could see that. The whips, the hatchets—it all had sinister overtones.

"They do shows for the tourists, but those are much tamer than what you saw." Mary leaned forward, speaking softly so that they couldn't be overheard by the people at other tables. "They always tone it down for the tourists."

Susan smiled, happy that Mary had accepted her as a fellow traveler, rather than just another tourist. She didn't know how she had earned the credential, but she was pleased to accept it anyway.

Their food arrived then—and Susan listened while Mary chatted with the waiter, asking a few questions about what was happening around town. Susan sipped her Guinness, feeling content.

She felt strangely comfortable with Mary. Unlike Alberta, Mary didn't quiz Susan about who she was, where she was from.

"So how do you like Bermuda?" Mary asked. "Is it what you expected?"

"Well, I don't know that I expected anything in particular. I won this cruise in a raffle, you see, and it seemed like the perfect thing to do. I needed to get away . . ." She hesitated. ". . . because I've been having a bad year."

"Ah," Mary said. "You needed a change of scene."

"I needed something. You see, my husband . . ." She stopped, not wanting to get into it in detail. She considered lying, but given the reaction to her last attempt, decided against it. Besides, she didn't want to lie to Mary.

"Don't say another word." Mary waved a hand, bracelet jangling. "I can tell you're still sorting out that story."

"What do you mean?"

"Your story, your version of what happened. The short version is simple: your husband did something dreadful and now he's no longer your husband. But you are trying to put the right words and thoughts to that story, the right emotional tones and resonance. You aren't ready to tell that story yet."

Susan frowned. "You make it sound like I'm inventing what happened."

"Of course you are." Mary said. "You are reinventing what happened. Reinventing who you are. We all do that all the time. Sort out the past, rearrange it, make it a little better, give it a bit of a plot." Mary shrugged. "Psychologists have done studies about human memory, and it turns out that people rewrite their memories all the time. You're always at the center of your own story—so you might as well make yourself the hero."

Susan shook her head, smiling. "That's funny. Just yesterday, someone was telling me that I should lie more often. Now you're saying that everybody lies—to themselves as well as to everyone else."

Mary cocked her head to one side. Her blue eyes reflected the light from the window, catching the tropical blue of the water in the harbor. "I don't think it's lying," she said. "It's more like revising. Rewriting a scene, so that you say just the right thing." She sipped her Guinness. "So who's been telling you to lie?"

"A writer named Max Merriwell. He's teaching a workshop on the ship. Do you know his work? He also writes books as Mary Maxwell," Susan said. "Wonderful books."

Mary smiled, as if Susan had told a joke. "Max Merriwell," she said. "Of course."

"You should come to the next workshop. Max is really a wonderful storyteller." Susan frowned, suddenly realizing that she'd made an assumption. "You are on the cruise, aren't you? I assumed . . ."

Mary nodded, still smiling. Susan wished she knew what the joke was. "Of course," Mary said. "Of course I am."

She was gazing out the window. The sky had clouded over. The fronds of the potted palms along the waterfront were stirring in the wind. "Looks like we're in for a shower," Mary said. "You'd probably better get back to the ship before the rain starts."

"Aren't you going back to the ship?"

"Later," Mary said. "I have a few errands ashore. But I'll see you later."

"I don't know—I haven't seen you until now."

Mary reached across the table and patted Susan's hand. "Don't worry—now that we've met, we'll meet again."

They said good-bye at the restaurant door. Mary headed down a side street and Susan headed for the ship. The wind was cool. She was halfway back to the *Odyssey* when the rain started: big, wind-blown drops that came thicker and faster as she started to run. Her sundress whipped around her legs; the rain pelted her arms and face. She felt exhilarated by the rain on her face, by her experiences in town. She was thinking about what she would tell Pat—what stories she would tell—and she felt, for a moment, like the wild adventurer in a story. Her own story or someone else's—it didn't really matter which.

ELEVEN

"Wheels have been set in motion," Gyro said. The pata-
physician shrugged. "Nothing that you or I can do about
that."
Ferris regarded the pataphysician with alarm. "What should
we do?" he asked.
"Wait and see."

—from *The Twisted Band*
by Max Merriwell

Tom was very tired. He had spent two hours that morning
with Mr. Perkins. It had been, as Tom had anticipated, a
waste of time. Mr. Perkins was now convinced that nothing
had really happened. "I'd been drinking a bit," he told Tom
with a sheepish laugh. "Those fellows must have just been
joking around."

From the database of passenger photos, Ian had sorted
out two hundred men whose age, hair color, and eye color
matched those of the men described by Mr. Perkins and the
bartender. Somewhat reluctantly, Mr. Perkins had glanced
through the photos, but he hadn't seen either of the men
he had been playing cards with. "I'm not very good with
faces," Mr. Perkins admitted.

Tom had politely thanked Mr. Perkins for his time, pin-
ning his hopes on the bartender. It was so simple. If the
bartender could identify the men, Tom could find them,
question them, and more than likely dispose of the matter
quickly and easily.

But Nic had no better luck. The bartender was motivated
to succeed—interested in a possible bonus—and he looked
through all the photos very patiently. He didn't find either
of the poker players among them, though he identified Mr.

Perkins as the man who had been with them.

Tom thanked Nic for his time and sent him on his way. Then Tom leaned back in his desk chair, sleepy and frustrated.

"Another cup of coffee?" Ian asked sympathetically.

Tom accepted a cup of coffee and the biscotti Ian offered along with it. "You're sure you included all the men in the right age range," Tom asked.

Ian nodded. "Every Caucasian male with a mustache over thirty and under sixty," he said patiently. "Passengers and crew."

Tom nodded wearily.

"Maybe it was a fake mustache," Ian said cheerfully.

"They both had mustaches," Tom pointed out, studying him with a level gaze. "Two men, both wearing fake mustaches, stage a fight for the benefit of a drunk."

"Sure," Ian said.

"Why would they do that?"

"A joke?" Ian shrugged. "I have to admit, I prefer my original explanation."

"What was that?"

"Max's fictional pseudonym is making trouble." Ian grinned. "He stabbed another fictional character, then tore the wires out of a fuse box to slow down anyone who was trying to find him."

Tom shook his head wearily. "Great—but I told you: I stick to nonfiction. If this turns out to involve paranormal occurrences in the Bermuda Triangle, I figure it's your department." Tom glanced at his watch. "I'd better check on the electrical work," he said. "That, I can deal with."

Tom spent the rest of the morning with a work crew, overseeing the installation of security locks on the utility panels, a precaution that had never seemed necessary before the vandalism of the previous night. Someone had yanked open the door to the utilities panel, torn out a handful of wires, seemingly at random, then splashed the box with Scotch, causing a blackout in the passenger areas of the ship.

Susan was drenched when she boarded the ship. She took a hot shower and by the time she was dry, the sun was out again. After her adventures in Hamilton, she was content to settle down by the pool with *Wild Angel* and read about Sarah McKensie and her life among the wolves. She had just started reading when she was interrupted.

"Hi."

Susan looked up to see Jody standing by her chair. Water dripped from the little girl's long brown hair and her red swimsuit.

"Good afternoon, Jody. How are you?"

"Nancy says I can't go swimming unless a grownup goes with me, and she's tired of swimming." Jody studied Susan with dark brown eyes, obviously sizing up her possibilities as a swimming partner. "Want to go swimming?"

Susan could see Nancy at the far end of the pool, toweling herself dry. The nanny waved cheerfully.

"No thanks, Jody. Not right now." Susan smiled at the girl. She had been in charge of the children's reading hour at the library, and she had always liked children.

Jody perched on the end of the lounge chair. "What are you reading?" she asked.

Susan thought for a moment about how to sum up the plot. "A story about a little girl named Sarah. She lived in California a long time ago. Her mother and father are killed by a very bad man, and Sarah is adopted by a pack of wolves." She stopped there, giving Jody a chance to digest this information. "Do you know what wolves are?"

Jody nodded solemnly. "I've seen pictures of them."

"Sarah lives with the wolves and learns to hunt with the wolves." Susan said.

"I'd like to live with wolves," Jody said.

"Really?" Susan smiled. Like Jody, she wanted to run off with the wolves. That was one reason she liked Mary Maxwell's work. It always seemed to address a desire that she hadn't realized she had. "You think it would be fun to live with wolves?"

Jody nodded.

"So do I."

"Yeah," Jody said. "Wolves can go swimming whenever they want."

Susan nodded. "I suppose they can."

"Where's that man?" Jody asked.

"What man?"

"The man who knows about the monsters."

"You mean Max," Susan said. "I don't know. I haven't seen him this afternoon."

"I wanted to tell him about Henry," Jody said. "He's not so scary after all."

"That's good," Susan said. "Max will be glad to hear that."

"Yeah," Jody said. "Not all monsters are scary."

"Jody!" Nancy was calling from the other side of the pool. "You need to get dried off."

Jody gave Susan a look that communicated her disdain for Nancy's rules, for being dried off, for all the things that were required of little girls but not of wolves.

"Jody!"

"Bye, Jody," Susan said and watched the little girl trudge around the pool. Jody's body language made it clear that Nancy's demand was a great and unwarranted imposition on her time.

Susan returned to *Wild Angel*. In an improbable but compelling series of events, Sarah McKensie was captured and jailed. Then she broke out of jail (with the help of an elephant and a mob of Clampers).

The sun was low in the sky when Susan closed the book with just a few chapters to go. She was eager to find out how the story would turn out, but reluctant to finish the book and leave the world of the wild girl just yet. Jody was right—wolves could go swimming whenever they wanted. So could wild girls.

Susan had always been a good girl. She had done her

best to please her mother; she had excelled in school; she sat up straight and ate her vegetables. Sitting by the pool, thinking about the wild girl, Susan wondered exactly when she had realized that being good wasn't making her happy.

It was a realization that had sneaked up on her. Maybe she had started to realize it when Harry had announced that he was leaving. She had been unhappy for a while before that, but she had thought that was because Harry was so unhappy. She had tried to deal with that by making Harry happy. She had cooked lovely dinners; she had taken care to look nice, even when she was just hanging around the apartment. But Harry hadn't even noticed and the effort didn't make Susan any happier.

Thinking about it now, she realized that being good had never made her happy. And it hadn't really kept her safe, either. She had been good, but Harry had left her.

Sitting by the pool, she decided that she might be better off trying to please herself. She might not be good, but perhaps she would be happier.

"Hey, Susan!" Pat was back from her scuba class, looking tired but cheerful. "I thought I might find you here. What are you doing?"

"Thinking about how being good has been a waste of time," Susan said.

"I told you that years ago," Pat said.

"Well, I've finally decided to listen."

Pat waved to the waitress and ordered a beer and French fries. "Now this is living," she said.

Susan told Pat about her adventures in Hamilton; Pat filled her in on the joys of scuba diving. Then Susan saw Ian standing by the pool bar. "Hey, there's Ian." She waved to the computer programmer, who came over to join them.

"You look comfortable," he said, pulling over a chair.

Pat nodded, smiling. "Any more notes from Weldon Merrimax?" she asked.

He shook his head. "No more notes. But an interesting development. Our pal Weldon seems to be making trouble." He told them about the poker game. "Mr. Perkins originally claimed that Weldon Merrimax had stabbed this other fellow, Patrick Murphy. Then he changed his story and said it must have been some kind of joke." Ian shrugged. "In any case, there's no way Tom can do much about it. No one can identify the alleged perpetrator nor the alleged victim." He grinned. "It's all quite mysterious."

Susan felt a chill, remembering the splash of red on the side of the ship. "That's weird," she said.

"What's weird?" Ian asked.

"Well, I was at the stern of the ship last night. And I saw something floating in the wake." She shrugged. "It probably wasn't anything."

Ian studied her face. "Sounds a little vague," he said.

"It was a little vague," she agreed quickly. "But there's another thing: What did you say the name of the victim was?"

"Patrick Murphy."

Susan frowned. "That's the name of a character in *Wild Angel*," she said. She flipped through the pages. "Yeah, here he is: 'Patrick Murphy, an agent of the recently formed Pinkerton National Detective Agency . . .' Weird coincidence."

"What does Patrick Murphy look like in the novel?" Ian asked.

"What difference does that make?" Pat asked.

Ian shrugged. "Just thought it would be interesting if the description matched."

"As I recall, he's a tall guy with a mustache," Susan said.

Ian laughed. "That's perfect. He matches the description of the victim. So a man who doesn't exist may have stabbed a character out of Mary Maxwell's novel."

When Tom arrived in the Ithaca Dining Room, everyone else was already at the table. Apparently Alberta and Bill had joined an official tour of the island. Alberta seemed miffed that Susan had gone off on her own.

"Don't you think it's dangerous go wandering around in a foreign city alone?" Alberta asked Susan. "Anything could have happened."

"There was nothing to be afraid of," Susan said. Tom noticed that she hadn't answered Alberta's question. She had evaded it rather neatly by stating a fact, rather than discussing how she felt.

Alberta had not noticed Susan's evasion. "Well I would have been afraid," she said. "I've heard so much about purse snatchers and pickpockets. You just can't wander about here like you can back home."

"Actually, armed robbery is more common in most American cities than it is in Hamilton," Tom interjected. "I had to do some research on the subject when the company was putting together a brochure on shoreside safety for passengers. You can wander about in Hamilton and be statistically safer than you are back home."

Alberta frowned, shaking her head, but Susan gave him a grateful smile. Then, as was so often the case, the conversation turned to food. Among the appetizers that night was a selection of caviar, which led Charles and Bill into a lengthy and tedious discussion of fish eggs.

Charles was apparently something of an expert on the subject. He treated the table to a prolonged discourse on the caviar of the spoonbill, a peculiar prehistoric fish that thrived in the waters of the Mississippi River. According to Charles, the caviar was quite delectable, but Tom wasn't convinced. To him, all fish eggs seemed better used as bait than dinner.

At last, they placed their orders and Charles turned to Tom. "So what was the story with that blackout last night," he said. "That sort of thing would never happen on Celebrity Lines."

"It appears to have been an act of vandalism," Tom said. "Someone went into a crew area, found a fuse box, and tore all the wires, blacking out three decks for just over an hour."

"Long enough to be quite inconvenient," Charles said.

"I thought it was fun," Susan said. "We went to the Apollo Lounge and had hot chocolate. But why would anyone rip out the wires in a fuse box?"

"I'll bet it was those dreadful Clampers," Alberta said.

"Clampers?" Susan looked startled, Tom thought. She glanced at Max. "Members of E Clampus Vitus? The society that's in *Wild Angel?*"

Max looked up from his brandy and nodded. "That's right," he said. "It seems there's a group of Clampers on board."

"They say they're interested in history," Alberta said in a disapproving tone, "but as far as I can tell, they are only interested in drinking."

Susan glanced at Max. "I thought you made them up."

"No need to do that," Max said. "The Ancient Order of E Clampus Vitus has been active in California since the Gold Rush. They're an historic drinking society."

"Or a drinking historic society," Tom said. He had had a few problems with the boisterous group already. "They do seem very fond of drinking."

"They were in the casino last night," Alberta said. "Gambling and drinking and raising a fuss." She shook her head, looking at Tom as if hoping that he would volunteer to do something about it.

Tom just smiled and nodded. According to Company Policy, there was nothing wrong with gambling and drinking in the Casino, that being the purpose of the establishment. Whether the Clampers had been "raising a fuss" was a judgment call. Alberta's judgment as to what constituted an unacceptable fuss clearly differed from that of the security staff.

Tom leaned on the railing of the Promenade deck, staring out at the waves. He was feeling restless, unsettled, and he thought a stroll might relax him.

Tom watched the lights of Hamilton sparkling in the distance. The pilot boat was gone and the *Odyssey* was leaving Bermuda behind, heading for the Azores. Ordinarily, Tom felt a sense of relief when the ship left a port. Usually, he felt most comfortable at sea, where the ship was a self-contained system, isolated from the rest of the world. But this departure was different. He felt uneasy, off-balance.

After dinner, Pat and Ian went out for a drink. They asked Susan to join them, but she decided to go back to the stateroom. It had been a lovely day. She went to bed early. Rocked by the gentle movement of the ship on the swells, listening to the soft humming of the ship's engines, she fell asleep.

She dreamed that she woke up. She did not really wake up, but she dreamed that she did. In her dream, she opened her eyes.

The stateroom was dark except for the moonlight shining through the glass door leading to the balcony. In the moonlight, she could see the outlines of the stateroom furniture: the desk, the chair, the closet.

Something wasn't quite right. Susan lay in bed, trying to figure out what had wakened her. The ship continued its easy rocking; the engines still hummed softly. She heard some people laughing as they walked down the corridor—drunks heading for bed after a late night in the bar, she thought. She looked toward Pat's bed, but it was still empty.

Susan sat up in bed, sniffing the air. She caught a faint scent of flowers—perhaps a floral perfume. Jasmine, she thought; it reminded her of jasmine tea.

Blinking in the dim light, she saw something draped across the back of the desk chair. She leaned over and switched on the bedside light.

She was alone in the cabin. A silk scarf hung over the

back of the chair. It wasn't hers and it didn't look like the sort of thing Pat would wear.

She noticed that the closet door was ajar, as if someone had dressed in a hurry and not stopped to close it. Through the opening, she could see a brightly colored dress, a blouse patterned with tropical flowers. Not her clothing.

Tentatively, she got out of bed and picked up the scarf, wanting to reassure herself of its reality. The silk was cool and smooth against her fingers. The sensation increased her unease. She did not belong here. This wasn't her cabin. How had she gotten into someone else's cabin?

She glanced at the papers scattered on the desk, ruled sheets torn from a spiral-bound notebook. The hand writing was sprawling and untidy, with looping, rounded letters that crossed the lines as often as they rested on them.

One sheet of paper caught her eye. At the top of the page was a set of lines, arranged like this:

The rest of the page was blank.

She recognized the lines as another hexagram from the *I Ching*. On the shelf above the desk, there was a copy of the *I Ching,* the same book that her college roommate had used to read fortunes. She took it down and found the hexagram. It was titled Chun: Difficulty at the Beginning. The name, the text said, related to a blade of grass, pushing against a stone as it sprouts from the earth.

She was sitting down in the chair, preparing to read more about this hexagram, when she heard the sound of a hand on the door. Startled, she stood up, just as the door was opening.

In Susan's stateroom, the door opened. Susan turned in

her sleep, rising toward wakefulness. She could hear Pat saying good night to Ian. For a moment, Susan blinked in the dark stateroom. Her stateroom. Then she closed her eyes and sank back into sleep.

TWELVE

"Sometimes dreams are simply dreams," Gitana said. "And sometimes, they are something more. It all depends on who is doing the dreaming."

—from *The Twisted Band*
by Max Merriwell

Ian looked up when someone tapped on the door. "Come in," he called. Max Merriwell opened the door and stepped into the office.

"Hey, Max," Ian said. "Good to see you."

The writer looked surprised to see Ian. "Hello, Ian. I was looking for Tom."

"We share an office. He's making the rounds of the ship. He'll be back in a few minutes. Sit down. Make yourself at home."

Ian was glad to see the writer. He found Max intriguing. "Would you like a cup of coffee?" Ian asked. "Osvaldo just brought a fresh pot. He knows how I like it, so it's stronger than most of what you get on board."

Ian poured Max a cup of coffee. He provided Max with a napkin and insisted that he try a biscotti. "Osvaldo's decided that I need to eat more, so he always brings cookies when I ask for coffee. Try one."

Max sampled a biscotti. "Wonderful," he said. "There's a little Italian deli near my apartment that makes biscotti, and I've missed them." He sighed and considered the cookie in his hand. "It's a very nice ship, but I do miss being at home."

"You live in New York City?" Ian said.

"In Greenwich Village," Max said. "I've been in the same apartment for twenty years now."

Ian imagined Max's apartment. Tiny, he guessed. Rent-controlled, of course. Crammed with books and papers. In *There and Back Again*, Bailey Beldon, the main character, lived in a cozy space in a hollowed-out asteroid—a warren of rooms packed full of interesting things. Ian imagined that Max's apartment was similar to that asteroid.

"Coming on this trip was an experiment. I felt I needed a bit of a change."

"Tom told me you were working on a new book," Ian said.

Max shrugged. "Still playing with ideas," he said. "Nothing solid yet."

"What brings you to see Tom?"

"I found another note under my door." Max pulled a scrap of paper from the pocket of his sports coat and held it out to Ian. "I thought Tom might like to see it. He was very interested in the other note I received."

Ian unfolded the paper. It had been torn from a spiral-bound notebook. Beneath a hexagram from the *I Ching,* a few sentences were scrawled in exuberant, looping handwriting: "A blade of grass pushes against a stone. A first meeting, beset by difficulties. Rain and thunder fill the air. When it is a man's fate to undertake such new beginnings, any premature move might bring disaster. To overcome the chaos, he needs helpers."

"Ah, that's appropriate," Ian said. "The lower trigram is K'an, the abysmal. Dark and dangerous water. The upper trigram is Chen, the arousing. Its image is thunder."

Max smiled. "You're a student of the *Book of Changes,*" he said.

Ian looked up from the hexagram. "I consult it on occasion. As I recall, the Wilhelm/Baynes edition of the *Book of Changes* says that this hexagram indicates the way in which heaven and earth bring forth individual beings."

"Do you recall the course of action suggested?" Max asked.

"Let me check." Ian called up the appropriate hexagram on his computer screen. "The commentary warns that times of growth are beset with difficulties, arising from the profusion of all that is struggling to take form. To bring order out of the confusion, the superior man must seek out helpers."

Max nodded. "Interesting," he said. He did not seem surprised by the note or its interpretation.

Ian considered the note again. "Do you have any idea who is sending you these notes?" he asked.

Max rubbed his beard thoughtfully. "Well, yes—I have some idea. I have seen similar handwriting," he admitted.

"You have? Where was that?"

"In my apartment. I sometimes wake up in the middle of the night and write notes about whatever I'm working on. In the morning, I never remember writing them." He chuckled. "Sometimes, the handwriting on those notes doesn't look like mine."

"Sometimes it looks like this?"

"Sometimes it does. And sometimes it looks like the writing on the other note I got."

"So you're writing notes to yourself?" Ian asked.

Max shrugged. "In a sense, everything a fiction writer writes is a note to himself. It's all part of the creative process. Every writer has his own methods. Perhaps mine is more unusual than some."

Max glanced at the clock on the wall, then set his coffee cup down, and stood up abruptly. "Look at the time," he said. "I'll be late to my own class if I'm not careful."

Susan woke up early. She had slept soundly and she was ready for breakfast. Pat was already gone—she had mentioned the night before that she might go for an early morning walk around the promenade deck. That girl had too much energy for her own good. Susan considered going to look for Pat, then decided that she would rather have breakfast by the pool and finish reading *Wild Angel* before heading for workshop.

It was early, but the day was already warm. The pool

sparkled in the bright sunshine. Susan chose a lounge chair in the shade, ordered a cup of decaffeinated coffee, a fruit plate, and a yogurt from the poolside waitress, and settled down to read her book.

She read to the end of *Wild Angel*, then closed it with a sigh. Like all of Mary Maxwell's books, *Wild Angel* had a happy ending. The villain was punished and the good were rewarded. The would-be Temperance lecturer ran off with the traveling circus, and Sarah turned her back on civilization, returning to her wolf pack. Susan was glad of that. Sarah belonged with the wolves, she thought.

She had just set the book on the table beside her when she saw Mary, the woman who had rescued her from the gombey dancers. Mary waved. "Good morning!" she called.

"Mary! How great to see you!"

Mary looked elegant and comfortable in shorts, sandals, and a crimson blouse. She carried a canvas beach bag; a scarf patterned with scarlet hibiscus was looped casually around the handle. It looked strangely familiar, but Susan couldn't place it.

Mary pulled over a chair from a nearby table and sat down. "What's that you're reading?"

Susan handed the book to Mary. "It's the latest Mary Maxwell book. I think it's one of her best. Or I guess I should say one of Max's best. Max described Mary Maxwell so well that it seems like she's real."

Mary leaned back in her chair, an odd expression on her face. "How did he describe her?" she asked.

"Let's see. He said she was totally fearless. She likes to travel and she's always getting into trouble—but she always gets out again. Actually, he said she liked to stir up trouble just for fun. She sounded a bit like my friend Pat."

Mary nodded thoughtfully.

"I'm going to be going to Max's workshop soon," Susan went on. "Why don't you come along? He's a very interesting speaker."

"No thanks," Mary said. "I have an appointment at the

beauty salon in half an hour." She pushed a hand through her hair. "I'm going to cut this mop off. I've heard the salon staff is excellent."

Susan pushed her own hair back, making a face. Her hair had once again escaped the clip at the back of her neck. In the warm weather, the curls were turning to frizz. She reached back and used both hands to lift the hair off the back of her neck so that the breeze could cool her. "In this weather, it would be great to have short hair."

"I think so. It's worth a try." Mary leaned back in her chair, studying Susan's hair. "Have you ever thought about cutting yours short?"

Susan hesitated, her hands full of hair, startled by the question. She had been wearing her hair long since she was in college.

"Let me hazard a guess," Mary said. "Your husband—your ex-husband, I suppose—liked it long."

Susan nodded. "That's what he said."

"Well, he's no longer entitled to an opinion, is he?" Mary leaned forward in her chair, studying Susan. Susan caught a whiff of her perfume—a familiar, floral scent. Jasmine? "He liked it long, but so what? What do you like?"

Susan released her hair, then pushed another wayward lock out of her eyes. When she was a child, her mother had insisted she keep her hair long. Harry had said her long hair was beautiful. Susan had always gone along with their opinions.

"I've always worn it long," she said. "I don't know what it would be like to cut it short."

"Unknown territory. Terra incognita. Here be dragons." Mary was smiling now. "Those are always my favorite parts of explorer's maps. The unknown seas where the dragons coiled, waiting and watching. You don't know what might happen, out there in the unknown."

Susan smiled back. How wonderful to compare something as simple as a haircut to an adventure into unexplored seas.

"Of course, you have to keep in mind that there are all

kinds of dragons," Mary went on. "In Western tradition, dragons are generally hostile, devouring maidens and laying waste to kingdoms. The Greeks and Romans didn't believe that—their dragons lived underground and didn't make trouble. But Christianity lumped those pagan Greeks and all their dragons together and made them symbolic of sin, grinding them under the heel of Saint George and his pals." Mary shook her head ruefully. "I prefer the dragon of the Far East, a benevolent, playful creature who flies without wings, a symbol of yang, the principle of heaven. I've always admired that sort of dragon."

Susan thought about dragons and unknown territory and her ex-husband and the disadvantages of being a good girl. It was definitely time for a change. "Maybe I'll get my hair cut," she said softly.

"I've always found that changing my appearance is a useful step when I'm changing my life," Mary said. "Do you want me to make an appointment for you?"

"Oh, I can't put you to that trouble."

"Don't be silly. I'll be there anyway. What time is that workshop over?"

"11:30."

"I'll make an appointment for 12. Would you like to join me for lunch, after?"

"That would be great."

Mary glanced at her watch. "I'd better be going. I'll meet you outside the salon at one." She headed off to the salon.

A few minutes later, Susan realized she had just enough time to get to the workshop.

Max was talking about character development when Susan slipped into the chair beside Pat, smiling apologetically. Max returned her smile, and kept talking.

"Some authors begin by observing people they know, writing long descriptions about what they wear and how they stand and the kind of car they drive," he was saying. "And that's all very well. It's useful to know whether your character wears faded jeans or three-piece suits. But I'm more interested in a character's interior landscape than in what they are wearing. What I want to know is how their clothes reflect and reveal that inner landscape."

Susan took out her notebook and pen.

"So we're going to try a little exercise in character development and description. I want you to choose one article of clothing that belongs to a particular character. Describe that piece of clothing in such a way that I know its owner, know something about how that character thinks and feels. I'll give you five or ten minutes to try it. Any questions?"

Alberta had a question, of course. She wanted to get the rules very clear before she could begin. Yes, he meant any article of clothing at all. A shirt, a shoe, a hat, a piece of lingerie. Well, yes, if she wanted to write about a shoe, she could write about a pair of shoes, since they could be viewed as a single article. Yes, she could choose to write about a pair of gloves instead, if she liked.

He was still fielding questions when Susan started writing.

"The silk scarf was looped carelessly around the handle of her bag," Susan wrote, "though she wasn't a careless sort of woman. Impulsive, perhaps, but not careless. She liked the scarf for its intense colors, reds and golds reminiscent of the burning embers in the heart of a fire. She liked the way it looked on the handle of her bag."

Susan hesitated, remembering a fashion article she had read a few months ago. Her mother had given her a subscription to the fashion magazine for her birthday. Susan had little use for its advice, but she dutifully paged through each issue. She remembered an article about learning to "accessorize," a word that Susan thought was awkward and ugly. The photos accompanying the article had shown cool, disdainful women wearing silk scarves. One wore hers in a graceful bow around her neck; another had hers knotted around her waist to make a stylish belt; a third wore hers like a shawl, draped elegantly over her shoulders. The heading on the page said something about the "amazing versatility of a simple scarf."

Susan remembered checking the prices of the scarves pictured. The cheapest had been 150 dollars. She knew that in her hands, all those expensive scarves would misbehave, knotting and crumpling and, no matter what she did, looking just plain silly. But in the hands of the fashion models, these scarves were versatile. Susan suspected that Mary accepted the scarf's versatility and took it farther than any of the fashion models would dare.

"She recognized the scarf as a square of fabric that had many possibilities," Susan wrote. "It was such a versatile article of clothing. She could wear it around her neck as a fashion accessory. In a medical emergency, she could fashion it into a sling. If she needed to make a daring escape, she could tie it together with bed sheets and throw it out the window as an improvised ladder, trusting to the strength of the silken fibers. Or, if a situation called for anonymity, she could fold her scarf into a triangle and tie it over her nose and mouth like a bandit in an old Western.

"So many possibilities. She was a woman who thrived on possibilities, on adventure, on mystery and unexplored territories. She would set off boldly, not knowing where she was going and not caring either. If you were lucky—if you looked like someone who might be interesting, who might be bold, who might be willing to learn how to use a scarf for purposes other than those described in fashion magazines—she might invite you along."

CONSIDERING GOOD GIRLS

My friend Susan told me last night that she had decided to stop being a good girl. I think this is an excellent decision on her part.

From what she's told me, Susan has always been a Good Girl. She listened to her mother, even when her mother was talking bullshit.

I hate to say it, but mothers do that sometimes. They may do it with the best possible intentions. Maybe they are trying to protect you from the dangers of the world when they say, "Oh, sweetheart, do you really want to . . . ?" Fill in the blank with whatever it is you really want to do: become a physicist, hitchhike across country, wear that sweater with those shoes. Well, maybe mom was right about the hitchhiking, but physics can be fun and magenta and chartreuse can go together in a clashy sort of way.

Very early in life, I learned when to listen to my mother and when to ignore her. But as far as I can tell, Susan has always listened to her mother and tried to be good. She went to college and married her first boyfriend—a control-junky asshole in my opinion, but maybe that's just me.

This cruise seems to be one of the first times she has ever broken loose. I was glad that she went off to explore Hamilton on her own. Seems like she had a great time.

I think Officer Tom is interested in her, but she denies it. The girl has such a rotten self-image. Officer Tom may be able to get past all that. I hope so, for his sake and for Susan's sake. He seems like a nice guy. A little stiff, maybe, but a nice guy.

Anyway, I'm glad that Susan has decided to become a Bad Grrl. I think I can be a fine role model in that regard.

THIRTEEN

"Don't put your faith in maps. The map is not the territory," Gitana explained to Ferris. *"In fact, the map only bears a faint resemblance to the territory. It leaves out far more than it includes."*

—from *The Twisted Band*
by Max Merriwell

Susan stared at herself in the mirror, watching as the beautician's scissors transformed her into another person entirely.

In the mirror, she could see another mirror on the other side of the small room. In the reflection of that mirror, she could see both a reflection of the back of her head and a reflection of her face in the mirror in front of the chair. In that reflection of a reflection of a reflection, she could see more reflections, marching away into infinity. In all the reflections, handfuls of her curly hair were falling in clumps as the beautician wielded her scissors.

Susan felt remarkably calm. The clip, clip, clip of the scissors blended with the calypso music that played in the background. She breathed in the fruity scent of conditioner—Annette, the beautician, had insisted on treating her hair to a moisturizing mango conditioner before the cut.

Susan felt the chill of the scissors as they snipped around her right ear. In the mirror, she could see her ear peeking through the curls. It looked small and pale, exposed to the world for the first time in decades.

"This hair was made to be short," Annette said.

"I always thought my face was too round for short hair."

Annette shook her head. "Whoever told you that was an idiot," she said.

Susan smiled. As she recalled, her mother had imparted that bit of information when Susan was twelve years old. Susan had always believed it was true.

"You're going to be a new woman," Annette said.

"That's good," Susan said, partly to Annette and partly to herself. "I was getting a little tired of the old one."

Half an hour later, Annette brushed off Susan's shoulders and neck, whisked off the smock, and sent her back into the world. Susan stepped out of the salon onto the deck and stopped for a moment at the railing.

The ocean breeze tickled the back of her neck lightly and she smiled. She reached up and ran her hands through her curls. So short. So bouncy. She shook her head. It felt so light without the weight of her hair. It felt so strange. It felt wonderful.

"Hello," Mary called as she walked toward Susan. Mary's dark hair had been cut to chin length. She looked great.

Susan smiled at Mary. "I should have done this years ago," she said.

Mary shrugged, smiling. "Well, you've done it now. Where shall we go for lunch?"

"Somewhere new," Susan said. "Terra incognita. Somewhere I've never been before."

"Your choice," Mary said.

Mary waited and Susan thought about the restaurants she had seen listed in the ship's directory.

"How about Penelope's?" she said.

"Sounds good to me," Mary said. "Lead the way."

Susan set off with great confidence. She had studied the ship's map to learn the way to the salon, and she remembered that it showed a companionway just to the stern of the salon.

She strolled beside the railing, letting the wind tousle her hair. They reached the stern, where a small sun deck held half a dozen deck chairs filled with sunbathers.

Susan stopped, baffled. "I thought the map showed a companionway down here." She frowned, feeling like a fool. Mary, she thought, was the sort of woman who could find her way without hesitation.

"Maybe we missed it," Mary said. "Let's try around this way."

"Well, I remember the map showed . . ."

"Oh, don't worry about the map. You can only trust a map so far. The map is not the territory, you know."

"I didn't mean to get us lost," Susan said apologetically.

Mary shook her head, smiling. "If we're lost, we're bound to end up somewhere interesting." Mary started out and Susan followed. As they walked along the railing, heading toward the bow of the ship, Mary told Susan about how she dealt with being lost. "On my first visit to Katmandu, I developed a strategy that worked quite well. The streets and alleys there twist and curve and meet at the most unlikely angles. I'd set out walking from the Katmandu Guest House, leave the main street, and be lost in fifteen minutes. Then I'd wander and explore. When I wanted to go back, I'd flag down a rickshaw, bargain for the fare, and tell them to take me to the Katmandu Guest House." She smiled. "I didn't need to know where it was. I just needed to find someone who did."

Susan nodded, trying to imagine herself using such a strategy. When she and Harry had visited Paris, she had suggested going out for a walk. Harry had consulted a map at every corner, insisting she look at it with him. "You have to know where you are," he maintained. Harry always knew where he was and it bothered him that she didn't.

At Harry's insistence, she had tried—she really had tried. On that trip, she learned that she could keep track of where she was if she paid close attention, remembering the street signs, remembering landmarks, looking back at where she had come from so that the way would look familiar when she returned.

She could do it. But the effort of remembering the way had spoiled the pleasure of taking a walk. She couldn't take the time to admire the fruits and flowers of a street vendor; she was too busy getting her bearings. She couldn't stare up at the architectural details of old buildings; she had to check the street signs and consult the map.

"I should have tried that when I was in Paris," Susan said. "Except there weren't any rickshaws."

"Flag down a taxi instead. That works in just about any city." Mary had found a door marked emergency exit. She had her hand on the knob.

"Wait," Susan said, fearing that an alarm might go off if Mary opened the door. But it was too late: Mary had the door open already. No alarm.

"The doors marked 'emergency exit' lead into crew areas," Mary said.

"But those are off limits to passengers, aren't they?" Susan asked.

Mary shrugged. "If we meet a crew member, they'll just ask if we are lost." Mary started through the door and up the stairs. "It's a short- cut."

"To where?" Susan said. The words had a familiar sound. She realized that they were Harry's words: he had asked that whenever she suggested that a particular route might be a shortcut.

Mary shrugged, smiling. "To adventure, to nowhere in particular, to somewhere interesting, to where we want to go. Let's check it out."

The companionway led to the aft portion of the recreation deck, where they found a basketball court, occupied by half a dozen sweaty, shirtless men, and a shuffleboard court where two teenagers in baggy shorts were playing a game of what Mary called "Sudden Death Shuffleboard" because the young men were playing it with such speed and intensity.

Mary led the way toward the bow, where they found another companionway. Eventually, after wandering past a sun deck and a wading pool, they were somewhere Susan recognized. "I've been here," she said. "Penelope's is this way."

Mary nodded. "I told you it was a shortcut," she said.

Mary took a table by a window, where they could look out at the waves that sparkled in the tropical sunshine. The bar was in the center of the room.

It was a bright, cheerful room. The walls were white. Mirrors above the bar reflected images of the room. Looking up at the mirror, Susan caught a glimpse of Mary. For a fraction of a second, she did not recognize the short-haired woman sitting across from Mary. Then she smiled at her own reflection. She looked like a new person—so relaxed, she thought, so happy with herself.

When the waitress came to take their drink orders, Mary studied the drink card on the table. Photos on the card showed frothy concoctions involving alcohol in various forms combined with coconut, pineapple, mangos, and other tropical fruits.

"Could I get a Flaming Rum Monkey?" Mary asked.

The waitress, a perky blonde, frowned. "I'll see if the bartender knows how to make one."

"All right. If he doesn't, I'll have a Flamingo Frappe."

Susan surveyed the list. The Flamingo Frappe involved apricot brandy, lime juice, gin, and grenadine. "I don't know," she murmured, staring at the card. She usually ordered a daquiri. But today she wanted something different.

"How about a Tropical Storm," Mary suggested. "Lime, rum, crushed pineapple, and grenadine."

"Sure," Susan said. She liked pineapple. "I don't usually drink at lunch," she told Mary as the waitress walked away.

"You're a new woman," Mary said. "You may find yourself doing any of number of things you don't usually do."

A few minutes later, the waitress returned with their drinks. "I'm sorry," she said. "The bartender doesn't have a recipe for a Flaming Rum Monkey. He suggested you try Aphrodite's Alehouse. Frank, the night bartender there, knows how to make every drink around."

Mary smiled, plucking the neon pink umbrella from her drink. "I'll do that."

As the waitress walked away, Susan asked, "What's in a Flaming Rum Monkey?"

"I don't know," Mary said. "It hasn't been invented yet."

Susan frowned. "What do you mean?"

"I made it up. You see, I've always thought cocktails have the most fabulous names. You've got swizzles and rickeys and fizzes and flips and smashes and shrubs and slings. Great words, all of them. Then you get into specific names, like the Beachcomber and the Side Car—and downright poetic ones, like the Fallen Angel and the Blue Devil and Mrs. Fizby's Fizz. Bartenders make drinks up and some go on to immortality. So I thought I'd make up a name, and see if I could find the drink that went with it." She grinned.

"So there is no such thing as a Flaming Rum Monkey?"

"Not yet. But I figure it's only a matter of time. It's such a catchy name. And it just begs to have variations. You could have your Mexican Monkey, made with tequila; your Irish Monkey made with Old Bushmill. And if you make an iced version, that would be a Monkey in the Snow." Mary gazed out the window, contemplating the possibilities. "I figure the drink probably involves coconut—the monkey connection, you know. In fancy places, maybe it's served in a half a coconut shell."

Susan studied Mary, marveling at this odd woman. "But if it doesn't exist, why ask if the bartender can make it?"

"I figure that one of these days, I'll find a bartender who is inspired by the name and wants to figure it out. Maybe Frank in Aphrodite's Alehouse is the man. We'll see."

She smiled at Susan, and Susan returned her smile. Mary seemed willing to include Susan in this adventure, and that made Susan happy. But she was a little skeptical. Inventing a drink seemed like fun—but baffling bartenders by pretending a drink already existed didn't seem to Susan like the best way to do it.

"Why not just tell him you want him to invent a drink?" Susan said. "Rather than pretending it already exists."

"Asking someone to invent something puts them under

a lot of pressure to be creative. I think I'm making it easier on them. All they have to do is match up a drink with the name."

"You think a bartender could figure a drink out, just from the name?"

"Oh, names are very powerful," Mary said.

"But in the meantime, you're spreading confusion," Susan observed.

"Exactly." Mary smiled. When Susan frowned, she went on. "A little confusion is a wonderful thing, don't you agree?"

"I don't know. I don't much like being confused myself."

"Most people don't. People like finding patterns in things—they like explaining things and learning how one thing relates to another. When you're confused, you can't see any patterns, and that's uncomfortable. So you start casting about in search of pattern, trying to make order from the confusion. Eventually, you sort it out and you fit whatever confused you into a pattern and then you're happy."

"Okay," Susan said slowly.

"But sometimes, it's good to be confused. I enjoy it. If you are confused often enough, you learn to be confident that you'll sort it all out sooner or later. You figure out methods for dealing—like hailing a rickshaw in Katmandu. You learn to relax with confusion—and that's a very powerful place to be."

Susan felt a little dizzy. She sipped her Tropical Storm and tried to relax with the confusion.

Mary was leaning back in her chair, studying Susan's face. "I think you tell yourself the wrong sort of stories," Mary said.

"What?" Susan said, startled, but trying to remain relaxed.

"You kick yourself for getting lost. You tell yourself that you don't look good with short hair. You avoid taking the shortcut. Little things, but they all add up. You don't trust yourself at all."

Susan didn't know what to say. "I suppose you're right," she began. "But . . ."

Mary held up her hand. "No buts," she said firmly. "You need to learn to trust yourself, to trust your abilities. There are so many possibilities for a woman who knows how to use her imagination." Mary sipped her drink, still considering Susan.

Susan bit her lip, feeling inadequate. Mary seemed to be taking her on as a sort of project, and Susan wasn't sure how she felt about that. She leaned back in her chair, wondering how she might distract Mary and take her attention off of Susan's shortcomings. That was when she spotted the man from the bar, sitting at a table on the other side of the restaurant. "It's Weldon Merrimax," she said.

Mary sat up straight. "What?" She followed Susan's gaze.

"Don't stare at him," Susan said, fighting the urge to look at him again. "Ship's security is looking for that guy."

"Why?"

"He's been claiming he's Weldon Merrimax. He cheated someone at poker. And he got in a fight at a poker game with a man named Patrick Murphy. He may have stabbed Patrick. It's kind of confusing," Susan said in a rush. "I've got to call Tom, the chief security officer."

Mary nodded. She was frowning. Her eyes were dark and unreadable. "You do that," she said.

"You stay here. I'll be right back," Susan said. She stood up quickly and hurried away, before Mary could ask any more questions.

It took Susan a few minutes to get the bartender's attention, and a few more minutes to explain what she needed. "Call Tom Clayton, the security officer. Tell him that the man he's looking for is right here. All right—I'll wait while you get him on the line."

Susan waited impatiently. Glancing across the room, she saw Mary, standing at the man's table. What was she doing? Mary was talking to the man, waving her hands angrily. The man was laughing. As Susan watched, he stood up and walked out of the restaurant. Mary followed him, still talking.

Susan considered taking off after them, but it seemed more important to get in touch with Tom. At last, the bartender placed a phone on the bar in front of her.

"Tom," she said. "It's Susan. That man you were looking for—that man with the identification problem—he was here in Penelope's a minute ago. He just walked out. I'm going to see if I can follow him."

"Stay where you are," Tom said. "I'm on my way."

"I've got to go," Susan said quickly and hung up. Mary had told her that she had to trust her abilities, and she figured she would start by following Weldon Merrimax or whoever he was. Besides, she was worried about Mary.

When Tom didn't find Susan in Penelope's, he searched the surrounding area. He finally found her on the observation deck, though it took him a moment to recognize her. She had cut her hair short, a startling change. She looked great.

"Susan," he said. "Where is this guy?"

She looked up as he approached. "He's gone," she said. "And so is my friend Mary." She shook her head. "I don't know where they went."

"Tell me what happened."

She told him about spotting the man. "I thought I'd better call you right away," she said. "While I was calling you, Mary went over to talk to him. I don't know why. Then he left and she followed him. And as soon as I got off the phone with you, I went after them. But they were gone."

Tom nodded. "Perhaps your friend Mary can help me out. What's her last name?"

Susan shook her head. "I don't know. I never asked."

"Do you know her stateroom number?"

Susan shook her head again. "We met in Hamilton. Then we ran into each other by the pool. She had an appointment at the salon, and she made an appointment for me to get my hair cut."

Tom nodded. The beauty salon would have a record of the appointment. It was a start.

Tom visited the beauty salon. He felt out of place in the turquoise and pink reception area. The air reeked of floral perfumes—the scents of lotions and conditioners and pomades. Allegedly, the salon catered to both men and women, but the buzz of conversation that came from the open room behind the reception desk was unquestionably female.

He told the receptionist that he was trying to locate a passenger who had had her hair cut that morning. "Her first name is Mary. I don't have a last name."

"Oh, I remember her," the receptionist said. "She paid cash. I told her she could put it on her cruise card, but she said she'd rather pay cash."

"Does that happen often?"

The receptionist shrugged. "Every now and then. Sometimes a woman doesn't want her husband to know exactly what she spent, but Mary didn't seem like that sort."

"What sort did she seem like?"

"The sort who wouldn't put up with guff from any man. Oh, don't get me wrong. She was a very pleasant lady. I just got the feeling she didn't let people push her around."

There was a touch of admiration in the receptionist's tone. The receptionist, Tom thought, seemed like the sort who did let people push her around.

"So you didn't get her cabin number?"

The receptionist flipped open her appointment book. "No cabin number. But you could look her up. I have her last name. Here she is: Mary Maxwell."

Tom stared at Mary Maxwell's signature in the appointment book. Large, looping letters, like the script on the note that Ian had passed on to him, the one that someone had slipped under the door for Max just that morning.

Back at the office, he asked Ian to check the passenger list on the computer. There was, of course, no one named "Mary Maxwell" listed.

FOURTEEN

"The universe is a much stranger place than you think,"
Gitana told Ferris. "Much larger, much stranger, and much
less predictable."

—from *The Twisted Band*
by Max Merriwell

Susan heard the shower running when she stepped into her
stateroom. "Hey, Pat," she called. "I'm back."

The sound of running water stopped and Pat called to
her from the bathroom. "Hey, girl. I ran into Ian when I
was checking my email in the business center, and we had
lunch together. He told me that your pal Max got another
note." Pat stepped out of the bathroom, wearing a robe, her
hair wrapped in a towel. "Wow! You look fabulous. What
a great haircut!"

"Oh, thanks," Susan said. She had almost forgotten about
the haircut.

"Really," Pat insisted. "You look like a different
woman."

Susan sat on the edge of the bed, studying her reflection
in the mirror on the wall. A stranger's face looked back at
her. The stranger looked puzzled. "Yeah, I do."

Pat was toweling her hair dry. "So what's the problem?"
she asked. "Don't you like it?"

"The haircut's fine. I just wish I knew what was going
on." Susan told Pat about going to lunch with Mary, about
seeing the man from the bar, about Mary's disappearance.
"I don't know what could have happened to Mary."

"Abducted by aliens," Pat suggested. She stood by the
bed, combing her hair so it stood up in random clumps, her
version of a stylish hairdo. "Or else she's one of those

women who will ditch a friend for the first dangerous man who comes along."

Susan shook her head. "I can't believe that. I wish I knew how to get in touch with her. I just want to make sure she's all right."

"So what did you talk about, before she disappeared?"

"What difference does that make?"

"Maybe it would give us a clue about how to find her."

"You've read too many mysteries," Susan said.

"Come on—give it a try."

Susan patiently related all that she could remember of her conversation with Mary—from rickshaws in Katmandu to Flaming Rum Monkeys. "I don't see how any of that could help," she said, when she finished.

"Well, here's an idea," Pat said, sitting beside Susan on the bed. "You said the waitress recommended Aphrodite's Alehouse as a place to get that flaming drink?"

"A Flaming Rum Monkey." Susan nodded.

"We'll go there and wait for Mary. She's bound to show up sooner or later."

Susan frowned. It wasn't a great plan, but it was better than anything she'd come up with. "I can't ask you to waste your time sitting around waiting for someone who might not show up."

Pat laughed. "Waste my time sitting around in a bar? Oh, twist my arm."

"What about dinner?"

"We can grab some snacks in the bar," Pat said. "Let's do it. I'll give Ian a call and see if he wants to meet us there. It'll be fun."

Susan hesitated in the entrance to Aphrodite's Alehouse. She surveyed the room, searching for Mary.

"Do you see her?" Pat asked.

"I'm looking," Susan said. A group of women sat at a table by the dance floor, but Mary wasn't among them. She wasn't at any of the tables by the fireplace, nor at the bar.

"No, no sign of her." She shook her head. "Should we get a table?"

"A table? No, we want to talk to the bartender, so let's grab a seat at the bar."

Susan followed Pat reluctantly and perched on a bar stool beside her. She would have been more comfortable at a table. The bar was in the center of the room and sitting there made her feel like she was on display. She reminded herself that she had given up being a good girl, that she was a new woman. It didn't help much. She still felt awkward.

The bartender, an older black man, set a beer and three rum swizzlers on a waitress's tray, then turned to greet them. The name tag on his shirt identified him as Frank.

"Good evening, ladies. What can I get for you?"

"A friend of mine was talking about a drink she had in Jamaica," Pat said. "Something called a Flaming Rum Monkey. Could you make one of those?"

Susan kicked Pat under the bar, but her friend just kept looking at Frank innocently.

Frank looked thoughtful. "You know, you're the second passenger who's asked for that drink."

"Really?" Pat said.

"That's right. A lady asked for a Flaming Rum Monkey earlier today."

"What did she look like?" Susan asked.

"Short, dark hair. Very friendly. I told her I'd see if I could find a recipe for the drink. She said she'd be back tonight."

"That sounds like Mary," Susan said to Pat.

Pat nodded. "She's the one who recommended the drink," Pat told Frank. "So you can make me one?"

Frank studied her and smiled. Susan thought he had the air of a man who had decided to go along with a joke—but wanted the jokers to know he hadn't been taken in.

"After your friend asked, I checked my bartender's guide, but I couldn't find a recipe."

"That's too bad," Pat said, her eyes wide and innocent. "I was really hoping to try one."

Susan spoke to Frank. "To be honest, Mary told me that she made the whole thing up. She just likes the name, and wants to know what the drink will taste like."

"I can believe that. She seemed like a lady who was fond of a joke." Frank's smile grew wider. "It's slow tonight. I could come up with a drink that you might call a Flaming Rum Monkey. And we could turn the joke around on your friend."

"Great idea," Pat said.

"She said she thought it would involve coconut," Susan said.

"All right," Frank said thoughtfully. "Better that than bananas."

Susan watched as Frank began pulling bottles from the shelf. Creme de cacao, coconut syrup, dark Jamaican rum, some brown sugar, some spices.

"Hello, Frank! Hi, ladies." Ian sat on the stool beside Pat.

"Ah, Ian. You're just in time for the first Flaming Rum Monkey." Frank smiled. "This is my friend Ian," he told Pat and Susan. "I asked him to search the Internet for a recipe."

"I should have known," Pat said.

"No luck," Ian said. "Plenty of flaming drinks, but no Rum Monkeys."

"Mary made the name up," Susan said. "She liked the name and she wanted to know what the drink would taste like."

"Mary Maxwell," Ian said, smiling.

Susan stared at him, and his smile grew broader.

"That's the name she gave at the beauty salon," Ian said. "Tom had me check, but she's not on the passenger list."

Susan didn't know what to say.

"Best to start with a hot drink, I think, since that will be easier to flame," Frank said. He had been considering his bottles while Ian talked. "So I'll begin with a hot buttered rum de cacao and go from there." He spooned some brown sugar into the mug, added cloves and nutmeg, stirred it with a cinnamon stick, then poured in a little boiling water.

"We're watching an artist at work," Ian said to Pat.

"Absolutely," Pat agreed.

While they talked about how underappreciated good bartenders were, Susan watched Frank and wondered about Mary.

Though he had to interrupt the task a few times to make other orders, Frank eventually completed a drink that included rum, creme de cacao, coconut syrup, and boiling water. Then he poured a splash of 151-proof rum into a ladle, ignited it, and added the flaming rum to the drink. As the blue flames flickered in the dimly lit bar, he handed it to Susan. "Give it a try."

Susan blew out the flames and sipped the concoction. It tasted like a Mounds bar, laced with rum. It was warm and sweet and potent. "This is wonderful," she said.

"Let me try." Pat tried a sip and passed it to Ian.

"Maybe a touch more coconut," Ian suggested.

"I disagree," said Pat. "I think any more coconut would spoil it."

"It's perfect just as it is," Susan said.

Frank had already put another Flaming Rum Monkey in front of Susan. When the flame flickered out, she sipped it carefully. Such a comforting drink.

"What's that you're drinking?" asked a tall man who had come up to the bar.

"That's a Flaming Rum Monkey," Frank said with a note of pride.

"Very tasty," Pat said.

The tall man ordered one, and Frank made another round for the group. By that time, Susan's mug was empty.

"Another Rum Monkey for my friend," Pat said, and Susan found herself sipping another drink.

The bar was getting noisier and more crowded. Susan noticed that the tall man with the Flaming Rum Monkey had joined a group of men—all in their thirties and forties—clustered around one of the tables near the fireplace. One of them was lifting his glass in a toast. "What say the brethren?" he called. The others cheered and shouted, "Satisfactory!"

Susan recognized the ritual question and response from Max's description of the Clampers in Wild Angel. "That must be a group of Clampers," Susan said. "E Clampus Vitus."

"Yes, I met some of them earlier at the poolside bar," Ian said. "They're having some sort of reunion and celebrating a noble feat of St. Vitus. Something involving a rescue and an elephant. It wasn't at all clear."

Susan blinked at him, remembering a scene from Wild Angel. The Clampers had created a distraction while members of the circus used an elephant to yank the bars from the window of the jail and free Sarah. Could Max have based this incident on some historical event? Or could the Clampers be celebrating their appearance in Wild Angel? "Wait," she said. "There was a scene like that in Mary Maxwell's book. I wonder if it was based on some historical incident."

"Let's ask the Clampers," Pat said. "They'd know. They're drunken historians after all, not just drunks."

Ian stood up to go with Pat. Susan shook her head. "Let me know what they say. I'll stay here and keep an eye out for Mary." She watched as a waitress carried a trayful of the flaming drinks to the table of Clampers. Apparently the drink had met with the tall man's approval and he had ordered a round for the group. Pat and Ian headed over to the table.

Susan was surprised to realize that she had finished her Rum Monkey. Before she could protest, Frank had made her another. He was just setting it in front of her when he looked over her shoulder.

"Ah," he said with satisfaction. "You're back. Just in time. Let me get you a Flaming Rum Monkey."

Mary slid onto the bar stool beside Susan. "Mary!" Susan said. "I was worried about you. I . . ."

Mary wagged a finger at Susan. "Later," she said. "Now we must give our full attention to the matter at hand."

Mary watched as Frank mixed another Flaming Rum Monkey, ignited it, and offered it to her with a flourish. She picked up the mug. The flames danced, then died. Mary took a sip while Susan and Frank watched. "Perfect," she said. "Just as I imagined it."

Frank winked at Susan. "As good as the ones you had in Jamaica?"

"Better," Mary said. "As good as I imagine the ones I wish I had had in Jamaica would have been—if I had actually had them."

Susan frowned, trying to follow that sentence and failing.

Mary smiled. "The imagination is a powerful thing," she said, lifting her glass to Frank. "And the Flaming Rum Monkey lives—thanks to you."

A waitress called to Frank from the far end of the bar—an order of Rum Monkeys for the ladies at the table by the stage. The band had started up again. Pat and Ian were surrounded by Clampers who were lifting their Flaming Rum Monkeys in a toast. There was no chance of getting Pat's attention just now.

"What happened to you this afternoon?" Susan asked Mary, speaking loudly to be heard over the din.

"I had a bone to pick with that fellow," she said. "Sorry I had to rush away like that."

"Ian says you signed in at the beauty salon as Mary Maxwell," Susan went on.

"That's my name," Mary said. "I had to talk with Weldon Merrimax. He's a dangerous man."

"Wait a second," Susan said. "Slow down. What did you have to talk to him about?"

Mary sipped her Rum Monkey, looking thoughtful. "A lot, actually. It's all about the nature of reality. And dreams, of course—it has a lot to do with dreams."

Susan blinked, more baffled than before.

"Come on," Mary said, taking her arm. "Let's go outside where we can talk without being interrupted."

Still clutching her drink, Susan let Mary lead her from the bar, out into the corridor, then through the double doors onto the promenade deck. The door swung closed behind them, shutting out the shouting of the Clampers, the music of the band.

A cool breeze blew from the ocean. Overhead, the stars were bright and still. Susan leaned against the railing. She felt drunk. She felt that she had the right to demand answers. She wanted to know what was going on.

"What the hell are you talking about?" she asked Mary. "Why are you pretending to be Mary Maxwell? Who is that guy who's pretending to be Weldon Merrimax? What's going on, anyway?"

Mary was gazing out to sea, where the dark water rose and fell in gentle swells. "So many questions," she said softly. "So much confusion. Isn't it lovely?

"I think some answers would be nice," Susan said.

Mary grinned, leaning back against the railing. "One more question, first. Have you ever read *Through the Looking-Glass,* by Lewis Carroll?"

"Many times." That had been one of Susan's favorite books to read aloud at the library's story hour.

"Do you remember when Alice meets Tweedledum and Tweedledee? They show her the Red King. He's sleeping— wearing a red nightcap and snoring. And Tweedledum says that Alice is just a thing in the Red King's dream."

Susan nodded. She remembered the scene. "Alice says she's not just a thing in his dream, she's real. She starts to cry and Tweedledum says, 'I hope you don't think those are real tears.' "

Mary nodded.

Susan went on. "In the end, the whole story is Alice's dream."

"Is that what you think?" Mary said. "It isn't really, you know."

"Of course it is," Susan said. "That's what the last chapter is all about."

"Oh, yes, the last chapter is Alice talking about how it

was a dream," Mary said. "And she thinks it must have been either her dream or the Red King's dream. But you know it wasn't really either one."

Susan stared at her. "What are you talking about?"

"It's really a story told by Lewis Carroll," Mary said. "Alice is imaginary and so is the Red King. So you could say it was Lewis Carroll's dream . . ."

Susan nodded slowly. "I could go along with that."

". . . but Lewis Carroll was imaginary, too," Mary went on.

"No, he wasn't," Susan protested. "He was a mathematician and a deacon in the Church of England. He was reputed to like little girls a bit too well."

Mary shook her head. "That was the Reverend Charles Lutwidge Dodgson," she said gravely. "He wrote as Lewis Carroll, but that's not the same thing as being Lewis Carroll, now is it?"

Susan hesitated, thinking of Max Merriwell and Mary Maxwell and Weldon Merrimax. "I suppose not," she admitted reluctantly.

"I'd say it was all a dream of Dodgson who dreamed of Carroll who dreamed of Alice who dreamed of the Red King. Or it could have been the other way around. Maybe the Red King dreamed up the whole thing."

Susan's head was spinning. "But what's real?" she asked.

Mary laughed. "Have you ever read the work of Chuang Tzu?"

Susan shook her head. The only thing that seemed clear was that Mary was not going to clarify matters.

"Oh, you must. It will help you come to grips with all this. Chuang Tzu was an ancient Taoist poet and philosopher. He wrote about dreaming that he was a butterfly. And when he woke, he wondered if he was really a butterfly, dreaming he was a poet." Mary shrugged. "There's no way to know. And as far as I'm concerned, it doesn't matter." She gazed into the distance for a moment, as if concentrating on something only she could see. "Listen," she said.

Susan heard a strange sound on the breeze—like the

wind howling through a gap. "What's that?" she asked.

"Sounds like wolves to me."

"Wolves?" Susan shook her head again. "That's ridiculous. We're in the middle of the ocean."

"Just a small pack," Mary said, as if the size of the pack made a difference. A chorus of distant howls rose and fell with the breeze.

"How could there be wolves here?" Susan said, bewildered.

Mary shook her head, looking amused. "You haven't been listening. Reality is a much more flexible concept than most people think. The borders are fuzzy." Mary shrugged. "It's all about the power of the imagination. The shifting nature of reality. The possibilities of the dream. You need to trust your imagination. You need to believe your dreams."

"This isn't a dream," Susan protested. "I'm really here."

Mary just smiled. She was looking over Susan's shoulder. "Look who's coming this way."

Susan turned to look, and she saw Max Merriwell approaching, walking along the railing and smoking his pipe. When she turned back, Mary was gone.

Max came up beside her. "Susan?" She turned to look at him. "It *is* you!" He studied her for a moment. "Quite a change. "You look very nice." He puffed his pipe.

She glanced around, looking for Mary.

Max was studying her, frowning. "Is something wrong?"

Yes, Susan thought, I'm going nuts. I'm imagining conversations with lunatics. I'm hearing wolves.

"No," she said. "No, I'm fine." She didn't want to ask Max if he had seen a woman disappear. She didn't want to try to explain what they had been talking about. "I . . . I just stepped out for a breath of fresh air."

"We missed you at dinner," Max said. "It was quite dull without you and Pat and Ian."

"Pat and I decided to make do with bar snacks," she said. She realized as she said it that they had never gotten around to ordering any snacks. No wonder she was feeling so drunk.

"Ah. Well, I'm meeting Ian for a drink at Aphrodite's before I turn in. Will you join me?"

She shook her head. "No, thanks. I've had enough for now." More than enough, she thought. She stared out to sea, feeling dizzy.

"I'll go in then. Come and join us if you feel like it later."

She heard a burst of music when he pushed open the door, silenced when the door swung shut. She closed her eyes. She had drunk too many Rum Monkeys. Mary's last name was Maxwell. There were wolves howling in the middle of the ocean. That made no sense at all. Her imagination was running away with her.

Now that Max was gone, Susan could again hear wolves howling somewhere above her. A sweet wild sound, stretched thin by distance. It couldn't be wolves, Susan thought. There were no wolves in the middle of the ocean. But it sounded like wolves.

It could be the wind, she thought. That was the only logical explanation, the only sensible thing to think. Mary was some kind of lunatic and the howling was just the wind. Susan tried to believe that it was the wind, blowing across a narrow opening and howling in a way that sounded just like wolves.

She tried to believe that, but she didn't want to believe that. When it got right down to it, she wanted to believe that there were wolves up there. There are, she thought drunkenly, so many possibilities for a woman who knows how to use her imagination.

Susan imagined members of the pack exploring among the deck chairs on the recreation deck, lapping water from the sparkling pool, bedding down in a heap of towels, overlooked at day's end by the towel guy. Something strange was happening, and she did not want to believe that there was a sensible, reasonable explanation for it.

She followed the sound, heading toward the bow of the boat. She found a door marked "emergency exit" that led

to a companionway, and she climbed the stairs. She pushed
the door open and stepped onto the silent recreation deck.

The poolside chairs had been stacked neatly, their cushions stacked beside them. Nets covered the swimming pool
and the Jacuzzis—a safety precaution, she suspected. The
cruise line didn't want a drunken passenger falling into a
pool and drowning. The water in the swimming pools
surged back and forth with the rolling of the ship, over-
flowing the pool and washing across the deck.

She circled the pool, peering behind the stacks of deck
chairs, searching for wolves. There were lights beside the
pools, lights on the ship's railings. Beyond those circles of
light, the ocean was dark. When Susan looked over the rail,
the only light came from the moon and the cold, distant stars.
The ship had seemed so large in New York harbor. Now it
felt tiny, insignificant in the vastness of the ocean.

The dark ocean surged and swelled. So much darkness,
all around them. Unknown territory, she thought. Terra
incognita. She sympathized with the ancient mapmakers
who had drawn dragons in the unknown seas. There could
be dragons out there, lurking just beyond the limits of her
vision. There could be sea serpents below the waves hiding
in the darkness of the deeps.

When she was in the bar, in the dining room, in her
stateroom, she felt like she was in a resort hotel, as safe as
she was on dry land. But out here—where the wind tousled
her hair and the stars gazed down with chilly indifference—
out here, she could feel the power of the ocean.

It was terrifying—and at the same time, it was fascinating. So many possibilities. So much to explore. So much
unknown territory. That was what she loved in Max's
books, in Mary's books. The sense that something wonderful or terrible might be waiting just around the corner.
You could find a gold ring and talk with dragons. You
might walk through a gate in a garden and find yourself
caught up in a battle between the owls and the ravens. (A
woman did that in Mary's book, *The Owl Kingdom*.) You
might experiment with a Möbius strip and get caught in a

dream that circles around and around, never letting you go. A man did that in Max's book, *A One-Sided Story*. You might fly across the galaxy or live among the wolves. Anything could happen.

This was all Max's doing, she thought. Worlds that Max had created were bleeding through into the reality of the cruise ship. Max had opened a door and strange things were coming through.

Susan walked carefully beside the swimming pool with its sloshing water, a miniature imitation of the ocean around them. She was drunk and she knew it. She was very careful.

She heard the wolves again, howling in the distance. Above her, always above her. An exhilarating sound, the sound of mystery, the call of adventure.

She climbed the stairs that led from the recreation deck to the observation deck. When she was halfway up the stairs, the howling fell silent and she heard a rattling sound—like claws scratching against the deck surface. But when she reached Cyclops' Lookout, it was empty. She listened for the wolves, and heard nothing. Only the wind of the ship's passage as it traveled across the face of the deep.

FIFTEEN

> *"You're not looking for adventure?" The pirate laughed.*
> *"That's no guarantee of a comfortable life. Perhaps adven-*
> *ture is looking for you."*
>
> —from *The Twisted Band*
> by Max Merriwell

Tom stopped by the security office after dinner. On his desk, he found a note from Ian: "I'm meeting Pat and Susan in Aphrodite's Alehouse for a nightcap—want to join us?"

Tom was tired, but restless. Dinner had been tedious—Susan, Pat, and Ian had been absent, Max had been quiet. That left Charles Rafferty and Bill Carver, supported by their wives, to dominate the conversation. They discussed, at great length, the quality of the wine list on various cruise lines. Charles had worked up quite a head of steam over the selections of merlot available on the *Odyssey*—apparently his educated palette required more than four choices.

Tom decided that a nightcap might be just what he needed. He headed for the bar.

Aphrodite's was noisier than usual; the crowd seemed drunker than usual. Tom watched a waitress carry a tray filled with flaming drinks to a group of ladies at a table near the stage. Some new invention of the company, no doubt. Tom couldn't keep track of all the cocktails served aboard the *Odyssey*—silly things with umbrellas and strange names like Juno's Revenge and Cupid's Sting.

Tom spotted Ian, Pat, and Max deep in conversation at one end of the curving bar and went to join them. "Hello, Tom" Ian called as Tom approached. "Pull up a stool."

Tom looked around for Susan. Perhaps she had stepped into the ladies room. He pulled up a stool.

Max looked up from his brandy snifter. He had been quietly drinking brandy at dinner, as well.

He looked rumpled and sleepy, Tom thought. He was not wearing his usual tweed sports coat, having finally surrendered to the tropical heat. He wore a knit polo shirt from the ship's boutique and he did not look entirely comfortable in it.

"Max was just telling us about a dream he had last night," Ian said.

"Strangest thing," Max said. "I dreamed I was in the ship's library and I saw a novel titled *Adventures in Time and Space with Max Merriwell*. I took it from the shelf, but before I could open it, I woke up." He shook his head.

"Who was the author?" Pat asked.

Max shrugged. "I don't know. I didn't look."

Tom watched the waitress carry another tray of flaming drinks to the table by the dance floor. "What is that drink?" he asked Ian.

"A Flaming Rum Monkey," Ian said. "It's a drink your friend Susan suggested to Frank."

Tom took advantage of the opportunity. "Where is Susan, anyway?" he asked.

"Frank said she stepped outside with her friend Mary," Ian said. "Maybe half an hour ago."

"A Flaming Rum Monkey?" Max said. "I didn't think that drink really existed."

"She left with Mary?" Tom continued, not willing to stop for Max's interruption. "A woman with short dark hair?"

Ian nodded. "That's what Frank said."

"I saw Susan on the promenade on my way in," Max said. "She was alone then."

Tom nodded. "Thanks," he said. "I'll go look for her."

As he walked away, Tom heard Max say, "I've always wondered what a Flaming Rum Monkey tasted like. I made up the name a number of years ago. It's Mary Maxwell's favorite drink, you know."

———

Tom walked the promenade that led around the ship. The night air was pleasantly cool, and he passed a few couples, but he didn't see Susan or Mary. He was thinking about checking some of the ship's other bars, when he got a call on his radio from one of the security staff. A woman was on Cyclops' Lookout, the observation platform at the front of the ship. She'd been there for the past hour. Did Tom want to check on the situation?

He went.

The woman stood at one side of the observation platform, staring up at the sliver of a moon. The wind tousled her curly hair.

"Susan," he said, and she turned to look at him.

"Hi, Tom. What are you doing out here at this hour?"

"Just checking up on things. Where's your friend Mary?"

Susan shrugged. "Abducted by aliens," she said solemnly. She was drunk, Tom thought. He wondered how many Flaming Rum Monkeys she had consumed.

"Ian said you left the bar with her."

"I did. Then she disappeared. Abducted by aliens." She was gazing at the horizon. "I heard some wolves howling and I came looking for them."

"Wolves?" he said.

"They sounded like wolves," she said. "I suppose they could have been drunken Clampers. There are so many possibilities."

Tom leaned against the railing beside her. She wasn't making much sense, but she seemed relaxed and cheerful and a little drunk. "So what are you doing up here?"

"Watching a UFO." She pointed up at a blinking light crossing the constellation of Orion. "I figure it could be the aliens who abducted Mary." She smiled, clearly joking.

Tom watched the blinking light in silence for a moment. "I could ask the navigator if he knows what it is. He pays attention to satellites and such."

"You could do that. But if he doesn't know, he'll just explain it away. Swamp gas, he'll say." She watched the blinking light for a moment. "What do you think UFOs are?" she asked him.

Tom frowned at her. "What do you mean?"

"Some people think that they're swamp gas. Some people think that they are filled with little green men who are coming to rescue us. Some people think they are filled with little green men who are coming to destroy us. What do you think?"

"Remember the other night when Max said that people lie," Tom said. "I don't think they always know that they're lying. I think sometimes, people make things up and decide to believe in them."

Susan nodded, staring out to sea. "Sort of like a dream that everyone agrees to believe in," she said.

"Sort of."

She turned her head and studied his face. "Did you ever watch *The Twilight Zone* when you were a kid?"

The summer that Tom was ten years old, he had watched *The Twilight Zone* with his father every Thursday night. It had been reruns, all reruns, but his father had loved the show.

Tom's father had been a plumber, a big, hard-working man with callused hands. Tom had two older brothers, but they had spent their Thursday evenings with friends, with girls, in the parks, on the street corners. Tommy had spent his days with friends, but on Thursday evenings, after dinner, he would sit with his dad on the battered brown sofa. He remembered it well.

He could hear his mother in the kitchen, washing the dinner dishes. His dad held a can of beer in one big hand, a cigarette in the other. Tommy could have had a glass of lemonade if he had gone into the kitchen to get it. But his mother would have put him to work—drying dishes, running an errand, something, anything. His mother thought TV was a waste of time. So Tommy stayed with his dad, laying low and hoping to escape her notice.

"Oh, this one's a good one, Tommy," he remembered his father saying. Every episode was a good one, according to

Dad. Thinking about it now, Tom wondered about why his father—a practical man who worked hard for living—had had such an affection for the show. "The strangest things can happen, Tommy," his father had said. "Anything is possible."

Tom watched the blinking light that Susan said was a UFO. His father might have agreed with her. "Yeah," Tom said. "I used to watch *The Twilight Zone* with my dad. He loved that show."

"Do you remember the part at the beginning," Susan said.

Tom smiled and mimicked the music of the theme song.

"Yeah, there was that," Susan said. "Then Rod Serling would say, 'You unlock this door with the key of imagination. Beyond it is another dimension.' You remember that part?"

Tom nodded. "Sure. This door would come looming out of the darkness."

"That part always made me shiver," she said.

Tom remembered how the eerie music and the looming door had affected him. "That was a scary door. Not quite as scary as *The Outer Limits*, where they took control of your television set, but it was still scary. I can see why you would shiver."

"It wasn't just that it was scary." Yes, Susan was definitely drunk, Tom thought. She was speaking with exaggerated care. She had the thoughtful air of someone who had drunk enough to make commonplace occurrences seem very profound. "That door made me think that anything was possible. I could step through the door and escape into somewhere strange and different. All I needed was my imagination."

Escape, he thought. Maybe that was part of the attraction for his dad. Escape from work, from his nagging wife, from the day-to-day chores.

"My mother didn't like me to watch the show," Susan was saying. "She said I already had too much imagination. She said I didn't need to watch that weird stuff."

"But you watched it anyway?" When Tom was a kid, he had defied his mother at every turn.

She nodded. "Every chance I got."

She fell silent, gazing out to sea. He watched her face. The wind caught her short hair, mussing it, but she did not reach up to try to push it back into place. He liked her new haircut. He liked this slightly drunk, much more relaxed Susan. He felt like reaching up and playing with her curls, but he fought the urge.

"Submitted for your approval," Tom said, mimicking Rod Serling's measured tones. "A cruise ship, passing through the Bermuda Triangle. The vacationing passengers are looking for sunshine and relaxation. They don't know that this vacation will take them into . . ." He paused dramatically. ". . . the Twilight Zone."

"That's all right," Susan said very seriously. "Some of us don't mind a visit to the Twilight Zone. What do you think will happen?"

He shrugged. "Hard to say. But as long as all the meals are served on time, most passengers won't even notice."

She glanced at his face. "You'd notice, though. You and Max. You're both always paying attention. Keeping an eye on everything and trying to make sense of it all."

"It's my job."

"Even if it weren't your job, you'd be paying attention," she said. She stared at the waves. "Ian told me that Mary signed into the beauty salon as Mary Maxwell. I know the guy you're looking for is Weldon Merrimax. What do you think is going on?"

He shrugged. "A couple of Max's fans are having some fun," he said.

"Do you really think so?"

He shrugged. "Best explanation I can come up with."

"There are other explanations," she said. "Suppose, just suppose, that those people really are Max's pen names. Somehow they are . . ." She hesitated, then went on. "Somehow they are leaking through from some other dimension. Like on an episode of *The Twilight Zone*. What are you going to do about it?"

Tom kept smiling, willing to go along with the joke. She was so very sweet and so very drunk. "Well, I don't see that I have to do anything, really. I can't confirm that any crimes have been committed. Oh, there was one drink that didn't get paid for, but that's minor. Max is getting strange fan mail slipped under his door, but he told me that writers have to get used to that sort of thing."

"Didn't Weldon Merrimax cheat someone at poker?"

Tom raised his eyebrows. Ian had been talking. "Nothing illegal about gambling on board," he said. "We're in international waters. It's against Company Policy, but all I can do is advise passengers of that."

"Didn't he stab Patrick Murphy?"

"As far as I can tell, no Patrick Murphy was ever on board. The man who reported that incident now says it never happened. So it's tough to make much headway."

She nodded. "Maybe it was just a dream," she murmured. Tom studied her face. She was smiling, but her eyes were drooping, like the eyes of a tired child who didn't want to go to bed just yet. "I'll think about it more in the morning," she said, stifling a yawn. "It's past my bedtime."

"Can you find your stateroom?" he asked.

"I'll just wander around until I find it."

"I'll escort you there," he said. "No telling where you'll end up if you get lost in the Twilight Zone."

"No telling," she agreed.

At her stateroom door, he said, "I'll check on your UFO."

"Okay," she said. "See if you can find out what galaxy it's from."

She closed the door behind her.

It was past Tom's bedtime as well, but he still felt restless. He headed up to the bridge, figuring he'd see if anyone on duty knew what Susan's UFO was.

The bridge was the highest point on the ship. A broad bank of windows offered a view of the observation deck below, the sun deck below that, and the dark ocean waters beyond them both. A light over the main control console spotlighted Michael, the officer on duty. Lights from instrument panels glowed brightly in the darkness. As always, a quartermaster kept watch through the windows. Lounging on a chair beside the quartermaster was Geoffrey, the ship's navigator, a lanky Brit. All three men grinned when they saw Tom.

"Hello, Tom," Geoffrey said. "You all done on the observation deck? I was planning to do my monthly sextant check and I didn't want to interrupt anything."

"Nothing to interrupt," Tom said easily. "Just having a pleasant chat."

"About the moon and the stars," Michael said. "I know where those pleasant chats lead."

A little romance between passengers and crew was not unusual. Some officers made a habit of it, keeping an eye out for single women who might be open to a vacation fling. Tom had never taken advantage of such opportunities. He'd been involved with other crew members—with an Irish woman who worked in one of the bars, with a back-up singer in one of the shows. Nothing serious; nothing that lasted beyond a few cruises. But he had avoided any involvement with passengers.

Tom shook his head. "We were talking about an unidentified flying object crossing our bow. Maybe a satellite."

"Where?" Geoffrey asked.

Tom stepped to the window beside the navigator. He scanned the sky, locating where the light had been and checking the area where he expected it to be. The blinking light had vanished. "No sign of it," he said.

Geoffrey shrugged. "Must have been your imagination."

Susan lay in bed, her thoughts swirling cheerfully, drunkenly. It had been such a confusing evening. She kept think-

ing about Mary Maxwell. She was just as Max had
described her.

As Susan drifted to sleep, she thought about Max's pseudonyms. It made sense that they would show up. Max had
named them, Max had believed in them. So here they were.
Just as naming the Flaming Rum Monkey had caused it to
come into being.

It made sense. Not that hard-edged logical sense that
Harry had always favored, but a fuzzy, intuitive sort of
sense. The sort of thing that Harry would say made no
sense at all. It made sense to her, and that was enough.

She fell asleep, soothed by Rum Monkeys, lulled by the
gentle rocking of the ship. She dreamed that she stood on
the recreation deck, surrounded by wolves.

The animals were all around her, but they weren't paying
any attention to her. They were exploring the area, sniffing
the stacked deck chairs. One of them found a towel and
picked it up; another grabbed the free end, beginning a tug
of war that involved several animals.

A big black male pawed at one of the ropes that held a
net over the swimming pool. When she stepped toward him,
he looked at her expectantly, wagging his tail.

"You want to go swimming?" she asked the wolf. She
always talked to dogs. The wolf kept wagging his tail.

She circled the pool, untying ropes. At the last rope, she
hauled the net out of the pool and piled it on the deck. The
first wolf was already in the water. Another joined him as
she watched.

She sat on the deck by the pool, dangling her legs in the
water and looking up at the stars. The UFO was there, a
blinking golden light. She wondered whether there was a
pattern to its blinking. Was it trying to tell herself something?

In her dream, she heard a sound—someone opening the
door that led out onto the recreation deck. The wolves had
already found the stairs at one end of the pool and gotten
out. As she watched, they blended into the shadows. She
wondered if she should go with them.

Pat opened the door to the stateroom quietly—but even so, she disturbed Susan. Susan did not wake, but she turned over in her sleep, leaving the dream behind. The wolves fled into the shadows. The recreation deck was empty.

BAD GRRLZ' GUIDE TO PHYSICS

BAD GRRL CONSIDERS MAX MERRIWELL

Things are a little strange aboard the *Odyssey*. And the strangeness seems to center on our friend Max Merriwell, the man with too many names.

Earlier tonight, Frank Robinson, the bartender at Aphrodite's Alehouse, made the world's first Flaming Rum Monkey—a lovely, tasty, and dangerous drink. Frank invented this drink because a woman named Mary—the same Mary that Susan met in Hamilton—requested one. Mary told Susan this was a drink that didn't exist. Mary had come up with the name and had decided to look for a bartender who could make one.

All well and good.

Then Max ambled into Aphrodite's and asked what that flaming drink was. He seemed startled and pleased to learn that it was a Flaming Rum Monkey. "That's Mary Maxwell's favorite drink," he said.

Strange. A woman named Mary asks for a drink that Max invented for a pseudonym named Mary. A product of the imagination takes on reality. The only question is: whose imagination was it? Max's or Mary's?

Then there is the matter of the Clampers and the elephant. Susan mentioned that *Wild Angel* describes a jailbreak involving a group of Clampers and an elephant. Tonight, the Clampers on board the *Odyssey* were celebrating some event from the Gold Rush involving a jail break with an elephant.

They weren't at all clear on the details. I asked three of them and got three different versions of the story—all including an elephant, a jail, an orphan, and a lot of drinking, but differing in other respects.

Max told us that he made up the story about the elephant and the Clampers. And when he found out that the Clamp-

ers told a similar story as historical fact, he smiled and had
another Flaming Rum Monkey.

Susan disappeared with her friend Mary; Tom went off
in search of Susan; Ian and I stayed in the bar with Max,
drinking Rum Monkeys and talking about coincidences and
dreams. After Max went to bed, Ian and I stayed up, drinking Rum Monkeys and talking about the intriguing Mr.
Merriwell.

As I jokingly told Ian earlier, Max lives in a vortex of
potentialities. He spins around and flings out possible realities, inhabited by Mary Maxwell or Weldon Merrimax,
populated by wolves and flying saucers. From what he told
Ian, he's been living alone in a Greenwich Village apartment for the past couple of decades. Plenty of time to generate possibilities.

And now these possibilities are manifesting themselves.
Why? After a few Rum Monkeys, Ian was claiming that
all the strange events could be blamed on the Bermuda
Triangle. I had had a few Rum Monkeys too. Under the
influence, I proposed a more scientific explanation: Max is
a man who is in touch with many potentialities. He ordinarily exists in a stable state, but something has destabilized
the system.

I wonder if that destabilization has something to do with
my friend Susan. I have always thought that Susan had
more than her share of unrealized potentialities.

All properties of quantum entities or systems are emergent properties—things that are about to happen. That's
Susan in a nutshell. She's loaded with emergent properties.

One other thing: when two quantum systems meet, their
potentialities overlap to make a new, combined system that
has different properties than either of the original systems.
The whole is greater than the sum of the parts.

Could it be that the quantum aspects of Max's life have
met the quantum potentials of Susan's and stirred up something entirely new? Could it be that I've had too many Rum
Monkeys? Doesn't matter. It's bedtime. Here, for future

reference, is the recipe for a Flaming Rum Monkey, cour-
tesy of Frank Robinson, Mary Maxwell, and yours truly.

FLAMING RUM MONKEY

Put a teaspoon of brown sugar, a sprinkling
of cloves, nutmeg, and cinnamon, and a teaspoon of coconut syrup (the kind used in piña
coladas) in a warm mug. Add a little boiling
water—just enough to dissolve the sugar. Let
the mixture steep for a minute. Pour in two
ounces of dark Jamaican rum and one ounce
of dark creme de cacao. Fill the mug with boiling water and stir.

Now for the flames! Put a pinch of brown
sugar in a big spoon. Fill the spoon with 151
rum. To warm the rum, hold the spoon over
the mug filled with the hot mixture.

Light the rum in the spoon. Tip the spoon
into the mug. The mixture in the mug will burn
with a lovely blue flame.

Don't singe your eyebrows. Don't burn your
tongue. Blow out the flames and try a sip of
your Rum Monkey. Hot, sweet, and touched
with coconut. Enjoy your Rum Monkey and
dream of possibilities.

SIXTEEN

I thought I was safe," Ferris said. "I didn't realize . . ."
"You find monsters where you least expect them," Gyro said.
"That's just the way it works."

　　　　　　　　　—from *The Twisted Band*
　　　　　　　　　by Max Merriwell

Tom woke up sneezing the next morning. He skipped his morning rounds and headed straight for his office. When he arrived, he was sniffling and wondering whether he could go back to bed. No such luck. He already had a dozen messages from the purser's office. Passengers with cabins on the recreation deck had been complaining of strange sounds in the night. "Drunks outside my window howling like a pack of wolves," one said. "Some idiots howling," said another.

Wolves, Tom thought, remembering Susan's drunken ramblings of the night before. A pack of Clampers, most likely.

Tom checked the security log. The guard patrolling the recreation deck had found the net off the main pool, something that happened every now and again when some drunken passengers decided to go for a midnight swim. The guard had put the net back in place, checked the deck for any passengers, and found no one.

Tom went to the recreation deck. The sky was overcast; the sun was a hazy patch of light beyond the gray. It was unlikely that the passengers would be rushing to the pool, but Ernesto, one of the deck stewards, had just finished putting out all the deck chairs. When Tom hailed him, he was placing a fluffy white towel on each deck chair, preparing for an eager throng of passengers. Ordinarily, Er-

nesto was a cheerful fellow, but that morning he was not
smiling.

"Good morning, Ernesto," Tom greeted him.

"Not a good morning," Ernesto said, shaking his head.
"Not good at all."

"What's the trouble?" Tom said, expecting to hear that
passengers had been partying on the recreation deck the
night before and had left a mess. It happened—drunken
passengers, broken bottles, dirty glasses.

"Animals!" Ernesto said, scowling. "I don't know what
they were doing last night."

Tom nodded sympathetically. "They left a mess, did
they?"

More than a mess, apparently. It took a while for Ernesto
to describe all the things that had been done. The pool was
full of hair—Ernesto showed him the pool filter. It was
clogged with short white, gray, and black hairs. Ernesto
showed him a towel that had been torn in several places.

Ernesto told him that someone had peed on the deck.
"Not just in one place," he said in an outraged tone. "But
there and there and there." He waved his hands to indicate
several spots around the pool. The deck was wet where
Ernesto had hosed it off. "There is a restroom just inside
the door over there," Ernesto said, waving his hand. "Just
a few feet away. And that is not the worst of it." Ernesto
beckoned Tom to a nearby trash bag, opened the top, and
gestured for Tom to look inside. In the white trash bag was
a pile of what was unmistakably shit. Dog shit, by the look
of it, from a very large dog. "Who would do such a thing?"
Ernesto asked. "Animals!"

Tom had no answers for Ernesto. He told the irate deck
steward that he would arrange for extra security staff on
the recreation deck. He called the purser's office and told
them the same thing.

Drunks, he figured. A drunken party that broke up just
before the security guard came through. A drunken party
of older men who were shedding their gray and white hair.

A drunken party of men who liked to tear up towels and had no compunction about where they peed.

Of course, that didn't explain the dog shit. Tom shook his head and blew his nose. The head cold was making him feel slow and stupid. There had to be a reasonable explanation. Once or twice, a crew member had smuggled a pet on board: a kitten once, a toy poodle another time. But the turd in the trash bag hadn't come from a toy poodle. That had come from a sizable animal, too big to be easily smuggled aboard.

Sure, it looked like a pack of wolves had been swimming in the pool and marking their territory on the deck, but that made no sense at all. There had to be an explanation, but he couldn't come up with it just now.

That morning, he met with security staff and told them about the problems on the recreation deck. He told them about the dog shit by the pool and advised them to keep an eye out for dogs. He increased the patrols on the recreation deck.

Not much else he could do.

Susan's eyes felt gritty. She had woken that morning with a dull pain in her head, the aftermath of too many Flaming Rum Monkeys. Ibuprofen had reduced the headache to a distant sort of throbbing—still there, but far far away.

She didn't feel quite herself. The rumble of the ship's engines was a steady trembling in her bones; it set her nerves on edge. She felt the movement of the ship as it rose and fell on every swell, a subtle shifting that left her disoriented and uneasy. She wasn't hungry—her stomach was unsettled.

She and Pat had skipped breakfast, stopping by Apollo's Court just long enough to pick up some coffee. They hurried to the library for Max's workshop and walked in a few minutes late. Max was already lecturing.

"Fiction is about people. As a writer, you use words to create people that live in your reader's mind. When people read your story, they should believe in the characters you created. They should feel that they know these people."

"How do you create people that the reader can believe in? You describe these people; you show how they react to events around them; you show them interacting with other people. These are all ways to make your characters real in the minds of your readers."

Susan sipped her coffee, wishing she had a firmer grip on her own reality that morning. Her memories of the previous night were somewhat blurry. She vaguely remembered talking with Mary. She vaguely remembered hearing wolves; she vaguely remembered talking with Tom about *The Twilight Zone*. The one thing she remembered quite clearly was drinking Rum Monkeys.

She blinked, aware she had lost track of what Max was saying. He was giving them a writing exercise.

"I want you to think back to the last time you witnessed an argument," Max said. "It doesn't have to be anything major—just two people disagreeing about something." He paused, giving people a moment to think.

Susan remembered seeing Mary talking to Weldon in Penelope's, gesturing angrily. That had been an argument, she thought.

"Now think about why the people were arguing," Max said.

Susan frowned. She didn't really know why Mary and Weldon were arguing. She didn't know what Mary and Weldon were doing on board. There was so much she didn't know.

She raised her hand timidly. "I don't know what the people were arguing about," she said. "I saw them arguing, but I didn't overhear what they were saying."

"That's perfect!" Max said. "That gives you more room to play with. You can make up the rest."

Susan nodded, doubtful but willing to try.

"As a writer, you need to think about why people do the things they do," Max went on. "That understanding is important to creating convincing characters." He leaned back in his chair, studying the group. "A cop once told me that there are really only three criminal motives: money, sex, and power. I would add a couple of other motives. Love— though if you're feeling cynical, you can put that down as a subset of sex. Desire for fame—though some would say that's a subset of power. Curiosity—that's an important one in science fiction."

He looked around at the class. "Now think about what motivated the people in your argument. The people may have very different motives, so it helps to consider each person separately. Take a moment, write the name of one person, and then write a little bit about his or her motives."

Susan wrote "Weldon Merrimax" at the top of the page, then stared at the name for a moment. She remembered her own encounter with Weldon in the bar. He had seemed happy when he accused her of being a liar. Righteously angry and happy to be making her uncomfortable. "I used to tell fortunes for a living," he had said.

She thought about what she knew of fortune-tellers. They preyed on people who were lonely and confused, weak and easily manipulated. She remembered what Max had told her about Weldon. Yes, she thought, he liked to manipulate people; he liked to feel superior. Under Weldon's name, she wrote, "Weldon is motivated by power. He was trying to put Mary in her place."

"Now consider the other person," Max said. "Write down their name and their motive."

"Mary Maxwell," Susan wrote. Then she thought about what she knew of Mary. She loved adventure. She was curious about the world. But those didn't seem like reasons she'd be arguing with Weldon. Susan thought about what she had told Mary about Weldon. She had told Mary that the security staff was looking for him because he might have stabbed Patrick Murphy. Patrick Murphy, Susan remembered, was a character in Mary's novel.

Susan frowned. Mary was angry because Weldon had attacked Patrick Murphy. Under Mary's name, she wrote,

"Mary wants to protect her characters from Weldon. She is angry that he attacked Patrick Murphy."

"Now that you have some idea of the character's motivations," Max said, "I'd like you to write a dialog between these characters. Just their words—you can fill in the rest later. In this dialog, the characters won't say anything about what motivates them, but the reader should be able to figure out the power dynamic from the dialog. Give it a try."

Susan looked at the page, then wrote. " 'You had no right to kill Patrick,' Mary said. 'No right at all.' "

SEVENTEEN

*You can't expect an adventure to be tidy," Gitana said. "If
you could get home in time for supper, it wouldn't be much
of an adventure, would it?"*

—from *The Twisted Band*
by Max Merriwell

After workshop, Pat and Susan went to the recreation deck.
They sat in deck chairs beside the great oval swimming
pool with its impossibly blue tile.

Susan felt detached, still absorbed by her account of the
argument between Mary and Weldon. The deck of the
cruise ship seemed unreal. The chrome railings sparkled in
the sunshine. Children splashed in the water. People at the
bar were laughing and talking. It was all terribly cheerful
and wholesome.

They ordered lunch. "You look a little under the
weather," Pat commented. "Those Rum Monkeys are lethal.
Oh, hey—you know what? Max claimed that he made up
the name 'Flaming Rum Monkey.' He said it's Mary Maxwell's favorite drink."

"Of course," Susan said, nodding wearily. "It's all too
weird." After a moment's hesitation, Susan said, "I probably shouldn't tell you this. You'll think I'm nuts."

"That's all right," Pat said. "I already think you're nuts.
And my dissertation advisor thinks I'm nuts. So go ahead."

Susan described her conversation with Mary. She told
Pat she had heard wolves howling and had followed the
sound to the observation deck. Tom had found her there.

Susan leaned back in her lounge chair, trying to remember all the details of her conversation with Tom. "I asked
him about Weldon Merrimax and Mary Maxwell."

"What did he say?"

"He said a couple of Max's fans were playing a joke. I suggested that maybe those people were leaking through from another dimension." Susan blushed, remembering that. "He was very polite about it."

"He didn't immediately say you were nuts? He must be in love."

Susan felt her face grow hotter still.

"Ah," Pat said, studying her face. "So you didn't just chat, out there on the observation deck under the stars."

"We did just talk," Susan said. "I pointed out a UFO and we watched that. But other than that, we just talked. He's a very nice guy."

"I see," Pat said. "And I suspect he thinks you're very nice, too, or he wouldn't have been hanging out with you while you talked nonsense about Weldon Merrimax and Mary Maxwell."

"He didn't say it was nonsense," Susan protested. "He just said he didn't think any crimes had been committed. Do you think it's nonsense?"

"No, but I study quantum mechanics, so you can't go by what I think."

"So what should we do?" Susan asked.

The poolside waitress approached, carrying a tray filled with drinks and food.

"I'm like Tom there—I don't see that we need to do anything. So I think we should eat lunch," Pat said. She grinned as the waitress set her plate on the low table between their lounge chairs. "Don't want to let these tentacles get cold." Pat had ordered the fried calamari.

Susan made a face. "I don't see how you can eat those things."

"They're very tasty," Pat said. "I've always been intrigued by squid. When Max asked us to write about monsters, I wrote about a giant squid. I was terrified of them when I was a kid. When I was in third grade, I read an illustrated children's book on sea creatures and there was this drawing of a sperm whale battling a giant squid. The

whale had one tentacle in its jaws; the squid had wrapped
the others around the whale's head. I can still remember
the giant squid's eye, about the size of a dinner plate, gazing balefully from the page. I always figured the squid won
that battle. The whale was bigger, but the squid looked so
mean. For years I was afraid to go swimming in the ocean.
I figured a giant squid would grab me and pull me under."
Pat speared a fried tentacle with her fork, lifted it and
smiled. "I order calamari by way of revenge."

As they were finishing lunch, Pat told Susan about her
plans for the afternoon. "I'm going to go play Bingo," she
said with enthusiasm. She pulled out a copy of the *Ship's
Log* and pointed to the notice about the afternoon Bingo
game in the Singing Sirens Theater. "Want to come?"

"No thanks."

Pat possessed an infinite capacity for enjoying odd pas-
times. In the past, Susan had accused her of choosing to
participate in impossibly boring activities for the exclusive
purpose of making fun of them later. Pat had not denied
the charge. She had merely defended herself by saying that
she was fascinated—in an anthropological sort of way—by
human behavior.

"What are you going to do, then?" Pat asked.

"Maybe just sit here and read Max's book," Susan said.
She had brought along a copy of *There and Back Again*
and she was looking forward to reading it.

Pat shook her head sadly. She gestured at the *Ship's Log*.
"How can you resist all these opportunities to be entertained?"

Susan shrugged, smiling. She had scanned the *Ship's Log*
the day before. The activities it offered seemed to fall into
four categories: self-improvement (aerobics classes), sales
opportunities (wine tasting in the Ithaca Dining Room), at-
tempts to match up singles (learning the "cha-cha" from
Lisa), and manufactured social activities (bingo, Ping-Pong
tournament, Scrabble in the games room). A few activities
fell into more than one category—the skin care seminar

promised self-improvement and also, she was sure, would include a sales pitch.

"Will power, I guess," she said. Pat left Susan to her book.

The hero of *There and Back Again* was Bailey Beldon. Bailey was a norbit—that being the name adopted by those who lived in the Asteroid Belt. A happy, home-loving bachelor, Bailey lived in a comfortable, cozy, hollowed-out asteroid. One day, he found a message pod that had lost its way. A mysterious adventurer named Gitana and a group of sibs from the Farr clone, the galaxy's largest, richest, and most famous clone family, came to claim the message pod. The message pod held an invaluable commodity—a partial map of the wormholes that were used in interstellar travel.

That's where Bailey's adventure began. The norbit was swept up on a quest that carried him far from his comfortable home, in search of the rest of the map.

It was a wonderful yarn. Bailey had survived several adventures and had just reached the temporary safety of Farr Station, home of the group of clones, when Susan realized that she was cold. The sun had vanished beneath a solid gray blanket of clouds; a cool wind was blowing. The children had abandoned the pool and the bar was almost deserted.

Susan closed her book and headed for the library. During workshop, she had noticed a number of comfortable-looking easy chairs, and she thought she would curl up in one of them.

A hand-lettered sign on the library door read: "Three o'clock: Children's Story Hour." Susan read the sign and smiled. When she had worked in the library, story hour had been one of her favorite times. She had loved to read aloud and had loved listening to other librarians read to the kids. There was something so soothing about listening to a familiar story read aloud. Susan stepped inside, anticipating a treat.

The library was in considerable disarray. Jody was there,

along with half a dozen other youngsters, ranging in age
from four to seven. The kids were playing some kind of
game that seemed to involve taking all the cushions off the
upholstered chairs and building a fort. Two little girls were
having a tug of war over one cushion and bickering loudly.
A little boy in a red T-shirt and overalls was bouncing on
a chair from which the cushions had been removed. They
were all, Susan thought, at that cranky, nasty, sleepy stage
that so many kids reach when they haven't had a nap.

Cindy, the member of the cruise staff who had introduced Max, was standing to one side, looking desperate.

During Max's talks, Cindy usually sat in the back and
looked bored. Susan thought she was rather rude. Cindy
never did any of the writing exercises that Max proposed;
she just stared out the window.

Now, she looked like she was on the ragged edge of
panic. She held a book in one hand and she waved the other
hand ineffectually at the kids. "Let's all sit down, shall
we?" she said. "I'll read you a nice little story."

"We don't want to hear a nice story," Jody said, speaking
loudly to be heard over the bickering girls. "I'm building
a house for little monsters."

Cindy looked like she might either burst into tears or
start screaming about little monsters. Susan decided she
should intervene before Cindy lost it. She strolled up to
Cindy.

"What are you going to read?" she asked, taking the book
from the young woman's hand. It was *There and Back
Again,* by Max Merriwell.

"Max said it would be good to read to kids," Cindy said.

"This isn't a kid's book," Susan said, frowning. She
thought about what she'd read so far. Parts might be a little
over the kids' heads, but nothing was really objectionable.
She looked up from the book and noticed that Jody was
listening. "In fact," Susan continued, "I don't know if you
should read this book to these kids."

Cindy looked startled. "What do you mean? I
thought . . ."

Susan interrupted before Cindy could say that she thought it was a nice book. "It's by that guy who knows so much about monsters," Susan said. "Jody's met him. It might be too scary for these little kids."

Jody had looked up from the fort she was building. "Are there monsters in it?" she asked Susan.

Susan nodded slowly. "Yeah, there are. And lots of other stuff that would be too much for such little kids." The girls had stopped fighting over the cushion to listen. "A book like this could give these kids nightmares," Susan said to Cindy.

"It's not too much for me," Jody said stoutly.

Susan gave her a considering look. "I don't know," she said. "Maybe you could handle it. But these little kids . . ." She waved a hand at the others.

"I'm not little," shouted the boy in overalls. He had stopped bouncing on the chair. "I'm four."

"I'm four and a half," proclaimed one of the little girls. Suddenly everyone was shouting his or her age and insisting on the right to hear this scary story.

Susan allowed them to persuade her. "Well, I suppose I could read some of it," she said.

"Yeah!" said the little boy. "Read the part about monsters."

"I'll sit here and read." Susan replaced a cushion on a chair and sat down. "Do you guys want to sit on the floor or on the chairs?" The question established that they would all sit, but gave them a choice about where they sat. "Everybody find a seat and then I can start reading."

Cindy—looking startled and grateful—helped the kids get settled. Jody curled up in a chair; the two little girls made a nest of cushions on the floor; the boy in overalls sat cross-legged on a cushion, like a meditating monk.

Susan read the first few chapters, describing Bailey's adventures. It was a fine book to read aloud. She particularly liked the section where Bailey and his friends were almost captured by the Trancers, a space-going cult that trapped interstellar travelers with music, playing irresistible tunes that made people dance 'til they dropped.

Bailey helped the Farrs escape and make their way to Farr Station. At that point, Susan looked up from the book and glanced at her watch. "I think that's all we have time for today," she said.

The smaller of the formerly bickering girls looked up from her nest of cushions. She had, Susan thought, been napping for the past hour. "I want to hear more about Bailey," she murmured sleepily.

"I'm still waiting for the monsters," Jody said.

"That's it for today," Cindy said, looking toward the door where another member of the cruise staff had appeared. "Here's Trudy to take you back to the Kid Zone for snacks." And all the kids trooped off with Trudy, into the foggy afternoon.

"Thanks so much for helping," Cindy said. "They were going to trash the place and eat me alive when you came along."

Susan smiled at her. "It was fun," she said. "When I ran story hour at the public library, I learned that there's an art to rounding up kids and getting them to settle down. The first rule is: Never tell them you are going to read a nice story. They don't want to hear a nice story. Tell them you're going to read something totally unsuitable for children. That's what they want to hear."

"I thought you were serious when you were telling me it wasn't a kids' book," Cindy said.

Susan shrugged. "It isn't. They won't get parts of it. But that's okay. I'll read ahead and make sure there aren't any sex scenes coming up."

Cindy nodded, looking relieved. "I don't usually run story hour. Usually, the librarian does that. But she quit when we were in New York, and we're shorthanded. I'm doing it so Trudy can get an afternoon break." She picked up *There and Back Again* from the table where Susan had set it down. "I guess I'll start tomorrow from where you left off."

"You'll need to remind them a bit about what has happened so far," Susan said. "Summarize the story, touching on the high points."

Cindy nodded, but Susan thought she looked a little nervous.

"If you like, I could stop by again and make sure you get off on the right foot," Susan said.

"That would be wonderful," Cindy said. "I could sure use your help." She frowned. "But you're a passenger and I really shouldn't let you . . ."

"I want to," Susan said. It was true. She did want to. She wanted to keep reading about Bailey. Though she could read the rest of the book to herself, it would be much more fun to read it to the kids.

Cindy nodded, returning Susan's smile. "If you want to, I can't stop you."

Susan headed for the door, leaving Cindy straightening up the library. In an easy chair right next to the door, she saw an elderly woman, sitting in the shadows. As Susan approached, the woman stood up.

"Such an interesting story," she said.

"I'm glad you liked it," Susan said, smiling.

The woman in the shadows was very old. Her hair appeared to be naturally gray, a contrast to the bleached blue-white hairdos that seemed to be favored by many of the older women on the *Odyssey*. She wore no makeup and when she smiled at Susan, her face creased into a labyrinth of laugh lines and wrinkles. She wore a loose silk tunic over baggy silk trousers. On the front of the tunic was a spiral, painted in gold.

The tunic and pants could be a sort of cruise wear, Susan supposed. Gold paint seemed to be popular on cruise wear. But the old woman's outfit looked far more comfortable than any of the cruise wear in the *Odyssey's* boutiques. The golden spiral had been beautifully painted with a single stroke of a brush.

Susan thought the spiral on the woman's tunic was a lovely coincidence. The pataphysicians, a fascinating group of philosophers featured in *There and Back Again,* used the spiral as their symbol.

"I thought the story you were reading did an admirable job of describing 'Pataphysics," the woman said. "The College of 'Pataphysics is so frequently misunderstood."

Susan was startled. "Wait," Susan said. "I thought 'Pataphysics was something Max made up."

"Max?" the woman asked.

"Max Merriwell, the author of the book I was reading."

"I'm afraid I don't know the man. But 'Pataphysics has been around for years and years. And Max did a lovely job of talking about it. So few people understand our philosophy."

"I see," Susan said, a little confused.

"So many people think it's a kind of joke." The old woman shook her head. "But that's not it at all. In fact, only a pataphysician is capable of complete seriousness. Pataphysicians take everything seriously. Absolutely everything. According to the Pataphysical Principle of Universal Equivalence, everything is just as serious as everything else. A battle to the death, a game of Scrabble, a love affair—all are equally serious."

Susan nodded. A character in *There and Back Again* had said something similar. "People confuse playing with not being serious," Susan said slowly, quoting from *There and Back Again.* "But pataphysicians are very serious about their play."

"Exactly," said the old woman, beaming at Susan. "We are playing the infinite game—where one plays simply in order to continue to play."

"That sounds like the way my friend Pat Murphy thinks about life," Susan said.

The old woman's smile grew even broader. "Your friend is named Pat Murphy. How lovely. That's my name, too. And she's quite right. Everyone is playing the infinite game. The pataphysical privilege is being aware of the infinite game that we are all playing. Perhaps your friend is a pataphysician."

Susan shrugged. "She's a physicist," Susan said. "She studies quantum mechanics."

"That's just a short step from 'Pataphysics," Ms. Murphy said. " 'Pataphysics is the science of imaginary solutions. Members of the college have noted that every event arises from an infinite number of causes. When scientists attribute cause and effect to a situation, they are basing that attribution on an arbitrary choice. That is where the imagination comes in. Scientists exercise their imaginations to choose a solution that fits the facts as they see them, valiantly trying to pin down one point of view as 'real.' " Ms. Murphy shrugged. "We feel that attempt is both heroic and misguided. In the College of 'Pataphysics, we welcome all scientific theories. They are all quite lovely and equally valid. We take all theories equally seriously."

"Well, I don't know if Pat would go along with that," Susan said.

The old woman smiled. "As a physicist, she has accepted that light is sometimes a particle and sometimes a wave. She can accept that an electron investigates many possible realities. It's not so far from that to understanding that the idea of truth is the most imaginary of all solutions."

Susan laughed. "You sound like you understand a bit about quantum mechanics," she said.

"Yes—it's an area of study that members of the College find quite interesting. Quantum mechanics, philosophy, and the overlapping areas between them."

"I haven't read much philosophy," Susan admitted.

"You really must," Ms. Murphy said. "It can be wonderfully enlightening, in a ponderous sort of way. Take, for example, the nineteenth century philosopher Hans Vaihinger, who extrapolated from Kant's epistemology the notion that all of our concepts—including those involved in both science and morality—are nothing more than useful fictions. I'm quite fond of that one."

Susan smiled politely, not wanting to be drawn into a

discussion of German philosophers. "It's been a pleasure meeting you," she told Ms. Murphy. "I'll suggest to Pat that she investigate the possibilities of 'Pataphysics."

"I think that would be a fine idea," the old woman said.

EIGHTEEN

*"Every now and then, I find it very useful to get lost," Gyro
said. "I find out the most interesting things that way."*
— from *The Twisted Band*
by Max Merriwell

At the entry to the dining room, Susan and Pat stopped to
admire the latest fruit sculpture.

"It's an edible Solar System," Pat said.

The sun was a cluster of candles, burning brightly in the
center of the bed of ice. The planets were suspended on
wires in a line that extended from the sun to the center of
the dining room. Mercury was a hazelnut; Venus, a green
plum. Earth had been carved from a turnip, with its oceans
painted on in blueberry juice. Mars was a dusty red, ripe
peach, and the asteroids were raisins. Jupiter was carved
from a watermelon; Saturn was a cantaloupe, with rings
formed of thin golden slices of melon, attached to the
planet with skewers. Neptune was a honeydew melon, cool
and green in the distance. Beyond Neptune was Pluto. Susan could see that distant planet, but could not make out
details of its composition. The shadows of the fruit planets
spun majestically on the distant wall, wavering in the candlelight.

While they were admiring the planets, Ian came up behind them. "How are you ladies this evening?" he asked.

"This is magnificent," Pat said.

Ian nodded. "Antonio is quite an artist. He did it in honor
of the new show in the Singing Sirens Theater."

"What's the show?" Susan asked.

"It's called *Space Odyssey*," he said. "I haven't seen it

myself. But I've heard that it includes a very impressive flying saucer."

The others were already at the dinner table, except for Tom, whose seat was empty. Ian informed the group that Tom had a nasty cold, and wouldn't be joining them that evening. Susan felt a little guilty about that. She figured Tom must have caught cold when they were out on the observation deck, talking about UFOs.

Dinner was dull without him. Alberta went on at some length about the day's Scrabble tournament. "Bill and I won quite handily," she said. She very proudly described her strategy for arranging for a triple word score for a word that used an "X."

Then she started in on the new show in the Singing Sirens Theater. "As a science fiction writer, you really should see it," she told Max. "It has a wonderful flying saucer." As near as Susan could tell from Alberta's description, the show was a bunch of variety acts cobbled together around a love story between a spaceship captain and a beautiful alien woman. It included singing, dancing, a magician, a juggler, and a flying saucer that landed in the middle of the stage.

After dinner, Pat talked Susan into attending the show with her. "It sounds kind of lame," Susan said.

"Oh, I'm sure it's completely lame," Pat agreed. "So lame that it has to be entertaining. We've got to see the flying saucer."

When Susan said nothing, Pat went on. "I figure we can sit through just about anything for an hour and a half. How bad could it be?"

Half an hour later, when women wearing silver-sequined bikinis, silver tap shoes, and bobbling antennae were dancing in front of a painted backdrop of glow-in-the-dark stars, Pat leaned over and whispered to Susan. "I shouldn't have asked."

Susan squirmed in her seat. The theater was too warm and the stuffy air reeked of perfume. She had been trying to imagine a dance number in which bobbling antennae

might be an asset, rather than a liability. She had not suc-
ceeded. "I don't know how much more I can take," Susan
whispered back. "Have you had enough yet?"

"I've got to stay until the flying saucer lands."

Susan considered this, weighing the possible excitement
of the flying saucer against the known tedium of the dancing and singing.

"If you have to escape, go ahead," Pat continued. "I'll
meet you back at the room."

The woman just ahead of them turned and gave them a
dirty look. Apparently their whispering was interfering with
her enjoyment of the antennaed dancers. Susan touched
Pat's arm and pointed to the exit, indicating that she intended to make her escape.

Outside the theater, Susan breathed a sigh of relief and
considered the best route to take back to her stateroom. It
was three decks up, directly above her. She could walk half
the length of the ship to reach the centrally located elevators, then retrace her steps. Or maybe she could find a shortcut. She was walking down the corridor toward the
elevators when she noticed a door marked "emergency
exit."

Remembering Mary Maxwell's observation that doors
marked "emergency exit" opened into companionways for
the crew, Susan pushed the door open. Sure enough, it led
to a landing, from which painted steel stairs led upward
and downward. A shortcut.

She headed up without hesitation. Her shoes clanged on
the metal stairs, and the sound echoed off the bare walls.
The hum of the ship's engines was louder in the companionway; there was no carpeting to muffle it.

The landing where she had entered had been brightly lit
by an overhead fixture. One flight up, a similar fixture was
overhead, but the fluorescent bulb was flickering, providing
a dim, intermittent illumination.

Just as she reached the landing, the light went out. Suddenly, it was dark. Not pitch-black—a little bit of light
filtered down from the landing above, but only a little. She

could barely make out the stairs in the darkness.

Good thing she was on a landing, she thought. A door let off the landing and she opened it, assuming it would take her into a passenger area. But it didn't. Rather than opening into a carpeted corridor, the door led into a service corridor, with painted metal walls and painted metal underfoot. It was lit by an overhead fluorescent light that flickered and buzzed. There was a service cart stacked with cleaning equipment parked by one wall, a few boxes of toilet paper on the floor beside the cart.

She hesitated for a moment, then decided to see where the corridor led. How wrong could she go? At worst, she would have to retrace her steps. She stepped through the door and started down the corridor.

The overhead light fixture hummed on a high note that was audible even through the rumble of the engines. The light was dim, and the corridor was even darker ahead. The air was stale, as if this corridor had been closed off for a long time.

Susan hesitated, peering into the darkness, then decided that perhaps she should go back. Nothing wrong with a little adventure, but she didn't like the look of this place. No point in being stupid.

She returned to the door that led back to the landing and tried to turn the knob. It didn't turn. She tried again. No luck. The door had locked behind her.

She'd have to find another way out. No problem, she thought, though her heart was pounding faster. It might take her a little longer, that was all. But when she turned to face the dark corridor, the light fixture made a crackling noise and went out, leaving her in complete darkness.

The corridor was silent, except for the sound of her own breathing. In the sudden darkness, she heard a sound—the rasp of metal scraping against metal—coming from somewhere in the corridor. She shivered in the darkness.

There was nothing to be afraid of, she told herself. She was just letting her imagination get the best of her. But she couldn't help remembering her account of the monster in the darkness, sharpening a knife. It was silly to think about that.

But even as she tried to reassure herself, she was blaming herself for being there. She shouldn't have come this way, she thought. She knew better than to try to take a shortcut. She always got lost. And getting lost could be dangerous, no matter what Mary said.

She could hear her own breathing, feel her heart pounding. This is ridiculous, she thought. She was scaring herself. It was just her imagination. But she smelled something rotten in the darkness. She swore she could hear stealthy movements coming closer.

"Is someone there?" she asked. She tried to sound matter-of-fact, but her voice trembled.

No answer. She fumbled in her pocket and found the squeeze light that she had purchased in Bermuda when she was concerned that there might be another blackout. Just luck she had it in her pocket. The bulb glowed, creating a tiny pool of bright light.

She saw a flicker of movement outside the circle of light. She shone the light around, but saw nothing but dark walls, dark floors. "Who's there?"

No answer. She faced the darkness, holding the light in front of her, but she reached behind herself to rattle the door knob again. It would not open. "Help!" Susan called. She pounded on the door with the hand that wasn't holding the flashlight. "Open the door!" she shouted, hoping that someone might be on the stairs, someone might hear her. "Help!"

She tried the knob again and it turned suddenly in her hand. The door opened. She almost fell onto the landing, but clung to the doorknob for support. Regaining her footing, she turned and slammed the door behind her, leaning against it and waiting for the sound of someone on the other side of the door.

All was quiet. After a moment, she turned to face the person who had opened the door. "Thank you," she began. "I got locked out . . ."

Her words died. In the dim light that filtered down from the landing above them, she recognized the man who was studying her. Weldon Merrimax. She stared at him in disbelief.

"You sounded like you needed a hand," he said.

"Yes," Susan said, her voice weak. "Yes, I suppose I did." She straightened up, standing with her back to the door.

"So what's in there?" he asked, glancing at the door behind her. "What had you so scared?" He studied her, his eyes cold and appraising.

"The light went out," she said. "That's all." She shook her head, not knowing what else to say. She didn't want to talk to this man. She was afraid of him.

"Scared of the dark?" he asked, smiling as if he liked the idea.

Susan shrugged.

"Nothing wrong with being scared of the dark," he said. "It's a sensible attitude, if you ask me. I think that's the first big lie that parents tell their kids. 'Don't be afraid of the dark,' they say. 'There's nothing to be afraid of.' What bullshit. There are lots of things to fear." He raised his eyebrows, still smiling at her. He looked like a rattlesnake, contemplating a mouse. "You step into the darkness and you don't know what might happen," he said, his voice still soft. "Anything could be out there."

"My imagination got the best of me," she said. "That's all."

"That's all?" His smile broadened. It wasn't a nice smile. "I wouldn't discount your imagination. The imagination is a very powerful thing."

"I've got to be going," she said, starting up the stairs.

"Oh, don't rush off," he said, walking alongside her. "I'm glad I ran into you. I think we got off on the wrong foot the other day. I have a bone to pick with Max, and I took that out on you. I just don't like Max taking credit for my work."

She kept walking.

"All those books you think are so bleak. Those are mine, not Max's. You understand that?"

She didn't answer. She reached the landing and pushed open the door. She breathed a sigh of relief as she stepped out into a carpeted corridor. She was in a public area one deck below the Calypso Deck and her stateroom. She could hear the music from the Lotus Eaters' Bar.

The man was still beside her. She stared at him, feeling more confident now that she was in a well-lit passenger area. She was trying to think of a way to contact Tom. "What do you want?" she asked him. "Why don't you leave me alone?"

"How well do you know your Bible?" the man asked her.

She blinked, startled. She hadn't read the Bible since she stopped going to Sunday school in sixth grade.

The man went on without waiting for an answer. "Do you remember where Satan came from. You know that story?"

She frowned. "He used to be an angel, then he was cast out," she said slowly.

"He was called Lucifer, the light-bearer. He was cast out because he had the balls to challenge the Creator by setting up a throne for himself, for thinking he was as good as the Creator. That was something God couldn't take. So God cast Lucifer into the pit." The man studied Susan with a level stare. "It's a question of who is going to be the Creator, that's all."

"I don't understand . . ."

"You don't want to understand," the man said, his voice laced with contempt. "And I'm afraid I don't have time to explain it all to you. I'm rearranging things a bit, so that they're more to my liking—that's all." He turned away, heading back into the companionway. He glanced over his shoulder. "By the way, when you see Max, tell him I'd like to talk to him." The door swung closed behind him.

Susan ran to the bar and asked the bartender to call security. "Hurry," she said. "Tell them I just saw Weldon Merrimax."

A security guard named Don came to the bar and rushed out to search the companionway, but Weldon was gone.

CONSIDERING THE COLLAPSE OF THE WAVE
FUNCTION AND THAT DAMN CAT

If you've been following me so far, you know that quantum physics describes a world of many simultaneously existing and sometimes contradictory possibilities. An electron orbiting an atom can be, simultaneously, in more than one place.

It really can. Trust me on this. Experiments have shown that the same electron is in two places at once. However— and here's the tricky part—the minute you try to measure the electron's whereabouts, all those potentialities collapse into a single actuality.

The easiest way to describe all this is to use Schrödinger's cat, a beast I find annoying but impossible to avoid.

Schrödinger's cat is a thought experiment. Let's get that straight at the start so that I don't get nasty letters from cat lovers. No one has actually performed this experiment with a cat. This is a theoretical cat—the brainchild of one Erwin Schrödinger, winner of the 1933 Nobel Prize for Physics.

So here's the imaginary experiment. Suppose you have a cat—let's call her Fluffy. You put her in a sealed, sound-proof box. You plan to keep Fluffy in this box for exactly one hour. There's plenty of oxygen in the box; Fluffy won't run out of air. But you have also placed in the box a Geiger counter and chunk of radium that emits gamma rays. Over the course of an hour, the radium has a probability of exactly 50% of tossing out a subatomic particle (a process known as radioactive decay).

Considered from the quantum mechanical point of view, the radium atom is in a superposition of decaying and not decaying with a 50% likelihood of doing either. Considered quantum mechanically, two realities exist: in one, the radium atom has decayed; in the other, it has not.

In the reality where the radium decays, the Geiger counter clicks. When this happens, a device breaks a flask that releases a poisonous gas that kills poor Fluffy.

In the reality where the radium does not decay, the Geiger counter doesn't click, and everything is OK. In that reality, Fluffy is fine.

Here's the part that tweaks the physicists. The radium atom is in a quantum mechanical state of superposition. It is simultaneously occupying two realities: decaying and not decaying. Since Fluffy's survival is linked to the state of the radium atom, the cat is also simultaneously occupying two realities: alive and dead. It is not that the cat is definitely alive or definitely dead and you just don't know which is true. It's weirder than that. Until you open the box and observe the system, the atom and the cat are in both states at the same time—the cat is oscillating between life and death.

Weird, huh? This is what makes my fellow physicists get twitchy. Strange behavior on the part of an electron or an atom is annoying enough. But Schrödinger's cat allows the weirdness of an electron to manifest itself on the macroscopic scale. You've got a cat that is simultaneously alive and dead—until you sneak a peek.

When you take a look, all the potentialities collapse to a single actuality. Physicists call this "the collapse of the wave function."

We know that the wave function collapses whenever we physicists try to measure or observe a system. The act of looking influences the system we are observing and causes all those lovely potentialities to become a single actuality. Open the box to look at the cat, and bingo—the cat is alive or the cat is dead.

Why should observation change a system? No one knows. Theoretical physicists call this the "measurement problem," and the whole thing has made lots of physicists terribly uncomfortable.

People have come up with some lovely theories to explain the measurement problem. The most popular among physicists is the theory proposed by Niels Bohr, one of Schrödinger's contemporaries. Bohr said that you can't describe a system unless you measure it, so you can't even talk about what it looks like between measurements.

As far as I'm concerned, Bohr's interpretation avoids all the interesting questions. It's sort of like he threw up his hands in disgust at the whole mess and just decided not to deal with it.

Then we have the Wigner Interpretation, proposed by physicist Eugene Wigner. Most physicists don't like this one much, but I love it. Wigner suggests that when someone looks at a system, their consciousness influences the system. The mind of the observer attempting to measure or observe the system triggers the collapse of the wave function.

Another theory I rather like is the Many Worlds Interpretation, first suggested by H. Everett in his Ph.D. thesis at Princeton and later developed further by physicist B. de Witt. This one ducks the question of what triggers the collapse by saying that there really isn't a collapse when someone makes a measurement. All the potentialities are realized as actualities, Everett said, but they exist in different universes, all branching out from the original point. There's a separate universe for every possible outcome.

Most physicists don't like this theory much—it smacks too much of science fiction. But Everett's approach offers some real advantages. Mathematically, it's solid—I can show you how Schrödinger's wave equation (developed by the same Schrödinger who came up with the cat conundrum) correctly describes the quantum mechanical state of the universe as a whole, including all of its branches.

As I mentioned before, my Ph.D. thesis deals with a mathematical model that connects Wigner's theory and the Many Worlds theory, showing that consciousness is what determines how and when the universe branches.

Maybe you're wondering what all this has to do with the *Odyssey* and Max Merriwell and my friend Susan. Could it be that Max has generated a mess of branching potentialities? If so, are we headed for the collapse of the wave function, where all these potentialities collapse into a single reality? If that's the case, will the reality when they collapse be our own? Or will the world as we know it cease to exist?

Or is the Everett–De Witt Many Worlds theory right? Do all these branching realities coexist, parallel realities that occasionally overlap?

I confess: I'm very curious about the answers to these questions. I think it's time to work out the math.

NINETEEN

"You never know what's going to be on the other side of the door," Gitana said. *"But you know you have to open it. Or you would wonder for the rest of your days."*

—from *The Twisted Band*
by Max Merriwell

The next morning, Susan woke early. Leaving Pat sleeping soundly, she went to Circe's Kitchen, on the chance she might find Max having breakfast. Luck was with her and he was there. His notebook was on the table in front of him, but it was closed. He waved when he saw her.

"Good morning, Max," she said. "Do you mind if I join you?"

"I'd be delighted to have your company. Please—sit down."

An overhead lamp cast a warm golden glow over the table; the air was scented with coffee. Though the restaurant was warm, Susan felt cold. Outside the window, the sky was overcast; the ocean waves were the color of lead—gray and impenetrable. Hard to believe that this dark water was connected to the sparkling, turquoise blue seas off Bermuda.

She ordered breakfast—bacon and eggs, coffee, toast—while trying to figure out how to broach the subject of Weldon Merrimax. But before she could, Max started talking.

"I found another note under my door this morning," he said. He took a piece of ship's stationery from his notebook and offered it to Susan.

She unfolded it. Another hexagram: five broken lines, topped by a solid line. Printed under the hexagram in the same angular handwriting as the first note was one sentence: "The dark lines are about to mount upward and overthrow the last light line."

"That sounds ominous," she said.

Max frowned. "Not necessarily. Considering darkness to be evil is a very Occidental perspective. Darkness isn't necessarily evil. There is always fluctuation between the dark and the light. The moon waxes and wanes; the sun rises and sets. The bright and the dark; the firm and the yielding; the yang and the yin."

Susan found herself remembering Mary Maxwell's discussion of dragons. "I met Mary Maxwell night before last," she said. "After drinking Rum Monkeys."

"Really?" Max didn't seem surprised. "I quite like Mary. She's a wonderful person."

Susan stared at him. "She's a real person then?"

Max shrugged, looking uncomfortable. "It's best not to examine these things too closely. It's all part of the creative process. Tricky stuff; that."

Susan shook her head. "I met Weldon Merrimax last night."

Max frowned. "Oh, that's too bad."

"He's real, isn't he?" she asked.

Max sighed. "That's a very difficult question, Susan."

"Seems simple enough to me."

"Might as well ask whether light is a particle or a wave," he said. "It's both, you know. Though not at the same time."

"What is going on, Max?"

Max stared down at his coffee for a moment, then said, "You have to consider the power of names. To summon a demon, one needs to know its name. To activate a golem, one writes the name of God on its forehead. Names are very powerful."

He looked up and met her eyes. "Mary Maxwell—the name came to me so easily, almost an echo of my own name. I dreamed of her and she told me stories. It was quite lovely."

He sipped his coffee and frowned. "I should have stopped there. That would have been best. But that fall, my agent suggested I write a crime thriller. It was a dreary autumn and the garbage men were on strike. All Manhattan stank like a Dumpster. I was in a bleak mood and I thought of Weldon Merrimax. Another echo of my name; a joke, really. I told my agent and he laughed. That night, I dreamed of Weldon Merrimax, an angry man obssessed with money and power. We talked, and he told me about crimes he had committed, about cons and swindles and frauds. He seemed to like talking to me. I listened and I wrote the first Weldon Merrimax book."

Max looked out the window at the gray ocean waves. "There's a question writers joke about. People always ask, 'Where do you get your ideas?' As if we had a clue. Oh, I can tell you bits and pieces of the process—someone mentioned this which led me to think about that and so I put these things together with a story from the *New York Times* and ended up over here. But where did Mary and Weldon come from? I don't know. I made up the names and invented the characters—or did I? Maybe they were already out there, waiting to be found. Maybe I called them up by invoking their names." Max shrugged. "Does it matter?"

"But what's going on now?" Susan asked.

"Well, I'm working on a new book," he said. "Writing a novel always involves a bit of turbulence."

Susan stared at him. "A bit of turbulence?" she repeated.

Max shrugged. "It's part of the creative process," he said. "The subconscious isn't a tidy place. I've been sleeping badly and I haven't been dreaming." He shrugged. "But I'm sure it will all work out."

"Weldon Merrimax said he wanted to talk to you," Susan said. "He said he was rearranging things so that they'd be more to his liking. He talked about God and Lucifer and said it's a question of who is going to be the Creator. He said to tell you he wants to talk to you."

"And so you have." Max did not seem perturbed. "That was the right thing to do."

"But what are you going to do?" Susan asked. "I think you need to talk to Weldon."

"Do I? I have nothing to say to him." Max shook his head. "If Weldon wants to sneak around leaving cryptic notes, that's his business. I'll just ignore him."

Max reached out and tapped a finger on the note in her hand. "The lower trigram is K'un, representing receptivity and the earth. The upper trigram is the mountain, which keeps very still. The superior man will wait quietly, avoiding action." Max folded his hands in front of him, smiling. "I believe that's the course the *I Ching* recommends."

"But he's very angry," Susan said.

Max did not reply. He glanced at his watch. "You know, we'd better hurry or we'll be late to class." He smiled at her. "Just relax. There's nothing to worry about."

Somehow Susan didn't believe him.

Susan returned to her stateroom before workshop, figuring she would wake up Pat. But when she got there, Pat was already in the shower. The dressing table was covered with sheets of notebook paper and the notebook paper was covered with equations.

As Susan closed the stateroom door, the sound of running water stopped. A moment later, Pat stepped from the bathroom. She was wearing one of the white terry cloth robes and toweling off her hair.

"What have you been up to?" Susan asked her, waving a hand at the drift of notebook pages.

"I ran into Ian last night, after the show. We got to talking about the weird stuff that's been going on. I came up with a theory to explain it, and I've been working out the math."

"The math?" Susan said, baffled.

"It's Everett's Many Worlds Interpretation with a few extra spins suggested by Roger Penrose's work. The influence of the conscious mind on the quantum state, that is. I can show you the math, if you like."

"That's okay," Susan said quickly. "Maybe you could just give me the overview."

"I figured I'd tell Max about it after workshop," Pat said. "Maybe we could all have lunch. I bet Ian would be up for it."

Though they hurried, they arrived at workshop late. Max was already lecturing.

"An important aspect of a story that beginning writers often forget is point of view. Who is telling the story? Whose eyes are you seeing the world through, whose perceptions are filtering the information you provide? You can tell the same story from two different points of view and get two very different stories."

He talked for a while about possible points of view. Susan didn't take very good notes. She was distracted. Every time a jogger ran past the window, she glanced in that direction, thinking it might be Weldon Merrimax.

"Now let's try an exercise," Max said. "Earlier on, you wrote about monsters. I asked you to write a scene where your monster was just out of sight. Today, we are going to try something a little different. I mentioned that writers have to get to know their monsters. One way to learn about something is to observe it from the outside. But as a writer, that's not enough. You need to know your characters inside and out.

"So here's what I want you to do. Imagine yourself standing by a closed door. It can be any kind of door you like: a spaceship airlock, a garden gate, the front door of your own home. You hear something at the door and you know that there's a monster on the other side. The monster wants to come in."

"I want you to write a scene from the point of view of that monster. You have to be the monster. Think about what the monster wants, what the monster needs." Max was silent, giving them all a chance to think. "Now I want you to write a scene from the monster's point of view."

Max waited while everyone got out notebooks and pens. As usual, Alberta had a question: "Does it have to be the same monster I wrote about before?"

"That's up to you. It could be a little different. You're getting to know your monster, and the version of it that you see today may be a little different from the version you knew a few days back."

Susan stared at the page. She didn't have to work too hard to imagine standing by a door with the monster on one side. She remembered the night before. But which monster should she choose to be: the monster in the dark or the monster who was Weldon Merrimax?

She thought about the dark corridor. She imagined herself as a monster, crouching in the darkness, watching a woman try to open a door. The door wouldn't open. The monster could smell the woman's sweat, the scent of fear. The woman was staring wide-eyed into the darkness, waving a silly little flashlight around. The woman was rattling the doorknob, calling out for help. Then the door opened and the woman was gone, rushing out of the darkness, slamming the door closed.

The monster was alone in the darkness.

"Think about how the monster feels," Max said. "What does the monster smell? What does the monster hear?"

How did the monster feel? "The monster felt strong," she wrote. "The monster could still smell the woman's fear. The monster breathed deeply, enjoying that scent. Such a foolish, weak woman, the monster thought.

"The monster could hear voices from the other side of the door. The woman's voice, high-pitched and trembling. Another voice, a man's voice.

"The monster went to the door and leaned against it. He did not push on the door—he didn't want to open it. He didn't want to go into the light, where she could see him. He liked it in the shadows and the darkness.

"He could hear her frightened voice—what a lovely sound. It would take so little to make her scream. She would cry out and ask for mercy. That would be good.

"Women were weak, the monster thought. He loved that about them. Such lovely playthings—they broke so easily.

"He smiled in the darkness, leaning against the cold metal door. The voices were moving away. The monster could hear the sound of footsteps on metal stairs, fading in the distance. The woman was gone.

"That didn't matter, the monster thought. He was patient. There would be other chances. No need to hurry."

At the end of class, Ian showed up at the back of the library. Pat waved to him, grabbed Susan's arm, and hailed Max before he could leave. "I thought maybe you would join us for lunch," she said. "I was hoping to talk to you about quantum mechanics and a few ideas I had."

Max looked a little startled, but nodded. "Of course," he said. "I'd be delighted."

They went to Penelope's for lunch and found a table by the window. Outside, the sky was still overcast. The ocean was a restless surging gray.

As soon as they ordered, Pat pulled out her sheets of equations, set them on the table, and launched into an explanation of her theory. "You know, of course, about Schrödinger's cat," she said.

Max nodded. "Yes, of course. Any science fiction writer worth his salt knows about Schrödinger's cat."

Pat glanced at Susan, and she nodded. Pat had explained the theoretical beast to her long ago.

"Now there are many explanations of what happens when you open the box, look at the cat, and find out it's either alive or dead," Pat continued. "You've got two potentialities—two different realities, if you will, superposed on each other. Then you take a look and you've only got one. Or do you?" Pat paused dramatically, glancing at Susan, then Ian, then Max. No one spoke.

"Not necessarily," Pat said at last. "Some have proposed that both realities continue to exist. In one, you are looking at a dead cat; in another, you are looking at a live cat. Two versions of you; two versions of the cat; two different realities. Each reality splits again and again, creating many parallel lines, each following its own course, branching repeatedly."

Max nodded. "Science fiction has done a great deal with parallel realities."

"Not just science fiction, Max," Pat said. "Physics, too. Everett and De Witt worked out the math." She tapped a finger on a series of equations on the topmost sheet. "But I've always had a problem with their theory. They postulate parallel realities, but no mechanism by which these realities are connected. If there are parallel realities, I think there must be a means of interconnecting them.

"That brings us to the work of Eugene Wigner," Pat said, "In an attempt to settle on what exactly caused potentialities to resolve into realities, Wigner proposed what is now known as the Wigner Interpretation. He suggested that the agent of this action was the mind of the observer. The conscious human mind influenced potentialities and brought about the collapse of the wave function, resolving all the possibilities into one reality."

"Now suppose for a moment that the parallel realities of Everett's theory could be connected by the action of the conscious mind, as suggested by the Wigner Interpretation. Consciousness provides the link between the parallel realities. The question I'm wrestling with now is—how does this link occur?"

"Through dreams." Susan spoke without thinking. Everyone looked at her. She bit her lip and ducked her head. "Just a thought," she muttered.

"Sure," Ian said. "In dreams, people from one reality visit other branches."

Pat blinked, startled at this contribution. "That's a possibility," she said slowly. "I don't know how to represent that mathematically, but it's an interesting idea."

"Ordinarily the connection is through dreams," Ian went on. "But maybe, when conditions are right, people from other realities can actually cross over into this one. Like maybe in the Bermuda Triangle." Ian grinned at Pat. "Do you think that's possible?"

Pat frowned. "I don't know." She tapped on one of her equations. "I mean—take a look here. There's a significant energy barrier between the parallel realities."

Ian kept his gaze fixed on Pat. He liked the ideas more than the math, Susan thought. "I don't know much about this," he said, "but what about the possibilities of quantum tunneling." He glanced at Susan and Max. "Quantum particles that should be confined to one area by an energy barrier sometimes show up elsewhere, as if they tunneled through the barrier rather than jumping over," he explained.

"That's quite a stretch," Pat said, frowning at her equations. "Equating a person with a quantum particle."

"A virtual person," Ian said. "Like a virtual particle." Again he glanced at Susan and Max. "Virtual particles are always popping in and out of the quantum vacuum," he told them.

"What's the quantum vacuum?" Susan asked, struggling to keep some kind of a grip on the conversation.

"It's the sea of potentiality that underlies everything in the universe," Pat said. "And Ian's right—virtual particles are always popping out of it, then disappearing again."

Max chuckled. "There's a lovely idea for a novel somewhere in there," he said cheerfully. "I'd say science fiction is ready to incorporate a little more quantum mechanics."

"Oh, it's not science fiction," Pat said. "The pressure exerted by virtual particles was measured experimentally back in 1996 by a fellow at Los Alamos. They're really out there."

"So a virtual particle pops into existence and then disappears again," Max said.

"Usually," Pat said. "But sometimes a virtual particle can stay on this side of reality. That happens if it collides with a real particle and steals its energy. Then the particle that was robbed disappears and the virtual one becomes real."

Susan gave up on trying to make sense of the equations and glanced at Max. She was startled to see that the writer looked concerned. But Pat had returned to her equations. "I suppose quantum tunneling is a possibility," she said. "Look here."

Ian leaned over to consider the equation.

Susan arrived in the library just a few minutes after the kids got there. She had rushed off, leaving Max with Pat and Ian, considering Pat's incomprehensible equations.

With Cindy's help, Susan got the kids settled relatively quickly. They were ready to hear more of Bailey's adventures.

She read the next couple of chapters, in which Bailey and his friends were captured by Resurrectionists, a group of space pirates who harvested human brains and nervous systems and used them in the construction of cyborg systems. Bailey's friends escaped, but Bailey was left behind to face a monster in the hold of the Resurrectionist ship.

The Rattler had once been human, but the Resurrectionists had dismantled her body and given her a new one of an original design: half organic, half mechanical. Rattler's spinal column stretched the length of a metal frame, supported by magnetized wheels, protected by the burnished steel carapace that housed her organs. She had half a dozen eyes set on stalks that swiveled, like the turret eyes of a chameleon. Metal arms equipped with mechanical claws extended from the front and sides and back of the frame.

Susan wet her lips. She had finally reached the part about monsters, and she found it a little disturbing. She glanced at her audience. Jody was paying close attention, eyes wide and fascinated.

The Rattler had escaped the Resurrectionists' labs and lived in the hold of the ship. She was more than a little bit mad. She hated the Resurrectionists, but she had developed a hatred of their human victims as well. She knew that they had something she lacked, something that the Resurrectionist had stolen from her during her reconstruction. She

wanted to take Bailey apart to see if he had what she
needed.

Susan found herself thinking of the monster that she had
written about, the one that lurked in the darkness and threatened women who had ventured out where they shouldn't
be. It seemed that her monster shared some attributes with
the Rattler. With an effort, Susan kept her attention on the
story she was reading.

Bailey was a resourceful norbit, and he managed to escape the Rattler. With the aid of a cyborg spaceship, he
rejoined his friends and went to the planet Ophir where he
met the Curator, an elderly woman who collected alien ar-
tifacts. Susan was startled to read the Curator's name: Pat
Murphy.

Susan glanced up and saw Trudy, waiting in the doorway
to reclaim her charges. "Hey, kids, storytime's over."

"But wait," Jody said. "We have to find out what happens next."

"You'll find out tomorrow," Trudy said briskly. "But
Halloween is almost here and it's time to make Halloween
costumes."

On her way back to her stateroom, Susan passed Aphrodite's Alehouse. As she walked by, she glanced through the
door and saw Max at the bar, drinking alone.

She hesitated, then stepped inside. The bar was quiet—
just a few people at the scattered tables. "Hey, Max," she
called. "I was just reading *There and Back Again* to the
kids at story hour. They love it."

Max looked up from his glass of brandy. "That's nice,"
he said.

She sat down on the bar stool beside him. He had the
relaxed look of a man who had been drinking steadily for
a while. He took another sip of brandy.

"I was surprised you had another character named Pat
Murphy," she said. "There was a Patrick Murphy in *Wild*

Angel. And in *There and Back Again,* the Curator was named Pat Murphy."

Max shrugged. Susan got the impression he wasn't really paying attention. "It's a common enough name," he said.

"I met an old woman named Pat Murphy yesterday who looked just like the Curator. I talked with her about 'Pataphysics."

Max sipped his brandy but did not reply. Frank Robinson, the bartender, came over. She thought he looked relieved to see her. "So nice to see you," he said. "I thought Max could use some company. What would you like to drink?"

"Just sparkling water, thanks."

While Frank was filling her glass, Susan asked Max, "Do you have any idea why there'd be a pataphysician named Pat Murphy on board?"

Max shook his head, staring down at his glass of brandy. "I have no idea," he said. "Unless it has something to do with the quantum vacuum." He looked up and met her eyes. "I've been thinking about the quantum vacuum," he said slowly. "Considering its implications. I've been telling Frank about it."

Frank looked, Susan thought, a little spooked—like a man who has been listening to ghost stories in a dark room. Not convinced, but not entirely comfortable, either. "Max has been telling me that everything in the universe is just ripples," Frank said to Susan.

"That's what Pat said," Max muttered. "Patterns of dynamic energy. Shifts and tweaks in the underlying field. Nothing's permanent; everything's changing. It's a great cosmic dance of changing realities. And that's all right with me. No surprises there. But I don't like that business of virtual particles becoming real. She says that can happen. A virtual particle can steal the energy of a real particle and become real. I don't like the sound of that."

Susan frowned. "He's talking about quantum mechanics," she told Frank. "It's all stuff that's too small to see. It's not like it's the real world or anything."

Max raised his eyes to meet Susan's. "That's not so," he said earnestly. "Quantum mechanics is at the heart of everything. The particles that make up everything in the universe are just tweaks in the field of the quantum vacuum. This bar . . ." He thumped on the polished teak. "This glass . . ." He tapped his brandy snifter and make it ring softly. "You. Me. We are all made up of particles that are just tweaks in the quantum vacuum."

Frank shook his head, looking at Susan. "I'm just a simple bartender and it sounds like fairy tales to me."

"The quantum vacuum is empty of things, a blank, a featureless void," Max went on. "It's empty of things, but it's filled with potentialities. Like a blank page, filled with possibilities, waiting to be called forth. Weldon Merrimax, Mary Maxwell, Max Merriwell—so many possibilities."

"Some possibilities are more real than others," Susan said. "This bar, this glass, you, me—we're really here."

Max shook his head, gazing at her owlishly. "Just tweaks in the vacuum," he said. "Called up in dreams. Always changing." He swayed on his stool. "Nothing you can count on."

"I wonder if you might want to help Max get back to his cabin," Frank suggested softly.

Max could walk, though Susan had to hold his arm to keep him on course. He fumbled in his pocket for quite a while, but managed to find his cruise card and use it to open his stateroom door. Then he muttered something about getting ready for dinner, and lay down on his bed. She covered him with the blanket from the foot of the bed and left him snoring quietly.

TWENTY

"What is the best defense against murder?" the woman
asked the pataphysician.
Gyro looked up. "Of the nineteen strategies for defense," he
said, *"the best is running away. Or, more simply, not being
there is the best defense."*

—from *The Twisted Band*
by Max Merriwell

The real trouble didn't start until later that evening.

Dinner was relatively civilized. Charles dominated the
discussion by complaining bitterly about the weather.
Charles seemed to hold Tom responsible for the cloudy
skies, asking repeatedly when Tom thought it would clear
up. Tom was still recovering from his cold. He had to keep
asking Charles to repeat himself, telling Charles that his
ears were stopped up.

Charles was perfectly willing to repeat himself. Susan
was impressed that Tom managed to remain so calm, explaining patiently that the weather was not within his juris-
diction as security officer. Charles went on to talk about
how much better the weather had been when they had
cruised with another cruise line.

After dinner, Tom disappeared—heading for bed, Susan
hoped. There was a party scheduled for the Atrium. At
about ten o'clock, Susan, Pat, and Ian stood on the second
level of the Atrium, gazing down at a towering pyramid of
champagne glasses that sparkled in the overhead lights.

Ian explained the workings of the champagne fountain
to Pat and Susan. At midnight, champagne would be poured
into the top glass, until it cascaded over the rim to fill the
glasses below. When those glasses overflowed in turn, they

would fill the glasses below them. Eventually, every glass in the pyramid would be filled with champagne.

"So what happens between now and midnight?" Susan asked.

"We're in for some spontaneous, organized fun," Ian said. "First, there's a limbo contest. Then the winner of the limbo contest will lead a conga line, dancing to the music of the Twisted Band." Ian gestured to the dance floor, where a guitarist, a sax player, and a steel drum player were setting up their equipment. "Then, for the grand finale, the winner of the limbo contest will be the first to pour champagne into the fountain."

"This should be interesting in an anthropological kind of a way," Pat said. "The limbo contest will be a hoot, and the Bad Grrl can make fun of it all later."

Susan shook her head. All through dinner, she'd been wondering how Max was doing. For the first time that afternoon, the writer had seemed genuinely concerned about what was going on aboard the *Odyssey*. She couldn't manage much enthusiasm for a limbo contest.

"Let's go down to the dance floor where we can see better," Pat said.

"You go on," Susan said. "I'll just watch from up here. Maybe I'll go for a walk."

It took a little persuasion, but eventually Pat and Ian headed for the dance floor, leaving Susan by herself. It had been a long day, beginning with her breakfast conversation with Max about Weldon, the power of names, the *I Ching*, and the creative process.

She watched Pat and Ian make their way down the spiral staircase, through the crowd of passengers in evening dress, and to the edge of the dance floor. It was easy to follow Pat's progress; her brilliant blue hair stood out in the crowd.

On the dance floor, Gene Culver had the microphone and he was encouraging the crowd to dance the Macarena, which blared over the loudspeakers. The people on the dance floor had begun to dance in a self-conscious sort of way.

Susan surveyed the crowd and spotted someone she recognized: the elderly Ms. Murphy who had known so much about 'Pataphysics.

The dancing spread, moving outward from the dance floor into the rest of the room. Viewed from above, it was a staggering spectacle of gyrating hips and waving hands as bald men in tuxes and ample women in sequins danced with enthusiasm. As Susan watched, Ms. Murphy headed toward the doors that led to the Promenade. Susan watched her for a moment, then caught a glimpse of someone else moving purposefully through the dancing crowd.

Weldon Merrimax was following Ms. Murphy as she headed toward the door. There was something ominous about his concentration on the woman. The elderly woman didn't know she was being followed. It didn't look good.

Susan looked for a security guard, but didn't see one. She looked for a way to get down to the Promenade level and intercept Ms. Murphy, but the spiral staircase was crowded and the dance floor was worse. She hurried to the glass elevators, but there was a crowd waiting there. Glancing to one side of the elevators, she spotted a a door labeled "Emergency Exit." Without hesitation, she opened the door and headed down the service companionway, passing a startled looking waiter carrying a tray of drinks. "This will take me to the Promenade level, won't it?" she asked.

"Yes, ma'am," he said, and she hurried past before he could stop her.

Jason Jacobs, the leader and songwriter for the Twisted Band, watched the limbo contest with thinly disguised loathing. He did not belong here, he thought. It was a cruel set of circumstances that had brought him to the *Odyssey*.

He had been working on a graduate degree in anthropology at the University of California at Berkeley and playing music in his spare time. A scout for a record company had heard Jacobs' band playing at a San Francisco club. The scout had been extravagant in his praise of the band.

He'd bought them drinks, promised them a record contract, said that they'd be an overnight success.

At that time, Jacobs hadn't been getting along very well with his dissertation advisor. Jacobs' dissertation dealt with the patterns of rhythm and melody that appear in ritual situations. He had studied the music used in Inuit shamanistic ritual and Voodoo ceremonies, Hopi dances and the gospel tunes sung in charismatic Christian sects.

In his study, Jacobs had found that certain patterns of rhythm and melody affect the human nervous system, inducing trance states that lead to the internal physiological repetition of the rhythm. Jacobs had become fascinated with these rhythms, incorporating them into his own music. His advisor had suggested that he might spend his time more profitably documenting his findings in the literature, rather than dabbling in pop music.

So the day after his meeting with the scout, elated and hung over, Jacobs told his dissertation advisor that he was fed up with the university's chickenshit attitude and he was moving on.

He had planned to take the music world by storm. But the scout was fired by the record company and no one else at the company seemed particularly interested in Jacobs' band. The band had landed a few club gigs, but that hadn't been nearly enough to pay the rent.

The sax player had a friend who knew someone who worked for Odyssey Cruises. And the steel drum player had heard rumors that London clubs were more receptive to new talent than the American clubs. One thing led to another and all those things led to this: Twisted Band was playing on the *Odyssey,* en route to London. And here he was, watching a buxom lady in a purple velvet gown and a white-haired lady in sequins limbo for the honor of leading a conga line.

The song that Jacobs had selected to play for the conga line that night was a new composition that incorporated the rhythms and melodies of ritual music. Jacobs surmised that this song, which he had titled "Dance All Night," would serve as a superstimulus for dancing. The crowd would not appreciate the artistry behind the composition, Jacobs reasoned, but at least it would get them to dance. That would make the cruise line happy, which would be useful if the band needed to arrange for a ride back to the States at some future date.

Jacobs watched the end of the contest. The white-haired woman—remarkably limber for her age—wriggled under a bar that was a good two inches below the buxom lady's best.

Gene Culver announced the white-haired woman as the winner, holding her arm aloft like the referree at a boxing match. Then he announced that Twisted Band would play an original dance tune, composed just for the conga line.

Twisted Band began to play, starting with a simple rhythm line on the steel drum. The guitarist echoed the rhythm, adding a simple, repetitive melody. The sax joined in, and then Jacobs began to sing:

> Sunbeams
> Moonbeams
> Nothing is the way it seems
> Your dreams,
> My schemes,
> Dancing through the night.

> One chance
> to dance
> Don't leave it to circumstance.
> A trance,
> A dance,
> Dreaming through the night.

The white-haired lady who had won the limbo contest beckoned to an elderly man in a tuxedo. He clasped her sequined waist and followed her lead. Another couple quickly joined them.

The service companionway had led to a kitchen area, from which Susan found her way to a passenger corridor that paralleled the Promenade. She was hurrying along the corridor, looking for a door that led outside, when she looked out a window. Her view was partially blocked by a stack of deck chairs, piled into a corner for the night. Beyond the chairs, she caught a glimpse of two figures in the shadows. She stopped, torn between the need to find a way out and the desire to see what was going on.

Was it Weldon Merrimax and Ms. Murphy, struggling in the darkness? Or just a honeymooning couple, necking in the shadows. Susan caught no more than a fleeting glimpse of the figures before they moved and were hidden by the chairs.

She rushed down the corridor. At the far end, she finally found a door that led out onto the Promenade.

Outside, the air was cold—a sharp contrast to the overheated air of the corridor. A layer of low-lying mist hid the waves; the ship seemed to be sailing on clouds.

Susan dashed back to where she had seen the shadowy figures. She found the stack of chairs beside a window, but no one was there.

Under normal circumstances, Ian did not dance. But the circumstances in the Atrium were not normal. It was strange how this music got into your head, he thought. Stupid words, but a catchy tune, and the rhythm seemed to be a part of him—as if his heart were beating in time to the music.

The white-haired lady had led the conga line in a circle around the dance floor, then off into the crowd. As Ian watched, a man set his champagne glass on the tray of a passing waiter and joined the end of the line, hands on the waist of a young woman in silver lamé. A matronly woman in an evening dress laughed, set her champagne glass on the edge of a potted plant, and joined the end of the conga line, hands on the waist of the young man.

"Come on!" Pat called. She was heading for the conga line, clearly planning to join in the dance. A little startled by her enthusiasm, Ian followed.

The music was very loud—Ian realized it wasn't just the music from the band. People were singing along with the vocalist. He found himself singing, too. Strangely, he didn't feel at all self-conscious about it. "Your dreams, my schemes, dancing through the night."

He tried to stop singing, but the music wouldn't let him go. The beginning of the conga line was moving out the doors that led onto the Promenade deck. He followed the others, dancing out into the cool air. He felt like he could dance forever.

Tom stood on the second level of the Atrium, surveying a scene of wreckage and confusion.

He had been asleep, laid low by the antihistamine he had taken, when a panicky call had wakened him. Don, his second in command, shouted over a pounding rhythm. "Tom! I need your help in the Atrium. The dancing . . ." Don was interrupted by a crash that sounded like breaking glass. "The dancing is out of control."

"What the hell . . . ? Dancing?" Tom said. The phone went dead in his hand. He had dressed immediately and rushed to the Atrium.

The band was playing an idiotic, repetitive song and someone had cranked up the volume, filling the Atrium with pounding sound. People were dancing, but it wasn't the usual, civilized, cruise-ship sort of dancing. No, this was your drunken, frat-party kind of dancing that leaves destruction in its wake.

A conga line circled the shattered remains of the champagne fountain—a heap of sparkling glass fragments, a puddle of champagne, and a half a dozen overturned champagne bottles. The conga line continued up the spiral staircase and out the double doors onto the Promenade deck.

The music was loud enough to penetrate Tom's stuffed up head, but just barely. Tom was too tired, the music was muffled by the cold. He could ignore it.

It was a party gone out of control. The dancing passengers were not actively engaged in any acts of destruction—Tom imagined that the champagne fountain was an accidental casualty. Even so, the cruise line did not approve of this sort of spontaneous fun. Fun, on the *Odyssey,* was an organized activity. Cruise-ship fun was sometimes silly, but that silliness was in the control of the cruise staff. This silliness was way out of control. It was Tom's job to restore order without, in any way, upsetting the partying passengers.

He looked for his security staff. There was Don, dancing in the conga line. There was Fred, also in the line. This just wasn't right.

Tom headed down to the stage to stop the music. He glanced around, searching for Gene Culver as he approached the band. He figured he would ask the band to bring this tune to a graceful end, then let Gene take over. But there was no sign of the cruise director.

None of the band members noticed when Tom joined them on the small elevated platform that served as a stage. The guitarist was staring into space, his eyes glassy and unfocused. The steel drum player continued the rhythm without hesitation, even when Tom stood in front of him and ordered him to stop. The sax player had his eyes closed; he kept playing the simple melody, over and over. The vocalist did not look at Tom, even when he tugged the microphone from the man's hand.

Tom jumped down from the platform and unplugged the band's microphones. Unamplified, the pounding of the rhythm lost its driving urgency. The shuffling of hundreds of dancing feet drowned out the unamplified music. But the people kept on singing.

Tom grabbed the radio on his belt and called the bridge.

"Sound the horn," he asked the officer on duty. "Three long blasts."

Susan heard people singing, heard the rhythmic shuffling of dancing feet. Coming toward her on the Promenade, dancing through the fog, was a white-haired woman in sequins, followed by an elderly man in a tuxedo, followed by a buxom woman in velvet. As Susan watched, more dancers appeared from the fog, a seemingly endless line of singing, dancing people.

These did not look like the sort of people given to excessive dancing. As they approached Susan and passed her, she noticed that many of them were sweating heavily, even in the cool night air. One man's hairpiece had come loose; it was half off his head, revealing a large bald patch—but he was oblivious, singing cheerfully and dancing with enthusiasm.

The words they were singing made no sense—something about dreams and schemes and dancing—but the tune was catchy. Susan found herself tapping her foot in time, caught by the rhythm.

As the dancers passed her, she spotted Pat and Ian in line and blinked. Pat was clinging to the waist of a paunchy, bald man and singing happily. She saw Susan and grinned at her. "Come on!" Pat called. "Join the dance!"

Just then, the ship's horn blared, cutting through the music, drowning out the words and the rhythm.

In the Atrium, Tom watched as the people in the conga line faltered, missing one step, then another. The guitarist blinked and looked around. The sax player stopped playing. Tom picked up the MC's microphone, which lay at the edge of the stage, and switched it on.

"Good evening, everyone," he said. "This is Tom Clayton, the ship's security officer."

The conga line was breaking up. The dancers were look-

ing around with the confused expressions of people waking
from a dream. A man tugged his tux jacket back into place.
A woman, whose hairdo had come loose during the dancing, fussed with her hair, frowning.

Tom hesitated, searching for the right words. On the *Odyssey,* the passenger was always right. He couldn't just order them all back to their staterooms. "We're glad that you
are all having such a good time."

Tom spotted Gene Culver halfway up the spiral staircase.
The Cruise Director had stepped away from the conga line,
as if to pretend that he hadn't been dancing. All those other
people had been dancing, but not him.

"We wanted to take advantage of this opportunity to
thank the man who brought you this evening's entertainment," Tom went on. "We want to thank the *Odyssey*'s own
cruise director—Gene Culver!" He waved a hand toward
Gene. "Come on up here, Gene." As Tom had expected,
the cruise director automatically snapped into entertainment
mode. He was smiling and waving to the crowd as he made
his way down the stairs.

"The party here is over," Tom said as Gene made his
way through the crowd, "but the casino is open, and there's
a fine show in the Singing Sirens Theater. And here's Gene
to tell you about all the ship's other entertainment opportunities."

Gene stepped onto the stage, holding his hands up as if
to silence applause. There was no applause. He looked
wide-eyed and disheveled. He smoothed his hair back over
his balding head. "Get them out of here," Tom whispered
in Gene's ear as he handed the microphone to the cruise
director and stepped off the stage.

It took more than an hour to clear the room. Tom
rounded up his security staff and they circulated through
the crowd, helping people find friends they had lost in the
dancing, directing people toward the theater, the casino, the
bars. Anywhere but the Atrium.

Sleepy from the antihistamine, debilitated by the cold,
Tom stayed for a time, directing the security staff and look-

ing for Susan in that vague and distant way that one looks for something lost in a dream. He didn't find her.

"I guess I got a little carried away," one man said to Tom, blinking owlishly. "I seem to have lost my wife."

"You were just having a good time, sir," Tom said. "Perhaps your best bet is to return to your stateroom. She'll probably do the same."

They called the ship's doctor to the Atrium to deal with a few minor injuries: a woman wearing sandals had cut her foot on broken glass; a man had twisted his ankle while dancing up the stairs. Tom contacted maintenance and a team of maintenance staff swept up the broken glass, mopped up the champagne.

People left humming the tune that the band had been playing.

Susan sat on a deck chair that Ian had pulled from the stack by the window. Pat sat on another one, rubbing her feet. "I don't know how it happened," she was saying. "One minute I was thinking about how I could incorporate the limbo into a discussion of quantum physics. The next thing I know I'm dancing like an idiot."

Other people who had been in the conga line were milling about. "Great dance music," one woman murmured. She sang softly, "Sunbeams, moonbeams. . . ."

"Don't!" said her partner, an older man in a tux. "I hope I never hear that song again."

"But it was such a lovely dance," the woman said.

"I don't like to dance," the man said.

"Everyone likes to dance," said the woman. Susan didn't catch the man's reply—the couple was walking away, following the rest of the crowd back into the Atrium.

"Everyone likes to dance," the woman had said. Susan remembered where she had heard that before. The Trancer in *There and Back Again* had told Bailey, "Everyone likes to dance."

Susan leaned back in the deck chair. The ship shifted

and rolled on the waves and she was glad that the movement did not match the rhythm of the song in her head. "Sunbeams, moonbeams, nothing is the way it seems." She had only heard it for a moment, but she could still feel the pull of its rhythm.

"Can't get that damn song out of my head," Pat said, echoing Susan's thoughts. "It just keeps repeating over and over."

"Certain patterns of rhythm and melody affect the human nervous system and induce trance states that lead to the internal physiological repetition of the rhythm," Susan said, quoting from *There and Back Again.*

"Yeah?" Pat said.

"That's from Max's book," Ian said. He was sitting in the shadows on a third deck chair. He was trying, Susan thought, to pretend that he had never been dancing. "Max wrote about Trancer music, songs that people can't help dancing to."

"Like that damn song we just heard." Pat made a face. "Trancer music, huh?"

"I thought Max had invented the Trancers and their music," Susan said.

"I thought so, too," Ian said. "But maybe not."

"How did you manage to escape the dance?" Pat said.

"I was out here when it started," Susan said.

"Yeah? What were you doing?"

Susan shrugged and reluctantly explained why she was on the Promenade deck. She had caught a glimpse of Weldon; she had seen a couple of shadow figures. Nothing really. "But I can't help worrying about Ms. Murphy. I hope she's okay."

Pat had a practical solution. "It's easy," she said. "We'll call the ship's switchboard and ask to be connected to her room. If she answers, we'll know she's okay."

Susan agreed.

They said good night to Ian and returned to their stateroom, where Pat called the switchboard.

"I'm sorry," the operator said. "You seem to be calling from stateroom 144 on Calypso deck."

"That's right."

"But that's Pat Murphy's room."

Pat laughed. "Right again. But I want to call the other Pat Murphy. There's another one on board."

"I'm sorry," the operator said. "You must be mistaken. We only have one Pat Murphy on the passenger list."

That night, Susan dreamed of Mary Maxwell. They stood together on the *Odyssey*'s observation deck, looking out over the sundeck. It was a warm, clear night.

Susan looked at Mary. "So who is dreaming now," Susan said. "I think it's me."

"I think you're right," Mary agreed.

"That means you aren't real," Susan said.

"You know, I've always felt most people have a view of reality that's much too confining," Mary said. "I think we'd all do well to listen to the Clampers. Their motto is *Credo Quia Absurdum,* 'I believe because it is absurd.' Quite an appealing notion. You must entertain all the possibilities, however absurd."

Susan shook her head. She knew she was dreaming, but she couldn't help arguing. "You can't do that," Susan protested. "Some possibilities make others impossible."

Mary frowned. "Are you saying that you can't believe in impossible things? I'll bet you do it all the time. You believed that a little girl could survive among the wolves in the Sierras, didn't you? That's really not possible, you know."

Susan thought of *Wild Angel,* then said crossly, "I suppose. But that's fiction. We live in the real world."

Mary blinked at her in mild surprise. "Do we? I live in a world I made up. It's like the monsters that live under the bed. You make them up; you give them power."

"There are real monsters in the world," Susan said, thinking of Alice and the monster who killed her.

"That's true. There are real monsters—but they're few and far between compared to the monsters you invent. It's the imaginary monsters that keep people from living the lives they want to live."

Susan frowned. "Is Weldon an imaginary monster?"

"Hard to say."

"Was he trying to kill Ms. Murphy?"

"Can you kill someone who isn't here?" Mary asked.

Susan shook her head in annoyance. "I don't care whether she exists, I'm worried about her. Weldon said this was a question of who was going to be the Creator. What does that have to do with Ms. Murphy? Or Patrick Murphy or my friend Pat, for that matter. And I'm worried about Max. I think he's in trouble."

"He's working on a new book," Mary said. "Writing is a creative process. It often involves a descent into madness."

Susan shook her head again. "I think there's more to it than that."

"You may be right. You see, there are times when pen names take on a stronger reality than the original name. Consider Mark Twain. You can know his name was really Samuel Clemens, but most people can remember that only with an effort. It's Twain that has the reality. Or Lewis Carroll. He's the fellow we remember, not that stuffy Reverend Dodgson. That Weldon—he's getting more real by the minute."

"What about you?"

Mary shrugged. "I'm not struggling for a place in Max's reality."

"And Weldon is?"

Before Mary could answer, Susan heard a sound—the toilet flushing. She blinked in the darkness as Pat crossed the room, returning to bed. Susan was in her stateroom, in her own bed, still without an explanation.

TWENTY-ONE

Scientist study the movements of particles and predict their paths. But who can predict the shifts and changes of the human heart?

—from *The Twisted Band*
by Max Merriwell

Susan stood on the observation deck as the ship approached the dock. She had woken early after a night of restless dreams. The day was bright and clear and cool, and she had come to the observation deck to watch the ship dock.

They were stopping for a day and a night in the town of Horta on Faial Island. Faial was part of the Azores archipelago, a group of nine islands in the North Atlantic. Susan had read about the Azores in her guidebook. Located 740 miles east of Portugal, the Azores were originally settled by that country and are now a part of Portugal.

From the observation deck, Susan considered the town of Horta. Whitewashed houses clung to the hills rising from the harbor, their red-tiled roofs shining in the sun. A gray horse pulling a cart ambled along the cobblestone street that followed the waterfront. It was still early morning, and she could see shopkeepers opening their shutters, setting out their wares.

The sun was warm on her face, and it looked like it would be a beautiful day. A light breeze tousled her hair. She was looking forward to getting off the ship, wandering through the town. She didn't want to think about Max or Mary or Weldon or quantum physics.

"Good morning."

She glanced in the direction of the voice and saw Tom,

crossing the deck toward her. "Good morning," she said, surprised to see him.

He gestured up at the bridge. "I was up there and I decided I'd better come down and protect you."

She looked up at the bridge. The sun shone on the windows, which reflected the brilliant blue sky. "Protect me from what?"

"From Geoffrey, the ship's navigator."

Susan blinked, startled. "The ship's navigator? Why do I need protection from the ship's navigator?"

"The other night, when you and I were watching that UFO, Geoffrey was up on the bridge." Tom gazed at the town, clearly choosing his words carefully. "Geoffrey is a bit of a ladies' man," he said slowly.

"Yes?" Susan was baffled. She didn't have a clue where this was going.

"Well, Geoffrey was up on the bridge just now, and he suggested that I ask you out to dinner. Well, actually, he said that if I didn't ask you out to dinner, he'd come down here, introduce himself, ask you out himself. I figured that it's my duty as a security officer to protect you from that." Tom shook his head. "You wouldn't want to go out with Geoffrey."

"I don't even know Geoffrey," Susan said. She was having a hard time getting a handle on this.

"Trust me—you don't want to know Geoffrey. Do you have any plans for tonight?" he asked.

Susan shook her head.

"I know a restaurant in a little village, not too far from here. I have the night off, and I thought you might like to get off the ship. This restaurant has the best seafood on the island."

She finally realized that he was asking her out on a date. How strange. She hadn't been on a date with anyone except Harry since college, when she and Harry had started going together. "Seafood," she murmured. She studied his face, then returned his smile. "And you're just asking me out to protect me. As part of your duty as a security officer."

"That's right," he said. "Of course, there are some duties I enjoy more than others."

She nodded slowly. "I guess if it's your job, I have to go along with it."

He nodded. "I suppose you do," he said solemnly.

She glanced up at the bridge. "Shall we wave to Geoffrey?" she suggested.

"I don't think so," Tom said. "I think it would just encourage him. I'll tell him you've been taken into protective custody."

Susan returned to the stateroom where Pat was just waking up. Susan told her friend that she'd be having dinner with Tom that night.

"That's great!" Pat said.

Susan shrugged. "I don't know. I haven't been on a date since before I married Harry. I never liked dating anyway."

"Yeah? Why not?"

"It always made me feel like I was participating in some kind of ritual that had rules I didn't understand. Seemed like everyone understood the rules except me. Getting engaged to Harry was such a relief."

"You make your own rules," Pat told her.

Susan nodded. That sounded like something Mary Maxwell would say.

"Or ask Tom what he thinks the rules are," Pat said. "Tom's a nice guy. You'll go out to dinner. Sounds like he has a lovely romantic evening planned. You'll have a fine time."

Susan hoped she was right.

Late that afternoon, Susan stood on the promenade deck, near where the gangway led down to the dock. It had been a lovely day so far. No sign of Weldon or Mary. No uncontrollable dancing. No wolves. She and Pat had left the ship and wandered around the small town, having lunch in a cafe by the waterfront. They hadn't talked about quantum physics at all.

A breeze carried the aroma of roasting sausage up from the dock below. A man had set up a grill at the end of the dock, and he was doing a fine business selling to the vendors who had come to offer their wares to the tourists.

Vendors selling jewelry, postcards, and souvenir trinkets had set up their stalls on the dock. They called out their wares in Portuguese and English; passengers shouted to each other over the crowd.

"Sam, come here and look at these bracelets," called a woman in a pink-flowered muumuu. "They're such a bargain!"

"Never buy anything at the dock," Tom said from the railing beside Susan. "It's never a bargain."

She turned to look at him. She hadn't seen him since early that morning.

He wasn't in his uniform. He was wearing a Hawaiian shirt patterned in turquoise blue flowers and his eyes looked very blue. He was wearing faded jeans, well-washed and comfortable. If he hadn't spoken before she looked at him, she might not have recognized him.

"You're out of uniform," she said.

"Out of uniform and off duty. At least, I'll be off duty as soon as I'm off the ship. When I'm on board, I'm never really off duty. But tonight, I'm leaving my pager behind." He grinned.

Seeing him in civilian clothes, she felt nervous.

"You're frowning," he said. "Why's that?"

"Just thinking," she said. She hesitated, then said, "I guess this is a date. This may sound silly, but I've never known how to behave on dates. It always seemed to me that there were some kind of rules that I never learned."

He frowned. "Only one rule," he said.

"What's that?"

"Once we're off the ship, we don't talk about the ship any more."

She thought for a moment. "I can manage that."

He spread his hands. "That's the only rule."

She smiled at him. "You look good out of uniform," she said.

She thought she saw an expression of relief flicker across his face. "You ready to go?" he asked.

"Ready when you are."

He led the way to the top of the gangplank, greeting the man who checked her cruise card at the security station. "Hey, Don, how's it going?"

"No problems." Don's eyes lingered on Susan for a moment. Then he smiled. "Have a good time."

Susan had the definite impression that she had been sized up. As they walked down the gangway, she said, "So I suppose Don will be asking you about me later."

Tom shrugged, looking sheepish. "Well, he's already congratulated me on asking you out. I think Geoffrey's been talking. Or maybe Ian." Tom glanced at her. "Sorry. Being on the crew of a cruise ship is kind of like living in a very small town." They reached the end of the gangway. "You ready to stop talking about the ship?" he asked.

"Ready."

"Then come on."

He took her arm and led her through the crowd, waving aside vendors who held out trays of jewelry, handfuls of postcards. He called out to them in Portuguese and headed in the direction that they waved.

"You speak Portuguese?" she called over the noise.

"A little. I speak a little Portuguese, a little French, a little Spanish, a little Italian, a little Greek. Just enough of every language to get myself in trouble around the world." He glanced at her, grinning. He seemed much more relaxed now than he had on the ship. "Just enough to find a cab. Here we are." They had reached the waterfront street. He waved to a battered black Toyota with numbers painted in yellow on the side. The car pulled over.

"Hello, my friend," the driver called through the open window. He was a gray-haired man wearing a cap tipped back on his head at a jaunty angle. His neatly trimmed beard and thin mustache gave him a roguish look. "Where are you going?"

Tom named a village and a restaurant and the driver smiled. "Very good," he said. "There is a festival in the village today."

Tom opened the taxi door for Susan, then slid in beside her. "What sort of festival?"

"Music, dancing, a carnival! It is to celebrate the miracle of Saint Erasmus. Five hundred years ago, he rescued all the fishermen of the village from a terrible storm. So today, the village feasts."

"Saint Erasmus," Tom said. "That's Saint Elmo, the patron saint of sailors."

"I've read about Saint Elmo's fire," Susan said. "But I've never seen it."

"Ah," he said. "I've never read about it. But I've seen it a few times."

She bit her lip, wondering if he was laughing at her. Then she decided that she didn't care. He could tease her if he wanted. "Then we have the perfect balance," she said. "Book learning and real life experience."

The taxi had turned away from the waterfront and was jouncing up a narrow cobblestone street. Through the open windows, Susan could see the whitewashed walls of the houses, so close she could have reached out and touched them. Where the whitewashed walls were chipped, Susan could see black stone.

The driver kept up a running commentary as he drove. "These houses, they are built of black lava rock, cut from the hills. They come from the fire of the volcano. The white—it comes from limestone, which came from the sea. So our houses come from fire and water, the volcano and the sea."

Children playing in the street scattered to the sides as the taxi approached, standing by the houses and staring in the taxi windows at Tom and Susan. When Susan smiled at them, they waved and called to her in Portuguese.

The taxi was approaching the edge of town when Susan

heard goats bleating. The taxi slowed and stopped. A herd of goats filled the cobblestone street. The goatherd, an old man with a crooked stick, shouted at his goats and urged them forward. The animals crowded past the car, peering in the windows with wide yellow eyes.

"It is good luck," the driver shouted over the bleating goats. "Meeting one goat on the road is good luck. Meeting so many—it is the very best luck."

Susan laughed as a goat stuck his head in the window, then leaned back as he stretched out his neck, trying to nibble on her shirt. She bumped into Tom and he put a hand on her shoulder to steady her. He was laughing, too. He reached past her and tapped the goat on the nose. "That's enough luck," he told the goat. The animal looked offended and withdrew. "I think it's even luckier to have a goat eat your clothing," Tom told Susan.

The car lurched, throwing them together, and turned a corner, leaving the goats and the houses behind. Suddenly, the harbor was spread below them. The *Odyssey* was a toy boat, sparkling white against the blue water. The sun was a flattened red disk, bisected by the horizon.

"Look," Susan said. "The sun is setting."

"Maybe we'll see the green flash. I've never seen it, but I've read about it in Bowditch's *American Practical Navigator*. When conditions are just right, the Earth's atmosphere bends the light of the setting sun so that the last bit of light is a brilliant green."

Susan laughed. "I read about it in a Jules Verne story, but I've never seen it either."

The taxi slowed, following a rough, winding road that ran along the top of a ridge. For a moment, they passed behind a clump of trees, and the sun vanished from sight.

"You've been looking for years," Susan said, "and you've never seen it? Are you sure it really exists?"

Tom shrugged. "Nope. Could be that someone with too much imagination made it up. But I'll keep looking anyway."

She smiled at him. "I don't think you're as practical as you pretend," she said.

The road emerged from the trees, and Susan saw the sun again, still lower in the sky, just a fraction of its bright disk above the horizon.

"Almost there," Susan said.

Another clump of trees blocked the view, then the road curved and the sun was visible again, just a sliver of red at the horizon. As Susan watched, the last touch of red disappeared and she saw a brilliant green light, just for a moment.

She turned to look at Tom. "Did you see it?"

He was shaking his head, looking startled. "I guess it does exist."

Susan grinned. Irrationally, she felt that she was somehow responsible for the green flash, as if by talking about it she had helped cause it to appear. As the taxi turned into a valley, she saw a cluster of lights below, a small village in a natural harbor.

The taxi took them to the main square, which was crowded with people and booths. The big stone church that formed one side of the square was decorated with tiny white lights; colored lights festooned the trees and the booths. As they got out of the taxi, Susan could hear music from the far side of the square—guitars and singing. Men in the booths were calling to the people—she couldn't understand the words, but she knew what they were saying. "Come try my game. Come buy my food. Come and spend your money and be happy."

When Susan was a child, the nearby church had held a carnival to raise money each summer. For a week, the church parking lot was filled with rides and cotton candy stands and booths where you threw coins on plates and rings over bottles and spun a wheel to win a giant stuffed dog. Susan had loved that carnival. Each year, that carnival transformed the mundane parking lot into someplace exotic and wonderful, a place where anything could happen.

"The restaurant is over this way," Tom said, taking her arm.

"Oh, let's go to the carnival first," she said. "Come on!"

She gave him no time to disagree. Without hesitation, she led him across the street, heading for the music, the barkers, the booths. Children with sparklers ran beneath the colored lights, calling to each other. The aroma of roasting sausage and barbecue and frying bread filled the air.

Susan stopped at the edge of a crowd that was watching a man demonstrate a set of kitchen knives. The man chattered at an enormous speed as he slashed an aluminum can in half, then used the same knife to cut a ripe tomato into thin slices. "I could swear that the same guy sold knives at the state fair when I was a kid," she told Tom, "except the guy at the state fair had a Brooklyn accent."

They walked past a game of chance where you could bet on a spinning wheel and win a garish clock. They passed a game where young men threw baseballs at targets to win stuffed animals for young women. Susan wondered whether Tom would stop to try to win her a toy. Harry would have done that. Harry would have insisted on winning the biggest stuffed dog, whether she wanted it or not. Susan was relieved when Tom glanced at the toys and kept walking.

A moment later, he stopped at a shooting game. The target was beside a puppet theater where marionettes hung lifeless. When Tom hit the bullseye, the theater lit up and the puppets danced. Tom smiled at Susan. "Better than an ugly toy," he said, and she smiled back.

Susan stopped at another booth, where people tossed coins at a stack of sparkling glassware. If a coin stayed on a plate, the person won that plate. Susan watched as a determined young woman tossed coin after coin, trying to get one to stay on the topmost piece, a spectacular cut-glass platter. Every coin the woman threw bounced off the platter and fell among the other glassware, ringing against the plates and cups as it fell.

"Do you have any coins?" Susan asked Tom. He pulled a handful from his pocket and held them on his flattened palm. He looked amused. He was humoring her.

"These things are impossible to win," he said.

She nodded, taking the coins from his hand and holding them out to the teenager who manned the booth. "Which one?" she asked him, and he pointed to three coins of the right denomination. The woman who had been trying to win the platter had stopped to watch Susan and Tom.

Susan felt good. She felt strong. She felt ridiculously confident. She wasn't sure why. If this was someone's dream, she thought, she would win the platter. If this was a story someone was telling, she would win. It was only right.

She took the three coins the teenager had indicated, and she returned the rest of the money to Tom. "The secret," she told him, "is not to throw it too hard."

He nodded, still smiling.

She tossed the first coin, lofting it high in a gentle arc that carried it to the platter. It hit with a musical "ping" and bounced away.

"A little too high," she said. "It had too much energy when it hit."

Tom nodded again. His eyes were narrowing and she could see that he was wondering how seriously to take all this. The woman who had tried to win the platter was still watching. Another woman came up. The first woman spoke to the second woman in Portuguese, then they both watched.

Susan tossed the second coin, going for a lower arc. It hit the platter and barely bounced, but it had too much forward momentum. It skidded right off the side.

"Too low," Tom said, and she nodded, holding the last coin pinched between her fingers. She faced the platter again, carefully measuring the distance with her eyes. Then she tossed the coin, lofting it high, but just high enough to reach the platter, giving it no more energy than it needed.

The coin hit, bounced, hit the platter again, and stayed.

The women and her friends cheered. Tom clapped her on the back. "You are a woman of startling talents," he said. The teenager who ran the booth stared in amazement as the women gathered around Susan, talking in Portuguese.

The teenager gave Susan the platter, pulling one in a box from beneath the counter. The box was dusty and battered. It had obviously been traveling with the carnival for some time.

Susan opened the box and slid it out, checking to see that the platter was the same as the one on the display. She smiled at the teenager and turned to the woman who had been struggling to win the platter.

"I'd like you to have this," she said, and handed the platter to the woman.

There was much conversation in Portuguese, much laughing and cheering. A translator was found—the woman's son, Susan thought. Speaking very careful, high school English, he thanked Susan for the woman.

Later, in the restaurant, Tom asked Susan how she had become such a master of carnival games.

The restaurant was on the second floor of a building beside the square where the carnival was taking place. Their table was on a balcony that overlooked the open square. The square below them was crowded with people, but Tom and Susan sat above it all—separate, isolated, private.

Susan frowned and looked down at the table, made suddenly self-conscious by Tom's question. Tom had ordered a bottle of red wine, and the waiter had filled Susan's glass. A single candle burned in the center of the table. The curved surface of the full wine glass focused an image of the candle flame on the tablecloth—a shimmering light in the center of the shadow of the glass. Susan studied the flame for a moment, considering what Mary had told her about telling your own story. You sort out the past, rearrange it, give it a bit of a plot. Susan wondered if she'd done that with her memories of childhood.

"Not all games," Susan said slowly. "Just that one. When

I was a kid, our church had a carnival every year and they had a booth like that one. They had a punch bowl that I thought was the most beautiful thing I'd ever seen. It was ceramic and it was painted with fruit and flowers. When I was ten years old, I wasted my whole allowance trying to win it for my mother."

She shook her head. "The next year, a month before the carnival, I took a plate from the kitchen and set it up on a TV tray in the back yard, behind some bushes where my mother couldn't see me practice. It was summer and I had lots of time. So I spent hours practicing."

She pushed her hair back out of her eyes, remembering that long, hot summer. In the first week, she missed the plate most of the time. Then she got to where she could hit the plate, but the coin always bounced out. She learned to toss it gently, so it had just enough energy to get to the plate, and not so much it would bounce out again.

"When the carnival came, I was ready. I took my whole allowance in dimes."

"So what happened?" She had his full attention. The candlelight shone on his face. His eyes were a very dark blue, a trick of the light.

She shrugged. "I won the punchbowl. And I gave it to my mother."

He leaned forward. "That's amazing. That's wonderful. She must have been so proud."

She shrugged again, feeling a tightness in her throat, a slight stinging in her eyes. She stared past him, focusing on the colored lights in the trees. "Not really. She . . . she didn't really like it." She managed a forced smile. "My mother had very good taste. And this punchbowl was the sort of thing only a kid could love. It was garish and bright and tacky. She thanked me politely and put it away in the cupboard and never used it for anything."

He reached out and touched her face, forcing her to look at him, studying her with those intense blue eyes. "Pardon me for saying it, but your mother was an idiot. Who cares if it was tacky? It was beautiful because you won it for her."

She nodded. She did not want to talk. She would cry if she talked too much, and she did not want to cry. It was a special evening, an evening where she was changing the rules, and she did not want to remember the time when the rules were bigger than she was.

"So that's why you won the platter tonight," he said. "You won it for someone who appreciated it, for someone who admired it, for someone who understood."

She nodded again.

"Your mother didn't understand."

His hand was still on her cheek. She leaned her head into his rough palm, glad to feel its warmth against her face.

The waiter came to take their order. Through the double glass doors that connected them to the restaurant, Susan could see a musician strolling from table to table, playing a sort of guitar. Instead of a round hole in the middle of the body, this guitar had two heart-shaped holes.

A moment after the waiter took their order, the musician came to their table and sang to them. All the people in the restaurant were smiling and staring out at the two of them sitting on the balcony. It could have been terribly embarrassing. Susan remembered a time when she and Harry had been vacationing in Mexico and a group of mariachis had serenaded them. She had wanted to crawl under the table.

But this time, sitting at the table on the balcony with Tom, she smiled at the musician, smiled at Tom, smiled back at the other diners. Everyone was so happy, and if they stared it was only because they wanted to share in Susan's happiness.

Tom reached across the table to hold her hand. She liked that—no need to talk, just the warmth of his hand on hers, the music of the guitar, the gravelly voice of the musician. She didn't understand the words of his song, and that was just fine.

The musician finished his song. Tom tipped him, and he strolled away. Susan sipped her wine and relaxed. Their dinner came, a wonderful seafood stew seasoned with chili. "The fire and the sea," she said to Tom, thinking of the taxi driver's description of the houses. "A little of both."

In the street below them, people were gathering. "It is the chamarrita," the waiter told them. "A traditional dance."

To the music of guitars, the dance began. The men were in one line and the women in another, but somehow, after dancing in an intricate pattern, they had rearranged themselves into laughing couples.

She told Tom—a little drunkenly, perhaps, after two glasses of wine—that she wished life were as easy as that. Just dance around and end up with the right partner.

After dessert, after a glass of port so sweet and smooth that it tasted like another dessert, it was time to go. Tom put his arm around her as they walked down the stairs to the street. He flagged down a taxi and they headed back for the ship.

From the top of the hill, they looked down on the harbor. The *Odyssey* sparkled against the water of the harbor, its lights bright against the darkness. Tom squeezed her hand— he'd been holding it since they left the restaurant.

"How beautiful," she said, looking down at the ship.

"Yes," he agreed, but when she glanced at him she discovered that he was looking at her, not at the ship.

Such a strange evening, she thought. She felt that she was somehow playing hooky, evading some responsibility. She had always been a very good girl, playing by the rules. But tonight, something had shifted.

"When we get back to the ship, will you be back on duty?" she asked.

"Not right away," he said slowly. He hesitated, watching her face. "I have a bottle of brandy in my cabin. Would you like to join me for a nightcap?"

Susan smiled. Was she the sort of woman who would go to a sailor's cabin on the first date? Apparently so. It was not the sort of thing she would ordinarily have done. But it was not an ordinary night. It was not an ordinary cruise. This was not an ordinary place. And she was beginning to believe that she was not an ordinary person.

"That sounds splendid," she said.

TWENTY-TWO

There are many kinds of pirates in the galaxy. There are businesslike pirates who are motivated by profit. There are sadistic pirates who crave power. And there are swashbuckling pirates who seek adventure. It is these last that capture the heart of the romantic. They are a wild, unpredictable, and ultimately compelling crew.

—from *The Twisted Band*
by Max Merriwell

Susan woke up early, feeling warm and relaxed. Tom was still sleeping, his arms around her. Tom's bed was barely big enough for two, but they had managed despite that. Susan had slept soundly.

A beeping sound woke her. Tom stirred in bed, flinging out an arm to silence the alarm. Four A.M., still dark. He had warned her that he'd have to be up early. They were leaving Faial that morning.

He clicked on the bedside light, and she blinked at the room. Their brandy glasses were still on the table in the corner. On the wall above the table were a few photos: Tom's brothers, his mother, his father.

She looked back at Tom. He was watching her. "Good morning," he said. "Trying to figure out what you're doing here?"

"I thought that was pretty clear last night," she said, and then bit her lip, wondering if she had been a little too bold.

He laughed. "You're right. It was."

She sat up in bed. It had all been so easy last night. Now she felt very awkward. Having thrown off the covers, she was aware of her nakedness—her clothes were tossed over one of the chairs.

"I know you have to work this morning," she said. "You warned me about that last night."

"I do," he said. "We sail in four hours. Lots to do."

"Well, I'd better be going," she said, reaching for her clothes.

He sat up and put his arms around her, stopping her before she could get out of bed. "Did I tell you that you are a woman of startling talents?" he asked.

She glanced at him. "You told me that last night, when I won the platter."

"I didn't know the half of it then," he said, grinning.

Tom walked her to her stateroom. He insisted on it, even though she assured him that she could find the way. The corridors were empty except for a lone steward bringing coffee up to the bridge. Tom greeted him. "Good morning, Osvaldo."

Susan gave Osvaldo a big smile. She knew that she looked like a woman who had just crawled out of her lover's bed. In movie love stories, the woman's hair was always ever so charmingly tousled the morning after, and she chose to imagine that her hair was tousled in just that way. She knew that Ian and Geoffrey and anyone else who was interested in Tom's love life would know how his date with her had turned out.

She didn't care. That startled her. She didn't care what anyone thought; she didn't care that her love life was a matter for public gossip. Her mother would be appalled. But she didn't care.

Tom kissed her good-bye at her stateroom door. He wished her a happy Halloween and warned her that he'd be busy that night. "I figure if Clampers are normally out of control, Clampers in costume will be worse," he said.

She slipped inside quietly, so as not to wake Pat. She undressed quietly and got into her bed, still feeling warm and sleepy.

———

Ian poured Max a cup of coffee and offered him a biscotti from the tray Osvaldo had brought that morning. While Max sipped his coffee and nibbled the biscotti, Ian considered the note Max had received.

Tom wasn't in the office yet. From what Ian had heard, Tom had had a fine night. Osvaldo had reported spotting him in the corridor with Susan very early in the morning. They both, according to the Osvaldo, had looked very happy.

"It was under my door, just like the others," Max said. "I thought I'd see what you and Tom thought of it."

He looked weary, Ian thought. As if he hadn't slept well.

Ian considered the note. A hexagram, of course: a stack of six lines, alternating broken and unbroken lines with a solid line at the top. Beneath it, someone had written, in a looping, exuberant handwriting: "Disorder prevails. One must move warily, like an old fox walking over ice."

"The lower trigram is K'an," Max muttered. "K'an, the abysmal. Its image is water. The upper trigram is Li, the clinging. Its image is flame. The fire and the water meet. The hexagram indicates a time of disorder and transition."

Ian called up the relevant page from the *Book of Changes* on his computer. He scanned the text quickly. "The hexagram indicates a time of transition," he said, "but it's a hopeful sort of transition. The Book compares it to spring, which leads out of winter's stagnation to the fruitfulness of summer."

"Yes, but hopeful for whom?" Max asked, frowning.

Ian read from the screen. " 'When fire, which by nature flames upward, is above, and water, which flows downward, is below, their effects take opposite directions and remain unrelated . . . We must first investigate the nature of the forces in question and ascertain their proper place. If we can bring these forces to bear in the right place, they will have the desired effect, and completion will be achieved. But in order to handle external forces properly, we must above all arrive at the correct standpoint ourselves, for only from this vantage can we work correctly.' "

Max nodded vaguely.

Ian went on reading. " ' . . . One must engage the energies of able helpers and in this fellowship take the decisive step. . . . Then completion will become possible.' "

Max nodded again, frowning. "I suppose that makes some sense," he murmured. Then he glanced at the clock. "Almost time for workshop," he said. "I'd best be going."

He wandered out the door, taking a biscotti with him and leaving crumbs behind.

Susan woke to the sound of the door to the corridor closing. Pat stood by the door, holding a tray, on which there was a pot of coffee and a plate of sweet rolls. Pat smiled when she saw that Susan's eyes were open. "Would you like some breakfast?" Pat asked. "Seems like you need to keep your strength up."

Susan grinned and stretched, the memory of the night before returning to her. "I did manage to work up an appetite," she said.

Pat sat at the foot of the bed and set the tray beside Susan. She poured coffee and Susan sat up in bed and helped herself to a sweet roll. Outside the sliding glass doors, the sky was overcast. Susan could see the island of Faial, but the ship was moving, leaving the harbor and heading back out to sea.

"So what's the story?" Pat asked. Her tone was light, but she was studying Susan's face, obviously concerned about her friend's feelings.

Susan hesitated, thinking about all that had happened the night before. She was feeling confident, happy, sure of herself. "We drove through the village and met a herd of goats in the street," she began. "The taxi driver told us that was a good omen. He was right."

She told Pat about the taxi ride, about the green flash, about the carnival, about the dinner. She got to the part where they were returning to the ship, and she said, "Then one thing led to another."

"That's the part that I like," Pat said. "The part where one thing leads to another. And I assume the other thing led to his cabin."

"Well, yes, it did." Susan grinned.

Pat leaned back in her chair, studying Susan's face. "Wow. You're not even blushing. You head off into the wilds with this guy and you come back a changed woman. That's amazing."

Susan laughed. She was startled by her own audacity, and pleased that Pat recognized it.

"So is he the kind with a girl in every port?"

Susan shrugged. "I don't think so. Can't say for sure."

Pat stared at her, astonished and delighted. "This is so out of character," she said. "I love it. So what are you going to do next? Are you going to run off to sea and become a pirate? Dance on the table at dinner? You're a changed woman."

Susan thought for a moment. "The pirate option sounds pretty good," she said. "I'm not much of a dancer."

"What about Tom? You think he's interested in being a pirate?"

Susan helped herself to another sweet roll, considering the question. "I don't know what Tom thinks." She poured herself more coffee. "And this may sound callous, but I don't really care."

"You don't care?" Pat was staring at her in amazement. "Wait a second. You always care. When you were with Harry, you seemed to care more about what he thought than you did about what you thought."

Susan laughed. "Uncharted waters," she said. "Unexplored territory. Maybe I'm really a loose woman at heart and I'm just realizing it now."

Pat smiled. "Not loose, but looser. I think it's great. Let me know if you need a first mate on your pirate ship."

"You think I'll be captain?"

"The way you're heading, I wouldn't be surprised."

———

The workshop was smaller that day. The knitting lady and the surly teenager hadn't shown up. Cindy blamed the rough weather.

The sky was overcast and the movement of the ship had changed. Susan couldn't describe the new movement as rocking—that was too definitive a word to describe such a subtle motion. This was a slow, almost imperceptible shifting. She found herself leaning ever so slightly in her seat, compensating for a tilt in the floor. Then she realized that she was leaning too far. Gradually, she shifted back to an upright position. Then, moments later, she found herself leaning in the other direction.

All this took place over the space of several seconds, slow enough that she could almost ignore it—except for the moments when the direction shifted and she almost overbalanced. Such strange sensation. It was a strange, dreamy, vertiginous sensation. It made her a little dizzy, a little disoriented.

"Today," Max said. "we are going to explore the power of the imagination." Max didn't seem to mind—or even to notice—that his class was dwindling.

"To write a story that others will believe, you have to believe in it yourself." Max cocked his head and considered the group around the table. It seemed to Susan that his gaze lingered on her. "You have to believe in your story, no matter how unbelievable it may be. And your belief will bring your story to life."

Alberta raised her hand, looking skeptical. "How can you believe in something that you know you made up?" she asked. "That doesn't make any sense."

"Oh, it's even more difficult than that," Max said. "Much more difficult. I'd like you to believe in things that you made up that most people think are quite impossible. As for how—well, believing in impossible things takes practice."

Susan stared at him, remembering what Mary Maxwell had said in her dream. "Are you saying that you can't believe in impossible things?" Mary had said. "Maybe you just need a little practice."

"To believe in something that's quite impossible, you have to consider it in great detail," Max was saying. "You must be very specific. The more unbelievable a situation, the more carefully you have to describe it. If you are writing a story that takes place on a sunny summer day and the sky is blue, that's easy. But if you are picnicking on Mars and the sky is pink, you need to be more specific in your description. Exactly what shade of pink do you mean—the pink of bubble gum? The pink of a freshly cut watermelon? Or the faintest flush of pink, like the Earth sky at sunrise?

"To make a story believable, you must create all the details in your imagination. The reality of your story depends on the power of your imagination." Max gazed around the table. "I want you to think of something unbelievable and make it real. A situation, an event, an object."

"What kind of event?" Alberta asked.

Max regarded her steadily. "Something that you don't believe in," he said mildly. "I can't tell you what it should be, since I don't know what you believe in."

"Like what?" she persisted.

Max shrugged. "Like a Scrabble tournament at which someone beats you and Bill. Whatever you like, as long as you find it difficult to believe." He looked around, but no one else had any questions. "Sit back in your chair," he said. "Close your eyes and think of something unbelievable. If it helps, start by thinking of a familiar place where this unbelievable thing could happen."

Susan closed her eyes obediently, wondering what she should imagine. Sleeping with Tom seemed unbelievable, but she didn't want to write about that. So she started with a place. She imagined standing on the observation deck, looking down on the sundeck at the bow of the *Odyssey*. What could happen there? She looked into the distance and saw a golden light on the horizon. A UFO, she thought. A flying saucer could land.

"Before you turn your attention to the unbelievable thing,

consider the details of the environment surrounding it," Max continued.

Susan thought about the maze of windscreens. The saucer is landing at night, she thought, so the deck chairs had been put away. It was, she thought, a dark and stormy night—that's when unbelievable things always happened in stories. Rain pounded on the deck. The ocean was rough. She imagined a wave splashing up against the side of the ship, sending an arc of spray over the railing. Lightning flickered in the sky, and thunder rumbled overhead. The ship's engines were humming, laboring to push the ship through the rough seas.

"Now think about the unbelievable thing," Max said. "See it in your imagination."

Susan imagined a glimmering golden light, blinking in the distance. Just a pinprick of light at first, like a star gleaming through the clouds. It grew larger—to the size of a grape, the size of her fist. Still it came closer—a glowing golden saucer, hovering over the sundeck. The saucer was shaped like a Frisbee—a little thicker in the middle than the flying toy, but generally Frisbee-shaped. It was about twenty feet across.

"Think about details now," Max said. "You've got an image of this thing in your mind. Now look at that image carefully."

There was a band of paler gold light around the saucer's center line. Staring at that band, she realized that the saucer was spinning—she could hear a high-pitched humming as it spun. Portholes, set on the saucer's center line, blurred in her vision as the saucer spun, creating the band of pale gold.

"Have you got it?" Max said. "Keep picturing your impossible thing for a moment, to get it settled in your mind."

In Susan's mind, the saucer's spinning slowed, then stopped, as the great ship came down, crushing three windscreens beneath it. The glass shattered, the metal frames crumpled.

The saucer's glowing form reflected in the remaining

windscreens. Its hum blended with the hum of the ship's engines.

"Open your eyes," Max said.

Susan blinked at him.

"Now open your notebook," he said. "Write down what you imagined," Max said.

Susan opened her notebook to a blank page and uncapped her pen, eager to begin.

The workshop ended at 11:30. By the time they left the library, the waves were slapping the sides of the ship with increased vigor.

Tom came up behind Susan and Pat as they stepped onto the promenade deck. "Thought I might catch you and warn you," he said. "The weather satellite says we're going to be in for some heavy weather. Careful what you have for lunch, if you're likely to get seasick."

Susan shrugged. "I don't know. I haven't been sick so far."

He took her hand as he walked beside her. It felt natural to have him there. "How do you feel about carnival rides—the ones that spin you around and around and upside down?"

"I don't mind them too much."

"You'll probably be all right then."

"We're heading for lunch now," Pat said sweetly. "Want to join us?"

Tom shook his head. "I'm on duty. Too much to do. Just wanted to say hi."

He headed off then, smiling what Pat called a "shit-eating grin."

"You made that boy very happy," Pat told Susan.

TWENTY-THREE

A cop once told me that there were only three reasons anyone did anything: money, sex, or power. I told him he was making it too complicated. When you got down to the core of things, there was only one reason: power.

—from *Tell Me No Lies*
by Weldon Merrimax

All morning long, other officers and members of the crew winked at Tom and nudged him in the ribs, grinning knowingly. Osvaldo had talked to someone and that person had talked to someone else and everyone was enormously entertained. When met with a grin or a wink, Tom just grinned back.

When Geoffrey asked Tom about his evening, he just said, "Gentlemen don't kiss and tell." Then he had to defend his status as a gentleman, which Geoffrey was inclined to dispute, but that was all right. Better spend his time defending his own credentials than deflecting questions about Susan.

The way the evening had progressed had taken him a bit by surprise. He was happy, no question of that, but he felt a little off balance. He was stunned by his good fortune, and he was wondering what might happen next.

The *Odyssey*'s departure from Faial went smoothly. No problems with port officials. They left on time and all was well.

He intercepted Susan and Pat on their way out of Max's class, then he headed back to his office to fill out all the company paperwork associated with departure from a foreign port. When he stepped in the door, Ian looked up from his computer and greeted Tom cheerily.

Tom sat down at his desk and tipped his chair back, studying Ian. "I assume your spies have filled you in," he said.

Ian grinned. "Absolutely. You'll be pleased to know that Susan and Pat ate a hearty breakfast, polishing off an entire tray of sweet rolls. By all reports, the young lady appeared to be quite cheerful. No buyer's remorse. No second thoughts."

Tom nodded, smiling. "Your spies are very efficient. But I already know that. I saw her on my way up here."

After lunch with Pat, Susan went to the library for story hour. Cindy was looking pale and grim-faced. The ship's motion was getting to her. She was grateful to see Susan, glad that she was willing to read to the gathered witches, cowboys, and monsters, the kids having already donned their Halloween costumes.

Susan read the next few chapters, in which Bailey dove down another wormhole and battled the enormous, metal-eating spiders that lived in the Great Rift Cloud. Then he and his friends were captured by pirates.

The story was exciting, but it was tough to keep the kids' attention. The ship was rolling. Every now and again, a wave struck the side of the ship with a hollow boom. Once, right after this sound, spray splashed against the library window, having cleared the railing and crossed the width of the promenade.

It started raining, a fierce downpour that rattled the windows. The ship's rolling turned to pitching, as the ship met the long swells head on. She rode up on the waves and slammed down again.

At about that time, Tom was attending a meeting of the ship's officers. Geoffrey was explaining that the ship had changed course in an attempt to avoid the worst of the storm, but they had not managed to dodge the bad weather altogether.

Gene Culver described Halloween plans. According to Company Policy, cruise activities were not to be canceled on account of weather. No matter that the tiles were sliding off the board, Scrabble would be played in the games room at four o'clock. Storm or no storm, there would be a big Halloween party in Penelope's. There would also be dances and other activities in the ship's other bars and restaurants.

Tom commented that he would be increasing security during the evening hours. He expected trouble, but the security staff would be prepared for it.

After story hour, Susan returned to the stateroom to meet Pat, who had gone to a workshop to make a Halloween costume. She had promised to bring some extra costume supplies back for Susan.

Susan stood at the balcony door for a moment, then slid open the door and stepped out onto the balcony. The wind was cold and it carried drops of water—spray or rain, Susan wasn't sure which.

The sky was dark gray overhead, darkening to black at the horizon. A great wave slapped the side of the ship, sending up a fountain of water. Susan retreated into the stateroom, just as Pat came through the door, clutching a shopping bag. "Hey," she said a little breathlessly. "I got all kinds of stuff. Hardly anyone was there. But I ran into your pal."

"My pal?" Susan asked.

"Weldon Merrimax." Pat upended the bag, scattering bandannas and patches and pirate hats and plastic daggers on the bed.

"You met Weldon?" Susan stared at Pat, shocked. "Where? Did you call Tom?"

Pat shook her head. She was picking through the costume stuff. "He was at the costume workshop."

"Weldon Merrimax was at the costume workshop?" Su-

san frowned, struggling to picture Weldon Merrimax con-
structing a Halloween costume. She couldn't quite manage
it.

"I didn't know he was Weldon Merrimax when I started
talking to him," Pat said. "I thought he was kind of interesting. Then he introduced himself. He has the most intense
eyes. Really sexy."

Susan stared at her friend. "What are you talking about?"
Susan said. "He's either crazy or dangerous."

Pat shrugged, still rummaging through the costume supplies. "Or a very clever joker. I asked him about that business about Patrick Murphy. He said it was just a
misunderstanding." She looked up from the costumes.
"Take it easy, Susan. All I did was talk with him."

"What did you talk about?"

Pat shrugged. "Halloween costumes, quantum mechanics, poker—the usual kind of thing. You're taking this too
seriously. Nothing happened."

"Why didn't you call Tom?"

"I figured Weldon would be gone by the time security
got there. That's what's happened every time you've called
Tom. Seemed like time to try another approach."

Pat picked a pirate hat and a dagger off the bed and held
them out to Susan like a peace offering. "I brought you
stuff for a pirate costume," she said. "You'll look great as
a pirate."

Confused and alarmed, Susan allowed Pat to dress her
as a pirate, placing the hat on her head, tying a red ban-
danna around her neck.

"I've got a hoop earring that will look great with that,"
Pat said.

"Aren't you worried about Weldon at all?" Susan asked
her.

Pat sat on the bed, studying Susan. "Doesn't seem necessary to me," she said. "After all, he hasn't really done
anything except leave notes for Max, play poker, and make
a little trouble. And I've never been one to avoid trouble."

Susan shook her head.

"He says he just wants to talk to Max," Pat said.

"Max doesn't want to talk to him," Susan said. "And I don't trust him."

Pat shrugged again. "He doesn't seem that bad to me. But then, I've had more experience with bad boys than you have."

TWENTY-FOUR

My hands ache when the weather is set to change. When I move, I feel a grating pain, as if there's sand in the joints. An old, familiar pain, it reminds me to be careful. Trust no one. Be ready to hurt them before they can hurt you. Because you know that they will. Just as sure as the sun will rise.

—from Tell Me No Lies
by Weldon Merrimax

At dinner that night, there was no sign of Alberta, Bill, Charles, or Lily. Rough weather and seasickness had laid low all but the most stalwart travelers. Tom had managed to arrange his schedule so that he could attend dinner, knowing that he wouldn't be able to spend any time with Susan that evening.

Pat had brought a bag of pirate paraphernalia. Tom declined her costume suggestions, saying his uniform was costume enough. But she convinced Max and Ian to accept a few accessories.

She placed a three-cornered pirate captain's hat on Max's head. He made a gentle, world-weary sort of pirate, with tired blue eyes and a wry twist to his mouth.

Ian wore a black eye patch and a kerchief. He declined both dagger and sword, claiming to be a conscientious objector in the pirate wars. "Besides," he said, "I'd probably just stab myself."

Susan returned Tom's smile, but he thought she looked a little worried. Buyer's remorse, Tom wondered, remembering Ian's phrase. But when he sat down beside her, she took his hand under that table, so that didn't seem to be it. Maybe just concerned about the storm.

The half-deserted restaurant was decorated for Hallow-

een, with orange and black paper streamers. In honor of
the holiday, Antonio had foregone the usual fruit sculpture.
Instead, he had sculpted a jack-o'-lantern from ice. A votive
candle burned in the center of the ice sculpture. Light from
its flame cast broken, flickering patterns on the bottles of
wine that surrounded it.

While Pat and Ian were exchanging pirate phrases ("Keel
haul the rascal!" "Har!" "Avast!" and the like), Tom talked
with Susan. "I'll be on duty until late tonight," he said.
"Unless all the Clampers decide to go to bed early."

Susan nodded, looking preoccupied. "Pat and I are going
to the party at Penelope's," she said. "I think Max and Ian
will be joining us."

Tom nodded. "I suppose there'll be some drunken
Clampers there." He grinned at her. "I imagine I'll have to
stop by and keep order."

"Har!" Pat interrupted. "The hell with the drunken
Clampers, matey. There'll be drunken pirates there."

"Then I'll definitely have to stop by and arrest any troublemakers," he said. He grinned at Susan and she smiled
back, but her smile seemed uncertain.

Susan hesitated in the doorway to Penelope's. The big room
was hot and crowded. The Clampers were there in force.
Many of them were dressed as pirates and gleefully behav-
ing in character, standing at the bar and demanding grog.
The pirates had patched eyes and peg legs and hooks for
hands. At a quick glance, Susan guessed there wasn't a
whole man among them.

Four men on steel drums were playing a lively Calypso
tune. Susan could barely hear them over the Clampers.

She lost Pat and Ian in the crowd by the bar. After the
third time a Clamper hailed her with a cheerful cry of
"Avast, you saucy wench!" she decided that she might as
well go back to the stateroom. It wasn't a good night for a
party, Susan thought. She was worried about Max—who
had declined to join them at Penelope's, saying he wasn't

in the mood for a party. She was annoyed with Pat for breezily dismissing her worries about Weldon. The party might be fun if Tom were there, but even if he stopped by, it would only be for a few minutes. She would have liked to talk with him—but he was working. She would have liked to go for a walk outside, but rain was pounding the deck and rattling the windows.

She was heading for the door when the steel drum music changed to a hauntingly familiar tune with an insistent and repetitious beat. Against her will, Susan found herself focusing on the music. Her mind filled in the words:

> Sunbeams
> Moonbeams
> Nothing is the way it
> seems
> Your dreams,
> My schemes,
> Dancing through the night.

She put her hands over her ears and pushed toward the door, hoping to escape before it was too late. But the crowd blocked the way and she could hear the music through her hands. A dozen Clampers had formed a conga line. They were singing loudly.

> One chance
> to dance
> Don't leave it to
> circumstance.
> A trance,
> A dance,
> Dreaming through the night.

Even as Susan tried to flee, she could feel her body moving to the rhythm. The conga line snaked out into the rain, passing her. The last person in the line, a smiling Clamper, beckoned her to join them.

The trouble started early for Tom. Tom's staff was occupied with drunken pirates and monsters and ghosts and goblins partying in the corridors and generally raising a ruckus. Tom had been heading to Penelope's when he found three drunken Clampers in a Jacuzzi. They were fully clothed and they were singing. "What Shall We Do With the Drunken Sailor?" improvising new verses, and acting them out.

"Dunk him in the hot tub 'til he's sober—early in the morning!" The Clamper who had been designated the drunken sailor seemed to be in danger of drowning when Tom stepped in.

Tom was explaining politely that the Jacuzzis were closed which was why the heat was turned off and the water was cold. He was explaining that it was dangerous to be on deck during a lightning storm, which is why the area had been roped off. He was helping the men out of the water, when he heard a distant chorus of drunken voices singing the tune that had started all the trouble a few nights back.

"Hey, it's that song again," one of the drunks said, and started to sing along. "Your dreams, my schemes, dancing through the night."

Tom stepped away from the man and radioed the bridge immediately. "Three long blasts on the horn," he said. "Right away."

The officer on watch started to argue. "It's kind of late for that, Tom, isn't it? Passengers are sleeping . . ."

"It's that damn song again," Tom said. "Who knows how long it's been going on. Sound the horn before the bridge is overrun by drunken Clampers."

They sounded the horn.

When the ship's horn blasted, cutting through the Trancer tune, Susan found herself standing on Cyclops' Lookout, surrounded by other dancers. She was being pelted by rain. Her clothes and hair were already soaked, but she wasn't cold—dancing had kept her warm.

She pushed her hair off her forehead and looked around, wondering whether Pat and Ian had been caught by the conga line. The wind sang in the lines over her head with a high whine, just at the edge of her hearing range. The sound set her nerves on edge. Lightning flickered, illuminating the sky for an instant. Thunder rumbled and the rain fell harder.

Around her, the Clampers were shouting. "Where's the bar?"

"Hey, I think we should get out of the rain."

"Look—some lunatics are on the sundeck. I thought that was closed off."

With a sudden feeling of dread, Susan stepped to the railing and looked down at the sundeck. In the glow of the bow lights, she could see the maze of glass windscreens. Beyond the screens, at the very bow of the ship, she saw her friend Pat, face pale, hair a brilliant blue even in the dim light. Pat's back was to the railing, and a man stood in front of her. Susan recognized him: Weldon Merrimax.

Susan gripped the railing, staring down at the pair, terrified for her friend. "Pat!" Susan shouted, but the thunder rumbled, drowning out her voice. As she watched, Weldon stepped forward, reaching out to grab Pat.

Pat braced herself on the railing and kicked at Weldon's groin, but he turned and Pat's foot did not connect with its intended target.

"Never kick for the balls," said a quiet voice beside Susan. "Men protect against that. Go for the knee instead. A much better target."

Susan stared at Mary, who leaned on the railing beside her. "We have to help her," Susan said. "We have to . . ." She looked down at the sundeck just in time to see Weldon strike her friend in the face with the back of his hand, knocking her to the deck. Susan gasped, lifting her hand to touch her own face in an unconscious gesture of sympathetic pain.

"Help!" she shouted, but no one heard her. She looked around, frantic to find someone who could save Pat. She and Mary were alone by the railing. She could see crowds of passengers behind her, all intent on getting out of the rain, on getting back to the bar. Clampers blocked the narrow walkways that led around Penelope's. There was no way to reach the companionways that connected the observation deck to the sundeck.

"Help is already on the way," Mary said quietly.

Glancing down again, Susan saw Max, stepping around one of the windscreens. The wind tousled his gray hair and inflated his tweed sports coat, puffing out the sleeves and making the coattails flap. The pounding rain splashed when it hit the deck, sending sparkling drops arcing as high as Max's knees.

In a flash of lightning, Susan saw Max's reflection in the windscreens around him—a dozen versions of Max, all walking forward with grim determination. On the bow ahead of him, Pat had struggled to her feet. Weldon had a grip on her shoulder and was pushing her back against the railing.

Then the lights went out.

When Tom got the call on his radio, he was at the stern of the ship on the recreation deck, dealing with the group of wet and shivering Clampers that he had extracted from the Jacuzzi. Bridge staff was calling to alert Tom: three people were on the sundeck, an area that had been closed to passengers since that afternoon, when the waves were at their worst. A high wave might still wash over the deck, carrying the fools with it.

Tom said he'd be right there. He pointed the Clampers toward the elevator and headed for the sundeck. Then the situation got worse.

Something happened down in engineering—something

bad. At the time, Tom didn't know just what had happened or how or why. All he knew was that alarms were sounding all over the ship; screaming sirens and ringing alarm bells drowned out the music and laughter.

The lights went out. The emergency generators came on, and the lights flickered for a moment. Then the generators died too, and the lights died with them.

Tom snatched the flashlight from his belt and headed for the bow of the ship.

In the sudden darkness, Susan stared in the direction of the bow, helpless. The railing was cold beneath her hand, a solid object to which she could cling in a dark and uncertain world. The ship shuddered beneath her feet and she heard a hollow booming as a wave struck the side of the ship. What was happening out there?

Lightning flashed, a brilliant bolt followed by an explosion of thunder. In the flash of dazzling blue-white light, Susan saw that Weldon had turned away from Pat to face Max. Susan saw the two men only for an instant in the lightning flash, but the image lingered in her vision after the darkness returned. Max's fists were clenched. Through fogged and rain-spattered glasses, Max glared at Weldon. He looked ridiculous, Susan thought—a short, gray-haired, pudgy man facing a thug. He looked absurdly brave, ridiculously courageous. Thunder rolled overhead, a deafening rumble.

"Max doesn't have a chance," Susan said. "It's impossible. If only there were some way to help him. If only . . ."

"Impossible?" Mary said. "Not at all. There are always possibilities."

Again the lightning struck—a series of bolts this time, illuminating the deck with a flickering light. Susan saw movement among the windscreens. Wolves. Sarah's pack of wolves. Their wet fur glistened as they ran toward the bow, circling around Max to attack Weldon from both sides. In the instant before the light died, Susan saw the wolves spring toward Weldon. Weldon grabbed Pat and threw her toward the animals, stepping away so that his back was against the railing.

"Possibilities," Mary said. "So many possibilities. All occupying the same space and time. As quick as lightning, as fleeting as a thought, as powerful as imagination."

Susan strained her eyes in the darkness, desperate to know what was happening. She could hear the hammering of the rain on the deck around her, the crashing of the waves, the rumble of the thunder. She was cold, so cold. The rain had soaked through her clothes and she was shivering.

"There are other possibilities," Mary was musing. "Maybe an alien abduction."

Through the downpour, Susan saw a distant light in the sky. Not the blue-white brilliance of lightning, but a warm golden glow. Just a pinprick of light at first, like a star gleaming through the clouds.

She had imagined this, she thought. The light grew larger—to the size of a grape, the size of her fist. Still it came closer—a glowing golden saucer, spinning over the sundeck. She could hear a high-pitched humming sound.

Susan could see Max now, his face bathed in the golden light of the saucer. Though he was still short and still pudgy, still wet and windblown, he did not look quite so ridiculous now. He looked like a man who knew what he was doing. He was smiling, his arms open as if to greet a friend as the saucer came in for a landing. The wolves sat at his feet, gazing up at the glowing saucer.

"Nice saucer," Mary said.

Susan stared at the saucer as it came down, crushing three wind- screens beneath it. The glass shattered, the metal frames crumpled.

The saucer rested on the deck, still humming. For a moment, nothing happened. Susan hadn't imagined anything more. She tried to think of how this alien invasion could help her friends.

Pat lay on the deck where Weldon had thrown her. She

had lifted herself up on one elbow and was struggling to her feet. Weldon stood at the railing, just a few feet away.

"What's next?" Mary asked.

Weldon was moving again. In the golden light, Susan saw him step toward Pat. Her friend, who had always seemed so strong, now looked small. Susan watched, frozen in horror. What was next? She didn't know.

A wave struck the side of the ship, sending up an arc of water that washed across the deck, drenching Weldon. Pat was standing now. She wasn't looking at Weldon anymore; she wasn't watching the golden saucer. She was looking past Weldon, looking over his shoulder out into the darkness where the ocean waves surged.

As Weldon stepped forward, a great tentacle—as thick around as a strong man's leg—reached over the side of the ship and wrapped itself around the railing. Then another tentacle, a great suckered rope of flesh, wound itself around the post that supported the railing. And then a third tentacle reached high over the railing and wrapped itself around Weldon's waist.

Susan couldn't hear Weldon over the hum of the saucer and the crash of thunder, but she saw his eyes widen in terror and his mouth open in a scream. The tentacle dragged him to the railing.

Weldon grabbed the railing. For a moment, he clung there—his great, broken hands locked around the railing in a desperate grip. Then with a mighty tug, the tentacle wrenched him free and hoisted him over the railing. He disappeared from view.

"Lovely," Mary said, clapping her hands together. "That was a possibility that hadn't occurred to me."

Susan stared toward the bow. The saucer was taking off again, leaving Max and Pat, alone in the rain. "We've won!" she said.

"Oh, but it isn't about winning and losing," Mary said mildly. "It's about possibilities."

Susan paid no attention. "Weldon's gone. Pat and Max are safe." She looked toward Penelope's. The walkways were empty now; everyone had retreated indoors. "I've got to get down there." She ran for the nearest companionway, not waiting for Mary to reply.

Susan yanked the heavy metal door open. It was dark in the service companionway. She fumbled in her pocket and found her penlight. It cast its beam on the painted metal walls—just enough light to show the way. She stepped inside, letting the door swing closed behind her, muffling the pounding of the rain and the rumble of the thunder. She headed down the stairs, hurrying to join Pat and Max.

Weldon was gone, but Pat and Max had to get in out of the rain. They were cold; they were wet. Pat was hurt. She had to help them.

Susan was halfway down to the next landing when she heard another sound, the ominous scrape of metal on metal. The stairs turned just ahead, and the sound came from around the corner. She stopped where she was. She could hear her own breathing, the soft dripping of water from her clothes. Then she heard another sound, the rattle of metal claws on the stairs. Her breath caught in her throat. The monster in the dark, she thought.

She could imagine the monster quite clearly now. Its body was the Rattler's, a construction of discarded parts imperfectly joined, flesh and metal meeting in an unnatural union. Its mind was the broken mind of a serial killer. It hunted for women who were alone and unprotected. It wanted to take her apart.

It wasn't supposed to happen like this. Weldon was gone. Max and Pat had beaten him. She should be safe now. This wasn't fair.

The air stank of rotting flesh. She heard the rasp of a knife scraping against a sharpening steel; she heard harsh, irregular breathing.

"Is someone there?" she called, trying to keep her voice steady.

"Where do you think you're going?" a hoarse voice

whispered in the darkness. "You can't go there."

She gripped the metal banister. The companionway had felt warm when she stepped into it, but she was shivering now. She had to keep going. "I am going to help my friends," she said, but her voice was weak.

"You can't go there," the voice in the darkness repeated. "You can't do that."

She heard a creaking and a rattling as the monster shifted its position. It was, she thought, on the stairs directly below her. She could not keep going down.

She thought of Pat, slumped against the railing. She thought of Max, wet and shivering in the rain. She had to help them. "I am going to help my friends," she repeated. Her voice was stronger.

"You can't go," said the monster. "Bad things will happen to you. I'll take you apart. I'll cut you into pieces."

Bad things—she thought of the bad things that happened to bad girls. Bad girls were raped; they were tortured. Killers stalked them; monsters threatened them. Madmen cut them apart with chain saws, with hatchets, with knives. Good girls stayed home where they could be safe.

"Go back," the voice said.

Go back? She couldn't go back. She had thrown away her wedding ring, jumped into bed with a sailor, talked with people who weren't there. She couldn't go back.

She shivered in the darkness. She did not want to go back. She was a woman of startling talents and she would not go back.

Take a closer look, Max had told them. You need to look closely at the things that frighten you. Mary Maxwell had said that it was the imaginary monsters that kept people from living the lives they wanted to live. Was this an imaginary monster?

Stooping, she shone the penlight through the gap between the steps, sending the beam toward the monster. The beam flickered across corroding metal, rotting flesh.

"No," the monster said. "Go back." She heard claws rattling on the stairs as the monster moved away from the light.

"I won't go back," she said. Her voice was strong, though she was still shivering. I have to see it more clearly, she thought.

"Bad things," the monster said. It seemed to Susan that its voice was softer.

Susan straightened and took three quick steps down the stairs, before she could hesitate. She turned on the small landing. The monster, she thought, was right below her, blocking the door to the sundeck.

She shone the light toward the monster. The beam flickered across a carapace of rusting metal that glistened with mucus from the flesh that had been joined to it. She caught a glimpse of a ravaged face: skin stretched taut over the bone of a skull; wisps of graying hair clinging to the pale scalp; broken teeth in a slit of a mouth; watery eyes glittering in the darkness. Then she heard claws scrabbling as the monster backed away from the light.

"You can't go here," the monster said. Its voice had a desperate edge. She took a step downward, shining the beam of light toward the monster. It retreated as she advanced.

She did not hesitate. The thin beam of the penlight before her, she rushed down the stairs and burst out the door, into the clean, rain-washed air, into the cold and the wet.

The deck was awash with rain. She made her way toward the bow through the darkness, clinging to the frames of the windscreens for support, lurching from one to the next. More than once, she slipped on the wet deck, thrown off balance by the ship's unpredictable movements.

She was halfway to the bow when lightning flashed nearby, illuminating the deck with a sudden brilliant blue-white light. She caught a glimpse of her reflection in the glass windscreens around her: dozens of images of herself, all of them drenched and wind blown, all of them grinning.

Grinning? Yes. She knew that she shouldn't be so happy—this was a serious situation, a dangerous situation, a frightening place to be. But she couldn't help it. This was an adventure. She had escaped the monster; she was going to rescue her friends. She was cold and wet and frightened—and she was right where she wanted to be.

She reached the bow of the ship. The flying saucer was gone. There were no wolves. Pat was slumped beside the broken frames of the windscreens that had been crushed beneath the saucer. Max stood beside her, feet braced against the movement of the ship. He was staring out over the bow. Rainwater dripped from his gray hair, his beard; his glasses were spattered with raindrops; his clothes were soaked. But his expression was ecstatic. Lightning flashed on the horizon, gleaming through his gray hair.

"What a wonderful ending!" he exclaimed when he saw her. "So unexpected! So powerful!"

"Pat! Are you all right?" Susan kneeled on the wet deck beside her friend. Pat looked up. A bruise was darkening around her left eye.

"Wasn't that a fabulous squid?" she murmured.

"Come on," Susan said. "We've got to get you out of here. Put your arm around my shoulders."

Susan had helped Pat to her feet when Tom arrived, flashlight in hand, looking large and efficient in a bright yellow raincoat. "What the hell is going on?" he asked, but he didn't wait for an answer. He did the practical things. He put his raincoat around Pat, who was shivering in the cold. He helped them across the deck—past the signs that said the sundeck was off-limits, back onto Calypso Deck, down a service companionway in which Susan saw no monsters.

By the time they reached the ship's infirmary, emergency power had been restored to the ship. The doctor was tending to an injured pirate—he had sprained his ankle while dancing in the conga line. Tom insisted that the doctor take a look at Pat and Max, though they both said it really wasn't necessary.

The bruise around Pat's eye was darkening. It looked like she would soon have a spectacular shiner, with colors that complemented her hair. "I slipped and fell," Pat said. "It was all my fault. I shouldn't have been out there anyway." She glanced at Max. "Isn't that so, Max?"

Max nodded, looking startled. "Yes, of course. Whatever you say. But it was such a wonderful storm."

"Let's get some ice on that bruise," the doctor said. He glanced at Max, who was still dripping rainwater. "And we'd best get you into something dry and warm."

The doctor bustled about, getting an ice pack and some towels, taking charge of the situation.

Susan glanced at Tom and found him studying her with skepticism. "She fell?" he asked.

She shrugged, remembering Max's advice. Sometimes it was easier to avoid telling the whole truth. "I wasn't there," she said. "I saw them from the observation deck and went down to join them."

"Because it looked like so much fun out there?"

She shrugged again. "It looked like they could use a hand."

They left Max and Pat in the doctor's care, and Tom took Susan to her stateroom. He only asked if she were all right.

"I'm fine," she said. "A little shaky, but fine."

"Could you tell me what was going on out there?" he asked.

She wet her lips and took a deep breath, deciding that she didn't want to lie to Tom. "Mary Maxwell and I were watching from the observation deck. Weldon Merrimax was trying to kill Pat. Max went to save her."

He nodded, looking skeptical. "What happened to those wind screens?"

"A flying saucer landed on them. That was my doing, I'm afraid. Mary sent in a pack of wolves."

"Of course," he said. He was shaking his head. "And where's Weldon now?"

"A giant squid reached over the railing and snatched him overboard. I think Pat made that up."

"A giant squid," he said dryly. "I should have guessed.

That would explain everything. And then you raced to their rescue."

"That's right."

He put his arms around her.

She leaned into his embrace, smiling. She considered telling him about the monster in the companionway, then decided against it. He'd had enough to deal with for one night.

WHAT THE HELL HAPPENED?

What do women want?

It's an old, old question. And I'm pleased to tell you that I know the answer.

What do women want? An explanation.*

That's really all we want. We just want to understand why. Why did he say that? Why, oh why, did he ever do that? And why was that giant squid on the sundeck, anyway?

Women—Bad Grrlz in particular—are interested in the answers to these questions. Like scientists of all kinds, we search desperately, persistently, for an explanation.

In the interest of science, I will explain a few things here.

What, you may ask, was I doing out on the sundeck with that thug Weldon Merrimax?

Well, when I met Weldon Merrimax, he was intriguingly mysterious about the goings-on aboard the *Odyssey*. He told me he couldn't explain it all to me just yet. But he said that if I met him on the sundeck at midnight on Halloween, he would explain everything. Who could turn down an invitation like that? A mysterious rendezvous with the promise of an explanation—how intriguing!

Oh, sure—it was stupid to meet him. I'll grant you that. When I went to the party at Penelope's, I hadn't really decided whether I'd go or not—but after a Rum Monkey it started to seem like a fine idea. I figured I'd just slip away and find out what Weldon had to say for himself.

Out on the sundeck, Weldon told me that he was going to kill me. I asked why. (What did I tell you: Bad Grrlz always want an explanation.) And he told me about a

---

*Some say that the answer is "a new pair of shoes"—and there are indeed days when that is the correct answer. But today, the answer is: "an explanation."

dream. He had dreamed he was in a library and he found a book titled *Adventures in Time and Space with Max Merriwell*. In this book, Weldon Merrimax was just a pseudonym of Max Merriwell. "It wasn't fair," he said.

"What does that have to do with me?" I asked him.

"The author was Pat Murphy," he said. Then he tried to grab me.

It was nice of Max to come to my rescue.

Apparently, he had wandered out of his cabin and spotted me in the corridor as I headed out to the sundeck. He decided to follow me. "I was worried about you," he told me in the infirmary. "I thought you might need some help."

So I was on the sundeck with Weldon and Max came to rescue me. My memory of events gets a little blurry right after Weldon punched me and I fell in a heap. I'll tell you: getting punched in real life is a hell of a lot worse than it looks in the movies. This spunky heroine did not immediately leap to her feet to fight back. That really hurt.

While we were in the infirmary, Max told me that I missed seeing a pack of wolves and a flying saucer. I remember blinking away tears just in time to see Weldon Merrimax coming toward me like the killer in a B-movie. He was, I think, going to toss me overboard. I saw a blast of spray shoot up behind him. And I thought about how nice it would be if a giant squid were to snatch him overboard. I imagined a tentacle grabbing the railing.

There it was, just as I had imagined it—a lovely tentacle wrapping itself around the railing. Then I imagined another tentacle, as thick and strong as the first. And there it was. Finally a third tentacle, whipping over the railing and wrapping itself around Weldon's waist.

As the tentacle dragged Weldon over the side, I managed to struggle to my feet and peer over the railing. I looked into the eye of the monster of my imagination—the giant squid. Its eye was the size of a dinner plate—as black as obsidian, as smooth and unreadable as an ocean swell. As I watched, another wave crashed against the ship. The monster released its grip on the railing and slipped back into the water, taking Weldon with it.

Max told us about the power of the imagination. I've always had a good imagination. I'm not sure how all these events fit into my understanding of physics. I'm not sure how to reconcile Schrödinger's cat and Pat's giant squid. I don't know how the mind of this observer influenced the potentialities to bring a giant squid up from the depths. But I think it's all quite intriguing.

After Weldon sank beneath the waves, Susan came running out to save us. Tom showed up just a few minutes later. Max and I spent an hour or so in the infirmary before Ian came to claim me. Apparently Tom had tracked him down and told him a little about what had happened. The doctor allowed him to take charge of me. We left Max chatting amiably with the doctor.

Ian tried to take me to my stateroom and tuck me into bed, but it takes more than a black eye to slow this Bad Grrl down. I took advantage of his efforts to comfort me. After a bit, his comforting hugs became something less platonic. I took him to his cabin and one thing led to another. (I made sure of that.) He was sleeping like a baby when I woke up this morning and slipped out of his bed. I came to the sundeck to survey the aftermath of last night.

This morning, the weather is clear. The sun is shining; the sea is calm. When I arrived on the sundeck, a workman was painting over the gray marks that the giant squid's tentacles had left on the white railing. Another was sweeping up the broken glass from the shattered windscreens.

I asked the man sweeping up the glass what had caused the damage, just to see what he would say. "Big waves," he said. "Fierce storm last night."

The fierce storm didn't explain the scorch marks where the saucer had landed, but they wouldn't be there much longer. The workman with the paint was heading for that patch of deck, preparing to cover over the evidence.

Last night, I asked Ian whether the folks on the bridge had seen what happened on the sundeck. He called up there

and asked. He told me that they talked about seeing ball
lightning, a rare form of lightning that takes the form of a
globe. I looked at him skeptically, and he shrugged. "People see what they want to see," he said.

The folks on the bridge apparently had nothing to say
about the wolves, the giant squid, or the passenger who
vanished overboard. Of course, there's no evidence that
Weldon was ever on board—he wasn't on the passenger
list—so he can go missing without provoking an official
inquiry. It's all very convenient.

I lingered on the sundeck long enough to watch the deck
crew eradicate all evidence of untoward happenings—
painting over the scorch marks, removing the twisted
frames of the windscreens. They are on the side of order,
after all. And last night's events were definitely on the side
of chaos.

TWENTY-FIVE

The descent into madness is an inevitable part of the process of writing a novel. You can't escape it. Just go with it. You really have no choice.

—from *On Writing Novels*
by Max Merriwell

That night, Susan slept soundly in Tom's bed, rocked by the storm waves, soothed by the rattle of rain on the window. She had waited up until he was off duty, and then joined him for a nightcap in his cabin. One thing led to another, as she had known it would. And she spent the night.

And as she slept, she dreamed. In her dream, she stood on the balcony of her own stateroom. The sea was covered with mist, as if they were sailing over clouds. She wondered what monsters the mist might be hiding, then decided it didn't matter. She could handle any monsters that might show up.

She heard the glass door slide open and glanced behind her, expecting to see Pat. Mary Maxwell stepped out. Through the glass door, she could see Pat still asleep in bed.

Susan smiled at Mary. "You're not gone," she said.

Mary shrugged. "Apparently not. Just thought I'd see how you were doing."

"I'm fine. Seems like all the troubles are over."

"You think so?"

"Of course. It was Max and Weldon that stirred everything up. Weldon's gone and Max seems okay now."

"So you think everything will calm down?" Mary asked.

"I think so."

Mary looked a little skeptical. She glanced through the glass doors at Pat. "She's sleeping so peacefully," Mary said. "She's dreaming. What do you think she's dreaming about?"

Susan shrugged. "I have no idea."

"About you, of course. About us, standing here talking. And if she stopped dreaming about you, where would you be?"

"Right here," Susan said.

Mary laughed. "You'd be nowhere at all. You're only a sort of thing in her dream. If she woke up, you'd be gone. Poof! Just like that."

"That's ridiculous," Susan said. "What about you?"

"Poof!" Mary said. "Just another thing in her dream. Ridiculous or not, it's true. I just figured it out myself. Why else would Weldon have been after her?"

Susan shook her head and turned away from Mary, looking out over the misty water. She shivered as a cold breeze blew on her face.

She blinked and she realized that she was in bed, cuddled up against a warm, masculine back. Tom turned over, then, putting his arms around her and pulling her close. In the darkness, she could see the glowing numbers of the digital clock. It was five thirty in the morning. Tom had to get up at six, she remembered.

"Good morning," Tom said. "I have to get up at six." He kissed her. "But we have a little time."

They made the most of the time they had.

"Be careful about deciding you want to be a fiction writer. It's not an easy path. You have to rely on your imagination—and your imagination is a dangerous thing." Max looked bright and alert, despite the alarms and excursions of the previous night. "Fiction writers are all a little crazy, and science fiction writers may be crazier than most. It comes, I think, from spending far too much time alone, imagining new worlds inhabited by strange people, making up stories, talking to yourself—and having conversations with your imaginary friends, people who don't really exist. It's not such a big step from imagining conversations to hearing voices."

At the end of workshop, Max smiled at Susan and Pat. "I was wondering if you'd like to have lunch," he said.

Pat nodded just as Susan noticed Tom and Ian stepping in the door. Tom waved to Susan. "I thought you might want to have lunch," he said.

"I'd love to," she said.

"Great," said Ian. "We'll all go together."

Susan frowned and glanced at Tom, thinking he might suggest that they break off from the group and have lunch alone, but he just nodded, going along with Ian's suggestion.

Susan sat between Tom and Pat, with Max and Ian on the other side of the table. Tom took Susan's hand, smiling at her.

She should be upset, she thought. It was the last day of the cruise. She had spent two nights with Tom, and soon they would be saying good-bye. They hadn't talked about what was going on between them. There hadn't been time for that.

But she was surprisingly relaxed. Something would work out, though she had no idea what.

"How are you feeling this morning?" Tom asked Pat.

The skin surrounding Pat's eye had darkened to shades of deep purple and blue, forming a spectacular shiner. But she was smiling. "Just fine," she said.

"How about you, Max?" Tom asked.

Max smiled. "Quite well," he said. "I think I've finally got a handle on the book I need to write."

"Can you tell us about it?" Ian asked.

Max nodded. "It's obvious, really. A serial killer on a cruise ship."

Susan stared at him. "An imaginary character who is a serial killer?"

Max shook his head. "Oh, no—an actual killer. Seems

to me a cruise ship is the perfect environment for a killer. It's so easy to dispose of the evidence. In the end, the killer turns out to be the ship's chief security officer." He smiled at Tom. "Sorry, Tom. It's just that you're the least likely candidate. I think it will be one of Weldon's best."

Tom nodded. "Speaking of unlikely," he said slowly, "I was hoping that the two of you might be able to explain what happened last night." He was looking at Pat and Max.

Max shrugged. "You know, I don't much care for explanations. I've found they usually just get in the way."

Tom looked at Pat, but Ian spoke up first. "I disagree," he said. "I love explanations. I like to have as many as possible. Then I can choose among them. Or pile them all together. Explanations are easy. We are in the Bermuda Triangle where strange things happen. Dreamers in parallel dimensions are dreaming overlapping dreams. We have tapped into a quantum reality where many possibilities overlap—and the overlapping realities are bleeding through into this one. Why have just one answer when so many are available?"

"But that's not satisfying," Pat said.

Ian shrugged. "Maybe not for you. It's satisfying for me."

Susan squeezed Tom's hand under the table. "Reality is a much more flexible concept than most people think," she said. "The borders are fuzzy. You can do a lot with a little bit of dreaming and a lot of imagination. Isn't that so, Max?"

Max nodded. "Absolutely," the writer said.

Tom shook his head. "What about all those cryptic notes?" he asked.

"Not cryptic," Ian said. "Ambiguous, perhaps, but that's the nature of the *I Ching*. It offers possibilities. What you do with them is up to you." He looked around the table. "As far as I'm concerned, there's only one question left now. What's next?" He smiled at Susan. "I wanted to talk to you about that. The ship needs a librarian, you see."

Apparently, Ian had been busy. It seems that the ship

needed a librarian for its winter cruise season in the Mediterranean. Ian had convinced both the Captain and the company that he had found the perfect candidate and now all he had to do was convince her to apply.

Susan listened in a daze. She looked at Tom, who was grinning. "So I'd stay on board the ship?" she said. She'd stay aboard, she'd have a chance to see if this thing with Tom was going anywhere, she'd sail around the Mediterranean and have adventures.

"You'd move to crew quarters, of course," Ian said. "And you need to fill out an application, but that's just a formality. It's all set, really."

"I don't know," she said. "I have an apartment in San Francisco. I don't see . . ." The sentence trailed off as she thought of the apartment. It wasn't really her apartment. It was Harry's apartment as far as she was concerned. With Harry's furniture and Harry's television and Harry's stereo. The books were hers, but the rest was Harry's.

"I figured that I could take care of your apartment until you get back," Pat said.

Ian and Pat talked about details while Susan listened, feeling that matters had been taken from her hands and handed over to someone much more competent. She was willing to give it a try.

Susan sat in the library, reading the end of *Through the Looking-Glass* to a group of children. Alice had returned home and was talking to a black kitten about her adventures on the other side of the looking glass.

" 'Now, Kitty, let's consider who it was that dreamed it all. This is a serious question, my dear, and you should *not* go on licking your paw like that . . . ! You see, Kitty, it *must* have been either me or the Red King. He was part of my dream, of course—but then I was part of his dream, too! *Was* it the Red King, Kitty? . . . Oh, Kitty, *do* help to settle it! I'm sure your paw can wait!' But the provoking kitten only began on the other paw, and pretended it hadn't heard the question."

"Which do you think it was?" Susan closed the book and set it down in her lap. She smiled at the children. "Any ideas?" she asked.

One little boy said it was the Red King and one little girl said it was Alice. Another little girl made a long and earnest speech about her own black kitten back home, which didn't really seem to relate to the topic at hand. And another boy said he didn't care whose dream it was but he liked Tweed-ledum best because he got to put a cooking pot on his head when he dressed up in armor (the illustration showed that), and the little boy thought that was a good idea. The discussion reached no conclusions, which was fine, since Susan hadn't expected that it would. Some children went with Trudy to the swimming pool, and parents came to reclaim others. One mother stopped to talk with Susan.

"What a wonderful job you have!" the young mother said.

Susan nodded. "I certainly do," she said.

"How on earth did you end up here?" the woman asked.

Susan thought for a moment, watching the woman's face. "Well," she said easily, "a month ago I decided to leave my husband and run away to sea. I sailed with the *Odyssey* to Europe. It was such a wonderful trip, I decided to stay aboard."

There are so many stories to choose from, Susan thought as she watched the mother leave with her children. You had to know when to say, "That's someone else's story, not mine." You had to know when to claim a story as your own, even if it didn't happen quite that way.

That morning, she had found a piece of paper slipped under her door. A hexagram and a note written in a looping, feminine hand: "When a door has been opened, one can undertake the most dangerous things."

· She didn't know what would happen next.

BAD GRRLZ' GUIDE TO PHYSICS

WHAT NEXT?

I've been thinking about my dissertation and thinking about my advisor and thinking about how little I want to deal with defending my ideas to him. I've been thinking about Max's comments on my theories, when he thought they were a science fiction novel.

So I have a plan. I'm going to write a novel. It'll be about a group of people on board a cruise ship. It'll be about a writer whose pseudonyms show up and make trouble. It'll be about reality and the stories people tell and the nature of both.

I think it will be an interesting novel to write. It contains so many possibilities. So far, all I have is the beginning.

A woman is wandering in a corridor, lost and confused. She is on a cruise ship about to set sail. She clutches a map, but the map doesn't tell her which way to go. In her experience, maps are not always useful. The map is not the territory. In fact, the map rarely shows the most interesting parts of the territory.

As she walks down the corridor, she hears a man talking about writing and talking about names and talking about who he is and who he isn't. She begins to listen.

That's all I have so far. I'm sure the rest will become clear in good time.

AFTERWORD
BY PAT MURPHY

"The scientists try to tell us that the universe is made up of atoms and molecules; actually, the universe is made up of stories..."

—Muriel Rukeyser

Max Merriwell is a fiction writer; Max Merriwell is a liar. So is Mary Maxwell. So is Weldon Merrimax. So is Pat Murphy. And so are you.

We are all fiction writers; we are all liars. Without knowing it, we make up stories about the world. And then we believe that our stories are true and ignore our own roles in creating the version of the world in which we live.

For the past eighteen years, I've been working at the Exploratorium, San Francisco's museum of science, art, and human perception. My background is in biology, but during my time at the Exploratorium I have written about all branches of science, including physics and chemistry and human perception. Learning about perception made me realize the fundamental truth of Rukeyser's statement.

When I came to the Exploratorium, I assumed (like most people, I think) that the world I see around me is the real world. After working at the Exploratorium, I no longer believe that to be true.

I see the world because light bounces off things in the world around me and enters my eyes. The eye's cornea and lens focus the light to make an image on the retina, a layer of light-sensitive cells at the back of the eye. The cells of the retina send a message to my brain. My brain interprets those signals to create a mental image of the world.

I don't see the real world. I see a mental image constructed by my brain.

Optical illusions—those tricky pictures where straight lines seem to bend, where sizes are distorted, where your eyes and brain are fooled into seeing the world as it isn't—reveal some of the limitations of this mental image. At the Exploratorium, you can watch a person shrink as they walk across a distorted room. Your brain expects the room to be rectangular. Unwilling to recognize that the room is an unfamiliar shape, your brain fabricates a plausible story to make sense of what it sees—the person is changing size. (You can see a version of this illusion by searching www.exploratorium.edu for "distorted room.")

Many people treat optical illusions as amusing tricks, but they are much more. Optical illusions actually reveal the profound workings of your visual system. Researchers into visual perception use these puzzling pictures to figure out how your brain fabricates its fictions about the world.

What you see is your brain's interpretation of the world. The same is true for what you hear, feel, taste, and smell. All your perceptions are constructions of your brain, stories that your brain tells you about the signals it receives.

What's more, the same is true of your memories. The work of memory researchers suggests that the memory of an event is malleable. Your brain constructs a memory from bits and pieces of what you saw and heard and felt at the time, then modifies that construction based on ideas and suggestions that come along after the event you are remembering has taken place. (You can learn more about the malleability of memory at www.badgrrlzguide.com.)

Essentially, your memories are stories that your brain tells and retells, rewriting as it goes along. This is something that many people find disturbing. Understandably so. Memory researcher Elizabeth Loftus writes: "Human beings feel attached to their remembered past, for the people, places, and events that we enshrine in memory give structure and definition to the person we think of as our 'self.' " If we accept that memory spills over into dreams and imagination, then how do we know what's real and what's not?

We don't.

Reality is a slippery thing. According to pataphysical philosopher Yves Rrognac, "The mind is a machine for manufacturing reality." So reality, in turn, is manufactured by the mind.

When I first realized how slippery reality was, I found the discovery to be rather disturbing. But eventually I came to realize that this slipperiness could be the source of a great deal of power and fun. That, I think, is when Max Merriwell, Mary Maxwell, and Weldon Merrimax came along. The book you are holding is the end of a three-year stint of playing with reality, which began with *There and Back Again (by Max Merriwell)*, continued with *Wild Angel (by Mary Maxwell by Max Merriwell)*, and culminated in *Adventures in Time and Space with Max Merriwell*.

Though I have had a great deal of fun playing with reality in this book, I have maintained a certain respect for the laws of physics. The science described by Pat Murphy (the character) in her Bad Grrlz' Guide is accurate. I did not make up any of the stuff about virtual particles popping in and out of the quantum vacuum. The physicists made that up on their own.

For more information on quantum physics, I recommend *Who's Afraid of Schrödinger's Cat?* by Ian Marshall and Danah Zohar. This is a book of nonfiction, but it contains concepts certain to delight the heart of any science fiction writer. Consider, for example, the following passage, an excerpt from the book's discussion of virtual transitions: "Particles can emerge from the vacuum only if they have sufficient energy to do so, but virtual particles continually spring into existence for a brief time before disappearing back again. They are like a cloud of impossibilities that cluster on the edge of possibility, and though 'unreal,' their presence exerts a subtle pressure on all material existing things. This pressure, which can actually be measured with sensitive instruments, is known as the Casimir effect."

Instruments that can measure the presence of "unreal" particles—what a wonderful thing! Though I am not working toward a doctorate in quantum physics, like Pat Murphy, the character, I plan to continue to follow the developments in this fascinating field. For more on my future endeavours, please check out my Web site at www. badgrrlzguide.com.

ACKNOWLEDGMENTS

This book is the end of a long process and many people helped me along the way.

The crew of Princess Cruises' *Dawn Princess* made my voyage with them quite enjoyable. Captain Attilio Guerrini, First Engineer Officer Martin Ross, and Security Officer Jimmy Green were kind enough to spare time from their busy schedules to tell me about their work.

Karen Fowler, Angus MacDonald, Daniel Marcus, Carter Scholz, Michael Berry, Richard Russo, Michael Blumlein, Ellen Klages, Richard Kadrey, Paul Doherty, Linda Shore, and Avon Swofford took the time to read and thoughtfully comment on all or part of this manuscript. I could not have completed this project without their help. Laurie Brandt offered support and insight along the way. My friend Gary Crounse provided a pataphysical point of view upon request, an attitude that proved invaluable in completing this project.

I want to thank Bad Girls Ellen Klages and Linda Shore for the good times we shared while working on the proposal for the Exploratorium's Bad Girls' Guide to Science. I hope someday we get to write the book! Special thanks to Ellen Klages for the memorable evening we spent inventing the recipe for the Flaming Rum Monkey, a dangerous drink for dangerous women.

I thank my husband, Dave Wright, who provided love and support throughout this long project. I thank Beth Meacham, my editor at Tor Books, for being courageous enough to see this project through to the end, publishing each book in turn, never wavering from the course. And I thank all my readers for coming along for the ride.